Indian Summer

James Mitchell

HEADLINE

First published in 1996
by HEADLINE BOOK PUBLISHING

First published in paperback in 1996
by HEADLINE BOOK PUBLISHING

10 9 8 7 6 5 4 3 2 1

ISBN 0 7472 5117 7

Printed and bound in Great Britain by
Cox & Wyman Ltd, Reading, Berks

HEADLINE BOOK PUBLISHING
A division of Hodder Headline PLC
338 Euston Road
London NW1 3BH

For Leila and John

PART I

PART 1

1

Like a snake, she thought, as she always did. Like an enormous snake that could crush giants in its sleep. Not that it would. This was a good snake, a kind snake, that one day would carry her away from Kalpur province, Kalpur town, with her mummy and her dolly, and take her to Calcutta or Delhi or Bombay, where they would live happily ever after. For this was a snake on wheels: a snake that ran on tracks: a snake called a train. All she had to do was remember her prayers: to the Blessed Virgin, to Baby Jesus, and away they would go.

Not daddy. She remembered her prayers to Kali, too, and Kali would not deny her. Kali did not forget, and daddy would be taken care of. The snake hissed; a great sigh of content. It knows, she thought. It will help us, and she said a Hail Mary as she nursed her dolly in the shade, until it receded, and it was time to move to another pillar that supported the station roof, and the sun could not reach them. Her dolly was very fair: pink cheeks, golden hair, blue eyes; and even if mummy had made her a wide-brimmed hat like the memsahibs sometimes wore, the sun could so easily hurt her. Not like me, she thought. I'm brown, even if mummy says I'm golden coloured. Even then. Because daddy doesn't even say I'm brown: he says I'm nigh on bloody black. Kali would remember that, too. She had reminded her often enough.

All over the station people were moving, shouting, drinking, eating. Men selling lemonade, puris, coffee; women selling oranges, shawls, charms. Men, women and children scrambling for tickets, or a seat on the great snake called a train: but for her it was peaceful. Nobody was beaten, nobody screamed in pain, nobody was drunk. She began to rock her dolly in her arms: it was time for her nap.

'What's your name?'

She looked up. A little memsahib all in white, except for the blue ribbons on her dress that were the colour of her eyes, a dress that Veronica coveted at once, though she'd have to change the ribbons. Seven, she thought. No more than seven. The same as me.

'Veronica,' she said.

'I am Miss Victoria,' said the fair child. Veronica waited. There would be more to come. With the sahibs and the memsahibs and the missy babas, there was always more to come.

'What's your doll's name?' the fair child asked.

Without hesitation Veronica said, 'Elizabeth Jane.' This was a lie, but the sahibs did not like to be kept waiting; nor did their wives, or their children. Her dolly's name was Sarah Brocklebank, but that was a secret shared by few. She had been named in honour of the daughter of Company Sergeant Major Brocklebank, a demi-god who

4

had been very unkind to daddy when he was in the army. She had given her dolly his daughter's name as a mark of respect, even honour.

'That's a stupid name,' said the missy baba, and Veronica gave no answer. There was simply no point in quarrelling with a white child. Whatever happened, she would lose.

'Where do you live?' the missy baba asked.

'Napier Street,' said Veronica.

'I bet it's awful.'

A living-room, a big bedroom, a little bedroom and a sort of cupboard where Pushpar the servant slept. Their one and only servant, who washed and cleaned and swept, and kept out of daddy's way when he was drunk. Awful just about described it.

'It's all right,' she said.

'Do you have an ayah?'

'Well, of course,' said Veronica. 'Everybody has an ayah.'

'Then where is she?'

'Gone to buy ice-cream.' If only it were true. But if they had been rich enough for Pushpar to be her ayah, she would have gone to buy ice-cream, because Pushpar was really jolly nice. She was the one who had told her about Kali, and how the goddess never forgot. Good or bad, she never forgot. And where's your ayah? Veronica wondered, but there was no point in asking. That would lead to a row, and the brown ones never won rows, even if they were really golden.

'What does your father do?' the missy baba asked, but before she had to lie again – because what did her father

5

do except get drunk, beat her mother, pay for whores? – the procession came by.

It was a sight she was used to, because the ghats were quite near Kali's temple and the railway station. A big crowd, Veronica thought, someone important, insofar as Indians could be considered important. She stood up to look at the procession across the street. A man of course. A big crowd, noisy and yet furtive too, priests, and a corpse on a bier. About her father's age, she thought. Forty or thereabouts, garlands of flowers all about him, and behind him, walking, a woman much younger, also covered in garlands. His wife. She looked dazed, Veronica thought, like her father when he was drunk, but it wouldn't be whisky. To get them to the ghats they often gave them bhang, Pushpar said. Poor thing. She turned away. This was no sight for Sarah Brocklebank.

'What is that?' the missy baba asked.

Really she knows nothing, thought Veronica, delighted.

'A funeral,' she said. 'They are taking the man to be burned at the ghats near Kali's temple.'

'And the woman? The one with all the flowers?'

'His wife,' said Veronica. She was no longer delighted: simply incredulous that such ignorance could exist.

'What will happen to her now that her husband is dead?'

She is making fun of me, Veronica thought. Nobody could be as stupid as that. Then she looked at the little memsahib and decided that she was. Even so . . .

'Happen?' she asked.

'Where will she live?' the other girl asked.

'She won't live,' said Veronica. 'She'll die.'

The wailing sound increased, and then the drums began: a pulsating crash that drowned out even the wailing.

'That's silly,' the missy baba said. Veronica hugged Sarah Brocklebank to her, and waited. The scream when it came cut through even the sound of the drums, but Sarah Brocklebank hadn't heard. Veronica had covered her ears. She looked at the missy baba. Miss Victoria was being sick. The white dress with the blue ribbons didn't look nearly so pretty. No need now to wish for it. It was a mess, but a mess she rather enjoyed until the missy baba's ayah came, took one look, and blamed everything on Veronica, scolding her until Miss Victoria interrupted her, demanding to have her dress changed *at once*, and her ayah led her away, still scolding over her shoulder in Hindi. Both little girls spoke Hindi as fluently as they spoke English, for this was India in 1907, at the height of the British Raj.

Veronica got up and looked at the road. There were bits of garlands lying there: even a whole one. She gathered up the best bits and began to make them into another whole garland as Pushpar had shown her. Two garlands. Kali would be pleased. For a moment she considered asking Kali to do something to that missy baba, Miss Victoria, and her ayah, too, but then decided against it. Kali, said Pushpar, was not interested in small things, and daddy's fate was a very big thing indeed. Best to save it all for him.

The giant snake hissed more loudly, but still it showed no anger, just writhed its way across the tracks and out of the station, off to a great city which daddy would never know. She would go at once to Kali's temple and pray, she decided: pray for daddy's destruction, which was what Kali was for; Kali the Destroyer, who always listened. Then afterwards she would go to the church and seek out the Goanese priest, Father Delemos, to see if he had any books she might borrow. He often had very good books for children.

Father Delemos worried about Veronica, but then he was a good priest, who worried about so many of his flock, and not without reason, he thought, but Veronica was different. To begin with she was such a pretty child: an extraordinary *mélange* of Irish and English and Mahratta and Goanese, yet with the possibility of a beauty that might outshine even her mother's, and before her husband had started to beat her Veronica's mother had been a very pretty woman indeed. The Goanese blood explained her ability to speak Portuguese, of course. She had talked it with relatives, now dead, and her mother, too, as well as with him. Talked it very well: but then she was also fluent in Hindi, Urdu and English; had even begun to pick up a little Latin by listening to the mass. In the Nativity play last Christmas she had been the most exquisite Blessed Virgin he had ever seen, but there had been a lot of trouble about the Infant Jesus. The Holy Child could hardly be portrayed by a doll called Sarah Brocklebank.

But with Veronica there was always trouble. Special prayers for example. No harm in Veronica saying a prayer to Saint Antony of Padua if she had lost something; or to her patron, Saint Veronica, for intercession, but to pray to Kali ... Father Delemos sighed. Over and over he had told her that it wouldn't do: that Kali was not Saint Kali, that her temple was not a church, and Veronica had said, 'Yes, father' and 'I understand, father', looking at him limpid eyed, then gone straight back to the temple as soon as he'd finished to ask the goddess to kill her father. Not that he could prove it, but he was certain it was true.

Not that her father didn't deserve punishment, and one day he might receive it if he continued to beat Veronica's mother as he did. Mary Dolores Higgins ... Well, the Dolores was apt enough. If ever a woman knew sorrow it was Veronica's mother, but it was the will of God that would resolve her pain, not the will of Kali. The child lied to him, of course she did, and yet he forgave her every time. Because she was special, he thought, and that is wrong, God forgive me, but God also knows that it's true. Not just pretty, but clever: quick to learn everything he taught her: languages, mathematics, music even. She had an aptitude for all of them, and an ability to listen, to concentrate, far beyond her seven years. But even so ... Kali. The goddess was in her mind and in her blood he thought, and it would take more than a couple of Hail Marys to get her out.

In fact it was Kali who helped her, though the goddess made her wait for eight more years, but the point was she did wait, offering garlands, praying in her temple, so that in the end Kali relented, but first her mother died. No, that wasn't true, Veronica thought. First her father murdered her mother.

Britain was at war with Germany then, had been for

months and months, and the effect on her father was extraordinary, for Michael Higgins, known to what friends he had left as Mick, turned out to be a patriot of the most bewildering kind. There was a union flag flying outside their house, and another on the living-room wall next to the Sacred Heart, and his Boer War medals were permanently on display beside a photograph of him in the uniform of the Royal Northumbrians, corporal's stripes clearly visible, just before Company Sergeant Major Brocklebank had had him reduced to the ranks. Nothing extraordinary about that. It was his obsession with reading newspapers ... Until then he'd never bothered, but when the war started he wanted every newspaper in English he could get, which meant that she and her mother had to work even harder at their dressmaking to find money for newspapers and magazines and books as well as beer and toddy and whisky.

The trouble was that daddy didn't know much about reading, and so when the words were big or he was too drunk she had to read to him, and if she hesitated or was unsure because a word was new to her, he would hit her. Daddy knew all there was to know about hitting, and if she cried he would hit her again. Daddy liked to watch her cry, but not too much. It interfered with their reading. Then when his brain was too fuddled to make sense of what she read he would make one of his speeches, or rather his speech, for he knew only one.

The superiority of the white man; the invincibility of the British Army. Death or glory. And it was true, she admitted to herself, that he had seen his share of both. This gross, shambling and sadistic wreck had once been lean and smart and brave. Slayer of his country's foes if you were British; a bloody murderer if you were a Boer. Then the speech would alter, like a change of key. The white man was great, honourable – invincible, if he was also British – and he had let the white man down. Let the whole bloody side down. And for why? Because he'd married a half-caste. A bloody chee-chee. At that point he usually cried himself, and then, if they were lucky, lurched out for a drink with another betrayer of the whites, and if they were very lucky, from there to one of his whores. They weren't always so very lucky. He couldn't always afford it. His army pension didn't go all that far, even with the kind of whore who would accommodate him.

The day it happened she was reading the *Times of India* to him, slowly and carefully, because he was already drunk at two-thirty in the afternoon, and she very much wanted to eat, though there was no chance of that until she had finished the newspaper.

'Major Brocklebank,' she read, 'Acting Commanding Officer of the third battalion, Royal Northumbrians, has been awarded the DSO for his courageous—'

'Let's have that again,' said her father.

'Major Brocklebank,' she read again, 'Acting Commanding Officer of the third—' He hit her then, using his clenched fist, and in a sense she was lucky. He knocked her unconscious. Mercifully her mother had been out, measuring the station master's wife for a new tea-gown, and Pushpar was at the market. When her mother returned she bathed her daughter's forehead, put salve on the bruise (her mother knew about salve as her father knew about beatings), and helped her to bed. Veronica's eyes closed, only to open because her bruise hurt once more. Her bruise hurt because her father was shaking her.

'What?' she said. 'What, daddy?'

'You'd better come and look at your ma,' he said. 'She's fallen down the stairs. Doesn't look well at all.' Even by his standards he was very drunk.

Veronica rose from her bed and went out. Her mother lay at the foot of the stairs, her face no more than one gigantic bruise. Veronica went down to her, took her wrist as the book said she must do, and waited to feel the pulse beat. There was none.

Oh, Kali, Kali, she thought. Soon I shall be fifteen and in all the years I've never forgotten you. Please . . . Please . . .

'Well?' her father said.

'Mummy's dead,' said Veronica.

'Drunken bitch,' said her father. 'Served her right.'

'Mummy didn't drink.'

Her father's fist clenched, then opened into a hand again. It seemed that he had other plans for his daughter. The hand reached out, found a bottle of toddy, and poured its remains over his wife, then put the bottle down.

'She was drunk,' he said. 'What was she?' The hand became a fist again.

'Drunk,' said Veronica. Nothing could hurt mummy now.

'Good lass,' said her father. 'You ask me, you're well shot of her. After all she's the one who gave you that smack on the face. Well?'

12

'Yes daddy,' Veronica said.

'Yes daddy,' said her father. 'You're doing grand so far. Now listen. I'm away out to find a copper or a doctor or something. You stay here. You understand me? You don't bloody move.'

'She should have a priest,' said Veronica.

'Chee-chees only see a priest when I say so,' her father said. 'Now mind I mean that.'

'Yes daddy.'

'Yes daddy. Them's the words I want to hear. And when I come back with the copper I want to see you crying.' Veronica nodded. She was crying already.

'Good lass,' said her father, and left her.

It all happened quickly. In India you had to be quick, because of the heat. A doctor pronounced mummy dead, a policeman sniffed at her face and smelt the toddy, and Veronica said what daddy had told her to say. Of Pushpar there was no sign. She's heard, thought Veronica. The neighbours' servants have told her, and she'll stay away until it's safe. And I don't blame her. Then Father Delemos was sent for, and together they knelt and prayed, said a rosary, her father as grave and devout as she was herself. Father Delemos didn't believe for a moment that a drunken Mary Dolores Higgins had assaulted her daughter, but was too compassionate to say so, not after one look at Veronica's face. It will be Kali, he thought, but how can I prevent it? If I say anything but my prayers the child will be beaten again. Instead he sent for ice to keep the body cool for the funeral next day. In India the corpses did not wait. Daddy used a piece of the ice to cool the next glass of toddy, and for some reason thought it was funny. When, Kali? she asked the goddess. When? When?

In bed she wondered if daddy might join her, now that mummy was dead, but that night he was too drunk, and next day he went to the whores instead. But he didn't sell the sewing-machine, Veronica noticed. That was now hers to use. To make the clothes mummy had taught her to make. She was not daddy's new bedmate: she was his new slave.

It could have been worse. For the first few days daddy was busy selling off mummy's clothes, what bits of jewellery she had left – even her wedding ring – and spending the proceeds on women and drink, leaving her to finish off the orders mummy had started, but after that was done she would have to find new work, and she wasn't nearly so good a seamstress as mummy, besides being far too young.

Father Delemos had buried mummy before a congregation of three: two customers who came because of kindness? curiosity? and herself. One of them gave her a rupee, and she used it to buy flowers for mummy's grave, and spent the change on a garland for Kali. No headstone. How could there be? She had no other money, and even to speak of it to daddy would be to invite another blow. No headstones for bloody chee-chees. But Father Delemos was kind and promised to pray for mummy every day, and a requiem mass too, and after the funeral Pushpar came back. As Pushpar swept and Veronica sewed, they gossiped in Hindi.

'I was so sorry,' Pushpar said.

And yet you weren't here, thought Veronica. You never

are here when daddy's in a rage.

'It must have been terrible.'

'Well, it was,' said Veronica. 'But please don't talk about it or I shall cry.'

'What shall we talk about?'

'Kali.'

Pushpar was old and work worn, surviving on the scraps that were all mummy could offer, but she had loved mummy almost as much as she feared daddy.

'Kali always listens,' she said. 'I told you.'

'Did you pray to her?'

'To Vishnu,' said Pushpar. 'She also listens. There is to be good news. I know it.'

But that was ridiculous, thought Veronica. How could there be good news in Michael Higgins' house? And yet there was.

2

It arrived next day. Pushpar was out, and Veronica had
had to make daddy's breakfast and look at the newspaper
in case it was one of their reading days. *Soon there would
be no money for newspapers.* Soon she would have to
persuade mummy's customers to order more clothes, and
some might do it out of pity: once, twice at the most,
because when it came to dressmaking she had been
nowhere near as clever as mummy. And the customers –
more bloody chee-chees – all knew that daddy had murdered mummy, and might be kind for a while. But none
of them were rich and one day there would be no more
sewing, and daddy would beat her.

There was the sound of a horse outside. Water cart,
she thought. But the cart or whatever it was stopped
outside her door, and newspapers or no newspapers, war
or no war, Veronica had to go to the door and look. It was
a gharri, the sort of carriage that waited at the station
for wealthy travellers, and in it Pushpar, and a giant of
a man who got out as she watched, a giant with a turban
and beard and an iron bangle: a Sikh. Once out he turned
to help down the third of the gharri's passengers, the

17

most beautiful woman that Veronica had ever seen. About my colour, she thought, and a little taller than me, but I haven't finished growing yet – and such hair, such eyes, and her dress that had to be silk, and the necklace and bracelets and ear-rings that could be nothing else but gold. She came towards Veronica and Pushpar followed, a slave following a queen, while the Sikh climbed back into the gharri that creaked under his weight.

When the queen reached her, Veronica curtsied, the way mummy had taught her, because what else can you do when a queen appears? But all she did was smile (her teeth were perfect too), and kiss her.

'Indoors, child,' she said. 'We have given the street enough to talk about.' And indeed the whole street was watching.

They went indoors, to the humblest, most unworthy of palaces, and Pushpar went at once to make tea, and Her Majesty asked, 'Do you know who I am?'

Veronica shook her head.

'I'm your aunt. Your mother's sister.' After a pause she added, 'Her younger sister.'

No need to tell me, Veronica thought. The way you look mummy could have been your mummy too.

'Mary Dolores never told you?'

'No miss,' said Veronica.

'You must learn to call me Aunty,' said Her Majesty, 'because that is who I am. Your Aunt Poppy ... Poppy Villiers.'

Veronica knew that her mother's maiden name was Foley, but who was she to argue with a queen? 'Yes, Aunty,' she said.

The woman smiled. 'Good girl,' she said, then looked at her watch. 'There isn't much time. May I ask you some questions?'

'Of course,' said Veronica.

Another smile. 'Such faith in me,' said her aunt, and then, 'First, do you wish to go on living here with your father?'

'Not wish, no,' Veronica said, 'but what else is there?'

Her aunt looked at her. 'Come here,' she said, and Veronica went to her. She knew she was safe.

Her aunt examined the bruise on her face. 'Your father did this to you?' she asked.

'He did worse to my mother.'

'So Pushpar told me.' Her aunt opened her handbag, and took out face cream, a powder compact and puff, and worked on Veronica's face as they talked.

'I live in Calcutta,' she said. 'Nice house. A garden with roses and lemon trees and a tank. All that. Would you like to come and live with me there?'

'Oh, yes,' Veronica said.

'But I might be terrible to live with,' said her aunt.

'How could you be worse than my father?' Veronica asked her.

Her aunt's eyes brimmed with tears then, but even her tears were like diamonds, Veronica thought.

'Then you'll risk it?' her aunt asked.

'Oh, *yes*,' said Veronica. 'But daddy may not want me to go with you.'

'Then I must persuade him,' said her aunt, and for some reason Veronica thought of the giant in the gharri. The thought was pleasing.

19

'Have you anybody you wish to say goodbye to?'

'Pushpar—' said Veronica.

'She will be here when you get back. Anybody else?'

'Our priest,' said Veronica. 'Father Delemos.' Her aunt
made a face. 'He's a very nice priest,' said Veronica.

'Then you must go to him.' Her aunt turned the compact's mirror so that she could see her face. Of the bruise
there was no sign. 'Hurry, child,' she said.

It was hard to explain it all to Father Delemos, but
already he had heard of the beautiful lady and the giant
(rumour spread faster than fire in India), and he gave
her a book as a farewell present, and let her go. It was
sad, but why keep an innocent child in the purgatory of
her father's making?

In spite of the heat Veronica ran to Kali's temple, to
make the namaskar, the bow, that showed her respect,
because that was all there was: she had no money for
garlands; then back to her own house where her aunt
sipped tea. Somehow she knew without asking that her
father was not in the house. Her aunt reached out for the
book.

'Shakespeare,' her aunt said. 'So you're clever?'

'I hope so,' said Veronica.

'Pretty too. Go and put on your best dress and leave
the rest. We'll buy new clothes in Calcutta.' Veronica ran
to her room.

When she came back her aunt said, 'That's your best
dress?' Veronica nodded. 'My poor child,' said her aunt,
and embraced her, and for the first time Veronica learned
to enjoy the feel of silk, the scent of perfume from
Paris.

'I should have done that before,' said her aunt. 'Do you know why I didn't?'

'No,' said Veronica.

'Because I was shy.'

'Oh, *Aunty*,' Veronica said, and hugged her once more.

'You won't see your father again,' she said. 'We have to catch a train. Does it bother you?'

'No,' said Veronica.

Her aunt nodded. 'But something's bothering you. What is it?'

Veronica looked to where Pushpar was washing up the teacups.

'All taken care of,' said her aunt. 'You don't suppose I'd leave her to your father's tender mercies? Once she's done the washing-up she's off.' She looked at Veronica. 'Don't worry. She won't starve. I told you it was all taken care of.'

The Sikh giant was called Jagadir Singh and after she had embraced Pushpar he rode with them in the gharri to the station. There was no sign of her father, no need for a bodyguard, but even so it was reassuring to have a giant with them, particularly one who treated Aunty with such respect. On the way they stopped at the bazaar, where Aunty bought Veronica the best shoes she could find, and a leather case to replace the sack which held the treasured possessions she had been allowed to bring. On the way to the gharri Aunty gave Veronica's old sandals to the first girl beggar they might fit.

The train was no longer a snake – she was far too old for that – but oh, it was magnificent. A private compartment (Jagadir Singh in the cheaper seats, but he would never

21

have trouble in getting one), and servants to bring more tea, and cakes, and jaggri, that delicious sugar-cane drink she liked so much and could never afford – until then.

As the train pulled out of the station Aunty said, 'Fill your new case, child. We can't have you arriving in Calcutta carrying a sack,' then watched as Veronica loaded books and more books into the case.

'A scholar,' said Aunty.

Veronica became frightened. 'You don't mind?'

'Of course not,' Aunty said. 'It's what you are.' Veronica sighed her relief and put her doll on top of the pile.

'But isn't a scholar rather old for dollies?' Aunty asked, and Veronica told her all about Miss Sarah Brocklebank. At first Aunty giggled helplessly, but then the laughter died.

'And that is why your father killed your mother and knocked you unconscious?' she said. 'Because his old CSM was good enough to become a major and command his battalion, and brave enough to win a medal?'

'Yes, Aunty.'

'What a swine he is,' said Aunty.

'I've been thinking about him,' Veronica said.

Gravely her aunt said, 'That's one thing scholars like you are for. To think. Tell me your thoughts.'

'Daddy wouldn't just let you take me away—'

'Of course not,' said Aunty. 'I bought you. For fifty pounds.'

'*Fifty pounds?*' Veronica could scarcely believe it.

'Cheap at the price, I know,' Aunty said.

'It's an *enormous* sum of money,' said Veronica. 'It's his pension for a whole year.'

'Then he'd better make it last,' said Aunty.

'Yes, but—' she hesitated, but her aunt motioned to her to continue. 'Once he's spent it all he'll come back for more. It's the way he is.'

Her aunt smiled: a smile like Kali's, thought Veronica.

'To see me he must first get past Jagadir Singh,' Aunty said. 'It isn't a very easy thing to do.'

Veronica giggled, then sat back content.

'Has the scholar any more thoughts?' her aunt asked.

'Two – if it's allowed.'

'We'll see,' Aunty said.

'First – how did you know mummy was dead?'

'Pushpar paid a letter-writer to tell me. She often sent word to me. I paid her, but it wasn't that. She was very fond of you both. And the other question?'

She found it very hard to ask, but already she knew that Aunty was one of those who believed in plain speaking. Cards on the table: that was the expression.

'Forgive me,' she said, 'but why didn't mummy tell me I had an aunt? Especially an aunt like you.'

'Because she was ashamed of me,' her aunt said.

Veronica's jaw dropped, her eyes rounded, and suddenly she looked about half her age, her aunt thought, but already the brain was working.

'And that's all I want to say about it for now,' her aunt said. 'We'll talk more when we get home.'

'Yes, Aunty.'

'Oh, so solemn,' said her aunt. 'It doesn't mean that I don't want you. I can't wait to dress you properly.' She opened her handbag, took out a gold cigarette case, matches in a golden box. 'Do you smoke?'

23

'When I can,' said Veronica.

'Then you can have one,' her aunt said. 'For a treat. But not too often, mind. You're far too young – and too pretty.'

As she puffed cautiously at her cigarette (she hadn't smoked very many; it was hard to steal cigarettes from daddy. It was hard to steal *anything* from daddy), she thought of what Aunty had just told her. There could be only one explanation she thought, and if she was right mummy had been foolish. That didn't mean that she loved her less, but mummy had been foolish.

They ate on the train, and drank too – her first champagne, which she adored – and when they arrived at the station in Calcutta Jagadir Singh collected their luggage and bustled off to find a gharri, while Veronica and Aunty made their way sedately behind him. And just as well to be sedate, Veronica thought. Calcutta was even hotter than Kalpur. But before they reached the gharri they passed four white people: a sahib and his memsahib, a girl of about her own age, and an army officer. The three civilians stared rather rudely. Do they think bloody chee-chees are too poor to ride in gharris? she wondered. The officer, however, did touch his cap with his swagger stick; not that Aunty noticed. She was far too busy telling her niece about the sort of clothes she would wear. Suddenly Veronica stopped dead.

'What's wrong?' Aunty asked. 'Don't you like rose pink? I know just the shade for you.'

'That girl,' Veronica said, 'I met her years ago. She was rude to me.'

'Memsahibs often are,' said her aunt. 'The answer is

for you to be rude to them – only you must be sure they don't realise it. They can make trouble for us. Fortunately they are often very stupid.'

'I don't know about making trouble,' said Veronica, 'but I got my own back.' She told Aunty about the funeral procession and the suttee, and Miss Victoria being sick.

'Terrible,' said her aunt. 'Aren't you glad you're not all Indian?'

'Yes, of course,' said Veronica. 'But I'm glad I'm not all white, either.'

'Whyever not?'

'You wouldn't be my Aunty.'

Aunty linked her arm in hers as they walked to the gharri.

Mark Beddoes had been obliged to go in the Lippiatts' car to their house to take tea. Rather a splendid car with an equally splendid chauffeur, but then Tom Lippiatt was the most tremendous swell. Burra sahib of burra sahibs. Pomp and circumstance all over the place, but Mark wasn't all that keen on tea. Cucumber sandwiches and Gentleman's Relish and small talk. On the other hand Lippiatt was a great chum of his uncle, Sir Charles, and Sir Charles was his only source of windfalls since his father had got through the family fortune at Deauville and Monte Carlo, then blown his brains out for an encore.

When they got to the Lippiatts' house it was at once apparent that they'd gone off him, and he knew at once why. Poppy Villiers. But that was ridiculous, he thought. They should know damn well that he couldn't afford her. Tom Lippiatt knew everything. Even so, he found it interesting that he should do nothing but resent Tom Lippiatt's disapproval, while his wife's held a certain piquancy. Pretty little thing, Maude Lippiatt. And that's quite enough of that, he told himself. Your life's complicated enough as it is.

'. . . Eurasians are a fact of life,' Lippiatt was saying. 'One we must accept, I suppose. All the same, that's no reason why one should acknowledge them in public.'

'I danced with Poppy Villiers at a couple of tea dances,' said Mark. 'No more than that. All the same, sir, if you think I shouldn't – acknowledge her—'

Two hits there, he thought. 'Sir' to remind Lippiatt that he was at least ten years older than Mark, and 'acknowledge' to remind him that he was being pompous. Even so, he took care to maintain an expression of wide-eyed innocence: the simple subaltern in the presence of a man rather older, and far, far wiser.

'The child she had with her,' Maude Lippiatt said. 'Would she be her daughter?'

Lippiatt shrugged.

'I mean,' said Mrs Lippiatt, 'whatever one thinks of the Villiers person she does dress rather well, whereas the child seemed positively dowdy.'

Mark Beddoes had no memory of what the child wore. All he could recall was that she blazed with beauty.

'Not a patch on your Victoria,' he heard himself saying, because it had to be said. At once Tom Lippiatt relented, and passed him a cucumber sandwich.

All in all it was good to get away. Look in at the mess, he thought. Have an early drink, maybe two. He could afford two. But when he got there he found he couldn't.

Rollo Sandyford was there, and not only was Rollo perpetually hard up, he was adept at conveying the idea that whoever was nearest should do something about it, and he, Mark, was nearest. He asked the mess waiter for two chota pegs and dear little Rollo smiled sweetly, but at the same time seemed to suggest that one whisky and soda was far, far less than he deserved. Mark waited. That there was more to come he had no doubt.

Rollo had a polo pony for sale. 'Acting on behalf of a friend' of course. Mark thought: if he concentrates he can just about distinguish one end of a horse from the other, and doesn't the idiot realise I can't even afford the fodder for a polo pony, never mind the bloody pony? And yet, and yet . . . The trouble with Rollo was that he was pathetic. Good looking in a pretty boy sort of way, but pathetic. Hopeless sportsman, rotten officer. The last man on earth from whom to buy a polo pony. Not that it would be a friend's pony. Selling on commission for some rich Indian, that was more Rollo's style.

'He really is a very good pony,' Sandyford said.

'No doubt,' said Mark.

'Well at least take a look at him. That's all I'm asking.'

So you can tell others I'm interested? Mark wondered.

Aloud he said, 'What would be the point? If he's that good I couldn't afford him and if he isn't I don't want him.'

'I thought you were rich,' Sandyford said.

'Not just at the moment,' Mark said. Or any other moment, he thought.

'I think I'll have a word with Rogers,' said Sandyford. 'If you'll excuse me—'

He left then, and Mark tried not to look too pleased about it. Sandyford should have gone to Rogers in the first place, he thought: a) Rogers could afford a new pony, and b) he might buy it. He was stupid enough. Still, the hurried exit had saved him the price of a drink.

He began to think of Poppy Villiers. A lot of chaps did that. Well obviously. She was incredibly beautiful, perhaps flawlessly so: dark eyes that were almost black, black and shining hair, exquisite figure, and even fully clothed she could generate an aura of eroticism which most women couldn't achieve stark naked. But it wasn't that. Even when he could have afforded her – well just about – he had felt no need to do so. Too long a queue?

It was the girl who was with her. Not child, not woman. Girl. About Victoria's age, he thought, but oh so different. Well of course. Golden, like Poppy, not peaches and cream. Looks like Poppy, too. The beginnings of elegance, even style, but poor. Even poorer than me, he thought, if that dress is anything to go by ... Poppy's niece, perhaps? Whoever she was, quite soon Poppy could have a rival.

3

Veronica loved Aunty's house, but then how could she not, after what she'd been used to? It was a bungalow, old and huge and rambling, and with a guest-house even more luxurious than the main building. The garden was vast, too: a great blaze of bougainvillaea, azaleas, roses, marigolds. There was even a tank big enough to swim in, and servants all over the place: gardeners, sweepers, a cook, bearers and, of course, Jagadir Singh: the watchman; the chokra, Aunty called him, but Veronica thought that he might have other duties too.

And to match the splendour of her new surroundings Aunty had bought her new clothes: silk and fine cotton dresses and underwear, silk stockings, hand-made shoes, a handbag, even jewellery: pearls and gold bracelets. They make me feel very grown up, she thought, but even more they make me feel loved, because not only did Aunty pay, she was happy to pay.

One night before dinner Aunty rang for champagne, and permitted one glass for Veronica.

'We ought to talk,' said her aunt.

'Yes, Aunty.' Veronica sat up very straight.

'Not so tense, please. There's nothing to be afraid of.'
Veronica relaxed a little. 'You're fourteen you say?' Veronica nodded. 'We must arrange a school for you. There is a convent school that takes girls of our sort—'

'Bloody chee-chees,' said Veronica, and then: 'Oh Aunty, I'm sorry. It just slipped out.'

'Who called you that?' her aunt asked.

'My father.'

'Idiot,' her aunt said. 'He didn't even have the sense to be proud of you.'

'He was ashamed of me. He was ashamed of mummy, too.'

'And mummy was ashamed of me,' her aunt said. 'But we'll get to that in a minute.'

She took cigarettes from her bag, and gave one to Veronica.

'Don't inhale too much,' she said. 'Just practise holding it and looking pretty. Because you are, you know.'

'Daddy said I was the wrong colour to be pretty.'

'And yet he married your mother. Don't interrupt. You're clever, too. Which is why you'll be going to the convent. Day girl. You'll get on. The nuns won't harm you.'

'Of course not,' said Veronica.

Her aunt looked at her thoughtfully, and was silent for a while. At last she said, 'We'll take a look at the place tomorrow. Your plainest dress and no scent. We can't have you upsetting the nuns.'

'Yes, Aunty.'

'We'll have to get you an elocution teacher too. Your accent's the only bloody chee-chee thing about you.'

'Yes, Aunty.'

'So meek and mild,' her aunt mocked.

'Why shouldn't I be?' said Veronica. 'You're telling me I must do all the things I want to do.'

'Just for that you can come and give me a kiss,' said her aunt, and when Veronica had done so, she continued: 'Now we come to why your mother was ashamed of me.' She drew a deep breath. 'I like to make things clear,' she said at last, 'but this one's damn difficult.' She ground out her cigarette, sighed again and said, 'Best get on with it I suppose.'

Veronica waited.

'I'm a prostitute,' said Aunty. So I was right, thought Veronica, and waited once more, because it wasn't the time to say anything. Not yet.

'A whore,' Aunty said. 'If I wasn't there'd be no money for this house, the servants, the convent school. All the same, that's why your mother was ashamed of me.' She looked at her niece, still silent. 'Well child,' she said. 'Have you nothing to say?'

Veronica also liked to make things clear.

'Just one thing, Aunty,' she said. 'If you're a whore you must be a good one.'

Her aunt blinked, then suddenly roared with laughter, poured out more champagne, and just a very little for her niece.

'Oh, I am, I am,' she said.

Nothing like those terrible far from sacred cows my father's so fond of, Veronica thought. And then: thank God.

'Let me explain,' said her aunt.

'Only if you want to,' said Veronica. 'I loved my mother – of course I did – but that doesn't mean she was always right. She was wrong about you.'

'Bless you,' Aunty said, 'but I want to explain. Since you live here I must. It's not something I can keep a secret.'

Again Veronica waited.

'When I was your age,' Aunty said, 'I was poor. I had nothing. Also certain people were – unkind to me. Very unkind.'

Nuns, thought Veronica, but did not say so aloud.

'So I ran away,' said Aunty, 'and found that men liked me. I also found a – colleague who was clever about money – and other things. Between us we started a business. A honeymoon business.'

'*Honeymoon?*'

'It's the only part of marriage most men really like,' said Aunty. 'But they do like that. Also they like a lady to be discreet, and with me discretion is guaranteed.' She yawned and stretched, and Veronica was at once aware of the lusciousness of the body beneath the elegant dress. I must learn to do that, she thought.

'You see, in India there are certain Englishmen who have always been rich. Quite incredibly rich,' Aunty said. 'Indians too. Maharajahs and so on – but they can be rather a nuisance. In emergencies, yes. But not otherwise. Englishmen are far less trouble.' She sipped her champagne. 'Where was I?'

'Rich Englishmen,' Veronica said.

'In England they live in country houses, or a London crescent or square. More often both. They have loads of servants and shoot deer and pheasant, and chase foxes in what they call the shires, whatever they are. They can be very boring about it, but then work often is. But they're rich, and they marry women who are often rich too, though not as rich as they are.'

'Why not?' Veronica asked.

'Because they're women,' said Aunty. 'Don't interrupt. And rich or not, they're often very boring in bed, but even so they do produce babies eventually, and if they're boys they're sent off to Eton before they join the Guards, or the Cavalry . . .

'And all their lives they have toys: toys that other men could only dream of buying. A pair of shotguns made by someone called Purdey, a yacht at a place called Cowes, a racehorse sired by a Derby winner. Beautiful, elegant things that cost the earth. Like me.' She looked at her niece. 'You don't mind if I call myself beautiful?'

'Of course not,' said Veronica. 'It's true.'

'Well, yes,' Aunty said, 'but a lot of people don't like the truth. Not that it need worry you . . . Where was I?'

'Expensive toys,' said Veronica.

'Me,' said Aunty. 'The most expensive toy of all. To go on honeymoon with Poppy Villiers is like riding the winner of the Oaks while firing a Purdey shotgun at a whole moor full of grouse.' She yawned again. 'Forgive me, child,' she said. 'I've drunk too much champagne and it always makes me sleepy. I've got a honeymoon next week, you see.'

Again Veronica waited.

'It's all nonsense, of course,' said Aunty. 'I'm good, but not that good. No woman could be. The thing is the clients

33

think I am. Well they have to, poor darlings. They pay me so much money.'

Veronica giggled, and her aunt said, 'You really don't mind me telling you all this?'

'You said you like to make things clear,' Veronica said. 'I'm glad.'

'You're not like your mother,' said her aunt.

'I think I'm more like you,' Veronica said.

Her aunt looked at her warily. 'We'll have to see about that,' she said. 'Have a word with Bridget.'

'Bridget?' said Veronica.

'Bridget Hanratty,' said her aunt. 'My colleague. She sort of looks after me.'

'Like a lady's maid?'

'Sort of.'

This wasn't making things clear at all. This was downright vague, and at once Aunty realised the fact.

'More like a companion,' her aunt said, and smiled. 'Another bloody chee-chee. She's visiting some cousin or other. She'll be back in a day or two.' Again she stretched and yawned. I really *must* practise that, thought Veronica. The stretching anyway.

'Dinner and an early night,' said her aunt. 'Oh and just one more thing. Higgins isn't a name I like. From now on you're Veronica Carteret. It's school tomorrow.'

No scent and her plainest dress, as Aunty had decreed, but her soap was scented too, and even her plainest dress wasn't all that plain, and anyway she was Veronica Carteret.

Her aunt inspected her. 'Oh dear,' she said, 'those

34

nuns will have their work cut out.'

In fact the nuns were no trouble at all. To begin with there was a uniform: plain blouse, grey skirt, low-heeled shoes, but she hadn't gone to the school to wear pretty dresses, she'd gone there to learn, and learn she did. English and mathematics and French and geometry: she gobbled them up like sweets from a box. And Sister Maria Angela was from Goa: there was even the chance to study Camoëns, the Portuguese poet whom Father Delemos had praised so highly.

At first the other girls in her class were wary of her. It seemed somehow unnatural for anyone to enjoy studying as much as Veronica did, but she was cheerful and good natured and always ready to help anyone who was stuck with their prep, and they forgave her. She was also the prettiest girl in the class, and they forgave her even that.

Aunty thought that studying was unnatural too, but she saw at once that her niece enjoyed it, and all that scribbling in books and practising the piano kept her out of mischief. She encouraged it. Aunty, bless her, was no problem. The problem was Bridget Hanratty.

Bridget was about five years older than Aunty, who Veronica reckoned must be twenty-seven; darker too, and smaller, and not so pretty, though pretty enough. The trouble was that Bridget was jealous. How could she be otherwise? Before I arrived, thought Veronica, she was the favourite: the one who controlled the house and the servants. Not that the servants gave trouble. They all knew how Aunty earned their wages – how could they not? – but they also knew they were paid every week, and that without Aunty they would have to seek far less pleasant jobs, even if Bridget Hanratty did nag a bit. In India servants expected to be nagged. It was part of the job. Even so, Veronica thought, *I* didn't expect to be nagged, and if Bridget doesn't stop it soon, steps will have to be taken: maybe even a visit to Kali. She had her father's temper after all, even if she tried jolly hard to hide the fact. It had got worse when Aunty had a client to entertain in the guest-house. They had far too much time to spend together. Still, there was piano practice and homework and a pony to ride. She adored riding that pony, and the syce had told Aunty she would do very well. And so I did, she thought, until I put her at a jump that just wasn't on and she threw me. Not that it was darling Rani's fault. I should have had more sense . . .

She sneaked back into the house and limped to her room. Cedric Richardson would be there soon to give her voice lessons. He was what Aunty called queer, but he had a beautiful voice, and was clever enough to make hers sound beautiful too: nothing like the voice she had used in Kalpur.

But this was India. You couldn't just sneak in unobserved where there are servants. The syce had told the sweeper probably, who'd told the bearer, who'd told Bridget. Like a parlour game. But whoever had told whoever, she had just come from her bath – bliss, that bath. It had at least done something to ease the pain – when there was a tap at her door and Bridget came in. And me in my drawers, thought Veronica. She might have waited. Still at least I'm worth a look. By the way she blinked, Bridget thought so too. Veronica reached for her camisole.

'I hear you had a fall,' Bridget said.

'I'm all right.'

'Maybe,' said Bridget. 'Show me where it hurts.'

'Are you a nurse or something?'

'I know about being hurt,' said Bridget, and somehow Veronica knew that it was true, and showed her. Bridget clicked her tongue and walked out, and thank God for that, thought Veronica, except that she came back almost at once with a bottle and a sponge.

'We'll try this,' she said. 'It won't hurt.' And then as Veronica hesitated: 'Trust me.'

Veronica did so, and found that the pain began to ease almost at once. When Bridget had done, she began to dress, and as she did so Bridget said, 'I hadn't realised. Somebody used to beat you.'

'My father,' Veronica said. 'Does it still show?'

'Almost gone,' said Bridget. 'But he must have been good at it.'

'He is. He killed my mother.'

'Oh, dear,' said Bridget. 'I knew she'd died – but Poppy didn't say how. I was away, you see. I'm sorry.'

'That's all right,' Veronica said, and discovered that she meant it. It *was* all right.

'My father beat me, too,' Bridget said.

'Did you get used to it?'

'You never get used to it,' said Bridget, and Veronica agreed. 'But I bet we were lucky compared with Poppy,' Bridget said.

'Her father beat her?'

Bridget shook her head. 'Her parents were good to their children, only they died in a cholera epidemic, and she and your mummy went to an orphanage. Your mummy was only there for a little while – she was older, old enough to marry – but Poppy was younger than you. They were beaten every day.'

'Who beat them? *Who?*'

Veronica was shouting, and Bridget smiled. The girl was in a rage, but it was a rage inspired by love.

'The nuns who ran the orphanage,' said Bridget. 'They weren't like the ones who teach you, Veronica. Apart from prayer their only pleasure was thrashing little girls.'

Simultaneously Veronica realised two things: why her mother had married her father, and why Aunty hated nuns. To send her to a convent school had been a generous gesture indeed.

'I would like to thrash them,' she said.

'No doubt the devil will do that,' said Bridget, then: 'Forgive me, my dear. I hadn't realised that you were one of us.'

'Us?'

'The ones who know about pain.' Veronica reached for her hairbrush and Bridget said, 'Better let me do that. We don't want your bruises to start aching again.' She was very good at doing one's hair, Veronica found.

'She ran away,' said Bridget.

'Aunt Poppy?'

'Of course. It's not easy to keep a hawk in a cage. She ran away and set up in business for herself.'

Which is why my mother was ashamed of her, thought Veronica. Darling, foolish mummy. Did you never think what the alternative was? You found out soon enough.

'Honeymoon on a short-term contract,' she quoted.

'Her favourite joke,' said Bridget, and then: 'I'm useful,

you know. I manage things for her. Jagadir Singh and me
– we take care of her.'

'Well, of course,' Veronica said.

Bridget looked at her warily, but it seemed as though
Veronica meant it.

'We shouldn't be enemies,' Bridget said.

'Much better to be friends,' said Veronica, and Bridget
offered her hand, but Veronica kissed her cheek instead.

It was time, the colonel said, for them to be off to the
war, and the mess growled its agreement, and quite right
too, thought Mark, especially for the likes of me. Here I
am with nothing to live on but my pay, waiting for somebody to die so I can be promoted, and there's a damn
sight better chance of somebody dying if we go to France,
and if it's me that dies it's all part of being a soldier. Like
that song the men sometimes sang on the march:

> It serves you right, you shouldn't have joined.
> It bloody well serves you right.

Then he looked down the table to where Sandyford sat,
his glass of port untouched. Rollo, it seemed, did not
share his sentiments.

Just time to give a farewell ball and fit in one more
game of polo, said the colonel. No playing polo in France.
All the same, they'd find the time to give those lancer
chappies one more hiding before the troop-ship came to
collect them next week. Rollo turned green. He's afraid,
thought Mark. Well, of course he is. Behind the bravado,
the all stout-hearted chaps together nonsense, we're all

afraid. But what can we do about it? It's what we're for.

Tom and Maude Lippiatt came to the ball, but not Victoria. She was far too young. Of course she was, thought Mark. All the same I wish that protégée of Poppy Villiers had come ... He had to dance with Maude, instead. Not that that was too great a hardship. She was still pretty, and pleasant to hold. Tom spent most of his time in the card room, which was perfectly fine with Mark. More dances with Maude.

They were sitting out, drinking iced punch, when she told him that she too might be going to England.

'Blighty,' she said. 'Isn't that what the Tommies call it?'

'That's it,' he said.

'Tom and Victoria too of course.'

'Leave?' he asked her.

'Tom's work. Something frightfully secret. To do with the war. Everything's to do with the war these days.' She smiled at him, but there was sadness in the smile. 'As well you know.'

He made no answer. He had no wish to turn green like Rollo Sandyford.

'Where will you stay?' she asked him.

'In France?' He seemed astounded, she thought: as well he might.

'No, no,' she said. 'In England. Surely you'll have a little time in England before—' her voice faded.

'The regimental depot's in Northumberland,' said Mark. 'My mother has a little house there. If I get leave that's where I'll go.'

'That's where your uncle lives, too.'

'Sir Charles,' said Mark. 'And my two cousins – when

we're not at the war, but that's where most of us are these days. It's all the rage.'

She grimaced. Sang-froid or whatever it was didn't seem to be to her taste, and come to think of it it wasn't to his, either.

'We may visit Charles Beddoes,' Maude Lippiatt said. 'He and Tom have been chums ever since they were at school together. Perhaps I – we – may see you there.'

'I hope so,' said Mark.

'But in case we don't – let me wish you God speed.'

Then Major Beresford came to claim the dance Maude had promised him. The waltz from *The Merry Widow*, Mark noticed. There were rather a lot of widows these days, but not many of them were merry. All the same, it was one of his favourites. Lucky old Beresford.

The next day was the polo match, and incredibly Mark had been asked to play. Rogers had been first choice – he had a string of ponies after all, and to be fair he was a damn good polo player – but he'd had a recurrence of the malaria which rather pestered him and offered Mark his place, and his ponies, which was damn decent of him. The ponies included the one Rollo was touting, which turned out to be a gallant little devil, if a bit long in the tooth.

At first it was one of the best afternoons Mark had had in a long time – he was playing well; scored twice in the second chukka – and it would be a long time before he got another game of polo. Perhaps he'd never – Mark blanked that one out of his mind and concentrated on the game. Almost he scored yet again but at the crucial moment that pony of Rollo Sandyford's – it would be –

stumbled, pecked and threw him and then kicked him. No malice aforethought, Mark admitted, but all the same it meant a hospital rather than a troop-ship. All the chaps were sympathetic, because it meant that he would be late for the war. All except Rollo Sandyford.

4

Veronica had been to the maidan and seen it all. She told her aunt about it.

'Hurt badly?' Aunty asked.

'Broken leg.'

'At least it'll keep him out of the war for a while.'

'He may not want to be kept out,' said Veronica.

'He may not,' said Aunty. 'Some men can't wait to be killed.' She looked at her niece. 'You're not – well – attracted to him, I hope?'

'Of course not,' Veronica said. 'It's just jolly unfair, that's all.'

'What is?' said her aunt. 'Try not to be vague, child.'

'Sorry, Aunty,' said Veronica. 'What I mean is – you have to be a man to ride a pony like the one that threw Lieutenant Beddoes.'

'You have to be a man to be shot at in France,' said her aunt. 'Is that what you want? To be a man?'

Veronica giggled. 'No, Aunty,' she said. 'I'm happy as I am.'

'So you should be,' said her aunt, and then, still not entirely sure, 'You're really not attracted to Lieutenant

43

Beddoes?' Veronica shook her head. 'Or anybody else?'

'I'm far too busy at school for all that,' said Veronica, and her aunt stared, bewildered. 'Unless you want me to be?'

'Early days,' Aunty said, and then, because she couldn't help it, '*School*?'

'Mother Agnes says if I go on like this I can take the Senior Cambridge next year.'

The Senior Cambridge, her aunt knew, was a difficult and demanding exam that often led to a place at a university. Her niece made it sound like the announcement of her engagement to a duke.

'And that's what you want?' she asked.

'Oh, yes,' said Veronica.

Her aunt sighed her relief, but wasn't there, despite her relief, cause for another kind of worry? 'I have some news for you,' she said.

'Yes, Aunty?'

'About your father. Pushpar sent me a letter. It came while you were out. He's dead.'

Veronica smiled as if she'd just passed the Senior Cambridge with honours.

'Of course she had to dictate the letter to a writer – but all the same it's clear how he died.'

'How, Aunty?'

'Drink,' said her aunt. 'And what she called the wounds of love.'

Veronica nodded. Pushpar would have called it his karma, she thought. Booze and VD were his destiny.

'Fifty pounds,' said her aunt. 'I might as well have handed him a loaded revolver.'

44

'Except that his way took longer,' Veronica said. 'Did he suffer?'

'Yes,' said her aunt.

Again the smile. The Senior Cambridge with every honour possible.

'You don't feel *any* pity for him?'

'You never heard the way he made my mother scream,' Veronica said. Or me, she thought to herself, but Aunty might think that was showing off.

Her aunt, who knew a lot about screaming in pain, left it at that. The child had no reason to mourn her father, and when you came to think about it, it had been fifty pounds well spent.

Next morning Veronica set off earlier than usual to go to school. There was a temple to Kali close by Aunty's house, and as Pushpar had told her, over and over, Kali never forgets: neither the good things nor the bad. She spent all her spare pocket money on garlands, then went to school. There were tests that day: English, French, maths, music, Portuguese, and even by her own demanding standards Veronica surpassed herself. The nuns were delighted.

His leg took its time, but he was young and fit, and it began to heal more quickly than he'd feared. The only thing was the plaster cast: in the Calcutta heat it itched unbearably, and the doctor recommended the Hills, where it was cool, but he'd turned that down flat. Suppose he was up there and they pronounced him fit, and he missed the next troop-ship because the Hills were far away and the troop-ship couldn't wait?

I'm reasoning like a fool, thought Mark. Only an idiot would like to leave India to go to France. An idiot – but not Rollo Sandyford. Rollo had had a quite extraordinary piece of luck – except that when one thought about it the reason for it was obvious. The Royal Northumbrians had been replaced by a native regiment. Gujaratis, and very smart and capable they were, except that one winter in Northern France would kill them to a man. The thing was that until they were settled in the Gujaratis needed a Royal Northumbrian to act as liaison officer, and the colonel had chosen Rollo. Without hesitation, thought Mark. The colonel's no fool, and if you've got men's lives to worry about, who needs Rollo? Not that Rollo was carefree. The liaison business was bound to end eventually, and when it did it would be la belle France for Rollo, too. Perhaps we'll travel on the same troop-ship, thought Mark, and then: Oh, my God I hope not.

There was to be a gymkhana, a charity affair to raise money for comforts to send to the troops. It was the wives of the ICS wallahs who organised it, and Mark was not in the least surprised when Maude told him that she was the organising committee's chairman. After all, she was good at organising, and she was far and away the most senior wife there, by rank if not by age, and anyway, her daughter was hot favourite to win the girls' jumping event. As Tom Lippiatt never tired of telling him, Victoria was a clipping little rider. The important thing was that he, Mark, was allowed to go. The surgeon had huffed a bit and puffed a bit, but the plaster was off at last, the bones had knit. He was even allowed to walk – a very little. The muscles of the leg that had been broken weren't nearly ready for a route march yet. Even so, he was allowed to go, with strict instructions to carry a stick and sit down as often as possible. After he'd walked to the waiting gharri he understood why.

The crowd at the maidan was huge. Lots of Indians of course, and most of them in the open air, mostly low-caste. The sun's heat was brutal, but a gymkhana was a spectacle after all, and, for those who endured the sun, it was free. The paying audience were those who had seats beneath canvas awnings that provided shade. The entire ICS, the Gujarati regiment's officers, quite a crowd of Eurasians, and far more Hindus and Muslims than he'd expected. Even Poppy Villiers was there. Not her young protégée, he noticed regretfully: school, he supposed, and no chance of leave. Not like Victoria, but then Victoria was competing.

The band of the Gujarati regiment thumped its way, often accurately, through the inevitable repertoire: Gilbert and Sullivan, *The Merry Widow, The Tales of Hoffman*, and Mark sat in the shade on his own, and without regret. Just getting to his seat had been exhausting; conversation on top of it would have floored him, but he didn't need conversation to tell him that something was up. The mass of poor Indians in the sun told him that, and so did the rich Indians in the shade. The sahibs and their mems looked uneasy, and the Eurasians were buzzing like bees.

And then it began. Musical rides, some rather inept dressage, and then the serious business: the jumps against the clock. Some of the competitors – men and women – were good, for this was India after all, and horse-riding was not for dilettantes. He found himself wishing, for the thousandth time, that he hadn't broken his leg. Against this lot he would have had a better than even chance . . . And then – show a bit of sense, Beddoes. If you hadn't broken your leg you'd be in France by now. There was a pause, and tea and biscuits, and the band thumped its way through gems from *Carmen*, and still the crowd buzzed, the ones with programmes consulted them for the umpteenth time. Whatever it is, thought Mark, it hasn't happened yet. Then the music stopped, tea things were collected, and it was the children's turn: boys over fifteen, girls over fifteen, and still the crowd stayed calm. Boys under fifteen: and there was a collective sigh, as if to the overture of a longed for drama . . . Girls under fifteen, and the audience again buzzed like bees, this time about to swarm.

Two girls who weren't bad, then one who was rather good, and the crowd watched, and some of them were yawning, thought Mark, and some were impatient, but these were not the girls they had come to see. The applause, even for the rather good girl, was apathetic at best. Then the MC called out 'Miss Victoria Lippiatt', and still the crowd were unimpressed, except for the ICS contingent, and they had to be impressed, thought Mark; this was the boss's daughter after all.

She was good, too. Good pony, well trained, but even so she was good: riding precisely as she'd been taught; never pushing her mount too hard, but keeping up the pressure even so. Pretty to watch. Not a rail fell. Clear round in fact, and a fast one. Even so, the applause was scarcely more than polite.

When it died the MC said, 'And now our last entrant, Miss Veronica Carteret.' When she came out Mark couldn't believe it. Veronica Carteret was the child – niece? cousin? protégée? – he'd seen with Poppy Villiers. Impeccably dressed – white shirt, jodhpurs, sola topee, but an Eurasian even so. Now the crowd were buzzing like hornets.

Her pony's a brute, thought Mark: surly and impatient by turns, and nothing like as clever at the jumps as Victoria's. But Veronica what's it knew it, and handled him in the only possible way, laying on the whip until he exploded into life, and she went at the jumps as if she were leading a cavalry charge.

Bridget Hanratty clutched Poppy's arm. 'Oh my God, she'll kill herself,' she said.

'Just be quiet,' said Poppy Villiers.

The pony tried to sulk again, but the whip took care of that, and he pounded on even faster. A rail rattled but stayed in place, and Bridget Hanratty shut her eyes. She was praying.

Another clear round: crude, even brutal compared with Victoria's, but according to the MC just as fast; and given the relative merits of the two ponies, crude brutality was the only weapon she had, thought Mark. That and courage. The way she'd ridden she could have broken her neck.

'The bastard,' said Poppy Villiers.

'Who?' Bridget Hanratty said.

'Tom Lippiatt.'

'Oh,' said Bridget Hanratty.

But it wasn't all bad news. In the first place, Veronica

had dead-heated with Victoria Lippiatt, and indeed how could it be otherwise, Poppy Villiers thought, with thousands of people watching? And so it was that a box of chocolates became two boxes of chocolates, and one certificate became two certificates, and both young ladies curtsied charmingly to Maude Lippiatt, though neither looked at the other. Moreover, Veronica's syce told her that Victoria's syce had told him that Victoria was furious. It wasn't all bad news. By no means.

Next day after school Veronica went to swim in the tank, and as she went her aunt called out to her to visit her afterwards, and bring the chocolates. She swam naked as she always did, at a time when there was nobody in the gardens except Bridget, who patrolled the flower-beds with a scowl that even Kali might have envied. (No clothes is best, Aunty had told her. Nothing like it for the figure.) When she had done she wrapped a towel around her like a sari, and almost at once was dry. The sun that day attacked like a tiger, but even so she remembered to take the chocolates from the ice-box. Her aunt hated it when you forgot things, but she was utter bliss to live with after daddy.

Aunty was lying on her bed, soaking up the punkah's swirl, clad in nothing but a shift of cotton so fine you could see straight through it, and golly she's gorgeous, Veronica thought, as she always did. Like those statues of Vishnu she'd seen in the ruined temple outside Kalpur. Firm breasts, a narrow waist, hips rounded just enough. But to it she had added a sense of style, a European elegance that announced that she could say no as well as yes.

'I thought we might have a little party,' her aunt said. 'A celebration.' She nodded to an ice bucket. 'Champagne.'

'We had some yesterday,' said Veronica.

'So we did,' her aunt said, 'and Bridget got tiddly. Today she's gone to see our stockbroker.' Veronica looked puzzled. 'Goose,' Aunty said. 'I don't just lie down for a living. I listen, too. When the clients make phone calls it's often about money.'

'Oh,' said Veronica.

'Oh is right,' said her aunt. 'I make more on the stockmarket than I do from honeymoons. Let's have a look at those chocolates.' Veronica handed them over. It was good to give something to Aunty for a change.

'At least they're the best,' her aunt said, and opened the box. 'Pour out some wine.'

Veronica poured, then offered Aunty her glass, and as she did so Aunty twitched away her towel.

'Well well well,' Aunty said.

Veronica had no idea what she was supposed to do, and so she did nothing. Not that she was afraid or anything. Aunty's gaze was no more threatening than that of an art critic looking at a statue. Not like some of those bitches who had gobbled up her father's fifty pounds. Their hands all over her. When she was nine: even less.

She waited until her aunt made the sign that she should turn in front of her, and slowly turned.

'We're growing up,' her aunt said. 'We're growing up very nicely.'

'Thank you, Aunty.'

'You're very like I was at your age,' her aunt said.

'Then I'm lucky,' said Veronica. Her aunt blew her a

51

kiss, then selected a chocolate, offered her the box.

'Lie down,' she said, and motioned to the *chaise-longue*, and Veronica lay down, because whatever else she was, Aunty was the boss, and in any case the *chaise-longue* was very close to the punkah.

'Turn,' said her aunt, 'and again, and again,' and Veronica turned. 'Now drink your champagne,' said her aunt. 'Have a chocolate.' Veronica did so. 'You're a problem,' her aunt said.

Veronica looked dismayed. 'I'm sorry, Aunty,' she said.

'Oh such distress,' said her aunt. 'Didn't you tell me just two days ago that you enjoyed problems?'

'That was algebra,' said Veronica.

'Well my problems are clients. Chaps,' her aunt said. 'And I can solve them every bit as well as you can solve those equations of yours.'

'Yes, Aunty.' Veronica smiled, warily.

'That's better,' her aunt said. 'My problem with you is what to do with you. I don't want to be rid of you, darling. I'll never want that.'

Veronica felt that she might cry, but it would be silly to cry when she had no clothes on, and Aunty had little time for tears whether she was naked or not. 'I thought you might want me to—' she hesitated.

'Join the firm?' her aunt said. 'I thought so too. Only if you wanted to, of course. You'd make a fortune, believe me. But that mother superior of yours—'

'Mother Agnes,' said Veronica.

'She says you're a natural-born academic,' said her aunt. 'If you did what I do you'd be bored to death in a fortnight.'

'So what am I going to do?' Veronica asked.

'Stay with Aunty. Be an academic,' her aunt said. It was everything she wanted. 'Just one thing,' her aunt added. 'When a chap comes along – a client so to speak – and the way you look they'll soon be forming a queue – I want you to tell me first before you make him blissful.'

'Yes, Aunty.'

'Your promise, child.'

'Word of honour,' said Veronica.

'That's all right, then,' her aunt said. 'Fill my glass will you, darling, and just one more sip for yourself.'

Veronica stood up and did so, and her aunt watched her with a sort of abstract delight. As if she were the filly that would win the Oaks her clients made such a fuss of, she thought, and talking of horses:

'That pony of yours yesterday,' she said. 'He wasn't much good, was he?'

'Stupid and stubborn,' said Veronica, 'but strong. If he'd been a little better I'd have won outright.'

'You gave him a bit of a leathering.'

'It was up to him,' said Veronica. 'If he'd done what I wanted I wouldn't have needed to use a whip.'

Her aunt chuckled. 'Maybe you should tell your chaps that,' she said, and then: 'A client got him for you. I know nothing about horses, and he swore to me it was a good 'un.'

'Then he lied,' Veronica said. 'Victoria Lippiatt's was a good 'un.'

Her aunt looked at her for a couple of seconds then asked, 'So how did you tie with her?'

'Because I hate being beaten,' said Veronica.

'Just like your pony,' said her aunt, and they both giggled, until her aunt said, 'All the same I owe you an apology. Next time I get you a pony I'll get better advice. Better pony, too.' And then, 'Bridget,' she said.

'She thought I should have won?'

'She thought you shouldn't have ridden at all,' said her aunt. 'She was worried sick.'

'But why—'

'Listen and I'll tell you,' said her aunt, and Veronica listened, not because she was afraid of Aunty: because she adored her.

'She doesn't understand about horses,' said her aunt, 'although I could say we both know quite a bit about riding.'

Veronica giggled again. Her aunt looked at her champagne glass, and giggled too.

'She's fond of you, you see,' Aunty said.

'I'm fond of her.'

'Good girl,' said Aunty. 'She never looked like you, but she knows a lot about love – the caring kind.'

Veronica said nothing – what was there to say? – but Aunty looked at her face and was satisfied.

'She was afraid you might be killed,' she said.

'On that slug?' said Veronica.

'As I said, she doesn't understand,' said Aunty, and then, 'Mahratta, Irish, English, Goanese.' For once Veronica looked bewildered, and her aunt felt a sense of triumph. It wasn't easy to bewilder her niece.

'The blood in your veins,' her aunt said. 'The English fought battles and marched to them on foot: no doubt the Goanese built churches and played music – it's what they

54

do best after all – but the Mahrattas and the Irish were horsemen. They would all have been proud of you yesterday, but especially the Irish and the Mahrattas. I know I was.'

'Thank you, Aunty,' Veronica said.

'I'm going to buy you a new dress,' said her aunt.

'Oh, *thank* you,' said Veronica.

'We've been invited to a dance next month,' her aunt said, 'and we can't have you going dressed like that, though you'd have no shortage of partners.'

Again Veronica giggled. No more champagne, she thought. She still had her homework to finish. French irregular verbs. Even so, 'A dance?' she asked.

'Mrs Lal,' said her aunt.

Mrs Lal was the widow of a successful jeweller, now a successful jeweller herself, who for some reason liked to give dances and parties that were a sort of No Man's Land where sahibs, Indians and Eurasians could meet and mingle. Even the more liberated kind of Indian females attended them, though of course they did not dance.

'You think I'm old enough?' Veronica asked.

'High time,' said her aunt. 'And anyway those dancing lessons of yours cost a fortune. It's about time I got some value for it. We'll go shopping on Saturday.'

'Oh, *Aunty*.'

'Get off to your homework,' said her aunt. 'I know you're dying to.' Veronica left the *chaise-longue*, graceful as a dancer, and her aunt said, 'I've been thinking.'

'Yes, Aunty?'

'We ought to have our portraits painted, you and I. In

the altogether. Would that bother you?'

'Not if you were with me,' Veronica said.

'Oh, I will be,' said her aunt. 'Not now, of course. But soon. When I can find a good painter, and those little peaches of yours have grown into pomelos.'

Veronica put out her tongue at her, and her aunt chuckled lazily. 'Good girl,' she said.

It was half-way through the pluperfect tense of *recevoir* that Veronica realised why her aunt had made her lie there naked: had been almost naked herself. It was to get her used to the idea: to show her that for them nakedness was a state of being rather than a state of mind, which meant that Aunty hadn't *quite* made up her mind about her joining the firm, whatever Mother Agnes had said.

5

The dress was of cream, not white, with a thin pattern of scarlet. Cream socks, too, not stockings, because she wasn't 'out' yet, no matter how you interpreted the word, but to make up for it there were dancing shoes of creamy silk with scarlet bows, and a ribbon of scarlet for her hair. And on top of all that Aunty took her to Mrs Lal's shop and bought her a ring: a gold ring with a ruby.

'Aunty, it's too much.'

'No, it's not,' said her aunt. Almost she sounded angry, then her voice softened. 'You went out on that pony – the one you called the slug, and quite rightly – and nobody thought you had a hope in hell. Especially the sahibs. But then you showed them. You tied for first place. Part of it was skill and the rest was courage – but who gives a damn what it was? You showed them. I'm proud of you.'

For a moment Veronica thought that she might cry, but somehow she knew that to cry would be to let Aunty down, and so she smiled instead.

For the dance she wore her new dress, her pearls, her ruby ring, and she knew she had never looked better because it was Bridget who told her so, and it was Bridget who had brushed her hair, tied in the ribbon, applied the tiniest touch of colour to her cheeks and lips. Perfume too. Light and delicate and elusive. Not like Aunty's scent at all. For that she would have to wait, but she didn't mind waiting. There was lots of time.

Aunty wore pink, but it was a pink like no other her niece had ever seen: deep and warm and sensuous, thought Veronica. Any deeper and it would have been scarlet. Aunty. The scarlet woman. Not that Aunty would have given a damn for that, either, but it might upset Mrs Lal, and so she wore pink, and a red-gold bracelet, red-gold necklace, diamonds in her ears. When they walked into Mrs Lal's drawing-room side by side the conversation stopped, then resumed frantically. Aunty never misses, thought Veronica, swelling with pride, but please God let some of it be for me, too.

Lots of sahibs, but not nearly so many mems, so that Mrs Lal had had to invite lots of Eurasians, too, though none who looked like Aunty. That pompous Collector or whatever he was – Lippiatt, that was it – had turned up, but he'd left his wife and daughter behind. Maybe she wasn't considered old enough for dances yet. Whatever the reason it was just as well. She hadn't been best pleased to share first place with me. Lieutenant Beddoes was there, and looking quite well, she thought. Handsome, too. Mess kit suited him. Not like the little chap he was talking to. In mess kit he looked like the Principal Boy in a pantomime.

Mrs Lal came to them, and said kind things about her looks, but that could be because of the ruby ring, and yet perhaps not. A lot of chaps were looking at her as well as Aunty. Then the band began to play. Well, quartet, anyway. Goanese. Aunty was right as usual. They were awfully good at music. The sahibs did their duty by their mems, or else headed purposefully towards the bloody chee-chees. It was a one-step, and quite fast, and soon the sahibs began to sweat. The sahibs were very good at sweating.

The one-step finished and almost at once the Goanese played a waltz. Lehar. The one from *The Merry Widow*. She played it too, on the piano at home, but not as well as the Goanese pianist. Not yet. Lieutenant Beddoes came up to them.

'Poppy,' he said. 'How nice.'

Aunty smiled. 'Good evening, Mark. I don't think you've met my niece.'

'Not met, no,' Mark Beddoes said, 'but I've seen her. At the gymkhana.'

Behind him, the Lippiatt person was looking far from happy. Veronica wondered if he would tell his daughter, and hoped he would.

Aunty smiled at her. 'She did well, didn't she?'

'First rate,' said Mark. 'Tell me, Miss—'

'Carteret,' said Veronica. 'Veronica Carteret.'

Gravely she offered her hand, and Mark took it, equally grave.

'Do you dance as well as you ride?' Mark asked.

'Now's your chance to find out,' said Aunty.

'May I?' Mark asked.

'Yes, of course,' said Veronica, and smiled. Eight out of ten for the smile, her aunt thought. Eight out of ten at *least*. Then her niece moved into Mark Beddoes' arms, and the score moved even higher.

It was the first time she had ever been in a man's arms – her dance teacher was a woman – but when you got to grips, so to speak, there was nothing to it. Lieutenant Beddoes was far more nervous than she was. But even so he was all right, and smelt rather more of cologne than of sweat. She found herself wondering what he would say if she told him that quite soon she and her aunt would lie down together stark naked to have their portraits painted.

'... absolutely fantastic ride,' the lieutenant was saying.

'I beg your pardon?'

'You,' he said. 'At the gymkhana. You tore round the course as if it was a cavalry charge.'

'With that pony it was the only way.'

'Yes,' said her partner. He sounded wary.

'Not like Victoria Lippiatt's,' said Veronica.

'Not in the least,' said Lieutenant Beddoes, and then: 'I say, I'm afraid this leg of mine is playing me up rather. You know I broke it?'

'Another damn pony,' Veronica said.

'Well yes. Would you mind awfully if we sat out and I got you a cup of coffee?'

Veronica said firmly, 'Ice-cream. Pistachio,' and Lieutenant Beddoes said, 'Of course.'

While she waited Veronica thought: That went well. He knows how I feel about Victoria and he didn't say a word when I said damn, so I know how he feels about me, and I know how I feel about him. He's nice, even sweet so far, but that's all he is. All the same, better not tell Aunty I said damn. She'd understand, of course she would, but that didn't mean she'd approve.

Aunty was dancing with the burra sahib, Victoria's papa, and for some reason he was making a hash of it. He wasn't a bad dancer – well not totally rotten – but he wasn't a good one either. But it wasn't just that. He looked nervous, even afraid: and the fear made him clumsy, so that he lurched about like a drunk. Not that there were any whisky-sodas to be had at Mrs Lal's. No champagne, either, she thought, but then Lieutenant Beddoes appeared with the pistachio ice-cream, which was just as good. Really he's rather good at fetching things, she thought.

Two days later he sailed on the troop-ship for Southampton. His leg wasn't a hundred per cent by any means, but the voyage home was a long one, and there was a doctor on board, and the troop-ship before the war had been a liner with a promenade deck: just the thing for a chap with a gammy leg in need of exercise. No Rollo . . . Now that was a bonus: rather a big one. Somehow Rollo had managed to persuade the Gujaratis' colonel that for the moment at least he was indispensable, which was odd when one thought of it. The Gujaratis knew their business. Even so he was spared having to take his meals with Rollo. Bliss.

Instead he thought of Veronica Carteret, if indeed that was her name. It sounded like an actress in musical comedy, but even so he thought of her. Over and over. Her and not her aunt. He'd danced with Poppy Villiers because no sane man would forego the opportunity. He'd danced with other women too: mems and Eurasians, because it was his duty, and for the look of the thing. He couldn't hover round Veronica Carteret all night like a wasp round a honeypot – and yet he'd gone back to her whenever he dared, whenever convention allowed: a one-step, two veletas, another waltz.

It was ridiculous: he knew it was. She wasn't even a woman – but she wasn't a child either, and that was the problem. When he had held her he had wanted her, every time, sensing the woman's shape beneath her dress. She could have wanted him, too, if she'd felt like it, he thought, but she hadn't. Of that he was sure. To her he was simply an older person who danced rather less than adequately because of his bad leg, but had a talent for fetching pistachio ice-cream. Nothing in that for him, and why the devil should there be? She was a *child* for God's sake. But not when he'd held her in his arms.

There was a swell in the Bay of Bengal, and that led to a bout of sea sickness that banished thoughts even of her, but she was back again as soon as the sea grew calm. The books about India he'd been determined to read – Lord Clive's biography, and Warren Hastings, Hickey's Diaries, and Wellington's Dispatches – none of them could keep her at bay. She ignored them all, walked prettily between the pages and just stood there and looked at him, and he melted every time. It was ridiculous and appalling and he couldn't help it. Maybe the war's the only thing that'll cure it, he thought. For a lot of chaps the war had been the cure for everything, good and bad, but at least he'd see his mother before he went to take his nasty medicine.

U-boat alarms in the Mediterranean, but God decided to let them live that time. The destroyers swooped, depth charges hurtling, and their water spouts sprayed like fountains, until one shot up black with oil. A goal for our side. And then one day it was cold, and it was the Atlantic not the Med, and the Germans scored the equaliser: torpedoed a tanker that blazed as if it were providing its very own Guy Fawkes' night. Yet still he thought of her: couldn't *not* think of her.

London was boring. None of his friends were there, his cousins too were with their battalion in France, and the one girl he wanted to see was in Calcutta – and that's quite enough of that, he thought, and went home instead. To mother, as if it were the school hols, except that now she lived in a neat little house in the village of Stonebridge in Northumberland, instead of the vast lump of decaying grandeur that she had brought to his father as part of her dowry, so that he might give it to the croupiers. Mark suspected that his mother preferred the neat little house, but he didn't. The mansion's grandeur hadn't been all that decayed, and he'd only found out how absolutely splendid it was to be rich when he ceased to be so.

She was pleased to see him of course. Kissed him and petted him and saw to it that Cook prepared his favourite meals; wore her most elegant dresses and what jewels she had left. She was still a pretty woman, he thought, and still had lots of friends, but he saw little of them. It's because I'm still alive and in England, and their sons were either in France or in hospital. Or dead.

Still he had news of them. There was a great pile of letters, and a lot of mummy's talk was about them, too:

the chaps in his regiment, the chaps he went to school with, except that it was more like a roll of honour than names of friends. Tony Bartram and Bob Elliott and Billy Fanshaw: all killed at Loos. Frank Denton, missing believed killed. Sam Forrest, blinded, and the colonel with both legs missing: yet the colonel, incredibly, had survived. On and on and on went the list, and though he and his mother tried desperately to talk of other things, somehow the war always reappeared, like an ugly and unwanted cat that sneaks in when nobody's looking.

When he couldn't stand it any more he'd take a gun out, or a rod. There was a wood nearby, and a stream, and the neat little house had shooting and fishing rights. It was autumn, and the pheasant were plentiful that year, because the men who should have killed them were doing their best to kill Germans instead. Plenty of brown trout, too, and for the same reason.

And just as well. There was to be a luncheon party before he took over his company, for he was a captain now, in charge of C Company of a newly raised battalion. Captain Beddoes. He said it aloud in the privacy of his bedroom. Captain Beddoes. Had a nice ring to it, he thought, and went into Hexham to have extra pips sewn on to his uniform.

He'd rather hoped that Sir Charles would be one of the guests. He was fond of his Uncle Charles, but his mother told him that Sir Charles was now living at his club.

'Why on earth should he do that?' Mark asked.

'He took it very badly when Francis was killed,' his mother said. Francis was his cousin, Sir Charles's elder son.

'Francis?'

His mother's hand went to her mouth. 'Didn't I tell you?' she asked. 'I know I wrote to you, but it must have been when you were on your way back here. Oh, Mark darling. I'm so sorry.' She began to cry, and he put his arms about her.

How can I blame her? he thought. It's true that Francis and I were friends: his brother too, but all I've thought about since I got here was the battalion, and God knows that was enough.

She left him to peer warily into the mirror. 'I look dreadful,' she said. 'Better go and repair the damage.'

Their lunch guests arrived before she came back. Tom and Maude Lippiatt, and their daughter Victoria. He'd been prepared for the parents, but the daughter came as rather a shock. Tom, it seemed, was home doing something frightfully important at India House, and not looking all that happy about it. He'd been given a week's leave, and was visiting relatives in Durham. Parsons probably, thought Mark, which may account for the unhappiness. Better give him a drink, quick. Maude on the other hand was looking delightful, and ten years younger than she'd seemed in Calcutta: an English autumn far kinder to her than the Indian sun. Her daughter, she explained, was with them because her governess had rather tiresomely developed appendicitis, and to leave her daughter in the care of a parlourmaid was out of the question.

A pretty child, thought Mark. Guinea gold hair, English rose complexion, her mother's pouting prettiness, but her eyes were her father's: shrewd, yet wary, perhaps ruthless

too. Then he looked again at her mother. Those eyes of
hers could be cruel too, he thought, if the need arose.
Victoria would be about fourteen, he thought. Veronica
Carteret's age, but the idea of holding her, touching her,
was unthinkable. Of Veronica it was best not to think at
all. He poured Tom Lippiatt a peg and went easy on
the soda, and sherry for Maude, then wondered about
lemonade for Victoria, but Victoria had discovered her
mother's spaniel Belinda, and asked if they might play
outside.

'Change after India,' said Lippiatt.

No servants, no punkah, no garden the size of a cricket
field.

'Yes indeed,' said Mark.

'Do you miss it?' Lippiatt asked, then: 'Silly question.
We all do. Especially Victoria.'

No ayah, thought Mark, no syce to groom her pony, no
other missy babas to boss in all directions because her
father was more king than commoner.

'She took it badly,' Lippiatt said.

'I beg your pardon?' said Mark. Lippiatt looked angry,
then realised that Mark was genuinely bewildered.

'The gymkhana,' said Lippiatt.

'Tying for first place,' said his wife.

Next week I have to go to camp and train a company
of raw recruits in about half the time it's going to need,
then take them to France and try to keep them alive, and
this man wants my sympathy because his daughter dead-
heated in a pony ride. And why hadn't they had a jump off
anyway? he wondered, and then he knew. It was because
Veronica would have gone round the course again in

66

exactly the same way, like one of those Mah̶̶̶̶
men who had given Sir Arthur Wellesley so m̶̶̶̶ ̶̶̶ ̶̶̶̶uble
in his early career.

'You should have seen it,' said Lippiatt.

'I did,' said Mark. 'My first outing after I broke my leg.'

'Riding like a maniac,' said Lippiatt. 'A bandit. A sword was all that was missing.'

So at least we're agreed on something, Mark thought. 'She didn't lack courage,' he said, and to his surprise Lippiatt agreed.

'What she lacked was decorum,' said his wife. 'It should be her aunt's business to teach her to acquire some, but since Miss – Villiers is it? – is totally without it herself, we must assume it to be impossible.'

It was a relief when his mother joined them, damage repaired.

A relief to join his company, too. The camp was on the moors near Otterburn: makeshift, like everything else connected with C Company, like the whole battalion come to that. Wooden huts eked out with bell tents, and latrines that were no more than holes in the ground screened with sacking. And yet the men were so keen. Volunteers every one of them, that was the reason, junior officers and men. The subalterns were all ex-OTC, most of them in their first job, or else fresh from university: one from his sixth form at school; and the men for the most part manual workers: bricklayers, miners, shipwrights. No need to toughen them up. They were harder than he was from the moment they joined. The trouble was that they were also totally untrained. They didn't even know one end of a rifle from the other . . . Except for the poachers.

It was a relief to see a familiar face: Horace Cheeseman, once his drunken and invincibly cheerful corporal, now his sober and pessimistic company sergeant major. Together they watched the company doing PT. Strong and well fed, physical training was no problem to them.

'They'll need a lot of work, sir,' Cheeseman said.

'That's what we're here for,' said Mark. 'The trouble is there's not an awful lot of time to spare.'

'Trouble is they don't know kit inspection from advance in open order,' Cheeseman said. 'Not that we've done much advancing just recently. Still, they're keen enough.' The thought of their keenness seemed to bewilder him.

'You find that surprising?' asked Mark.

Cheeseman thought about it and said at last, 'Not really, sir. No. They haven't been there.'

'Neither have I,' said Mark.

'I thought about that, sir,' Cheeseman said, 'and I took the liberty of telling them how we saw action up on the frontier.'

Skirmishes, thought Mark. Tribesmen with weapons so old you could auction them at Sotheby's, even if they were damn good shots.

'Hardly the Western Front, sergeant major,' he said, 'from what I hear.'

'No, sir,' said Cheeseman, 'but they don't know that. And you've been shot at. That's what counts. Been shot at and shot back. That's what they respect.'

Cheeseman, Mark knew, had been in France since the

battle of Loos, first as corporal, then sergeant. Done well, too, which was why he held the rank of CSM. It was also, his colonel had told him, the reason he was alive. If he'd stayed in France he might well be dead.

'That bad was it, sergeant major?' he asked.

'Like you wouldn't believe, sir.'

'All the same you'd better tell me,' said Mark. 'We'll be there soon enough.'

And so Cheeseman told him, and it really did seem incredible. A special kind of hell after the polo and tiger shoots, mess dinners and balls.

'Good God,' said Mark.

His company had finished their PT, and marched off to the makeshift wash-house, and as they marched they began to sing.

> It's a long way to Tipperary
> It's a long way to go.

'Gawd help them,' said Company Sergeant Major Cheeseman.

He had received a letter: not from mummy, not this time. Maude Lippiatt. She was staying near Otterburn, it seemed, because the Germans had started bombing London from airships which they called zeppelins, and Tom had been worried about her safety, and Victoria's, and as they both had lots of relatives nearby they had rented a little house in Northumberland. So much safer than London. Why not drop in for tea? . . . Might as well, thought Mark. The CO seemed to be pretty decent about

leave of absence if one didn't overdo it, and even if his
junior officers still had a lot to learn, Cheeseman would
keep an eye on them. Delighted to do it in fact. In the old
days Cheeseman had never been bossy, he thought, but
then in the old days Cheeseman had never experienced
a near miss from a shell, either.

The mess had a motor bike, a BSA, which was used
sort of communally inasmuch as anybody who was free
could use it, provided he filled it up with petrol afterwards. It was good to get away from the camp: from
the unrelenting cheerfulness of his company that clashed
head on with Cheeseman's unrelenting pessimism. Good
to ride through the countryside too: the gaunt beauty of
the fells and woods where the colours were brown and
red and gold: already preparing for winter. Good to have
a little feminine company too, he thought: even Maude's
and Victoria's. Khaki, polished buttons, gleaming boots
were all very well in their way, but it would be a treat to
hear the rustle of a dress once more. He wondered
whether Maude Lippiatt might have invited his mother
over, too. A delightful surprise that would be.

The house was near a village called Stallyford, and
finding it without a map was a feat in itself. To find
the house was easier: down a lane before you reached the
village. A former rectory, he thought. The church was no
more than a comfortable stroll away, no matter how well
the parson had breakfasted. But where was the parson?
he wondered. Off to the war to say prayers, bring comforts? From what Cheeseman had told him it seemed
unlikely. Parsons were no keener on being shelled by
Germans than anybody else. He rapped on the knocker,

and almost at once the door opened, not very wide: rather warily, he thought, and Maude Lippiatt looked at him. She looked prettier than ever, and not terribly sober, which was ridiculous.

'How punctual you are,' she said. 'The politeness of princes. Do come in.' Not ridiculous at all. He followed her down a hallway to a living-room. She was wearing a garment his mother was fond of, something called a tea-gown. His mother rather liked it because wearing it meant that by doing so she was, in the army phrase, 'excused corsets'. It seemed that for Maude Lippiatt to wear a tea-gown meant one was excused everything else as well.

It was a garment of pink silk. Rather sheer pink silk, he thought as he followed her. Not transparent, but opaque at best, and, depending on her movement and the light, quite often translucent, so that from time to time he was aware of the neat roundness of her buttocks, the long shapeliness of her legs. It was autumn in Northumberland and he'd just got off a motor bike. Even so he found himself sweating. In the living-room she turned by a window to face him, and the late sunlight pierced the pink silk like a torch in the darkness. Her breasts too were memorable.

'It's the maid's day off,' she said. 'Cook's gone to visit her mother, and Victoria and her governess have gone to a matinée in Newcastle.'

'I see,' said Mark.

'Goodness I hope so,' Maude Lippiatt said, and then: 'I very much want you to kiss me. But not while you're wearing all that leather and brass. I bruise rather easily.'

He took off his Sam Browne and uniform jacket, and if I'm clumsy who can blame me, he thought. All I was expecting was tea.

She came into his arms and kissed him with a delicate skill that was as unexpected as it was exciting, and his hands moved inevitably inside the tea-gown, which seemed designed to encourage just such an exploration.

'Oh, good,' said Maude.

'I think so,' said Mark, stroking, squeezing.

She arched her back helpfully. 'I mean, you're not shocked or anything?' she said.

'Just delighted,' said Mark.

'Then we'd better go to bed at once,' said Maude. 'Sooner or later cooks have to leave their old mums and cook dinner, and the curtain falls at last, even on Newcastle matinées.'

By the taste on her lips it had been gin, he thought, but it hadn't affected the delight of her kisses. He followed the teasing pink silk up the stairs to her bedroom.

The tea-gown came off at once, and the body beneath it was firm, rounded: a little chubby perhaps, but still noteworthy. He reached for her.

'No no,' she said. 'Not with your clothes on. Fair's fair after all. Let's see the body beautiful.'

'I'm doing that,' he said.

'In these affairs the lady's entitled to some fun too,' said Maude. 'Off with them.'

He undressed and she looked at him, rather like a farmer inspecting a bull he'd just bought and who'd decided it was worth every penny.

'Oh, yes,' she said. 'My goodness yes.' And then she

smiled at him and he knew that there was affection too.

'Come here, sir,' she said. 'Come here at once.'

And so, after the most delicious hors-d'oeuvres, he progressed to the main course: Maude Lippiatt, Tom Lippiatt's mem, Tom the friend of Sir Charles Beddoes, and the fact had never crossed his mind, because she was skilful and inventive and altogether delightful.

While they rested, she said, 'Surprised you, didn't I?'

'Well, yes,' he said, 'but surprise wasn't the first thing.'

'What was the first thing?'

'Bliss,' he said, and she kissed him.

'Was I good?' she asked.

He kissed her in his turn, choosing the places, and she shivered. 'You know you were,' he said.

'I'm not always,' she said, then her hand went to her mouth. 'Oh, my God, I don't mean I've had lots of lovers.' He waited, but she said no more, and neither did he. She was giving him what he needed. Why question the gift?

'What a dear man you are,' she said, and began to caress him. It took time but at last he responded, and she mounted him in a way that was as delicious as it was novel.

When they had done he said, 'Where in the world—'

'You're the first,' she said, 'and probably the last. It wasn't a chap.'

'A book?'

'No, no,' she said. 'A book wouldn't have been quite the thing, would it? It was a temple, and the statue of a naughty god and an even naughtier goddess.'

She sprawled on the rumpled bed and yawned. At last I understand the meaning of the word wanton, he thought. It's a much nicer word than I thought it would be.

'Well, I've done it,' she said.

'You certainly have.'

She slapped his face, but gently: a slap that was also a caress. 'Not that, silly.'

'What then?'

'My war work,' she said. 'I've done my bit. Well a bit of my bit. Did I shock you?'

'You delighted me.'

'When I can dispose of a daughter and a governess and a cook and a maid I'll delight you again,' she said.

On the way back to camp he thought about it. Not the loving: that took care of itself. The reason for it. She was fond of him of course. My God she must have been: but it wasn't just that. Tom Lippiatt, that was the problem, or he would be if he allowed him to become so. Was I good? she'd said, and when he'd assured her that she was wonderful, 'I'm not always,' she'd said, and what could that mean but Lippiatt? Better to forget it, but it wasn't an easy thing to forget.

Think how formidable she was, she who he'd never imagined could be formidable, at tea dances, balls, croquet matches. And yet she was. Positioning daughters, governesses, cooks, maids, like a general positioning troops: positioning herself too, for his delight, and great delight there had been. She was what? Thirty-six? thirty-seven? – and her body still pretty. Remarkably so. What the devil was wrong with Lippiatt, he wondered, to alienate all that prettiness, that skilful and charming lust? Leave it Mark old chap, he thought. There isn't any *point*, and tried to coax a little more speed from the BSA so that he could reach the mess in time for a drink before dinner.

They managed to meet three times more. She was as demanding as she was skilful, so that he was glad of the route marches and exercise that kept his body in condition. To give her what she wanted was a mark of respect, affection, even, in a small way, of love. The last time (Cook's day off, maid given leave to see her sister's new baby, governess and daughter at riding school), he told her his news because it was impossible not to, and how on earth could Maude Lippiatt be a German spy, even if she was so good at the *femme fatale* part?

'Will it be soon?' she asked.

'Next week.'

She gasped as if he'd hit her. 'You should have told me earlier.'

'I didn't know earlier,' he said. She looked at him and nodded at last, sure that he spoke the truth.

'There have been rather a lot of casualties recently,' he said. 'That's confidential.'

'Of course,' she said, her voice impatient: an Oh do get on with it voice.

'And so General Haig's sent for us.'

'But your men are scarcely trained,' she said.

'More so than most. And anyway – we're all there is.'

She began to cry then, the tears rolling down her cheeks and on to her naked breasts. 'My poor baby,' she said, and her arms came around him. It was the best time of all.

On the way back to camp he wondered, Is that what I

am? Her baby? Not that I give a damn. Whatever I am it was a pleasure.

At the camp his company bustled as if they were preparing for a week at the seaside. The whole battalion bustled: CSM Cheeseman the only pessimist.

'Lambs to the slaughter, sir,' he said.

'Not all of them surely?' said Mark.

'Where they're going's one big bloody abattoir,' said CSM Cheeseman.

That night his CO invited him to take a glass of port, as he'd done with A and B companies' commanders, and no doubt would with D's when the time came.

'How's the leg?' he asked.

'Top hole,' said Mark.

'Jolly good.' The CO brooded for a moment. 'Your chaps are shaping up well,' he said at last. 'You've done a good job.'

'Could have done with a few more weeks, sir,' said Mark.

'That's rather up to Jerry,' his CO said, 'and he wants us out there now.' He brooded again. 'Make sure they keep their heads down. The German snipers are lethal. And if we go over the top – *when* I should say – tell them open order means what it says. Don't let them bunch together. The German machine-gunners are lethal, too.' He finished his port. 'That's about it, I think.'

'Sir,' said Mark, but before he could stand his CO said, 'You come from these parts, I'm told.'

'Yes, sir.'

'Pop over to visit your mamma from time to time?'

'Other friends too,' said Mark.

'Quite so,' said the colonel.

In the army it was impossible to have a secret, thought Mark. Not that he gave a damn. Not with all those German snipers and machine-gunners so urgently demanding his presence.

'I should pop over and see her again on Monday,' the colonel said. 'We'll be rather busy after that.'

'Thank you, sir,' said Mark.

His mother was delighted to see him, and so was Maude Lippiatt. Formidable as ever, she had contrived to visit Mrs Beddoes on the day when, she knew, he would come to Stonebridge to say goodbye. She had even contrived to see him on his own. Mrs Beddoes it seemed had taken Victoria to the wood to see some red squirrels. She came to his arms at once when the parlourmaid left them. Strange to embrace her fully clothed, he thought, and so many clothes: day dress and petticoats, and corsets too by the feel of her: not like the tea-gown at all, though she kissed with the same delightful skill, then broke free at last.

'Your mother and Victoria will soon be back,' she said. 'There's not all that much fun in watching squirrels. When do you leave for France?'

'Tomorrow,' said Mark.

'Oh God,' she said. For a moment he thought that she might cry, but somehow she regained control.

'Do—' She paused. 'For a moment I was about to say something unbelievably stupid,' she said.

'Do be careful?'

'Yes,' she said. 'I'm sorry.'

'Why?' he said. 'It's good advice, and I fully intend to take it.'

'How sweet you are,' she said, 'but I daren't risk kissing you again, however much I want to. Come back to me.'

'It's what I want most in the world,' he said.

'Perhaps not that,' said Maude Lippiatt, 'but just for the moment I rank fairly high on your list of priorities. I know that.'

What a perceptive woman she was, he thought, and how cleverly she manages to hide the fact. Then her daughter and his mother came in.

'Darling, what a delightful surprise,' his mother said, and he kissed her cheek. As he did so he could see Victoria look from her mother to him, her eyes alight with an intelligence he had once thought she had inherited solely from her father. She's on to something, he thought. She's as sharp as she's pretty, but he couldn't imagine holding her. For the first time that day he thought of Veronica.

'See lots of squirrels?' he asked.

'Heaps,' said Victoria. 'All squabbling over hazel-nuts.'

'Soon be tea-time,' said her mother. 'If we don't leave now we'll miss the bus.'

Victoria made a face. In Calcutta they would have sent for a gharri.

'Must you go?' said his mother.

It's what she wants most in the world but she's being so sweet about it, Mrs Lippiatt thought.

'I'm afraid we must,' she said. He was her son after all.

When they had gone his mother said, 'This surprise isn't really delightful at all, is it?'

'We leave tomorrow,' said Mark.

'Oh, God,' said his mother, but unlike Maude Lippiatt, she didn't say it aloud. Instead she said, 'Let's have some tea. There's a chocolate cake. Your favourite.'

6

On his first leave he was fine, Maude Lippiatt thought.
Tense, of course, like a violin string stretched as far as it
would go, but otherwise fine. And gracious me, such
ardour, which made her think he'd been in rather a lot of
danger, but never once did he tell her so. She had gone
back to London, zeppelins or no zeppelins, because it was
far more convenient for her to meet him there or in some
south-coast resort before he set off to see his mother in
Northumberland, and Victoria would simply have to take
her chance like the rest of London. Tom too, for that
matter. Not that she was all that bothered about Tom.
Besides, if she was in London or thereabouts they could
manage an extra night together before he caught the boat
train.

After that first time, Victoria came to see her. A little
agitated, thought her mother, which made her even prettier than usual.

'I didn't know you were going away,' she said.

'I'm back now,' said her mother.

'Seeing a relative?'

'A friend,' her mother said.

'Mark Beddoes?'

Her mother shrugged: an elegant, sensual movement that Victoria longed to imitate.

'Does daddy know?'

This time her mother didn't even bother to shrug. She merely smiled.

'I bet he doesn't,' said her daughter, and then: 'I saw a pair of ear-rings in Bond Street while you were away. Pearls. Quite – demure – is that the word? Just the thing for a virgin.'

You've been rehearsing this for days, her mother thought, and then: My God, you want him too, but just for the moment he's mine.

'I thought you might buy them for me,' Victoria said, and still her mother was silent. 'Of course I could always ask daddy.'

'Why not?' said her mother. 'He's the one who'll have to pay.'

'I'd sooner they came from you.'

Again her mother shrugged. I really must practise that, Victoria thought, now I've got a bosom.

'Very well,' said her mother. 'You can take me to the jeweller's and I'll have a look at them, and if they're as good as you say we'll have your ears pierced. That can be painful sometimes, but you won't mind that, will you darling? Not if it's something you really want.'

Another leave and another, which meant an aged aunt in Bournemouth and an ailing friend in Eastbourne, and the violin string tuned even tighter. He was drinking, too, drinking rather a lot. At Eastbourne he'd been far too drunk by bedtime to make love to her, but they'd made up for it in the morning. It was at Eastbourne that she realised she was falling in love with him, and that just wasn't on, she thought, but what the hell am I supposed to do to stop it?

Then he came back again, far too soon. Wounded. He'd got a nurse to write and tell her so from a hospital in Sussex. 'Dear Aunt Maude,' the letter began, and that was fair enough. At least he'd ended with, 'Your loving nephew Mark.' He'd even managed to scrawl a kiss. He really was a nice man.

Of course she went at once, but before the cab came she told Victoria. Since she loved him too she had a right to know. The child came in and she motioned her to a chair. There simply wasn't time for fainting.

'Mark's been hurt,' she said, and at once Victoria's hands doubled into fists. But what would be the point of attacking me? Maude wondered.

'Are you saying he's dead?' her daughter asked.

'No,' said Maude. 'If he were dead I would tell you – and far more tactfully than this. He's got rather a lot of shrapnel in him and he's been sent to England to have it removed. You have a right to know that, which is why I'm telling you.'

There was a pause, then, 'Thank you, mummy,' Victoria said. In the street a cab horn sounded, and the two of them embraced. It had been a long time since they had embraced.

'Does daddy know?' Victoria asked.

'Not from me,' said her mother. 'You can tell him if you want to.'

* * *

Incredibly he looked cheerful. Weak, battered, bandaged, and smiling all over his face. But then he was out of it: for a while, anyway. Warily she kissed him.

'If you knew how I've missed that,' he said.

'That's all you'll get for quite a while.'

'I've got memories,' he said. 'And expectations.' She kissed him again. 'Iron diet,' he said. 'I never thought it would be quite like this.'

'Lots of it?'

'They say I'll look like a pin-cushion for a while, but it'll heal eventually. Most of it anyway. I just hope I won't be too ugly for you.'

'So do I,' she said. 'But I doubt it.'

'You know I've been thinking,' he said. 'Nothing like an iron diet to start you thinking.'

'May I share your thoughts?'

'Masculine thoughts,' he said. '*Egotistical* masculine thoughts. There we were, the two of us, going at it hammer and tongs—'

'Not even Shakespeare could have put it better,' she said.

'—and it never crossed my mind that you might become pregnant.'

'Don't let it worry you,' she said.

'But surely—' he began.

'Because it doesn't worry me. Except that it hurts. Having a baby I mean.'

Then she kissed him again and left because his mother was coming, and when a mother arrived a mistress's place was elsewhere. Still, he was alive.

His mother was appalled, and did her best not to show

it, but it wasn't a very good best. Just as well none of that flying metal hit my face, he thought. Naturally she asked him if it hurt. Only when I laugh had been the answer of the wounded Tommy in the cartoon, but he couldn't say that: not to her.

'Now and again,' he said. 'But not nearly so much as it did.'

'The nurse says they'll have to operate.'

'Tomorrow,' he said.

At once she looked anxious. 'So soon?'

'The nurse says it isn't a dangerous operation,' he said. But then the nurse isn't going to have the operation, he thought. Still, better not go into that.

'Oh, good,' said his mother, then looked at the vase by his bed. 'What lovely roses. Who sent them?'

Maude of course, but better not go into that, either.

'They came for my predecessor,' he said.

'Oh, dear,' said his mother. 'He didn't die, did he?'

'Convalescent home,' said Mark.

'Will you have to go to one as well?'

'I'd sooner come home,' said Mark, and for that he got a smile, but even so the worry soon returned. She really is devastated, he thought, to the point where she just can't cope with it. Even her conversation was haphazard, aimless.

'I'm sorry I forgot to bring flowers,' she said. 'The only thought in my head was to get to you.'

'And get to me you did,' said Mark. 'Much better than flowers.' Another smile, and then she rose, and he willed himself not to show his relief.

'Where will you stay?' he asked her.

'There's a hotel quite near. Shall I come tomorrow?'

'Better phone first,' he said. 'Chloroform and all that.'

'I'll say a prayer,' she said. 'Do you want me to let Sir Charles know?'

'So that he can say a prayer too?' No smile that time.

'The thing is he's still at his club,' said his mother, 'and I've forgotten which one it is.'

'White's,' said Mark.

'I'll write to him.'

When she left he found that he was sweating. It wasn't pain: it was coping with his mother's devastation. I love her very much, he thought, which is why I'll go to her house like a dutiful son, but I'll go back to London before I get back to the company. I'll go back to Maude's kisses. All you'll get for some time, she'd said, but he'd heal eventually and then there'd be more, but it wasn't just that. He was very fond of her: wished he could love her: he couldn't.

Well at least he was out of it for the time being, he thought, and thank God for that. In the real hell, the one in the life hereafter, there would be no leave, according to the parsons, and certainly no hospitals: not even a burns unit. But from the hell in France there was occasional – respite? Wasn't that the word? Even if the price you paid was a load of old iron. Still it was worth it, for what you got in exchange were clean sheets and bird-song and a nurse who, even if she was bossy, was pretty too. And C Company would be all right. He was sure of that. The chaps who ran it – the temporary gentlemen as the regulars called them, not that there were all that many regular officers left – had learned their business quickly and well: the bank clerks and the junior managers and the undergraduates from the wrong sort of university. The chap who took over the company had been a commercial traveller. Haberdashery, he said. Ladies' underwear said everybody else. The point was he was good. A damn sight better than me, thought Mark, but then I never should have been a soldier in the first place. I'm conscientious enough, but I lack the talent. And then: CSM Cheeseman was right. The Western Front was every bit as bad as he said it was. Sometimes, incredibly, it was worse.

The pretty, bossy nurse looked in on him. Asleep, and no nightmares. Not like some. And just as well that he could sleep, she thought. Tomorrow's going to be a busy day for him. Not that he'll know it at the time.

Maude and Tom Lippiatt dined alone in the flat in Bryanston Square. Victoria shared a rather grand version of nursery tea with her governess and was glad to do it. Dinner with her parents was far too often an ordeal. That night it was mulligatawny soup, whitebait, a brace of partridge sent by friends in the country and some sort of pudding that even Cook found it hard to define. The parlourmaid put a decanter of claret in front of Lippiatt, and left them. Her husband poured himself a glass. Rather a generous one, thought his wife.

'I'll have some of that,' she said, and again he poured, meagrely this time. 'More,' she said, and he filled it to the brim.

'That's better.' To hell with him and his polished irony, she thought. What I want is a drink.

'Victoria tells me you've been visiting the sick,' Lippiatt said.

Maude took a mouthful of soup. Not bad. Really, so long as you didn't take her out of her depth, Cook was more than adequate – except when it came to puddings.

'I told her she could,' she said.

'She needed your permission?'

'She got it anyway.'

'Beddoes? . . . Your impoverished captain?'

'The very same,' said Maude. 'Though whether he's mine or not – but you know all about that, don't you, Tom? Is she, isn't she? But the odds against you are rather longer than mine.'

Lippiatt gulped at his wine. 'A bit high handed, wasn't it?' he said. 'Disappearing like that and leaving it to our child to tell me? Not even a note.'

'Why, Tom,' she said. 'I didn't know you cared.' Somehow the cliché seemed justified. The parlourmaid brought in the whitebait, and just as well, she thought. This time he really might have hit me.

When she'd gone Lippiatt said, 'There's another thing. Those pearl ear-rings you bought Vicky.'

'Well actually you did,' said Maude. 'I thought they suited her.'

'They were damned expensive,' said Lippiatt.

'Goodness,' said his wife, 'you're not implying we're destitute?'

'Not that, no,' Lippiatt said, 'but—'

'Good,' said his wife. 'Our way of life may be lacking in – shall we say – warmth, but I fail to see why that means my living in poverty. Or your daughter.'

Lippiatt poured himself more claret.

'I think we'd better have another bottle,' said his wife.

The operation might not have been dangerous, but it was decidedly painful. His whole torso was one comprehensive ache. Black and blue, too. Other colours as well. And stitches. Like some aboriginal tribesman with a taste for masochism. Far too ugly for Maude Lippiatt. Not that he could have even tried. Northumberland in the autumn once more, that was the ticket. Wholesome food and gentle walks and mummy's friends in for bridge and church on Sundays. Then as his body recovered and the bruises faded, first a trout rod, then the twelve bore, with Belinda to prove that she could still retrieve a pheasant. Soon be middle-aged, Belinda, but she knew her business. Then down to London, he thought, see the medical board. See Maude Lippiatt, too. Maybe they would go inland this time. Bath, perhaps, or Cheltenham. After that the battalion was moving to a new location. A place called the Somme.

'I think I may have fallen in love,' Veronica said, 'but I'm not sure.' Come to think of it she was looking even prettier than usual, *and* rather flustered. It could be love at that, thought Poppy.

'What's his name?' she asked.

'Captain Hepburn.' She went to the mirror in her aunt's bedroom and peered into it, still flustered, but that was ridiculous. The girl was gorgeous.

'Which regiment?' her aunt asked.

'He isn't that sort of captain,' Veronica said. 'He's in the navy.'

Not a client, Poppy thought, and just as well.

'You don't have to look in the mirror to see how beautiful you are,' she said. 'You've got my word for it.'

'You mean that? Honestly?' Veronica asked.

'Well, of course. It runs in the family,' said her aunt. 'Now sit down and tell me all about it.'

There had been a polo match at the maidan four days ago and she'd gone to watch, and it was a beastly shame girls weren't allowed to play polo. Some of those ponies were super.

'Oh, get on with it,' said her aunt.

He – Nicholas – had been watching too, but he didn't seem to know very much about it. Probably because he was a sailor.

'Good looking?' her aunt asked.

'Oh yes,' said Veronica. 'Grey eyes. Dark hair. And the *most* attractive uniform. All in white.'

But you're the one who's a virgin, thought her aunt. 'Old? Young?'

In his thirties, her niece thought. Well in, if he's a captain RN, thought her aunt.

'Next day we met there again, and today. Then he took me for a coffee at the Laguna,' said Veronica.

'People stared at you I suppose?' They always did when a chee-chee went there, but they didn't throw you out. Not if you had money.

'I expect so,' said Veronica, 'but I didn't notice.'

'Whyever not?'

'I was looking at him.'

A serious case, obviously. 'He won't marry you,' Poppy said. Veronica shrugged.

'He's too old anyway,' she said.

'What then?'

'Now,' said Veronica. 'I want him now.'

'Not just like that,' said her aunt. Veronica knew that voice. When she spoke like that, you listened. She sat and waited.

'First I must meet him and we'll talk, then we'll see,' her aunt said.

'I never knew it was possible to feel like that for a man, but it is,' said Veronica, 'and after all I'm seventeen now—'

Her aunt held up her hand. 'I didn't say I'd forbid you,' she said. 'Maybe I couldn't stop you.' Veronica was silent. 'But if you disobeyed me – then we're finished. Do you understand, child? Do you?'

'Yes, Aunty.'

'Send him to me. I've no doubt you know how to reach him.'

'Oh, yes,' said Veronica. 'But you'll have to see him today. He'll be away tomorrow for a couple of weeks at least.' Her lower lip trembled.

There was a German cruiser loose somewhere near, so Poppy had heard. The gallant captain's job would be to find it. *Stay off that.*

'You know what the sahibs say,' she said. 'Absence makes the heart grow fonder.'

'But it could be three weeks,' Veronica wailed.

'I take it that it's bed you're after?' Veronica nodded. Of course it's bed, the nod said.

'Then three weeks is just what you need – *if* I agree. It'll take that long to prepare you.'

'Prepare me?'

'You don't think I'd send you to him like some missy baba who doesn't know what to do? When he comes back to you – *if* he comes back to you – you'll be ready for him.'

'You make it sound like a fight,' said Veronica.

'Sometimes it is,' said her aunt. 'That doesn't mean you won't enjoy it – but if we train you properly you'll win. Or fight a draw at least.' She looked again at her niece. The little peaches were definitely pomelos now. 'But you'll win – if it happens. I know it. You're like me. When it comes to love you were born a winner.'

'Thank you, Aunty.'

'The first thing is to let Bridget take a look at you,' her aunt said. 'Make sure it's all as it should be. Try not to be embarrassed. It's necessary.'

'Of course I won't be embarrassed,' said Veronica. 'Bridget's my friend.'

'She'll come to you after supper,' said her aunt. 'Just now she's busy with our broker. Send word to your captain to come and see me, then get on with your homework.'

'I'm not to see him?'

'Maybe three weeks from now.'

Veronica trailed from the room as if her favourite pony had died.

Captain Hepburn knew all about Poppy Villiers, even if he'd never so much as seen her. All the local sahibs knew about her, and quite a few had wanted her, but not too many had had her, it seemed. She was far too expensive.

When her bearer ushered him into her living-room he understood why. She was every bit as beautiful as her niece: rather more mature, much more sophisticated, but no less and no more beautiful. To the exact same degree.

She motioned him to a chair and offered him a drink. He asked for a whisky and soda, and she poured it for him herself. She, he noticed, was drinking champagne.

'So you're after my niece,' she said.

'I am.' His voice, like the rest of him, was pleasant, and at least he didn't stare at her as so many of the clients did, as if she were a bowl of his favourite curry.

'Love at first sight in fact.'

'Exactly that,' Captain Hepburn said.

'With no possibility of marriage.'

'How can there be?' he asked, and she respected that. At least it was honest. 'I'm twice her age and the wrong colour.'

'But not married.' He shook his head. 'May one ask why?'

'I like women too much,' he said, and she laughed. Her laughter was as delicious as the rest of her.

'So all you want is the honeymoon,' she said.

'I want to be with her, to make love to her, of course, but to talk and listen, too. She's enchanting to talk to.'

'Yes,' said Poppy Villiers. 'She is. But it would all be part of the honeymoon.'

'It's a sort of madness,' Hepburn said. 'I've known her for less than a week. Met her three times. And yet from the moment I saw her—'

He says it so calmly, she thought. His mind's on fire, body too, and yet he stays so calm. He's preparing himself in case I deny him the one thing he needs.

'The French call it *un coup de foudre*,' said Hepburn. 'A thunderbolt.'

And there's one for you, Poppy Villiers, she thought. That's the first time in your life a man looked at you and told you he'd fallen head over heels for someone else, even if it is your niece.

'Madness it may be,' she said, 'but you'll have to control it.' He waited. 'It would be a honeymoon in another sense too,' said Poppy Villiers. 'She's a virgin.'

'So I should have thought,' said Hepburn, 'but I meant what I said. I *like* women. I like doing what they like, and not many of them like being hurt. She'll be all right with me, I promise you.'

'Word of a gentleman?'

'Word of a gentleman.'

She looked at him: a long, hard, appraising look: the sort of look his navigation officer had given him when he was a midshipman.

'Very well,' she said at last. 'You can come to her when you get back. Use the guest-house.'

'Who told you I'd be away?' said Hepburn.

'She did.'

'Does she know why?' Poppy Villiers shook her head. 'But you do?'

'Of course,' said Poppy. 'Whores like me always know things like that. It's the German cruiser.'

'Indeed it is,' said Hepburn, 'but the way you describe yourself does you less than justice. You're a courtesan, certainly, or better still what the Ancient Greeks called a hetaera, which as far as I can remember means a lady companion, because I'm quite sure you're both. A companion and a lady.'

For a moment Poppy envied her niece: in fact for two pins she'd – but that wouldn't be fair. After all, Veronica had seen him first.

'It's agreed then,' she said.

'Thank you,' said Hepburn. 'I'll come round as soon as I get back. If indeed I do.'

'My God, is it that bad?' she asked.

'It could be,' Hepburn said. 'The German cruiser's good, and so's her captain. But then mine's good too, and I've thought up a couple of tricks that may surprise him.' He rose to his feet. 'I hope so. I long to get back to that niece of yours. She—' He shook his head at a bewilderment so complete that there were no words to express it.

'I wish you luck,' said Poppy, and kissed his cheek.

'Thank you,' said Hepburn. 'I've no doubt I'll need it. But please don't tell Veronica.'

'She's all right,' Bridget said.

'Was she embarrassed?'

'A bit giggly at first,' said Bridget, 'but afterwards quite matter of fact. Even businesslike, so to speak.'

'Not just book learning,' said Poppy. 'Common sense as well. She'll need it.'

Bridget drew on her cigarette. 'In a way you could say she's lucky. All that charging about on horseback like a Mahratta warrior – at least she won't feel much pain.'

'Good,' said Poppy, and Bridget shrugged.

'You wouldn't say that if she fell off the wretched animal and broke her neck – or even a leg.'

'She won't,' Poppy said. 'She wasn't born into this world to fall off horses.'

'Not her karma you mean,' said Bridget.

'Call it her destiny,' said Poppy. 'The child's not a Hindu after all. Not often, anyway.'

A bit cryptic, Bridget thought, but that one would keep.

'She's lovely,' Bridget said. 'I had a good look at her – all over – and there isn't a part that isn't perfect. Just like you.'

'So we know what her destiny is?' said Poppy.

'I thought so,' said Bridget, 'but you keep saying she's not coming into the business.'

'All those brains, those books,' said Poppy. 'She'd start to read Shakespeare and forget she had a honeymoon to go to.'

'And yet you're giving her to this Hepburn.'

'She's seventeen,' said Poppy. 'Curious. Got the itch. He'll do it well, believe me.'

Bridget sighed her relief. About that of all things, Poppy would know.

'Talking of books – there was something else. A long time ago, before she came here. Back in that railway town.'

'Kalpur.'

'Her father had a taste for cheap whores.'

'Indeed he did,' said Poppy.

'Some of them used to touch her.' Poppy began to swear in Hindi: fluently, comprehensively. 'I dare say,' said Bridget, 'but she was no more than nine and terrified of what her father would do if she said no. Besides—'

'Go on,' said Poppy.

' "I was a reader even in those days," she said, "and books cost money." '

Poppy Villiers laughed aloud, a harsh and bitter laughter that was the ugliest sound Bridget had ever heard her make.

'So she's one of us after all,' she said. 'She started even younger than me.' Then her voice softened. 'The poor darling child.' She yawned and stretched, and Bridget saw at once how Veronica would look ten years from then.

The next three weeks didn't give her much time for brooding, thought Veronica. All that preparation, and her homework, too. A new kind of maths, for a start. Spherical trigonometry. Sister Clare was very keen on it, and indeed it did have its own fascination, but there was so much else. Lots of swimming – so good for the pomelos, darling, said her aunt – and for some reason Aunty insisted on her riding her new pony, too. A great improvement on the one she'd had to wallop at the gymkhana, but even so – what with that and make-up and what Aunty called deportment, which meant getting up and lying down with very little on, not to mention Mozart and Mallarmé, Keats and Camoëns... Not to mention the weird exercises Bridget made her practise, either. Did it really take all that to be kind to a man – even a man as delightful as Captain Hepburn?

There were even books to be read – as if darling Nicholas was an examination paper she might fail if she didn't study hard enough. And such books. Some were ridiculous, she thought, and some made sense. The one called the *Kama Sutra* contained both, but it interested her more than the others. Quite a lot of it was just men showing off, which was something they did all the time, and in bed as much as anywhere else, according to Aunty, even when they had nothing much to show. On the other hand some of it was really useful. Not so much advice to the lovelorn as advice to those about to do it, which no doubt explained Bridget's insistence on those weird exercises. There was even, here and there, a kind of poetry. The description of the Padmini, for instance, the perfect woman: 'Her face is pleasing as the full moon; her body, well clothed with flesh, is soft as the shirar or mustard flower, her skin is fine, tender and fair as the yellow lotus, never dark coloured. Her eyes are bright and beautiful as the fawn, well cut, and with reddish corners. Her bosom is firm, full and high; her nose is straight and lovely, and three folds cross her middle about the umbilical region. Her yoni resembles the opening lotus bud, and her love seed is perfumed like the lily that has newly burst.'

Goodness they don't want much, these chaps, she thought, then took off her robe to walk to the mirror as Aunty had taught her and examined her naked body.

Be honest, she told herself, and was, and even so realised that she was one of those whom men desired, like Aunty, though the lily that has newly burst department would be up to Captain Hepburn.

She put her robe back on. When the honeymoon's over, she thought, I'll translate that Padmini stuff into Portuguese. Try to turn it into a poem. But I'll have to find a way round the umbilical region. Then she put the *Kama Sutra* back on the shelf and opened the book on spherical trigonometry.

7

Captain Hepburn too applied himself to spherical trigonometry. Without it navigation was impossible, and he had to get it right. There were only three days left to find the *König Friedrich*. Admittedly the German cruiser weighed ten thousand tons, but the Pacific was a damn big ocean. Seeking her was like trying to find a rowing boat in the North Sea. And his own ship, the *Sovereign*, was just about as big, and gulping down oil the way the desert swallows water. Two more days and he'd have to head for home. *König* and *Sovereign*, he thought. King against king – when all he wanted to do was head back to Calcutta and his gorgeous little princess.

Leave that, he thought. Leave it. Start thinking about Veronica and you'll be useless. Better, far better, to think of his German counterpart. He'd have his problems too. Fuel the top of the list, then supplies, especially ammunition. And prisoners. The Germans mightn't worry too much about killing Chinese, or Russians, or Indians – or even Portuguese – but most of the ships the *König Friedrich* had sunk had had British crews, and even Jerry might have qualms about killing them. Even in 1917. Veronica was part Indian.

For God's sake man, he told himself. Get back to your duty. Otherwise you may never see her again. He began to pace the shady side of the deck and the officer of the watch relaxed a little. Old Nick was beginning to think at last, he thought, and that was a good sign. Old Nick was good at thinking.

If I nail this bastard I'll get a leg up, he thought. Maybe even commodore. And if I do that I'll die an admiral, even if the war ends next week. What's more, I think I know how to do it. The German cruiser's got to have a supply ship. Got to. And from the way it's been dashing around sinking British tonnage that lagged behind the convoy, it's about due for supplies. There had been a big Swedish tanker in Djakarta not all that long ago – not that the Dutch were all that bothered. They were neutral, too. All the same – Swedes and Dutch. Little countries, worried countries that Germany could stretch out her hand for and crush if they didn't do precisely as they were ordered. Moreover it was a *tanker*, and according to his last information just a little off course for the Med, and the Atlantic, and Stockholm. On the other hand if it was on its way to the Hermanos, that little group of uninhabited islands five hundred miles from anywhere, the Swedish ship was exactly on course: and the Hermanos were uninhabited because there was nothing there. No water, no vegetation, nothing, which was why nobody had bothered with them, not even in 1917. Just the place for a German cruiser to rendezvous with a Swedish tanker. Not that it would be Swedish. Not if he was right.

There was radio silence, because who was there to talk to now that the destroyer he had asked for had been diverted elsewhere? Even so his wireless operators listened as if their lives depended on it, because they did, and his look-out watched, not through the usual telescope, but with a pair of his own binoculars; the best in the ship. They were German.

The wireless operator got something, but what it was he had no idea, and sent Hepburn a chit to tell him so. Hepburn scurried down to the wireless cabin and stared at the incomprehensible mixture of letters and figures the operator had written down. Code, he thought. I'm right. I know I'm right. He went back on deck and summoned the gun crews for one more drill.

Two days later the *Sovereign* limped into Madras harbour, because it was the nearest, and the *Sovereign* was in no condition for a long sea voyage, but under her guns was the 'Swedish' tanker. It hadn't even begun to discharge its oil when the German cruiser sank, and had surrendered when the first shell from the *Sovereign* screamed across her bows. A full cargo of oil and supplies, twenty-nine British merchant sailors, and a crew that didn't have five words of Swedish between them, though their German was fluent enough.

'No survivors from the *König Friedrich*?' said the port admiral.

'None, sir,' said Hepburn.

'Was it quick?'

'Not quick enough,' said Hepburn. 'We think our fourth salvo hit an ammunition hoist – she went up like Bonfire Night – but before that she clipped us a couple of good 'uns. Still, I've been over the *Sovereign* with the engineer officers. It's their opinion she looks worse than she is, and I'm inclined to agree.'

'You'll give your men shore leave?' the port admiral said.

'They've earned it, sir.'

The port admiral looked at him. Captain Hepburn. Old Nick, they called him, and he could understand why. 'No survivors?' 'None, sir.' Just that. A cruiser's whole complement, scores and scores of men, blown to perdition or drowned or both, and just two words for an epitaph. Still, he'd spoken well of his men.

'And you?' he asked.

'I'd rather like some leave too, sir,' said Hepburn. 'Urgent personal affairs in Calcutta.'

'You've earned it,' the port admiral said. 'From the dock-yard reports your ship will be out of action for some time. We can spare you for a week.'

'Thank you, sir.'

Hepburn saluted and left him, and the port admiral wondered if urgent personal affairs was yet another euphemism for Poppy Villiers.

It had been delicious, there was no denying it. Every bit as good as Indian sweets, even pistachio burfi. When it came to bursting lilies, Captain Hepburn was your man. Darling Nicholas. At first she had been just a little shy about some things: nobody except Bridget and Aunty had seen her naked since she was a little girl, but when it was obvious how much he enjoyed it she wasn't shy at all. Just pleased with herself. Even proud. And quite right too, she thought. I mean, look at him. And then being undressed. By a man. At first she'd questioned that, but then he'd explained that that too was a pleasure for him, and so she'd let him get on with it. Not that she was wearing all that much in the first place. But then she discovered that it was a pleasure for her, too, because to undress her he had to touch her, and being touched by Captain Hepburn was so delicious she'd called out loud. Darling Nicholas.

She hadn't yelled when he'd come into her that first time. She'd nearly done so, but Aunty had warned her, and the sound she made was no more than a gasp, and anyway the pain went as quickly as it came, and after it there was the first promise of pleasure, and when they'd done he'd taken her to the bathhouse, bathed her and dried her and kissed her all over till she'd gasped again. But not in pain. Not that time. Then they lay together and she coiled against him, and he looked at what he held. All of it young, rounded, enchanting. Where every prospect pleases, and only man is vile, he thought. But I wasn't vile. Not really. I was as careful as I could be. How could I hurt what I'm holding?

'You're a very brave girl,' he said. She shrugged, and that too was delightful.

'Because I didn't yell? But if I'd yelled you might have stopped and I didn't want you to stop.'

'Didn't you?' he asked.

'I wanted you to finish nasty chapter one and get on to lovely chapter two and you did.'

He began to touch her again and it was bliss. Being touched by darling Nicholas was as delightful as quadratic equations. Then she called herself to order. She had things to do in the touching line as well. Aunty and Bridget and all the books were agreed on that ... She didn't get a yell out of him, but he made some very satisfactory noises, and when they'd finished he'd gone to the ice-box. Champagne of course, for her first time. Like launching a ship. But there was pistachio burfi too. Her favourite. Darling, *darling* Nicholas.

'Your aunt tells me you're still at school,' said Hepburn and she nodded. Mouth too full to speak, he thought. Shovelling it down as if there was no time to spare. 'Do you like it?'

She swallowed. 'Love it,' she said. 'We're just starting spherical trigonometry.'

'I do a bit of that myself,' said Hepburn.

'Oh yes of course. Navigation,' said Veronica. She finished the burfi, took a sip of champagne, and walked as Aunty had taught her to a desk at the end of the bedroom. She wore nothing but a pair of high-heeled mules.

I've never seen anything more beautiful, he thought. Indian roundness like temple statues, but controlled by a European elegance that combine to make perfection. And a face to match the body. Hair so black it gleamed, eyes the colour of oloroso sherry, straight little nose, delicious mouth – and a chin that meant trouble for anyone who crossed her. A pretty little chin with a dimple, but there was determination in it, courage, perhaps even cruelty. Rather a lot to see in a chin, but he was sure it was true. Never mind the chin, he told himself. Look at the rest of her. Then she bent to look into a drawer and he thought I can't take much more of this. And then: Oh yes you can. You'll take all you can get.

She walked to a *chaise-longue*, legs moving slowly, elegantly, hips just swaying, shoulders back to make her breasts even firmer, rounder, then sat, knees together as a young lady should, and all of her a rosy gold colour he hadn't thought possible. She was carrying a notebook and pencil.

'Come and sit here,' she said. 'There's something I want you to explain to me.'

'About what?'

'Spherical trigonometry,' she said, and he thought, Dear God she means it. This is the most wonderful night of my life and she wants me to help her with her homework. And why not? It was all her, and all to be enjoyed. Even so he took the champagne and the glasses with him.

It didn't take him long to discover that she was a far better mathematician than he was, but even so he knew enough to help solve her problem. The trouble was that he was sitting beside her, smelling her perfume, sensing her nearness. Spheres, he thought. Globes. He reached out to cup and gently squeeze, watch the nipple bridle and darken. Veronica finished the note she was making and closed the notebook, turned so that his other hand too could cup and gently squeeze.

'Yes, all right,' she said. 'But once we've finished I'll have more questions to ask.'

'Yes, miss,' said Captain Hepburn.

She looked down at him. He was starting to get big again, and it was up to her to help him, and anyway he had been very good about the spherical trigonometry.

Besides, she wanted him. Tenderly, lovingly she touched, and gracious, how he responded. Veronica giggled.

'What's funny?' he asked, enjoying it all.

'Men have no secrets, do they?' she said. 'You wouldn't know about me unless you touched me, but this—' She gave him a kiss.

'We're ridiculous,' Hepburn said. 'I admit it. Sticking out like a sore thumb, so to speak. But we can't help it. And anyway—'

'Yes, Nicholas?'

'Let's save the laughter for later. There's something else I want us to do now.'

That was all a honeymoon was, it seemed: doing it, champagne, and her favourite food sent over in a tiffin carrier – except that now and again he helped her with her homework. She insisted on that. It would never do to neglect her homework. He proved very good at French and Latin, but he was hopeless at music, though he liked to hear her sing. Once she sent word to clear the garden and they went to the tank to swim naked together.

'So good for the pomelos,' she said.

'The what?'

'These,' she said, and touched her breasts.

'You must have spent half your life in the water,' he said. What a darling he was.

She spread their towels on the grass and the bulbuls sang and the flowers smelled sweet. Like me, she thought. Especially the lilies.

Then the time came when she lay in his arms and he stroked her and said, 'I go back tomorrow.'

'I know,' she said.

'Will you miss me?'

'Of course,' she said, and it was true, but it would be good to play Mozart again.

'There's something I want to tell you,' said Hepburn.

'Oh, yes?' Not ask, she thought. Not 'Will you marry me?' I'm not nearly ready for that yet, even if he is. Maybe I never will be.

'At first I wasn't going to say anything,' Hepburn said. 'It would have seemed like showing off, but the news will be out soon and you'll hear about it anyway.' He told her about the *König Friedrich*.

'But that means you're a hero,' she said.

Her first time and it was with a hero! But she had the sense not to say that aloud.

'The whole crew were heroes,' he said.

'But you led them. The greatest hero of them all. Heroes deserve special treatment.'

'My treatment's been special since I came here,' he said, and he deserved a little extra for that, too. That business with the scented oil, perhaps . . .

Next day, when it was time for him to leave, he looked at his clothes as if he'd forgotten what they were for, and she put on what little she had. It wouldn't do to tease him when he said goodbye. He looked so sad, and she too wept a little when he had gone, then dried her eyes and went to see Bridget. Aunty had reminded her twice, and it didn't do to dawdle after two reminders from Aunty.

Bridget examined her carefully, her hands impersonal as a surgeon's. 'Your friend's a gentleman,' she said at last. 'An officer and a gentleman.'

And a hero, thought Veronica, and put on her pretty

clothes and went to tell Aunty. (On Monday it would be school uniform again.) But of course Aunty already knew.

'But how?' Veronica asked.

'Hetaeras always get to know everything first,' said her aunt.

'Hetaera!' said Veronica. 'It's the perfect word for you. Who told you it?'

'Your captain,' said her aunt.

'Darling Nicholas,' said Veronica.

'Was it scrumptious?' her aunt asked.

'Oh, *yes*,' said Veronica, meaning it.

I chose well for her, her aunt thought. Pleasure after pain. A lot of pleasure by the sound of it, from a man who knew what he was doing, and yet no despair when he had gone. No longing for what couldn't possibly be. She offered her niece a cigarette.

'Want to talk about it?' she asked.

'I have to,' said Veronica. 'I mean I know you told me it would be nice, but it wasn't. It was bliss. Oh you are good to me.' She jumped to her feet and embraced her aunt.

'All I did was give my consent,' said her aunt. 'The rest was up to him.'

'But you gave it,' said Veronica.

'Did he hurt you?'

'Hardly at all.'

Bridget had been right, it seemed.

'And afterwards it was what you said. Scrumptious . . . He must have done it an awful lot.'

'Not with anybody like you,' Poppy said.

'How do you know?'

'Because there aren't any more like you,' her aunt said.

Veronica embraced her again. 'You're the best Aunty in the world,' she said.

'Cupboard love,' said her aunt. 'Go on about your captain.'

Veronica thought. 'He made me laugh a lot,' she said.

'What about?'

'Oh, lots of things. His thing come to that.'

'You laughed at it?' Aunty sounded horrified.

'Well, he'd been explaining this problem in spherical trigonometry—'

'In *what?*'

'Spherical trigonometry. Sailors have to do it too. It's part of navigation,' Veronica explained earnestly. 'Only neither of us had any clothes on and he started to get excited and it was all sticking out and I said "Men have no secrets, do they?"'

'And what did he say?'

'Well, first he laughed, then he said, "Sticking out like a sore thumb as you might say. But we can't help it."'

It was her aunt's turn to giggle. 'You're a very lucky girl,' she said.

'Well I know that.'

'Not that way. That was fine. But it's partly my fault. I forgot to warn you.'

'Warn me?' Veronica looked bewildered.

'About men and that thing of theirs. It's important to them. When it gets up like that they're all so pleased with themselves. In fact when I'm working I always pretend I've never seen one like it. For them it's like what the king holds.'

'The king's thing?' said Veronica. 'I never thought of that. But he must have one. He's a man after all.'

'His sceptre,' said her aunt repressively. 'Shows how important and strong they are.'

'Symbol of power,' said Veronica.

'Exactly,' said her aunt. 'And you went and laughed at it.'

'So did he,' said Veronica. 'It looked funny and I said so, and he agreed. But what it looked like wasn't important. It's what he did with it.'

'Just don't do it to your next chap,' her aunt said.

'No rush,' said Veronica. 'And anyway my captain may be coming here again when he gets his strength back.' She smiled. '*He* said that, too. He said so many funny things.'

'You're a very lucky girl,' said her aunt once more.

'It's all you,' said Veronica, and then Jagadir Singh came in, escorting a quite obviously terrified messenger from Mrs Lal's shop. Mrs Lal's shop meant jewellery, and when it came to the kind of jewels Miss Poppy received, Jagadir Singh left nothing to chance. But this time he was wrong. The neat little package was for Veronica.

'Open it, child,' her aunt bade her when the Sikh had gone, and Veronica ripped and tore. She was no believer in untying knots. A leather box, and an elegant one. What was inside must be rather good. She opened the box, and gasped. What was inside was a necklace of heavy gold, its centre-piece a ruby: rounded, glowing, and beside it a card. 'Now you've got three,' her captain had written, 'but don't let it bother you. This one's detachable. I hope – oh how I hope – to see you soon. Love. Nicholas.'

She giggled, then took the necklace and card to show Aunty, and Aunty giggled too.

'So naughty,' she said, then: 'Take off your top for a minute,' and Veronica obeyed at once. Aunty would never do anything to embarrass her, never mind hurt her. Nor did she. Instead, 'Such pretty pomelos,' she said, and put on the necklace for her. 'He has a good eye too,' she said. 'Go and look in the mirror.'

Veronica went. The ruby glowed between her breasts: the necklace gleamed. 'It's witty,' she said, 'but there's a kind of poetry too,' and put the top back on. 'May I keep the necklace on please?'

'For now,' her aunt said, 'but not to go to the convent – if you did all your classmates would be yelling for honeymoons.' Veronica giggled once more.

'Talking of honeymoons,' said her aunt, 'do you remember Rollo Sandyford?'

'The little soldier with the clammy hands?'

'That's the one. He wants one.'

'And will you?'

'Of course not,' her aunt said. 'He's far too poor to afford me. Wants to pay by instalments.' Her voice was outraged, and Veronica wanted to giggle again, but that would have been asking for trouble. Instead Veronica tried to look outraged too.

'Idiot,' she said. 'Why isn't he in France anyway?'

'Because he's as cunning as he's cowardly,' said her aunt, and waved her hand. Sandyford was dismissed.

'But there is another chap,' Aunty said. 'Not a stunner like your captain, but nice. Really awfully nice. He's a box-wallah.'

A box-wallah meant trade, and the soldiers and the ICS and perhaps even her darling Nicholas despised persons in trade.

'He must be rich,' Veronica said, and knew that she was safe. When it came to money Aunty was as big a realist as Bridget.

'Yes he is,' said her aunt. 'Very rich. He's also very keen on me.'

'So I should hope,' said Veronica.

'Yes, but he's had to go to Bombay,' said Aunty. 'Not much good being keen on me in Bombay while I'm in Calcutta. Except—'

'Yes, Aunty?'

'Oh, hell,' said her aunt. 'You told me everything. Why shouldn't I tell you? He doesn't like sharing.'

'He's in love with you,' said Veronica, and her aunt looked at her sharply.

'You're clever all right,' she said. 'But love – it's something I don't know a damn thing about. It could be true – I think I even want it to be true, but he's a sahib even if he is a box-wallah. What chance have I got?'

Veronica went to her and kissed her. 'I shall say lots of prayers,' she said, and her aunt embraced her.

'Aspasia,' said Veronica.

'And what's that when it's at home?' her aunt asked.

'I looked her up in the encyclopaedia,' said Veronica. 'She was the wittiest, most graceful hetaera of all. Pericles, the ruler of Athens, adored her. That's who you are. Yours must be quite a box-wallah.'

'Well he is,' said her aunt, 'and if things work out maybe you'll meet him. We'll see. Just now he's paying me a retainer.' Her niece looked puzzled. 'No more honeymoons till he gets back. I'm a lady of leisure. Well, a hetaera of leisure.'

Then Bridget came in to help them drink some champagne. The bank and investments again, it seemed. It must be a jolly decent retainer. Her aunt told Bridget all about the captain's thing and the laughter, but Bridget didn't laugh. Far from it. Honeymoons were a serious business. Cash in the bank. And nothing was as good as cash in the bank. It was a saying of the sahibs themselves.

'But it wasn't a honeymoon,' said Veronica. 'Not the way you mean it. All the same he sent me this,' and she showed her the necklace. Bridget was mollified at once.

'It must have cost a fortune,' she said.

'He's not just a hero,' said her aunt. 'He's a rich hero. Owns a lot of a place in London called Earl's Court. Hence the necklace. And you and he were sort of on honeymoon after all. Groom and blushing bride.'

'I'm hopeless at blushing,' said Veronica. 'I'm the wrong colour.'

8

In March 1918, Mark got what his brigadier called his second wound stripe, but which Mark preferred to think of as his second wound. It was *his* body after all. The Germans' last big push, and the battalion had run out of lieutenant colonels and he was the senior company commander, so they'd promoted him to acting major and put him in charge of the battalion. They'd given him an MC too, but that was because he was a regular. All the regular officers who weren't raving or dead got a Military Cross. Good for their peace-time careers. The fact that the war-time officers, the bank clerks, shop managers and schoolmasters, so rarely did was beside the point. When the war was over they'd go back to being civilians.

He'd lasted three days, then there'd been an open order advance and a German machine-gunner had put three bullets in him: shoulder, hip and thigh. He'd only put one in Sergeant Major Cheeseman, but Sergeant Major Cheeseman was dead. Better not to think about that. Not till his particular hell ended, if it ever did.

The thing was that the bullets that hit him had missed what his rather pompous MO kept calling the vital

115

organs. (The one that had got Cheeseman had hit his heart, and for a bullet in the heart there was no cure.) What he got was gangrene and a spell in a French hospital, where the gangrene got worse, then Blighty and another Home Counties hospital, and an operation and antiseptics, and rather a lot of pain. And Maude. Dear Aunt Maude once more, and Your loving nephew Mark. And another X for a kiss, as shaky as the first one.

She was round like a shot, as he'd prayed she would be: sensible, compassionate, *listening*, that was the thing, because this time he couldn't stop talking. It was his fear of course, that was more like terror, but she listened as if it were no more than gossip about some rather odd chums in France, and nasty foreigners making rather a nuisance of themselves. So long as she was there to listen he was all right, but even when she wasn't his body began to heal until at last the time came when he could go back to Northumberland to convalesce. Fly fishing and shooting and Belinda, he thought, and mummy too, because this time his mother hadn't come to visit him. She'd developed bronchitis it seemed, and long train journeys, so her doctor had told her, were Out Of The Question. It didn't bother him. He loved her as much as ever, but to have mother hovering over him in hospital distressed them both. Not like Maude Lippiatt.

The house was as it had always been: calm and cheerful and welcoming, and about as remote from the trenches as it was possible to be. He walked up the path doing his best not to limp: pretending that the stick he leaned on was no more than the prop for an outmoded dandy's swagger, but she was at the front door long before the parlourmaid, and hugged him and hugged him.

At last she said, 'I needed that.'

'Me too,' said Mark.

'So bad of me not to come to see you, but I really was rather ill.'

'Well of course,' said Mark. 'Otherwise you'd have been on the first train. I know that.'

'So I'm forgiven?'

'What's to forgive?' said Mark. 'You've been ill and I've been ill. Now I'm rather better. How about you?'

'Oh, lots,' she said. 'So long as I stay out of the cold.' Mark took her arm, urging her into the house, and sat her in a chair.

She looked at him and thought Oh, my God, he's *better*? His skin was brown, certainly, but that was because he was out of doors so much. Otherwise he was a stone under weight at least, his hands trembled when he put down his stick, and his eyes seemed to be staring at nothing but horror.

'Is it so very bad?' she said.

'Some of it,' said Mark. 'But there are good things too.'

'Tell me.'

She wants me to say I won't have to go back, he thought, but that won't be possible: not till God makes up His mind.

'Well I'm a major,' he said. 'Acting that is, but even so I've got the battalion. And I've got this.' He touched the ribbon of his MC.

'You've got those, too,' said his mother, and gestured at the wound stripes: one fading, one brand new.

'At least I'm alive,' said Mark.

117

'Oh, my God!' said his mother, and her son thought, What now? 'Your Uncle Charles,' she said.

'What about him?'

'Tim was killed,' said his mother. 'The same day that you were wounded.'

Tim, the younger son. Just his age. And Francis, a year older, but already more than two years dead.

'I'll write to him,' said Mark. 'At White's.'

'He's back here now,' said his mother. 'At Brampton Hall.'

'On his own?'

'He wrote to me. Told me he doesn't want to see me. Doesn't want to see anybody. Except you.'

'Me?'

'He said in the letter he wants to look at a survivor. I don't think he's quite—'

'Sane?' said Mark, and his mother nodded. What a marvellous way to convalesce . . .

'There's a letter for you, too,' his mother said. 'From India.' She fetched it from a drawer in her desk. 'You read it while I have a word with Cook about dinner. I'm sure you must be starving.'

No mummy, he thought. What I am desperate for is a very large whisky, but that will have to wait until I go up to my room.

'I am rather,' he said, and opened the letter. It was from Rollo Sandyford, and reeked with friendship and *bonhomie* of a kind so false he had to read it twice to be sure he'd read it correctly. All about how glad he was to hear he'd got C Company now. Just the man to keep them in order . . .

118

I've got rather more than that, he thought. I've got the fucking battalion. And then – I mustn't use words like that here. Not even inside my head, because if I do and have a couple of whiskies I'll start saying them out loud, and how could I start explaining that to mummy? How could I explain it to anybody who hadn't been there? He read on.

Rollo's liaison job with the Gujarati regiment was almost over, it seemed, which probably meant they'd see each other soon ... Of course, thought Mark. He's been sent to C Company, and he's touting for a job behind the lines where those nasty Germans can't hurt him. There's no such job, Rollo my boy. Old comrades in arms, Rollo wrote. Pals really. Mark winced. Who in their right mind would want Rollo for a pal? Chaps who could rely on each other. Now we're getting to it. Please please please don't let the Germans get me, Rollo was saying. What a waste of time, he thought. I can't even rely on myself ...

Then some odds and ends of gossip to sweeten the pill. Cricket and polo and Mrs Lal's dances, and Poppy Villiers still taking on all and sundry and making her fortune. But not taking you on, Mark thought, otherwise you wouldn't be so nasty. And her niece still at the convent school, it seemed. And what a waste of time. God knows she's beautiful, but she'll end up as big a whore as her aunt, or Rollo missed his guess. Mark crumpled the letter and threw it into the fire. If Rollo was ever dragged kicking and screaming to C Company he'd have an absolutely bloody awful time. Even worse than mine, thought Mark. I'll see to that.

* * *

The butler – Truelove was it? No of course not. Truscott. That was it – said, 'I'm afraid Sir Charles is not receiving at the moment, sir.'

'He's receiving me,' said Mark. 'He asked me to call.'

The butler looked at him more closely. It was all on his face. Good God, he was thinking. It can't be – and yet it is.

'Mr Mark?' he said.

'Well, yes,' said Mark, 'though nowadays I'm Major Beddoes as well.'

Again the astounded look, followed by impassivity almost at once. Truscott was a good butler.

'Yes, of course, sir,' he said. 'I shall inform Sir Charles. Would you care to wait in the gun-room? We don't use the drawing-room just at present.'

He led, and Mark followed. As if I were a deb at a dance, thought Mark.

'May I get you a glass of sherry?' said Truscott.

'Whisky,' said Mark.

Once again the impassivity slipped. Truscott didn't look at the clock, but both men knew it wasn't yet midday.

Mark swigged at the whisky, topped up his glass, swigged again and looked at the guns. Francis' pair of twelve bores, and Tim's, and Sir Charles': all hand made by Holland and Holland, but then Sir Charles was rich. Five thousand acres, two coal mines, and shares in God knows what. And a fat lot of use that is to Francis and Tim, he thought, and topped up his glass again; but this time he sipped. He was still sipping when Truscott came for him.

'You don't look very well,' said his uncle. They were in his dressing-room: Sir Charles in pyjamas and, for whatever reason, a smoking-jacket. Overweight, thought Mark. He'd always been so lean. Restless, fidgeting, and even madder than I am.

'It's because I was wounded, Uncle Charles,' he said. 'Francis was killed. And Tim.'

'My mother told me. I asked her to write to you.'

'She did,' Sir Charles said. 'Why didn't you write?'

'I'd been wounded then, too.'

'You're a very lucky feller,' Sir Charles said.

'*Lucky*?' It was possible, even necessary, to feel sympathy for Uncle Charles, but there were limits.

'You're the one sitting there,' his uncle said. 'Not Francis. Not Tim. You.'

Mark stayed silent, because what was there to say?

'Mind you they keep in touch,' said his uncle.

Séances? Mark wondered. Mediums? A lot of parents turned to that stuff for comfort. 'We're happy here,' the departed told them. 'All is peace.' After the Somme and Beaumont Hamel and Second Ypres peace would make anyone happy.

'They look in on me sometimes,' said Sir Charles, and Mark willed himself into a passivity modelled on Truscott's.

Sir Charles, baulked of a reaction, said at last, 'Look into my mind, I mean. I'm not mad, you know.'

'Well, of course not, uncle,' said Mark, and thought to himself, Any more than I am.

His uncle grunted, then said, 'There's whisky in that cupboard there. Pour us one apiece, and don't stint.'

Mark poured and thought: It takes one to know one, and Sir Charles gulped and said, 'They tell me things.

Usually when I've had a few of these.' He held up his glass.

'Yes, uncle?'

'It's marvellous where they are, they tell me. Hunting and point-to-points. Shooting, too.'

But not at Germans, thought Mark.

'And cricket. And the weather's always right for whatever you want to do. You think I'm crazy, I suppose?'

How can I judge? thought Mark. I'm that way myself.

'No, uncle,' he said.

Sir Charles grunted once more. 'Top us up,' he said, and when Mark had done so, 'I liked you, you know. Liked a lot of people once, but you more than most. Trouble is—'

'Yes, uncle?'

'You're alive.'

'For the moment,' Mark said, and his uncle sighed.

'Going back soon?'

'Couple of weeks.'

'Truscott says you're a major now,' his uncle said.

'Acting, anyway. It's because I've got the battalion.'

'And two wound stripes. And a Military Cross by the look of it.'

'Yes, uncle.'

'And still alive.'

'For the moment,' Mark said again. It was a difficult, even terrifying, thing to say, but he said it. The old boy deserved that much.

'You'd better go,' his uncle said. 'I'm tired.'

'Very well, sir.' Mark stood up, and waited to see if Sir Charles would offer him his hand. He didn't, so Mark left him, but he finished his whisky first.

* * *

Victoria said, 'You're off to see Mark again.'

'Of course,' said her mother.

'And daddy knows?'

'I told him,' said her mother, and Victoria shook her head in bewilderment. And who should wonder? her mother thought. The whole thing's bewildering. But so's the bloody war.

'Does daddy know where?' Victoria asked.

'Of course,' said her mother. 'He has to. Suppose the house caught fire. It's Cheltenham Spa.'

'Golly,' said Victoria, and for some reason looked ready to cry.

She wants to take my place, her mother thought, and maybe some day she will, and how will I feel if she does? But that's the least of my worries. To take my place Mark has to be alive . . .

She was almost sure that the rose-pink tea-gown was in the smaller case, but she'd better check. Mark loved her in the rose-pink tea-gown, and even more when he'd helped her take it off.

Her daughter said, 'I saw a bracelet the other day.'

'Really,' said her mother.

'Yes, really. Nothing vulgar. Just a gold band with sapphires.'

Gold like her hair, sapphires like her eyes, her mother thought.

'Sounds terribly you,' she said, and her daughter gaped at her. Maude chuckled. 'Don't look so surprised, child,' she said. 'Here's your mother gadding about all over the place and your father not lifting a finger. You've got to have some kind of compensation.'

Her daughter gaped again, but still contrived to look pretty. 'Thank you, mummy,' she said.

'Don't thank me,' said her mother. 'Just remember to be nice to daddy while I'm away. After all, he's the one who'll be paying.'

She always looks so pleased when she's going to make daddy fork out, Victoria thought. As if she were making him pay a fine or something.

Cheltenham Spa was rather good. Mark wasn't drinking nearly so much, though she got the idea that he'd been on the most colossal bender before he came south, but even so the rose-pink tea-gown worked its familiar magic, and he achieved heights that Tom didn't know were there to be scaled. That was death, she thought, moving closer by the day. But goodness, how sweet he was, when he wasn't being strong. Sweet in talk and kisses and touch; trying and failing not to tell her about German machine-guns, and their grenade the Tommies called a potato masher, and Sergeant Major Cheeseman . . . She listened because it was good for him, and afterwards they would go back to bed. But the days flew by and it was time to go so soon.

They took the train to London and sat decorously apart, and when she left he kissed her cheek as if she really was his aunt, then waited till she had gone and bought a bottle of whisky to help him cope with the boat train and men going back reluctantly to despair: men who had had enough and more than enough, and a grey and heaving sea that was like a moat to separate him from happiness.

* * *

The sea was cold: not far from freezing in fact. After all, the nearest land mass was Greenland, and the month was March, but even so he swam on. What else was there to do? His destroyer was sunk, or if she wasn't, it would be a bloody miracle. A bloody miracle to have a lifebelt round him come to that. And yet . . . He hadn't done too badly. A left foot almost detached from his leg when last he saw it, a hole in his side he could lose his fist in, his ship foundering, or foundered. And yet . . . And yet . . . Captain Hepburn swam on and counted his blessings while there was still time. And he had been blessed, that was the point. Commodore in command of a destroyer squadron – three of them – with a free hand to sink U-boats in the North Sea any way he could. Naval Intelligence said there were five of them and he'd got four. Until this. Four to one. Not bad odds. The thing was, he'd taken Admiral Fisher's advice: sink everything. That meant that before they'd even started the hunt he'd made the destroyer commanders swear they'd go for the enemy no matter what. Including their commodore ending up in the drink. A U-boat destroyed was infinitely more important than a dead sailor. Or fifty dead sailors come to that. And if they hadn't been picked up by now, there'd be fifty dead sailors at least. The price that had to be paid . . . If he'd lived he'd have become an admiral sooner or later, but that wasn't important either. And anyway he'd sooner have had Veronica.

Captain Hepburn swam on. The cold seemed to be relenting, but that wasn't possible. It had lost its power to reach him, which meant that he was dying, but at least he couldn't feel his left foot, if he still had one, or the hole in his side . . . From behind him there came the sound of what might have been the biggest banger on Guy Fawkes' night, then the huge, slapping sound of water falling in a deluge. And another. And another. The other two destroyers, he thought: after the last U-boat like terriers after the last surviving rat. Then one more boom, one more deluge, and then silence. This time the terriers have won, he thought. His game plan had worked.

A lot of it had depended on navigation, and a lot of that had depended on spherical trigonometry, and he would never have got it right if it hadn't been for Veronica and the other two honeymoons they'd had. Not that he'd told her. Of course not. For her they'd been no more than mathematical games played between bouts of the most exquisite passion he'd ever known. The diamond honeymoon (ear-rings and a necklace) and the sapphire honeymoon (a bracelet). Rubies for the first one: red, white and blue. A gift for a patriot. And she would never know. Or would she? She was so quick. Sometimes she had a way of looking at him that – Leave it, he thought. Just leave it. Whether she knows or not she *is* a patriot, and what other mathematician could you trust? What other mathematician could you go to bed with for that matter? But oh, my God, what bliss it had been to go to bed with her, and for that my God I thank you.

As the words came he knew that death was very near: that there was no point in the lifebelt any more. Somehow he got rid of it, and swam on as best he could; not diving down, just waiting. And suddenly she was with him: naked in that chilling sea, except that it didn't chill any more. It was as warm as the tank in Calcutta. She swam to him, grasped his shoulders and wriggled beneath him, deft as a mermaid, then her arms came round him, and she drew him down, down, into the kindly dark.

Suddenly it was over: a war which had become as much a part of his life as the seasons, just stopped. Of his original company perhaps a score of men, two sergeants and three corporals survived. Even so they had been winning when it ended. Eleven a.m. on the eleventh of November 1918. Not that it was the final end. An Armistice, the staff called it, and they'd advanced fifty miles in their counter-attack in ten days. Jerry had had the stuffing knocked out of him, not that they were the sort of Germans he'd faced in 1916. Stunted, some of them, all but useless, far too young or far too old; like my battalion, he thought. He hadn't believed it possible that troops like that could win anything – until he saw the opposition.

All the same they made no advance on the eleventh of November. Snug in their trenches they stayed, made a brew, had a smoke, and his German counterpart came to the same decision. From a distance they could hear the boom of artillery, even the rattle of machine-guns, even at five to eleven; but he and his battalion kept their heads down, and so did the Germans who faced them. Not cowardice, a gentlemen's agreement. Nothing else made sense. Then the five minutes passed and the silence came: the first silence in Northern France for four years, and incredibly it was followed by bird-song: the only noise until the men began to cheer. Even so he let five more minutes go by before he stepped on to the parapet, let himself be seen, and an instant later the German CO did the same. Together they scrambled out of their trenches and walked to No Man's Land. There were arrangements to be made. The war really was over.

The next day Lieutenant Sandyford joined the battalion. Twelfth of November 1918. Say what you like about Rollo, his sense of timing was remarkable, thought Mark. Two years to move from Southern India to Northern France. Something to do with bunions in Calcutta and tonsillitis in Catterick . . . Oh dear. All the same he sent him to a platoon in C Company, now commanded by Captain Handyside, once a bank clerk, now an officer with two years' service, two wound stripes and a Military Medal. (Captain Handyside had been promoted from the ranks.) Rollo had smiled bravely when Mark broke the news, then tried his best not to shudder when Mark introduced him to Handyside. He was out of it and he knew it. The other two in faded, dusty uniforms, medal ribbons, wound stripes, and he in a uniform glittering clean and no embellishments at all. He could never, ever belong. The men of his platoon looked at him hungrily and Mark left them to it. They deserved a treat . . .

Besides, he was due for leave, and a medical, it seemed. He wrote at once to Maude Lippiatt. 'Dear Aunt Maude,' et cetera, then 'Your loving nephew, Mark.' But this time the X beneath his name didn't wobble at all. His wars were over.

This time they went to Brighton: the perfect place for naughtiness, Maude said, and naughtiness there was in quantities, and not nearly so much whisky.

'Go easy with the tea-gown,' she said. 'It hasn't all that

much life left in it. Not like you.'

'Let me buy you another,' said Mark.

'We'll see,' she said, and then: 'When do you go back North?'

'After my medical,' he said. 'Next Friday.'

'Do you expect us to romp all the time till then?'

'That's up to you,' he said.

'Then we will,' said Maude. 'Except – do you think we should? It's a medical, after all.'

'It's to find out if I'm fit enough to go back to India. Business as usual. All that.'

'And are you?'

'I think so.'

'Oh, good,' said Maude. 'Tom's been ordered back to India, too. More business as usual. All kinds of business. Maybe we'll be in the same boat.'

'We'll always be that,' said Mark.

'How sweet you are,' Maude said. 'Just for that we'll do something reprehensible.'

'I doubt if I can just at the moment.'

'Let's find out,' she said.

He was fit enough, which in a way was a relief. A lot of regulars with two wound stripes were told they weren't, and that meant the scrap heap. And even before the wounds there'd been the broken leg, but after all that had happened playing polo, so that perhaps it was a ladder rather than a snake. *And* he'd got a DSO – for no particular reason that he could think of. A prize for surviving when there was a prize going free. Anyway his mother was delighted, even if he was going to leave her again soon. There'd be no more shrapnel, no more machine-gun bullets. The only cloud on mummy's horizon had been Sir Charles, because he hadn't sent for Mark again.

Not that I'm surprised, he thought. I survived the lot. Not like Francis and Tim: what other emotion could he feel for me than resentment? Even so, it would have been pleasant to be the next squire: send in his papers when the time came, kiss the regiment goodbye and do some serious reading. He wasn't all that keen on the regiment nowadays, but it was all he had.

Belinda put up a pheasant and he killed it with the first barrel, and Belinda looked at him.

My goodness you've come on a bit, the look said.

'You weren't there,' he told her. 'Either you learned quickly or you didn't learn at all.'

Belinda, feeling her years, trotted sedately to retrieve the pheasant. India, he thought. Business as usual. Maude in a tea-gown, Maude out of a tea-gown, and he wondered how he would feel when he saw Tom Lippiatt again. Not to mention Victoria.

When the news came she had cried for him. Of course she had. Three wonderful honeymoons – even if she'd had to play what Aunty called 'Let's Pretend' now and again so that he'd get it over with and they could get back to spherical trigonometry. Not that he'd ever found her out: not even suspected. She was far too fond of him to let that happen, and anyway she was there to make him happy and she *had* made him happy. It was a question of priorities, nothing more. All the same, she thought it might be better not to tell Aunty: not unless she asked outright. When Aunty asked things outright it was best to tell the truth, because Aunty knew all there was to know about detecting lies.

Veronica leafed through the spherical trigonometry notebooks he had left behind: rough jottings, unfinished calculations, abandoned ideas. The good stuff, the fair copies she had made for him he'd taken away after their last time, and was now at the bottom of a cold, dark sea, swapped you might say for a diamond necklace and earrings and a sapphire bracelet, but that was all right. It was all affection. And she'd known what he was after, though he had never told her, and that was all right too. He knew she knew, she was sure of it, and what he'd asked her to do was an honour, a privilege: help him plot the destruction of the Empire's enemies. She'd been useful, she was sure, and that was a good feeling too. Five U-boats sunk, and her darling captain a posthumous VC. He had saved many of his crew's lives, so the newspapers said, but not his own. She would miss him dreadfully, she thought, and then – he died in the cold. And alone. All the time we were together we were warm, even under the punkah, and only the trips to the bathhouse and the tank to keep us sweet – and even when I rubbed the scented oil on him he was a man, a real man: just as when he rubbed it on me I was a real woman. She breathed a long, shuddering sigh. Time to stop snivelling, she told herself. It's over. He's dead.

Her aunt came in, and her eyes went at once to the notebooks. 'You're going to burn them?' she asked. Veronica shrugged: a movement modelled precisely on her aunt's.

'They're just figures; ideas that didn't work,' she said.

'All the same, burn them,' said her aunt. Veronica waited.

'Yesterday I had my hetaera's dress on,' her aunt said, 'and it stayed on. I'm still faithful to Arthur. All the same I went to a party – Arthur doesn't mind that – and I heard gossip. About your captain.' Still Veronica waited.

'The sahibs think he was the greatest hero since Nelson,' her aunt said.

'Nelson died in battle too,' said Veronica.

Her aunt looked at her sharply. 'Clever girl,' she said. 'When you're dead you're no longer a threat. Is that it?' Veronica nodded.

'All the same they're proud of him. Besides, he was clever, too. Not a lot of the sahibs are clever. All that maths.'

'Spherical trigonometry,' said Veronica.

'They think he must have found some sort of teacher here. Sort of a guru. A Brahmin maybe. But it was you, wasn't it?'

Veronica nodded once more. 'Does anybody know?' she asked.

'No,' said her aunt. 'A few think he must have come here because of his reputation, but that would have meant he came to see me, and there would have been no point in asking because I never tell and they know it. Was it hard, what you did?'

'Hard?'

'Difficult,' said Aunty.

'Sometimes,' said Veronica, 'but it had to be done. It

meant he was able to kill an awful lot of Germans.'

'That doesn't bother you?' said Aunty. 'After all you could say you killed them too.'

'Of course it doesn't bother me,' Veronica said. 'They were the enemy.'

'Good girl,' said her aunt and opened her handbag, took out a buff-coloured envelope. 'This came for you,' she said. 'That captain of yours was clever all right. Three envelopes, one inside the other. The first was to our bank and they opened it. The second was to Bridget and we opened that together. The third – this one – is for you.' She handed the envelope over. It was stiff with sealing wax. 'Shall I leave you?'

'Oh no,' said Veronica. 'Please.' Now was not the time to be alone with her darling captain.

This time she couldn't rip and tear: the wax defied her, but she opened the envelope at last with a nail file, and read its contents.

'Darling, darling Veronica (she read),

'If you ever read this it means I'll be dead, but we all have to go some time and what better way than fighting the enemy? – and without you I couldn't have fought them nearly so well. For this, as for so many things, I thank you.'

Veronica read on. It was lovely stuff, and almost she wanted to cry again, until, 'Oh, Aunty,' she said. 'Come and see. I'm in his will.'

Her aunt came and read. Fifty thousand pounds, she thought. For three honeymoons. And all the other stuff too. It got some men like that. She had one herself and sometimes wished to hell she hadn't. Or did she? But

Veronica had made hers into a hero, even if he was a dead hero.

'– to the most distinguished mathematician of my acquaintance, Miss V. Higgins,' Aunty read aloud, 'to be used in any way she thinks appropriate.'

'But how could he know my real name?' Veronica asked.

'Because he asked me and I told him.'

'But why?'

'Because I knew what he was after. I just hadn't thought he would be quite so generous.'

Despite all her good intentions Veronica found it necessary to wipe her eyes, but her aunt approved of even that.

'A real man,' she said. 'He deserves your tears. But promise me you'll burn those notebooks.'

'Of course, Aunty,' Veronica said. 'It's all in here anyway.' She tapped her forehead, and her aunt looked at her, awestruck.

'But how can it be?' she said at last.

'It's so beautiful,' said Veronica. 'How could I forget it?'

Only one thing to do, Poppy Villiers thought. Change the subject. 'I've decided to retire,' she said.

It was her niece's turn to look awestruck. 'You've made so much?' she said.

'Hark at who's talking,' said her aunt and then: 'I've done all right. Not enough to run this house and all the servants and your pony – but all right.'

'There's the captain's money too,' said Veronica.

'No, there isn't. That's yours,' her aunt said. 'And stop interrupting.'

'Sorry, Aunty.'

'Yes, well,' said her aunt. 'Where was I?'

'Living comfortably.'

'Well, that's just what we're not going to do – you and Bridget and me. I adore being rich and so do you. We'd hate to live comfortably.'

Her aunt became silent, which was most unlike her, thought Veronica, until she realised that for once Polly Villiers was tongue-tied, and the kindest thing was to wait. The wisest, too.

'Oh, sod it,' her aunt said at last. 'I'll have to have a drink first. Ring for the bearer.'

Veronica rang, and the bearer scurried to them. In Indian households servants always knew when not to dawdle. Wary and prescient as antelope, thought Veronica.

'Champagne, Jeldi,' said Aunty. The bearer took off and was back in seconds, and the champagne was poured.

Her hand is shaking, Veronica thought. Oh, my God, she's not ill is she? Baby Jesus please don't let her be ill. But after the first swig of champagne Aunty smiled, and sipped like a lady.

'It's all new to me you see,' she said.

'What is?'

'Love,' said her aunt.

'You're in *love*?' Veronica seemed astounded, but then why shouldn't she be? Her aunt ignored it.

'Blest if I know,' she said.

'Is it Mr Nugent?'

'Well of course it is,' said her aunt furiously, and Veronica thought that it might well be love, then her aunt drank more champagne, swigging again. 'Sorry about that,' she said. 'The thing is that *he* loves *me*.'

'Sensible chap,' said Veronica.

'I've got it in writing. He also wants to marry me. I've got that in writing, too.'

'Golly,' said Veronica.

'I know what you mean,' said her aunt, 'but the thing is Arthur's not some stupid rich subaltern who doesn't know which way is up. When he puts things in writing he means them. Like a contract.'

'You've accepted?'

'Not yet,' said her aunt. 'He's still on his way back from Bombay. But I will. I don't know a damn thing about love, but I know about liking people, and I like him almost as much as I like you.'

Veronica went to her and kissed her. 'Congratulations,' she said, and then: 'Is he really that rich?'

'He's a millionaire,' her aunt said. Veronica's wine slopped in its glass. 'Started small,' said her aunt. 'Owned a print shop. Then came over here: box-wallah. Sold printing materials for a while. Then it was deals. You wanted to make something – Arthur would find the money. Steel, cotton, leather, it's all the same to Arthur. Rice, coffee, grain. You need money – he'll sell you some.'

'He sells *money*?' said Veronica.

'It's always in demand,' her aunt said. 'The trick is to know how much to charge for it, and Arthur knows that to a ha'penny. Bridget thinks the sun shines out of him. A cross between Carnegie and the Lord Krishna.'

'But he's nice?' said Veronica.

'Super,' her aunt said, 'when he's not making money. At the moment he's talking about going back into printing as well.'

'Does he say why?'

'Ask him yourself,' said her aunt, and topped up their glasses. 'He's dining with us on Saturday. Just imagine. My own niece playing gooseberry.'

Veronica said severely, 'Chaperone if you please, Aunty,' and her aunt giggled.

'There was something else,' her aunt said. 'What was it? Oh, yes. The Royal Northumbrians are coming back to India. Including that sad admirer of yours.'

'Mark what's it,' said Veronica.

'Beddoes,' said her aunt. 'You should at least *try* to remember their names. It's only polite.'

Veronica shrugged. Because Captain Hepburn's dead and Mark Beddoes is alive? her aunt wondered. There's nothing we can do about either condition.

'Is Lippiatt coming back too?' Veronica asked.

Her aunt looked at her. She never gave clients' names to her niece – except for Arthur, who was no longer a client but a fiancé.

'Who?' she said.

'Victoria Lippiatt's father,' said Veronica. 'There's talk of another gymkhana soon and if she comes out, this time I've got a pony I won't have to wallop.'

'I'll ask,' said her aunt, and then: 'Are you going to practise the piano tonight?'

'If you don't mind.'

'I don't mind at all. I thought I'd just mention that Arthur's very fond of Chopin.'

'*Acha*, memsahib,' said Veronica, and this time it was her aunt who put out her tongue, then said, 'I may get word of a painter, too.'

'A painter?'

'For you and me. In the altogether.'

'Oh super,' said her niece. Life with Veronica was never dull, thought her aunt. 'Except that I may wear my ruby necklace,' Veronica said.

'In that case I'd better get Arthur to buy me a bauble too,' said her aunt. 'Don't forget to burn those notebooks.'

9

That meant going out to the kitchen, where the dinner smells were promising, and then the music room and Chopin. Bang Crash Wallop, she thought. Still it was nice to get out the sledge-hammer occasionally, and then Mozart's *Rondo alla Turca* as a reward for duty done. Really there were so many things that were just as nice as doing it, but still she missed her darling captain.

When the gong sounded and she went in to dinner, Aunty was alone.

'No Bridget?' Veronica asked.

'Migraine,' said Aunty. 'More like sulks if you ask me.'

Then the bearer came in with the soup and they gossiped about the gymkhana till he'd gone, then, 'What's she got to sulk about?' asked Veronica.

'My retiring and you not even starting,' said Aunty.

'But you're not going to get rid of her, surely?'

'Of course not,' Aunty said. 'It's just—'

The bearer returned to collect the soup plates and present a dish of curried crabs. More talk of the gymkhana and Veronica's pony's prospects.

When he'd gone Aunty said, 'Bridget will have nothing

to do, you see. She can't stand having nothing to do.'

'She can help me look after my money.'

'I rather think Arthur will expect to do that.'

'Golly!' said Veronica. She really was coming up in the world. A millionaire for a financial adviser.

The bearer came in with a sweet of gulab jarmans and they talked of fashion. Aunty had seen a dress she rather fancied. Rose pink and cream, and rather a lot of lace.

They took coffee in the music room and played the gramophone. Tunes from a musical comedy called *The Bing Boys*, which Aunty liked very much. As they listened Aunty sipped a brandy and soda because Bridget had been rather trying. When the record ended she said, 'She'll get over it. Bridget, I mean.'

She knew the bearer wouldn't bother them. He disliked Western music. All the same: 'Let's have the other side,' she said, and so Veronica turned the record and Aunty offered cigarettes.

'And she *does* get migraines,' her aunt said. 'Usually when she gets excited about things. It was wrong of me to call it sulks,' then in the same breath she added: 'You need some new dresses too.'

'But I've got masses,' said Veronica.

'You're a rich woman. Rich women never have enough dresses. Besides—'

'Yes, Aunty?'

'I reckon you're "out", as the memsahibs say. No more missy baba. My God, after what you and your captain got up to how could there be?'

'It was more fun than curtsying to the king would be,' said Veronica.

'Never mind the king,' Aunty said hastily. 'We're discussing clothes.'

'You mean really grown-up clothes?'

'I certainly do,' said her aunt. 'You've spread your wings already. Now you can really fly. Just as well it's your half-term.'

'You mean tomorrow?' Her aunt nodded and smiled.

'Oh, *Aunty*.'

'I told Arthur I had a beautiful niece,' she said, 'and we're going to prove it.'

Veronica was silent.

'Something bothering you?' said her aunt. 'Frightened you might make me jealous?'

'Of course not,' said Veronica. 'It's you he wants. You he wants to *marry*. It's just—'

'Let's have it, child.'

'Won't it be a little tricky? Announcing your engagement to a white man here?'

'It'll be a bit tricky anywhere,' Aunty said. 'But I grant you Calcutta will be trickier than most. Arthur doesn't give a damn.'

If that's true, thought Veronica, he's every bit as much a man as my captain.

'But I do,' Aunty said.

The troop-ship *Gloriana* docked, and the men filed ashore. Not too hot, not yet; no more than eighty degrees, and so the colonel had decided on a march through the city: not that there were any signs of trouble, but the sight of a battalion of British regulars, bayonets fixed, reduced the possibility of trouble even further, and so march they did, the band blaring 'Tipperary' and 'Pack Up Your Troubles' and 'Blaydon Races', and evoking memories that were infinitely more distant than the other side of the earth: more like another planet. Even so C Company marched well: regulars who were glad to be back to square bashing and open-order drill and a gallon of beer on Saturday night. Only Rollo looked miserable, he thought, but then Rollo always looked miserable these days.

It was on Chowringhi that he saw them.

'Goodbye Piccadilly' (the band blared), 'Farewell Leicester Square', but of course the men marched at attention. In Indian terms this *was* Piccadilly, and there they were, the two of them, as if they'd just emerged from lunch at the Ritz. She looked older of course, because she *was* older, but Poppy Villiers seemed to be exactly as before: as if for her time had stood still, but then between the two of them they could have stopped the stars in their courses. Poppy in rose pink and cream, he noticed, and Veronica in a dress of blue and white, and diamonds in her ears. As they approached their motor (gracious how rich Poppy must be), a brigadier general came out of Cox's and King's and looked around for a gharri. There wasn't much opportunity for wit on the march, he thought, but now was his chance.

'Eyes left,' bawled Mark, and his company obeyed as one, and the brigadier general, delighted, returned a full salute, but it had all been for Veronica. The drums thundered and the tune changed. Sousa this time. 'Bollocks – and the same to you,' but not on Chowringhi, not with ladies present. And then a glimpse of more old friends.

142

Tom Lippiatt and his daughter, Victoria, who still looked like a schoolgirl, whereas Veronica looked like a goddess . . . No eyes left for him, either. He was just a civilian after all. No DSO, no MC . . .

In the lines he showered and changed, and almost at once his bearer brought him a chit. Just an address and five words: Come at once. Aunt Maude, and after the name a firm and somehow splendid X.

Their love-making had been even better than usual, he thought. No fear of imminent death, and a mixture of heat and the coolness of the punkah that only old India hands could know.

'I'd better get dressed,' he said.

'No rush,' said Maude, and grabbed him, and he lay still. No arguing with that.

'Tom,' Mark said. 'Victoria.'

'Tom is out – what do you military chaps call it? – reconnoitring,' said Maude. 'He's taken Victoria as camouflage.'

'Reconnoitring?'

'He's trying to find out what's happened to Poppy Villiers.'

'Nothing's happened to her. I saw her in Chowringhi when we marched to the lines.'

'And her delectable niece?'

'They were together, yes.'

Her fingers pleased. For him at least her revenge was sweet, but there still could be bitterness too. He willed himself to lie impassive and let it happen.

'He wrote a chit to her,' Maude said. 'I don't know what he wrote – I can't keep track of *all* he writes – but the

chit went off before he'd even finished unpacking.' Her
fingers pleased even more. 'But I did see her reply. The
bloody fool didn't even have the sense to burn it straight
off.' He waited. ' "Miss Villiers regrets that she is no
longer at home to Mr Lippiatt." And that was it. *Tout
court*.' Suddenly the movement of her hand changed and
impassivity took its toll.

'Maude *please*,' he said, and she looked at him.

'Oh, you poor darling,' she said. 'But just let me finish.
Tom's out palely loitering for a glimpse of Poppy Villiers
and just missed her by the sound of things – and Victoria's
out with him for a glimpse of a pony she's heard of.'

'Suppose they come home?'

'They won't,' said Maude. 'Not for another hour anyway.'

'How can you possibly know?'

'I told him not to,' said Maude. 'He's very biddable these
days. It worries me sometimes.' She looked down at him
then, and released him.

'My dear, you positively vibrated,' she said. 'Like a
water diviner or something.'

'A love diviner,' said Mark, and she wriggled beneath
him. It wasn't true, but it deserved a little extra effort.

'So good to be back in India,' she said. 'All this heat. So
good for *l'amour*.'

Her husband did not agree with her. He had just seen
Poppy Villiers and her niece drive past him, and as
always the sight of Poppy generated the mixture of rage,
loathing and frantic passion that was so difficult to hide.
As usual the two of them were gossiping and laughing so
that it was hard to tell whether Poppy had seen him or
not, but if she had she gave no sign. All the same – 'No

longer at home to Mr Lippiatt.' As if she were white and a lady instead of a rotten brown whore.

'Did you see who that was?' his daughter asked.

'Hm?' He tried to look abstracted but it wasn't easy, the way he was feeling.

'In that *vast* motor car?' said Victoria. 'It was that chee-chee Villiers and that niece of hers.'

'The one who—' he checked himself just in time. He'd almost said tied with you '—who behaved so badly at the gymkhana?'

'The very same,' said Victoria. 'Well, next time she can behave as badly as she likes because I'm jolly well going to beat her. Which reminds me – we ought to take a look at that pony.'

Like her mother, he thought. My mind's made up so do it now. All the same the child was riding well enough to deserve a new pony, and anyway, quite a lot of their money had once been his wife's, and yet he was the one who signed the cheques. It wasn't total consolation, but it helped.

Back to the mess for a peg or two before dinner. Being a major for a while meant he had a few quid to indulge himself with, and he rather liked indulging himself. The mess waiter brought him his Scotch and soda, and he sipped. A novelty sipping Scotch from a glass instead of gulping it from a bottle. He must have been mad. Well of course. They were all mad at Beaumont Hamel and Vimy Ridge and Passchendaele, some of them so mad they didn't even know it. Compared with the Somme, Calcutta was a haven of sanity; sacred cows, fakirs, holy men and all.

Billy Smith-Hatton came to him. Once a subaltern in B Company, now its company commander. He hadn't seen him in months.

'Well, well,' he said, and noted with relief that Smith-Hatton already carried a well-charged glass. There was a limit to the amount of indulgence he could offer to others.

'Haven't seen you in ages,' Smith-Hatton said.

'My very thought,' said Mark. 'Not since that rest camp in Poperinghe. February 1918 would it be?'

'It would indeed,' said Smith-Hatton. 'Seems odd, wouldn't you say?'

But Smith-Hatton also had a couple of wound stripes – and an MC ribbon and bar on his jacket: at least a match for his DSO and MC.

'I think we took it in turns to be wounded,' he said.

'No doubt,' Smith-Hatton said. 'Jerry *would* do it, no matter how we reasoned with him.'

He looked across the room to where Rollo Sandyford nursed a Scotch and soda as if it would have to last all night.

'Who's the naked man?' he asked. 'Isn't he one of yours?'

'One of my platoon commanders,' said Mark. 'Name of Sandyford. He looks perfectly well clad to me.'

'Not a medal ribbon in sight,' Smith-Hatton said, 'and if memory serves me right no wound stripes either.'

'He had tonsillitis,' said Mark, 'but they don't give you a wound stripe for that.'

'And the medals? Mean to say – not even a campaign medal.'

'He left it a bit late for that.'

'*Late*?' Smith-Hatton said.

'He'd been left behind here doing liaison work with the Gujarati Rifles, and by the time he finally rejoined the company it was the twelfth of November 1918.'

'Good God,' said Smith-Hatton. 'What on earth does he find to talk about?'

'He doesn't,' said Mark. 'He's alone most of the time.'

10

'May I bother you?' Bridget said.

Me in bodice and drawers *again*, thought Veronica, and then looked at Bridget's face. How sad she looked.

'Yes, of course,' she said. Bridget came into the bedroom.

'I was wondering—' she said.

'Yes?'

'I don't have all that much to do these days. I thought I might be your lady's maid.'

Veronica looked at her, aghast, so that Bridget said: 'Why do you stare like that?'

'You want to be my servant? I couldn't possibly—'

'I do it for Poppy,' Bridget said.

'But she's your *friend*.'

'I thought you were my friend, too,' said Bridget.

She's reminding me of darling Nicholas, thought Veronica, and oh, so tactfully.

'Well, so you are,' she said. 'You know you are,' and kissed her cheek. 'And if it's just a friend helping a friend, of course I accept. Aunty says there's no one to touch you.'

'Let's find out,' said Bridget.

The dress she and Aunty had chosen for dinner that night was of white silk with a delicate pattern of blue, and very grown up. Mid-calf in length, and with a discreet *décolletage*. Blue silk evening slippers with white bows, and sheer silk stockings, not socks.

'Very nice,' Bridget said. 'Who chose it?'

'We both did,' said Veronica, and Bridget nodded. Two of a kind, the nod said.

'And jewellery?'

'The captain's sapphires – and these,' said Veronica, and opened yet another box from Mrs Lal. Sapphire drops for her ears. Once again just like her aunt, thought Bridget. If she knew how to make it she knew how to get rid of it too.

'No necklace?'

'I thought a necklace as well would be a bit much,' said Veronica.

'And you were quite right,' said Bridget. 'But it needs something. Let's get you dressed while I have a think.'

'What about Aunty?' Veronica asked.

'I've dressed her already,' said Bridget. 'Don't worry. She knows.'

Aunty always knows, thought Veronica.

All the same, it was nice to be dressed by somebody who knew exactly what they were doing. Like her darling captain in reverse, she thought. Putting on instead of taking off: calm calculation instead of carefully controlled passion. Stockings just so, petticoat hems adjusted, buttons fastened by fingers that had done it all before. Then the towel around her shoulders, a hint of rouge, rather more than a hint of lipstick, and her eyebrows plucked into delicate arcs. A bit much, that last bit, but an Indian servant would have made her yell out loud.

And then her hair brushed: firm yet soothing strokes that relaxed her: made her ready for gossip instead of Mozart.

'Have you met him?' she asked.

'Mr Nugent? Not yet. But if Poppy fancies him—'

Bridget left it at that, and Veronica rather wished she hadn't. If Poppy fancies him he'll be – gorgeous? a bit of a handful? someone we'll just have to get used to? She wasn't to know. Instead Bridget began to talk about Veronica's pony.

'Ashoka you've called him?' Veronica nodded. 'A great king. Strong. Determined.'

'Like my pony,' said Veronica.

'Now you be careful,' Bridget said, then went out into the garden and came back at last with a corsage of blue orchids, pinned it into place. They were almost exactly the colour of the captain's sapphires. Veronica went to the cheval mirror in the corner of her bedroom and looked long and hard. Both women knew that she had never looked better.

'Darling Bridget,' said Veronica, 'it's absolutely marvellous to have a friend who's a lady's maid as well.' Then she went to the stairs. Seven-thirty, Aunty had said, and it wouldn't hurt to be a couple of minutes early, especially as Aunty was nervous. Drinks in the music room where Mr Nugent and Aunty were waiting, and Chopin too – and possibly Mozart if she was lucky. Slowly, walking as her aunt had taught her, she went into the room, and

Aunty looked at her and grinned in pleasure.

'Good God, child, you're gorgeous,' she said, and turned to the man beside her. 'Isn't she, Arthur?'

'She certainly is,' said Arthur Nugent.

A powerful man, well muscled, like a scaled-down version of Jagadir Singh, and a face that somehow combined a look of good humour and total determination. Strong and determined, in fact. Another King Ashoka.

'My niece, Veronica Carteret,' said her aunt, 'Mr Nugent. Mr Arthur Nugent.'

He offered his hand at once, and she could sense the power he so carefully controlled.

'A pleasure,' he said. 'A real pleasure. There won't be another man in Calcutta with two such lovely ladies. Not in the whole of the Raj, for that matter.'

His voice, like the rest of him, had a kind of controlled power, and he smiled like a schoolboy who's got exactly what he wanted for his birthday.

Oh, Aunty, why were you so nervous? Veronica wondered. He's gorgeous too.

'We've got something to show you,' said her aunt, and held out her left hand. It was a diamond. Somehow she had expected a coloured stone, but the diamond was perfect: a huge and glittering solitaire with a hint of blue that made her think of fire and ice together.

'Aunty,' Veronica said, 'it's absolutely fantastic,' and went to her and hugged her. 'I never knew Mrs Lal had anything like that.'

'I doubt she does,' said Nugent. 'I had to send to Amsterdam for that.'

'And the setting?'

152

'Paris,' said Nugent.

'Cartier,' said her aunt.

'Mr Nugent, it's the most wonderful diamond I ever saw,' Veronica said.

'There may be a few maharajahs who'll have one like it but there won't be many. And anyway I'm a maharajah myself now. Leastways I've got a maharani.'

Again the lucky birthday schoolboy grin, but this time aimed squarely at her aunt, who wriggled and looked demure even if she was wearing an orange satin dress that had never been demure in its life.

'All the same there's a problem, Miss Carteret,' Nugent said.

'A problem?'

'You call Poppy "Aunty" don't you? And very soon I'm going to marry her. Now where does that leave you and me? Like I say – a problem.'

'I don't think so, Uncle Arthur,' she said.

'Veronica, you've got it solved in one,' her Uncle Arthur said, and kissed her cheek. If I'd been a few years younger he'd have patted my head, she thought. Uncle Arthur's got all the women he wants, and her name is Poppy Villiers.

Dinner was splendid – well, of course it was; a love feast if ever there was one, and afterwards they left Uncle Arthur with his port in solitary splendour (not that he would be long, Veronica thought), and returned to the music room.

'You really like him?' her aunt asked.

'I really do,' said Veronica. Her aunt sighed.

'It'll mean changes of course,' she said cautiously.

Veronica waited. 'What I mean is the engagement,' said her aunt at last. 'We are engaged of course—'

'Of course you are,' said Veronica. 'No man would give you a diamond iceberg unless he meant it.'

Her aunt smiled. 'Thank you, darling,' she said, 'but what I mean is as long as we're in India it's a secret. I don't wear the iceberg in public no matter what Arthur says.'

'You mean you'll be leaving India?' Veronica said. But what about me? would have been her next words, but she bit them off in time.

'I mean all three of us will be leaving India,' said her aunt. 'And Bridget. If you want to come, that is.'

Veronica didn't hesitate. They had been a family of two, and now they would be a family of three, and one of them a man. Just right.

'Well of course I do,' she said.

'Without even knowing where we're going?'

'It'll be somewhere nice,' said Veronica. 'They're the only places you like.'

Her aunt grinned: a schoolgirl to Uncle Arthur's schoolboy. 'So now we've got another secret.'

'I'll keep it,' Veronica said.

'Of course you will,' said Aunty. 'You kept all the rest.' A pause and then, 'Arthur's voice.'

'It's a lovely voice.'

'Well, I think so,' said her aunt, 'obviously. But it's not what you'd call public school, now is it? None of that Eton and Harrow stuff.'

Nor was there. Uncle Arthur's voice had sounded almost classless, if such a thing was possible in an Englishman. Not that he gave a damn about that, either.

'Where do you think he came from?' her aunt asked.

Careful, Veronica told herself. This is tricky stuff, but Aunty wants the truth, and she must have it.

'Sometimes he speaks a bit like my father did,' she said.

'Clever girl,' said her aunt. 'They were born in the same town. Does it bother you?'

'Oh no,' said Veronica, 'but we won't have to live there, will we?'

'Certainly not,' said her aunt, and as she spoke Uncle Arthur joined them. 'Play for us, child,' said her aunt.

The *Polonaise Militaire* to make sure they were awake, then a couple of waltzes, and a mazurka at last to make sure they hadn't nodded off again. When she had done Uncle Arthur said, 'Those looks, and so gifted, too. Just like your aunt.' It was Veronica's turn to look demure.

'Just one more,' said her aunt. 'You choose.'

And so Mozart walked in as if he owned the place, but then Mozart owned every place he walked into.

'That was never Chopin,' said Uncle Arthur.

'Mozart,' she said. 'The *Rondo alla Turca*.'

'By lad,' said Uncle Arthur. 'I've got a lot of catching up to do.'

'One cigarette,' said her aunt, 'and then it's bedtime.'

'Yes, Aunty,' said Veronica. 'I don't want to be late for mass tomorrow.'

But for once her aunt smiled. She was going to say thank you to Baby Jesus and His Mother, and her aunt knew it.

Her aunt said, 'I've told Veronica we'll be leaving India.'

'You don't mind?' Uncle Arthur asked her.

'Not so long as I'm with you both,' Veronica said.

'You can bet your bottom dollar on that,' said Uncle Arthur.

Veronica said, 'If you don't mind I'll finish my cigarette upstairs. I'm so sleepy.'

'Off you go then,' said her aunt, and she kissed them both and left.

In fact she wasn't sleepy at all, but Bridget would be dying for a full report, and Aunty and her new uncle would be impatient to be off to the guest-house. After all they were *engaged*.

The chit said 'Kindly see me in my quarters immediately. Stafford OC,' and it didn't augur well despite the 'kindly'. The colonel didn't send for you to tell you how well you were doing. He didn't like being kept waiting either. Mark stepped out briskly to the colonel's door, was told to enter, and did so. The colonel was alone. No adjutant, so it couldn't be too bad.

'Ah, Mark,' said the colonel. 'Take a pew.'

'Mark' meant that whatever it was, it wasn't him. He sat bolt upright.

'That little feller in C Company,' the colonel said. 'Sandyford. What do you know about him?'

'Not a lot, sir,' said Mark. 'He didn't join the company until the day after Armistice Day. I never actually saw him in action.'

'Tonsillitis,' said the colonel. 'Bloody silly affliction when chaps like you were collecting wound stripes.' Mark waited.

'He plays a lot of cards,' said the colonel. 'Snooker, too. Damn lucky they tell me.' The colonel brooded for a moment on Rollo's good fortune. 'How good an officer is he?'

'About average,' said Mark.

'By which you mean rotten,' said the colonel. 'Don't tell me. I've watched him. His men don't care for him much either.'

'No, sir.'

'Because they know he wasn't shot at?'

'Not just that, sir.'

'What then?'

'Money, sir.'

'*Money*?'

The colonel couldn't have sounded more outraged if he'd said homosexual affairs.

'He hasn't any,' said Mark, 'apart from his pay, and an allowance from some relative or other, but I rather gather that's contingent on his being in the army.'

'You don't even have that,' said the colonel.

'But I enjoy what I do, sir,' said Mark. A whopper, that, but the colonel grunted: Mark gathered the lie had succeeded.

'And Sandyford doesn't like what he does?'

'He detests it, sir. And the men know it. They resent it because it means he detests them.'

'Not a very clever idea, to let them know it.'

'I don't think he is very clever – not in an analytical sense.'

'Just good with cards.' Again Mark waited.

'You know what I'm getting at, don't you?' said the colonel.

'Yes, sir,' said Mark. 'Have there been any complaints?'

'Not to me,' said the colonel. 'I want him stopped before there are.'

'You're quite sure it's what we think it is? I mean he is lucky, sir.'

'Lucky? How?'

'He dodged the entire war,' said Mark.

'What a shit he is,' said the colonel. 'I'd do better to get rid of him, but the relative who pays his allowance is a junior minister. You want to have a word with him – or leave me to do it?'

'Leave me to do it' was a warning; perhaps even a threat.

'I'd sooner handle it myself, sir.'

'Good man,' said the colonel. 'Put the fear of God into him. You can't dodge a whole war unless you're a colossal coward – not if you're a soldier as well.'

Mark went to the card room. Rollo was playing piquet with Rogers. Rogers and his money had both survived the war, though a lot of the money now seemed to be Rollo's.

'Unlucky in love no doubt,' said a voice behind him. It was Smith-Hatton. 'Feel like a game of billiards?'

'Why not?' They went into the deserted room.

'When it comes to cards Master Sandyford is a very lucky chap,' said Smith-Hatton.

'Too damn lucky,' said Mark.

'Too consistently damn lucky,' said Smith-Hatton.

'There's talk?' said Mark.

'Here and there,' Smith-Hatton said. 'Among the brighter ones. But nothing you could call proof – except that he doesn't drink when he plays.'

'That's hardly cheating.'

Smith-Hatton selected a cue. 'All the same, old boy,' he said, 'he hardly enhances C Company's reputation.'

Mark had an idea. 'If Sandyford asks, I want you to tell him I'm hopeless at snooker.'

'But why should he ask me?'

'Because we're friends.'

'But you're brilliant at snooker,' Smith-Hatton said.

'I want it to come as a surprise,' said Mark.

'Our painter's coming tomorrow,' said Aunty.

'Oh good,' said Veronica.

'Dying to let a man see you with no clothes on?' her aunt asked.

'Not dying, no,' said Veronica, 'but it might be interesting.'

'Not with this one it won't,' said her aunt. 'He's a fairy.'

'Ah well,' said Veronica. 'At least we won't have to fight for our honour.'

'From what I hear you'd have to fight for his,' said Aunty. 'His name's Matthew Burton. Arthur reckons he's good.'

'Uncle Arthur knows about pictures?'

'He knows about money,' said her aunt, 'and this one charges the earth because he can afford to. That's how good he is.'

'All girls together,' Veronica said.

''Fraid so. And this one's rather a dreary girl.'

'Do tell.'

'Well from what Arthur says he only has one joke. You

see all he paints are animals and pretty women – and the animals are mostly cats and the women are as bare as the animals.'

'Well, so will we be.'

'Yes, but there's his joke. The one and only. He'll tell the press: "I'm here to paint cats and pretty women. They're not entirely unrelated after all."'

'Will he say that about us?'

'He may think he will,' said Aunty, 'but he hasn't met Jagadir Singh yet.'

'There is just one thing,' Veronica said.

'You're not getting nervous, I hope?' said her aunt.

'Of course not. And anyway you'll be with me,' said Veronica. 'It's just that I was wondering – why are we doing this picture in the altogether?'

'Partly for our old ages,' said Aunty. 'To remind our chaps what they once had.'

'I haven't got a chap.'

'You will,' said Aunty. 'Don't interrupt. And partly because one of these days it'll go on exhibition – bound to – and a lot of sahibs we've never even met will be driven frantic.'

'So they will,' said Veronica, delighted. More pomelo expansion in the tank, and an excuse note to the convent: 'Veronica is sitting with me for a family portrait,' and then Matthew Burton RA arrived. He was quite small, but what he lacked in height he made up for in pomposity. Fuss, fuss and more fuss, when all the time he knew that the drawing-room was perfect for what he wanted. The light just right and multi-coloured cushions all over the place like a soft, exploded rainbow. But Aunty put up with it because she knew all there was to know about men, and that even included fairies. Oberon? Veronica wondered. Puck? But he acted far more like Pease-Blossom. At last Aunty decided that he'd been indulged enough.

'Time we made a start,' she said, took off her robe and nodded to Veronica, who took off hers. Fairy or not, Matthew Burton gasped aloud.

All the younger woman wore was a gold necklace with a perfectly set ruby as a centre-piece, and all her aunt wore was a diamond ring – if it was a diamond. It looked far too big to be real.

'Now,' said Poppy Villiers, 'where would you like us?' and her niece giggled, which did disturbing things to her breasts. Not that he wanted to touch them, but they had to be still. The trouble was that the women were too beautiful: too perfect. Who on earth would believe even their colour, that glowing rosy gold – but that wasn't his problem. This was for a private collection. The critics wouldn't get near it, which was all very well in a way, but on the other hand Matthew Burton found that he was sweating as he posed Poppy Villiers on her side to show both breasts and the incredible line of one buttock, hip and thigh: made Veronica kneel and twist to show every possible curve: buttocks tightened by her posture, breasts tightened too as she raised one arm so that a bird could alight on her finger.

'I hope it's not a kite,' Veronica said in Hindi, and her aunt chuckled. Burton sweated even more. The fact that he couldn't understand made it worse, he thought, and yet he knew this was the opportunity of a lifetime. Never again would he see such beauty in women and he knew it: each curve firmly, inevitably in place, each breast rounded, perfect, proud; the nipples as dark and glowing as the younger one's ruby. I've got to get it right, he thought. Got to. He began to sketch.

Aunty said in Urdu, 'He sweats a lot.'

'The sahibs always do,' said Veronica in Hindi, and her aunt chuckled again.

They mustn't do that, Burton thought. *She* made them wobble this time – but how soon they settled back into shape. He worked on grimly.

It was a kind of purgatory. Vaguely he realised that they spoke to each other in three languages – Urdu, Hindi and Portuguese – which was a damn sight more than he could do, with occasional asides in English. It was the English he dreaded. The end came when Veronica again spoke in – Hindi, would it be? and her aunt wobbled in a way that would drive a normal male demented, then said in English, 'His is rather large, wouldn't you say?' Burton's charcoal stick snapped under his fingers.

'Oh dear,' said Veronica, 'we were just saying what a big pencil you have, and now it's broken. Such a pity.'

'I'm afraid your chatter distracts me rather,' said Burton. 'If you could be silent for a while—'

'We will if you'll get on with it,' said Poppy Villiers.

Burton knew a life-line when it was thrown. He grabbed it.

When he was finished for the day the women resumed their robes.

'I'll let myself out,' said Burton, covering the portrait before gathering up paints and sketching blocks.

'I wouldn't dream of it,' said Aunty, and rang a bell. It was the polite thing to say after all, but it hadn't sounded polite.

'Jagadir Singh will show you out,' she continued.

Best keep it light, thought Burton, and said, 'Did I tell you I also paint pictures of animals? Mostly cats. I—'

Then Jagadir Singh came in. 'How interesting,' the older woman said, then to the Sikh: 'Take care of Mr Burton for me.'

Burton found that he was looking at the biggest man he'd ever seen: a man of enormous strength. Handsome, too. And then – Good God, he thought. He's even more queer than I am. From the corridor came the sound of women's laughter. It was as seductive as the rest of them and he hated it. It was directed at him.

The big man said, 'No sketches, sahib.'

'I beg your pardon?'

'No sketches. Of the ladies. Miss Villiers' orders.'

'But dash it I need the sketches to work from,' said Burton.

'Of course,' said Jagadir Singh, 'but they stay here.'

'Oh very well,' said Burton and took three drawings from his heavy leather bag that contained his materials.

'Thank you, sahib,' said Jagadir Singh, and Burton went to shut up his bag, but the big man prevented him. 'Allow me, sahib,' he said, then neatly and without fuss he emptied the bag, went through its contents and found eight more drawings. 'I am thinking you are a most forgetful fellow, sahib,' Jagadir Singh said reproachfully.

'I'm afraid I am sometimes,' said Burton.

'Miss Villiers thought you might be. But she told me to

tell you that you must not be forgetful while you are working here. Especially in the matter of sketches.'

'Very well,' said Burton, and Jagadir Singh picked up the leather bag as if it were no weight at all, then turned to face him.

'One question if you please, sahib,' he said. 'Where do all sketches of the ladies stay?'

Burton said miserably, 'In this room.'

'You are one very quick learner,' said Jagadir Singh.

On the way to the door Burton could hear the sound of a piano: a Mozart sonata, he thought, but he didn't want Mozart sonatas. What he wanted was a very large gin.

11

He was playing billiards again, against Rogers this time, but Mark's conscience was easy: Rogers was far better at billiards than he was at cards, and besides, it had been Rogers' idea. All the same they only had a quid on the game. Good as Rogers was, Mark knew himself to be better, and so it proved.

Smith-Hatton watched, and Sandyford walked up, stood beside him.

'Mark's awfully good, isn't he?' he said.

'At billiards, certainly,' Smith-Hatton said, and thought, Here we go. Dear Lord, help me to lie like a Christian.

'Not snooker?' said Sandyford.

'Not any more,' Smith-Hatton said. 'Le Cateau would it be? Where he got his first wound, wherever it was. He can still make cannons as you can see—' there was a ripple of applause as Mark brought off a tricky one, 'but potting's a problem. His arm seizes up if he goes on for too long. Not that he'll admit it.'

What a stupid thing to say, he thought. But then Sandyford *is* stupid.

'Poor chap,' Sandyford said. 'And to think he lost all his money, too.'

But Mark had forewarned him. 'Beddoes?' he said, incredulous. 'Lost his money?'

'He told me himself,' said Sandyford. 'Just before we went to France.'

That 'we' was unforgivable. He could tell all the lies he wished to.

'He lost relatives in France, too,' Smith-Hatton said. 'Mark isn't poor. Not now.' Somehow he contrived to appear bewildered, and looked at the glass in his hand. 'Mind you, that's confidential,' he said.

'Yes, of *course*,' said Sandyford.

It took him three days to persuade Mark to play snooker. Company business; friends to see; arm not what it was: but in the end they played, and Mark alternated between short flashes of brilliance and long, long intervals of ineptitude. Not that it seemed to bother Rollo: not least, thought Mark, because he was far too busy taking money off him at snooker to take money at cards from Rogers, or anybody else ... At last the time came for Rollo to ask for a settlement, and he did so, quite bravely really, but then it was a debt of honour.

'Yes, of course,' said Mark, 'but how about one more game first?'

'As you like,' said Sandyford, trying not to look greedy. 'How much?'

'Double or quits,' said Mark.

He didn't even look sober, thought Sandyford. After all he'd been in the mess since before dinner, and it was after eleven. And I've never had a thousand pounds in my life. Not all at one time.

'Done,' he said.

He was racking up the reds when Smith-Hatton wandered in.

'Oh, sorry,' he said. 'I didn't know you chaps were playing,' and turned to leave.

'Bit of a needle match,' said Mark. 'Don't go. Stay and referee.'

'Needle match?' said Smith-Hatton.

'Thousand quid,' said Mark.

'Big stuff,' said Smith-Hatton, and sat. All the better, thought Rollo. Smith-Hatton's as honest as day. He broke off.

Not bad, Smith-Hatton thought. He hadn't left poor old Mark much, and even so Mark muffed it. Sandyford didn't. He sank the red and then the pink, and just missed a second red. Mark missed it too.

And so it went on, to the point where Smith-Hatton almost began to believe his friend *was* a rotten player, until suddenly, like a man who had remembered he had a train to catch, Mark emerged from his trance of ineptitude and sank everything in sight. When he had finished, so was the game. There was nothing left for Sandyford to pot.

'Looks like you owe me a thousand quid,' said Mark, 'but as I already owe you five hundred I'll settle for half.'

You crafty devil, thought Smith-Hatton, and kept his eyes on Sandyford. It was fascinating. The feller was changing colour like a chameleon: from red to yellow to a kind of oily green. Suddenly he looked at Smith-Hatton and turned red again.

'You told me he was a rotten snooker player,' he yelled.
'I?'

Just one word, one letter, but it told Sandyford that he was doomed. He went back to the oily green colour.

'You know you did.'

'My dear feller,' Smith-Hatton drawled – he had been to Harrow and was very good at drawling – 'I wouldn't dream of telling you such an obvious lie.'

And he hasn't even lied himself, thought Mark. Smart chap, Billy Smith-Hatton.

Sandyford turned back to Mark. 'When you played badly it was all play-acting,' he said, still yelling.

'Out of practice,' said Mark. 'There weren't any snooker tables at Vimy Ridge.'

'Very true,' Smith-Hatton said.

'You cheated me,' Sandyford yelled.

Even Smith-Hatton snorted at him: Harrow or no Harrow.

'You will keep your voice down,' Mark said, and waited. 'Well?'

'Yes, sir. Sorry, sir,' said Sandyford.

'Again.'

'Yes, sir.' Once more Mark waited. 'Sorry, sir,' said Sandyford.

Mark nodded. 'Now about the money you owe me—'

'I haven't got it,' said Sandyford.

'Then you'd better start looking for it,' said Mark. 'But not in a pack of cards or a billiard table. Until you've paid your debt of – you'll forgive the expression – honour, you will not gamble again. In the mess or anywhere else. Is that clear?'

'Yes, sir,' said Sandyford.

'Cut along then,' said Mark, and Sandyford left.

'Well, well,' said Smith-Hatton. 'You did learn a few tricks at Vimy Ridge.'

'I think we both did,' said Mark.

It had been a horrendous experience, yet lucrative, too. Like being stretched on a solid gold rack he was allowed to keep when the torture was over. The women themselves were the cause, he thought. Not that he wanted them – how could he, the way he was? But night after night he'd wake up sweating (nothing easier than to sweat in Calcutta) because he thought he'd exaggerated their shape, their colour, their perfection, and every morning they would shed their robes to show that he'd underestimated them. Hard to say which one of them he hated most. The young one had the more waspish tongue, but her aunt had a way of looking at him, particularly his crotch, as if she couldn't believe a man could be so deprived. Then there was Jagadir Singh. That there were such things as erotic dreams he knew, indeed was grateful for them as and when they happened, but now he'd started to have erotic nightmares, all with Jagadir Singh as the only other participant . . . He painted on doggedly and at last it was done, except for the copy Miss Villiers had demanded.

'It's finished,' he said, and the two of them came over to look, not even bothering to put on their robes: treating him for what he was, and perhaps there was a kind of compliment in that.

'It's marvellous,' said Poppy Villiers.

'Wonderful,' said her niece. 'I was going to say you got it exactly right, but that would have sounded like boasting. Not that it would have been meant to be, except about you.'

Burton found that he was blushing. A compliment, from *her*. Her aunt rang for Jagadir Singh, and they put on their robes.

'Shall we go for a swim?' the older woman asked.

'So good for the pomelos,' said her niece, and the two of them laughed; that delicious, gurgling sound he hated to hear. He would have to ask his nephew what pomelos were, but first he would have to be searched by Jagadir Singh.

'You did well,' the colonel said. Three days had passed, and Sandyford had not gone near a card table or a snooker table.

'Thank you, sir,' said Mark.

'Will he give up gambling, do you think?'

'He will if he values his reputation,' said Mark.

The colonel grunted, and left it at that.

'I got a chit about you from Sir Robert Laver,' he said. Laver was their divisional commander, and very high powered indeed.

'Sir?' said Mark, and again the colonel grunted. The boy wasn't acting; he couldn't have been more astounded if a monkey in a ballet skirt had wandered in.

'He was at school with your uncle,' he said. 'Sir Charles Beddoes.'

'Yes, sir?'

'Urgent family affairs, he calls it. *Your* family. It seems

– I'm sorry, Mark, but it seems your uncle's desperately ill. He wants to see you. It's all very irregular, of course, but I think you'd better go.'

'Thank you, sir.'

'First ship,' said his colonel. 'Ten days from now. After the gymkhana. You going?'

'Yes, sir.'

'They tell me Tom Lippiatt's girl's a racing certainty over the sticks. You'll have time to get a bet down if you can find any takers.'

'Thank you, sir.' But his money would be on Veronica.

'You'd heard Lippiatt's been recalled to London too?'

'No, sir, I hadn't,' said Mark.

'Last chance his girl's got for the Gymkhana Cup,' said the colonel.

And that was it, thought Mark. No further word. He wondered if Maude knew she was going to London. Tricky if they took the same ship.

On his way out he shut his mind to any thoughts of why Uncle Charles had sent for him. It could be good news: it could be no more than self pity. Just hope to God he was home in time, whichever it was. Besides, there was something else to think about. The colonel had been far too quick with his congratulations. Still, at least he knew who his informer was. Billy Smith-Hatton. It had to be. Not that it mattered. Smith-Hatton was a friend of his . . .

He'd finished the second picture, and Jagadir Singh had searched him for the last time, and a thorough and humiliating business it had proved to be, despite the fact that they'd both rather enjoyed it. After that he'd taken his nephew out to dinner before setting off to Bengal to paint tigers. In cages of course. He'd add the jungle later . . .

Funny chap, his nephew. Full of fizz when he first arrived: full of questions about his models too, but one look at Jagadir Singh and Burton had turned into a clam. In the end he'd been paid on the nail, *and* in cash, and that was all that mattered – except that his nephew had somehow got word of it and was at once on the cadge. Runs in the family, thought Burton, not without pride. All the same – five hundred pounds. Chaps of his nephew's age should learn to live more modestly. Even so he'd lent him fifty, but he insisted on a receipt for it.

'Your Uncle Arthur says he doesn't like the mynah bird,' said Aunt Poppy.

'Whyever not?' Veronica examined the fit of her jodhpurs in the cheval glass. Soon it would be time to go to the gymkhana in Uncle Arthur's *vast* Rolls-Royce. Now was not the time to quibble about mynah birds.

'He says he'd sooner look at us,' said her aunt, then her hand went to her mouth. 'Oh my God,' she said.

'Aunty, what's wrong?'

'I never asked you if I could show him the picture. I forgot.'

'But one of them's yours anyway. How could I stop you? Besides, I don't mind. Honestly.'

'He says you let him see what I must have looked like ten years ago,' said Aunty.

'Then I'm lucky,' Veronica said, 'but it's you he wants

172

to look at. What did he say about the jewellery we wore?'

' "Nice touch," he said.'

'He's just the critic we need.'

'The wages of sin,' said her aunt, and laughed: the low and gurgling laughter that Burton had hated and Arthur Nugent adored.

'The sinning was fun too,' said Veronica, 'which reminds me: when *is* Uncle Arthur going to make an honest woman of you?'

'Not on the ship,' her aunt said firmly. 'I might be sea sick. We thought in Paris.'

'Why Paris?'

'Better food,' said her aunt. 'Darling, you don't mind, do you? It's just that Arthur's got rather a lot of business in London and I do so want to get married. Arthur's sent for tickets on the first ship he can get.'

'What sane girl would mind going to Paris?' said Veronica.

Her aunt hugged her, and said, 'I hope you win.'

'So do I,' said Veronica.

It was unfortunate, but it happened. As the Rolls-Royce sailed up to the marquee on the maidan, Victoria and her mother arrived in a gharri, and such a gharri, old and crumbling, with an inept and stumbling horse that moved like a clown, and a driver who had smoked so much bhang as to be oblivious of any reality. It was Victoria's mother who had reined in the horse . . . But when the Rolls-Royce arrived, servants came running at once, to guide Poppy Villiers and whoever it was to their seats and direct that Carteret bitch to the competitors' tent. Not only that but Mark Beddoes arrived immediately afterwards, and went to Veronica – to wish her well, no doubt. It was all so beastly unfair. Mark hovered like anything, but at last was aware that she and her mother were there, and turned to them, but she wasn't having that. No second-hand good wishes.

'See you later, mummy,' she said, nodded to Mark, and walked straight at Veronica. 'Get out of my way,' she said.

Veronica stepped aside, then looked at Mark. That she knew the cause of this rudeness was all too obvious, thought Maude. Victoria went up to her fellow competitor, an old chum from the riding academy for white children only.

'My father says there ought to be a separate entrance for half-castes,' she said. 'He's quite right.'

Oh, *dear*, Maude thought.

Mark looked like a very bad actor pretending he hadn't heard a thing, which is what he is, thought Maude. 'Tom not coming?' he said at last.

'Separately,' said Maude. 'He had a meeting.' Which he often does, she thought, and jolly convenient for you and me it is. They went into the marquee, where the band of the Royal Northumbrians was playing gems from Gilbert and Sullivan, and Poppy Villiers' latest was chatting with the Collector, who for once was trying to do the polite, even the jovial. Who the devil could Poppy Villiers' latest be? She looked at the lady herself, and goodness what a surprise; who should be talking to her but her very own husband? Not just a bloody fool, but an obvious one. Oh, dear. He muttered something, and she answered, not muttering; her voice audible and clear.

'No,' she said. 'How many more times? Besides, I'm leaving India quite soon.'

He turned at that and left her, left the marquee come to that. His best yet in fact, thought Maude: his wife ten yards away and he didn't even see her.

'It rather looks as if you're stuck with me,' she said.

'Bit of luck for me,' said Mark.

For no reason at all she thought: If there's any luck going spare today I want some.

Ashoka looked good, but then her syce knew his business and Ashoka was a handsome pony, a bay gelding with a white blaze on his forehead and an effortless power that hadn't failed her yet. She kissed the white blaze and spoke in Hindi.

'Hear me,' she said. 'Today we win. *Hear me.*' Ashoka snorted. Winning was what he was for. Nearby was The Begum, the missy baba's horse. A mare. It would be. Not that Ashoka had any need of mares, but all the same: 'Today we win,' she said again, and went to the tent reserved for the female competitors: all the missy babas *en fleur* so to speak, all chattering and giggling until she came in, then instantly silent. It didn't bother her. The half-caste jibe had hurt: cut like a whip in fact, but she hadn't shown it and now it was over. No need even to go into the tent, except to show that she wasn't afraid – and to upset them of course. That was important, too. From the pocket of her jodhpurs she produced a powder compact, and looked at her face in the mirror. She was all right: looking well and she knew it. Even so she produced a lipstick and touched up her lips, then left them.

Something else for them to gossip and giggle about.

Victoria had drawn last but one, and she was last. Again. Good and bad. Victoria would have to get a move on since she knew who was behind her, but on the other hand she would have to get a move on too if Victoria had a good round. Ah well. It was now all up to Baby Jesus and the Lord Krishna. And Ashoka and herself, of course.

The missy baba did well, and there was no point in pretending otherwise. A clear round. The mare jumped rather better than she had thought, and the missy baba rode better too. 'Miss Veronica Carteret on Ashoka,' a huge voice bellowed, her syce tossed her up into the saddle and she leaned forward to stroke Ashoka's mane. Even so, still in Hindi she said, 'Remember what I told you.'

They went into the arena and Ashoka lengthened his stride and she held him in tight. She didn't want any showing off, not the first time. Ashoka snorted, but did as she bade him, and Veronica had a clear round too. Another tie, but this time there'd be a jump off, thought Maude Lippiatt, and Ashoka is far and away the faster horse and that half-caste bitch knows it. But where was the sense in calling names? Her own daughter had already done that, and now Miss Veronica Carteret was about to punish her for it. She'd asked for it and she was about to get it: of that Maude Lippiatt had no doubt, but after all, she *was* her daughter. And darling Mark had scarcely bothered to look when Victoria rode, but when it was Veronica's turn he'd had eyes for nothing else. And yet she loved *him*, too. But then so did her daughter.

Victoria didn't quite achieve another clear round. She had a faster time, but the mare didn't like to be hurried and clipped the last fence but one; the pole fell. Four faults, the huge voice bellowed. Victoria hated that voice, just as she hated the mare and herself and the entire world.

'Miss Veronica Carteret on Ashoka,' the voice bawled, and more than anyone else she hated Miss Veronica Carteret.

Miss Veronica Carteret came out exactly as she had done at the last gymkhana, except that she didn't have to wallop Ashoka into doing what she wanted. He was doing what he wanted, too, going flat out and treating each jump as a stepping stone to the next. Easy and flowing like a river in springtime, jump after jump. But a river in spate, that was the point, and before he jumped Veronica yelled: Hi! Hi! Hi! And the sahibs and memsahibs winced, but Ashoka loved it, and when at last the final jump came, 'Haaiii,' screamed Veronica, and Ashoka flowed over it like a stream over boulders, and the great voice boomed, 'Clear round,' then after a pause, 'My God. The fastest time yet.' Even the sahibs and memsahibs applauded.

There was a cup, of course, an ugly lump of silver that she could keep for a year, but more important there was a little silver statuette that she rather liked, a horse and rider who knew their business. She took Ashoka back to the syce, and fed him mangosteens and sugar cane, both of which he adored, then went to the missy babas' tent for the last time. Anything else would have been cowardice. She walked straight into Victoria Lippiatt's wrath. That the white girl hated to lose was understandable, but so much? And then she remembered. Mark Beddoes had been there: Mark Beddoes had seen her lose. Bitch and chee-chee and no better than she should be, and living off that aunt of hers who lay down for money – and no doubt she did too when the nuns weren't looking. I'll have to think about who told you that, Veronica thought, but not yet. She's still got a lot to say. Show off and riding as if a gymkhana was a circus, and eyes only for men: men who despised her, were far too good for her, men who had no time for tainted blood: the pure, the *sacred* Anglo-Saxon race. The other missy babas watched in awe until Victoria ran out of breath at last, and Veronica said affably: 'I understand. Of course I do. You lost, and you hate to lose, and so do I. But never mind. You can have this anyway. I honestly don't need it.' She gave Victoria the ugly silver cup, but hung on to the statuette. Victoria threw the cup the length of the marquee, and even her best friend looked shocked.

Outside the tent Bridget was waiting, and Veronica looked at her warily. She wasn't at all sure that she was ready for Bridget.

'I thought you were working,' she said.

'So I was,' said Bridget. 'Settling for the tickets on the ship. We're taking an awful lot of stuff... But I fixed it. Nothing to worry about.' She smiled then, the smile Veronica loved, because while it lasted Bridget was beautiful. 'So your aunt suggested I bring a change of clothes for you,' she said. 'She's giving a party for the champion.'

She took Veronica's hand and raised it in the air: a champion indeed.

178

'Yes, all right,' said Veronica, 'but I have somewhere else to go first.'

'May I ask where?' Bridget asked.

'Kali's temple.'

The party was good, though 'party' was rather a grand word for it: just Bridget and Aunty and Uncle Arthur and herself, and champagne and pistachio burfi and cigarettes. Bliss. And so it was bliss for a while. The visit to Kali had helped to calm her – or so she'd thought. She'd left the goddess festooned in garlands – but then, from nowhere, it all came back to her. Bitch and chee-chee and Aunty lying down for money and her too. Suddenly she was so angry that she ran from the room, and Aunty and Bridget took off after her. Uncle Arthur, a realist, poured more champagne and wondered vaguely about dinner. He was very fond of the child but there was nothing he could do.

Veronica was sick: Pol Roger and pistachio burfi staining the toilet bowl. What a waste. She flushed it and went to her bedroom where her aunt and Bridget waited.

'I'm all right,' she said.

Her aunt looked at her closely. 'No,' she said.

'No,' said Veronica. 'I'm not. I'm absolutely flaming mad. Do you know what she said about you – about us?'

'Bridget told me,' said her aunt. 'You are right to be angry. You want to hurt her, I'm sure.'

'I am going to hurt her,' said Veronica, and began to curse in Urdu, in Hindi, in Portuguese, but all the time remained dry-eyed as the other two women listened to words that would at any other time have earned instant rebuke. When she ran out of breath Bridget went to her and touched her forehead.

'No temperature,' she said.

'It's over,' Veronica said. 'Please may I have a cigarette?'

Her aunt gave her one. 'When you've finished it I want you to bathe,' she said. 'Wash it all away. Then go to bed. Even if you can't sleep you can rest.'

'I'll sleep,' Veronica said. 'I think I know how I'm going to hurt her.'

Maude Lippiatt thought it had been quite a day. She had heard every word of her daughter's invective. She'd been on her way to hand out sympathy by the jugful when Victoria had started screaming. Not that sympathy would have been the slightest use, she thought. It would take chloroform at least. Mercifully Victoria was going to her best friend's house, so she could go to Mrs Lal's tea dance with Mark. Tom, too, if he'd recovered from his sulks, which she doubted. And so it proved. Still, it meant she could spend more time dancing with Mark, and that odious little tick Sandyford and the impenetrably stupid Rogers and one or two others as well, for to dance only with Mark would be to invite every kind of disaster. But there was time for a chat over tea and bikkies.

It seemed he knew that Tom was going home: his colonel had told him. Now that was interesting, perhaps even ominous, as if his colonel were telling Mark that *he* was going home for a good reason (the possibility at least of a baronetcy), and that Tom wasn't. (Accounts muddled at best, because Miss Villiers was expensive. Very. It was part of her charm.) Mercifully Tom was far too clever to be indicted or impeached or whatever it was: merely moved out of harm's way. A wasp removed from a honeypot. Not that she minded going back to England, not when Mark was going back too. Nor would Victoria . . .

Mark had wanted to escort her back to the bungalow, but she had refused. And just as well, she thought. As soon as she went in she knew that something was wrong. To begin with there were no servants. The place was as silent as a grave. True, they had been given leave to go to the gymkhana and cheer Victoria's triumph – not that the poor child had had one – but that had been hours ago, and now there were rooms to clean, dinner to cook. Trouble, she thought. Native servants always knew when there would be trouble: knew too when to keep away. Methodically she went from room to room, knowing that it would be bad, but it was only when she went into what he called his book room that she discovered precisely how bad.

It was also his gun room, and there dear, thoughtful Tom had shot himself through the head with a Webley revolver. The bullet had blown quite a large portion of his head away. The desk would never be the same again, but then the desk was government property. Someone else's worry now. For a moment she thought she would vomit, but there simply wasn't time for that. She forced herself to go closer to the desk. At least the bloody fool hadn't left a note, but what else could it be but suicide? She'd have to do something about that.

First she took down the pair of shotguns from their

rack, then the Mannlicher rifle he used on tiger shoots, then the gun oil and the polish and the rest of the paraphernalia he used to take care of his arsenal, then cleaned one of the shotguns, left the other and the Mannlicher in line waiting their turn. Then she went through his papers. A recent will leaving his little all to his darling daughter. That would never do. She put it aside and looked further. A letter signed 'Guy': the governor himself. 'Grave disquiet' and 'best if he quit India at once' and 'no further action because of his splendid service in the past'. She put that aside too and searched further, found the previous will that made her sole beneficiary, and why not? she'd earned it, and a lot anyway was hers, and put it into the nearest drawer, then took one last look. The whisky decanter. Of course. The idiot had emptied it before he'd pulled the trigger. It was a miracle he hadn't missed. She took it back to the drawing-room and half filled it from a bottle in the drinks cupboard, then took the new will and the governor's letter to the kitchen. There was just enough heat left in the stove to burn them both, but she broke up the shards with the poker even so, then looked at her hands. They were shaking. Champagne, she thought. Time for a party. Dear Tom always did enjoy a party. She found a bottle in the ice-box and drank off one glass, refilled it, then went to the telephone and asked for dear Tom's assistant. He answered at last and wasn't best pleased, until he learned that it was Mrs Lippiatt.

'Edward,' she said, 'the most ghastly thing has happened. I think you should come here at once.' Somehow she managed to coax a sob into her voice, then hung up the ear-piece, and swallowed what wine was left in the glass. She could always finish the bottle when the uproar was over. After all, she'd earned that, too.

PART II

PART II

12

It had been a rush: packing and storing, and finding a good home for Ashoka, but she'd taken care of that herself. Ashoka was far too special, too beautiful, to go to anyone who didn't love him, and so he went to a fourteen-year-old missy baba who stared at Veronica in awe because she had seen her ride at the gymkhana, which explained why she'd shouted 'Hi' in a well-bred sort of way when she put him over a hurdle, Veronica thought. Not that Ashoka minded: he liked a little enthusiasm when he was working, even if he considered the hurdle a bit of a joke: but the missy baba kissed the blaze on his forehead, and Veronica knew that he'd found another devoted slave.

The bungalow was not to be sold. Both Aunty and Uncle Arthur were agreed on that. Uncle Arthur had friends and colleagues who came to Calcutta from time to time, and the bungalow, with Jagadir Singh in charge, would be far more comfortable than any hotel. A favour owed. Veronica wondered what use could be found for the guest-house, now that its principal adornment was off to Paris to be married, and that led to thoughts of Captain

Hepburn and honeymoons, champagne and pistachio burfi and spherical trigonometry. The trouble was that darling Nicholas had been so good at it – lilies bursting like billy-oh – and when she wanted another chap, as she was sure she would but not yet, how could she find one like Nicholas? And suppose he wasn't? How boring that would be. Especially getting rid of him. She'd have to ask Aunty, but again not yet. There were still all her books to pack.

The ship was splendid. P&O of course: *The Empress of the Indies*, and that could only be Aunty, Uncle Arthur said, and quite right too. They had the biggest, most luxurious suite, she, Aunty and Bridget, but then Uncle Arthur owned rather a lot of shares in P&O. He had a cabin next door to them, but he hardly ever used it, not when Aunty was in the suite . . . They dined at the captain's table, she and Aunty, chee-chees or not. (Bridget contrived her own arrangements, which ended in her making one of the purser's staff the happiest man on board – apart from Uncle Arthur.) The missy baba and her mother were on board too, and so was Mark, but not at the captain's table. One for our side, she thought: one for the bloody chee-chees, and even if it is all Uncle Arthur's doing, here we sit: dressed in silk, bejewelled and perfumed. Veronica looked at the purser's table where Victoria sat, staring hard, hating her still. Nice little dress but so *young*, she thought, and pearl ear-rings just right for a virgin. Suddenly she had an idea. When Bridget came in that night to undress her, she told her what it was. Bridget chuckled.

'You're wicked,' she said.

'But you'll help me?'

'Of course,' said Bridget. She had heard every word at the gymkhana.

And so the missy baba's torment began at last. Every night Veronica would wait in her underwear while Bridget went to the saloon to see what Victoria was wearing, then come back to report. After that there were two choices: if Victoria's dress or jewellery resembled some that Veronica had then Veronica would wear hers, because hers were better. If not she would wear something in the starkest possible contrast: darling Nicholas's ruby necklace for example, on the night that Victoria wore a little gold locket and chain.

The best night of all was when Victoria wore a dress of blue and white, and the slender gold bracelet with its pretty little sapphires. Bridget didn't even have to be told: she went at once for the white dress with the blue pattern, and the sapphire ear-rings Uncle Arthur had given her for winning the gymkhana, the sapphire bracelet darling Nicholas had given her because of spherical trigonometry and other things. It was a remarkable bracelet: a great hoop of intertwined white and yellow gold, the sapphires flawless, glowing, gleaming, and so *big*.

'Oh super,' said Veronica, and willed herself to patience as Bridget brushed her hair.

To reach Aunty and Uncle Arthur in the saloon she had to walk past the missy baba and her mother, and walk she did with the demure yet elegant step that Aunty had taught her, shoulders back because of the pomelos. By the time she reached them half the saloon was watching, and Veronica stopped, her free hand revolved the bracelet on her wrist so that the sapphires flashed.

'Why, Miss Lippiatt,' she said. 'How pretty you look tonight.' Then she nodded and went to Aunty with that same demure yet elegant step.

'Bitch,' Aunty said softly, and grinned at her. 'I'm proud of you.'

'I'm leaving,' said Victoria.

'Up to you,' said her mother, 'but if you do you're telling her she's won.'

'She has won.'

'I thought you had more guts,' her mother said.

All very well for you, thought Victoria. You have to be in mourning, and anyway you look good in black, but how can I compete with *that*? But even so—

'You're right,' she said. 'I'll stay.'

'Good girl,' said her mother, but then her daughter went and spoiled it.

'Daddy wouldn't have wanted me to run away,' she said.

My poor child, Maude Lippiatt thought. Your father legged it the first chance he got, but how can I tell you so? She looked around for Mark, who of course was looking at Veronica what's it, and at once saw her daughter's point of view. Life could be damned unfair sometimes.

Aunty said, 'It'll be cold in Paris.' They were in the suite's drawing-room, waiting for tea.

'We bought stuff for that,' said Veronica. 'The stuff they wear in Darjeeling. Heavy coats, thick dresses.'

'Wool,' said her aunt. Veronica made a face.

Her aunt reached out for the fashion magazine Veronica had been reading. It was in French.

'Does this say anything about cold weather clothes?'

'Russian boots. Fur hats. Fur coats,' said Veronica.

'What sort of fur?'

'Sables are supposed to be the best,' said Veronica, 'but mink and silver fox are nice too.'

'Arthur will buy us some,' said Aunty, and the doorbell rang. Bridget responded at once and the steward brought tea as Bridget fled. Her young man by now would be simmering nicely.

Veronica said in Hindi, 'Honeymoon?'

'No,' said her aunt in the same tongue. 'Not for money – though no doubt he'll give her a present when we get to Egypt. She'll see to that. Just keeping her hand in as you might say.'

Veronica giggled.

'Bridget can be awfully generous at times,' said her aunt. 'When it suits her.' She motioned to her niece to pour out tea. 'Arthur wants a word,' she said. Veronica waited. 'Not because you've been naughty or anything, although you have,' said her aunt, 'and serve the silly little bitch right. It's about England.'

'What about it?'

'All that mathematics and languages and music,' said her aunt. 'He thinks you'll want to go on with it.'

'Well – yes,' said Veronica.

'He's got an idea,' said her aunt. 'Not Oxford or Cambridge or even London. Not yet anyway.' Then she added vaguely: 'Honeymoons . . . All the same I think it's a good idea.'

'Will you be there?'

'He wants to do this himself,' said her aunt. 'Because he likes you. Loves you, maybe. Like a daughter I mean.

Though I'd have had to ripen pretty early, the age you are. Where was I?'

'Uncle Arthur,' said Veronica. 'My education.'

'In the drawing-room,' said her aunt. 'Seven-thirty. Don't keep him waiting.'

'No, Aunty,' said Veronica. Uncle Arthur hated to be kept waiting every bit as much as Aunty.

But Bridget came to her early. The purser's assistant was beginning to wilt, it seemed, so that by seven she was made up, hair just so, darling Nicholas's ear-rings and necklace pure and glittering against the deep pink of her gown. She went on to the promenade deck because there was a breeze, and because she wanted to think about translating the description of the Padmini into Portuguese. Mustard flowers, yellow lotus, lilies bursting: that was fine, but the three folds of flesh about the umbilical region – it didn't *begin* to sound like poetry: not even in Portuguese . . .

Maude Lippiatt came up to her. 'Good-evening,' she said.

Veronica looked at her. Easy, and to all appearances relaxed, yet the older woman was nervous, Veronica was sure.

'Mrs Lippiatt,' she said.

'May I join you for a moment?' Maude Lippiatt said.

'Of course,' said Veronica. She was wary, but she wouldn't run away. That would never do.

'Not to chat,' Maude Lippiatt said. 'For us to pretend to chat would be ridiculous.' Veronica waited.

'It's about Victoria,' Maude Lippiatt said, and Veronica waited once more. She has learned the value of silence, the older woman thought: what a powerful weapon it can be. 'She insulted you dreadfully.'

'Yes,' said Veronica.

Whatever I get I'm going to have to work for it, the older woman thought, and damn the child anyway, but she is my daughter.

'I apologise for that, I really do,' Maude Lippiatt said, 'but – forgive me – don't you think she's been punished enough?'

'Yes,' said Veronica. 'And so does my aunt.'

That one hurt. The girl was reminding her how Victoria had insulted her aunt as well: how silk dresses and a convent education and ponies had been paid for.

'We've decided that I'll stop,' Veronica said.

'We', Maude Lippiatt thought. Her aunt was still in this.

'It's up to your daughter now,' Veronica said. 'If she leaves us alone I'll leave her alone.'

'Us', Maude Lippiatt thought. The plural again. How the girl must love that aunt of hers.

'Thank you,' she said.

'But only if she leaves us alone,' said Veronica.

'Your aunt says you like Pol Roger,' Uncle Arthur said.

'My favourite,' said Veronica.

'In that case I think you'll enjoy this.' He took a bottle from an ice bucket, filled her glass, and his. They sipped.

'But this is even better,' Veronica said. 'What is it?'

'Krug,' said Uncle Arthur. 'But we mustn't drink it all. Poppy's going to look in later.'

'She said not.'

'That was before she knew I'd ordered Krug,' said Uncle Arthur, and grinned. Nobody she'd ever known could grin quite like him: conspiratorial, mischievous, cunning and happy all in one. Then he called himself to order. 'Let's get the business over first,' he said.

'Business?'

'This idea of mine. You know I'm rich?'

'Aunty told me.'

'Poppy told you I'm rolling in the stuff. Not a hobby of mine as it happens, but I could if I wanted to. Not the Nizam of Hyderabad, but doing very well. Not that I'm boasting.'

'Of course not, Uncle.'

'It's just – I want it clear, you see. Between us. Every time I spoil you and Poppy rotten I can afford it.'

'But I've got my own money,' said Veronica.

'And it's staying yours,' Uncle Arthur said. 'Dammit you're my niece.'

'Yes, Uncle Arthur.'

'Also you're the best thing that ever happened to Poppy. I can never repay you for that – not with money anyway, but at least I can try, so no more nonsense. Right?'

Veronica cast down her eyes, looked meek. 'Yes, Uncle Arthur,' she said again.

Uncle Arthur chuckled. 'I own things. Did Poppy tell you that?'

'She said you sold money.'

'Not a bad way of putting it,' Uncle Arthur said, 'but I buy things too. Like newspapers.'

'In India?'

'England too. I'm part of a group that's bought Empire

194

Publishing.' Veronica looked puzzled. 'Trade magazines mostly. But it owns the *Daily Messenger* as well.'

Now that was something. The *Daily Messenger* was one of the biggest dailies in the country. There was a *Sunday Messenger* too.

'So don't worry about fur coats,' Uncle Arthur said. 'You'll get them.'

Them? Veronica wondered.

'You look nice,' Uncle Arthur continued. 'You deserve to look nice. And Poppy says you're to be her bridesmaid.'

'If it's all right with you,' said Veronica.

'Of course it's all right with me. You've been wonderful to her, considering how—'

'Never mind that. She's been wonderful to me,' Veronica said. 'No matter how she lived.'

'Quite right,' Uncle Arthur said. 'Not that I give a damn. I'm the one that's got her now.'

That he meant every word she had no doubt. It seemed that Uncle Arthur rarely gave damns. 'Anyway that isn't the point. Your aunt says she told you what we think you should do.'

' "Not Oxford or Cambridge," she said. "Or London." '

'Not much to go on,' Uncle Arthur said. 'She meant universities.'

Honeymoons, thought Veronica. Of course. Quite a lot of undergraduates' fathers would have found brief bliss with Aunty.

'But Durham's got a university too,' Uncle Arthur said. 'Good one, they tell me. And you would be near us. I've hired a house there.'

'You think I'll get in?' she asked him.

'Of course you'll get in,' Uncle Arthur said testily. 'I'm endowing a scholarship.'

'And you want me to try for it?'

'You've got it,' said Uncle Arthur.

'But how—?'

'Because I'm paying,' Uncle Arthur said. 'And anyway – you'll be the cleverest one there, as well as the prettiest.' Then Aunty came in for her share of the Krug.

After dinner they danced, Aunty always with Uncle Arthur, as was only right and proper, she with anyone who was passably good looking and could tell a waltz from a one-step. They were all sahibs of course, and as they'd reached the Red Sea they all sweated a lot, but she couldn't sit out all the time. Young sahibs for the most part. The elders disapproved because she was a bloody chee-chee and because some of them had their doubts about Aunty, and therefore about her, too. The young ones had no such inhibitions. What they wanted was to put an arm round her waist, hold her hand, smell her perfume, try to make her smile, and sometimes she did. Like Bridget she could be generous at times, but only in a small way. No lakhs of rupees: five annas at best.

It was Mark Beddoes who asked for the lakh of rupees, or rather grabbed for it. When he asked her to dance she accepted at once: she knew his feelings for her but he wasn't a grabber, not usually, and even Mrs Lippiatt couldn't regard one waltz as more punishment for her daughter.

The trouble was that Mark had had rather a lot to drink that night (too much conjecture about what his uncle wanted from him), and because of it he behaved rather badly, Veronica thought. All she'd wanted to do was waltz, and think about the *Daily Messenger* and Durham University and what kind of fur coat (coats?) Uncle Arthur had in mind, when Mark's hand started wandering, and then his knee. That wouldn't do at all.

The trouble was that she'd had her fair share of the Krug, and a glass of claret at dinner. She wasn't in the mood for a grabber. Darling Nicholas would never have grabbed on a dance floor, or anywhere else, she thought. He'd simply have led her to a bedroom, taken her clothes off and got on with it, but definitely no grabbing. *Darling* Nicholas – but by this time Mark was grabbing like anything. Then she remembered the trick Aunty had told her about. Keep smiling, that was the thing: don't let the gentleman know that *you* know, so to speak – and then, if it's a waltz, he's yours. Those new dances are far too fast. But it was a waltz, Waldteufel's 'Les Patineurs'. Busily twirling, Veronica eased away, and Mark frowned, then she moved back to him, and the frown vanished. And no wonder, she thought. My thigh between his, and moving to the music: one two three, one two three. And the touch of silk, Aunty had told her. Silk on top of silk, and below it her thigh that was even silkier still. One two three, *one* two three.

Then the music ended and Mark said, 'I'm sorry. Excuse me. I'm afraid I'm about to be sea sick.' The sea was like a mill pond.

'Oh, what a pity,' she said. 'I was so looking forward to the next one.' And in a way that was true.

He hurried to the door. Darling Nicholas was absolutely right as usual. Sticking out like a sore thumb, even under his trousers. She sat the next one out.

It got to be a habit. At first she did it only to the ones who mauled her, always with success, and that set her wondering if she could do it every time. Not with a fairy, of course. With someone like Burton it couldn't work, but then she didn't want to use it on someone like Burton. No fun at all. It was the heterosexuals she was after, whether they mauled or not, and it did work, every time. Looking up at them wide-eyed, watching them sweat, then one two three, one two three, till they sweated even harder, and had to run for it. Sea sickness. Forgotten handkerchief. Collar stud working loose. Any and every pathetic excuse, until her aunt called her to order.

Uncle Arthur was being fawned on by a man who wanted to buy some of his money, so that they could talk without being overheard, which was as well.

'What on earth's got into you, child?' her aunt asked. 'Child' was bad. It meant her aunt was displeased.

'It was Mark Beddoes who set me off,' said Veronica. 'He was mauling me so I used that trick you taught me. He wouldn't have mauled a white girl.'

'You haven't danced with Captain Beddoes since Tuesday,' said her aunt, 'and you've been knocking them over like ninepins ever since. It's got to stop, child.'

'Sorry, Aunty.'

Her aunt looked at her. 'Why?' she said at last. 'They can't all have mauled you.'

'Quite a few did,' said Veronica. 'But it wasn't that.'

'What then?'

'I told myself it was to see if it worked every time and it did. But that was foolish.'

'Then why?' said her aunt. 'You'd be the talk of the ship if I hadn't put a stop to it. "That little chee-chee cock-teaser".'

Veronica winced. Aunty seldom used words like that.

'That's why,' she said.

The band was playing 'They Didn't Believe Me' and a young man walked hopefully towards them, then Aunty looked at him and he kept on walking.

'I did it for our side,' said Veronica. 'The bloody chee-chees.'

'Go on,' said her aunt.

'You told me I'm pretty—'

'You're beautiful,' said her aunt. 'Get on with it.'

'I know my gowns are good because you chose them, and my jewellery's good too, but – but when the sahibs dance with me – it just suddenly came to me – they don't treat me the way they treat the young mems. You know. Attentive. Polite. All that. Not even Mark Beddoes.'

'How do they treat you?'

'As if they were doing me a favour.'

'All of them?'

'Except two. Uncle Arthur – and Nicholas. Nicholas loved me no matter what colour I was.'

'Mark Beddoes?'

'He wants me. I know that. And sometimes he acts as if he deserves a medal because he doesn't tell me so. He doesn't treat missy baba Victoria like that – and then when he was drunk he mauled me too.'

Once again her aunt looked at her. 'Are you going to cry?' she asked.

'No.'

'Because I wouldn't blame you, darling. Honestly I wouldn't. But not here. Not with all the memsahibs watching.'

'Darling' meant she was forgiven.

'No, Aunty,' Veronica said. 'Don't you see? If I cry it means they've beaten me, and they haven't. They never will.'

Her aunt said, 'It started with your father, didn't it?'

Veronica nodded. 'He beat me all right,' she said. 'Made me cry, too. But he didn't defeat me. None of them will.'

Her aunt patted her hand. 'That's my brave girl,' she said.

'You still love me?'

'Of course,' said her aunt. 'But no more making ninepins.'

Uncle Arthur joined them at last. 'How's the price of money?' Aunty asked.

'Still going up,' said Uncle Arthur.

They left the liner at Alexandria then went to Cairo, goggled dutifully at the pyramids and the Sphinx, and spent a couple of nights at Shepherd's, then back to Alexandria and a French ship that took them to Marseilles. Egypt had been as hot as India, but Marseilles by their standards was barely warm, and Paris was freezing, the heavy cloth coats not nearly heavy enough, but Uncle Arthur was ready for that. It was September and they were cold. After a night at the Crillon he took them to a furrier and bought them fur coats: sables, mink and silver fox. Hats too. 'Three apiece is enough for now,' he told them sternly. 'We don't want to overdo it.' Then on to a shoemaker for Russian boots, and back to the Crillon for lunch. There was a coat for Bridget too, of Persian lamb, that was at once smart and luxuriant.

'And mind you wear it,' Uncle Arthur said. 'We don't want you catching pneumonia. You're far too useful.' Bridget was in ecstasies, but Veronica gathered she *was* useful. Not just as a lady's maid to Aunty and herself. Uncle Arthur had long since discovered that Bridget had a head for business, and was well above average when it came to selling money. He pays her quite a lot, Aunty told her, but then she's worth it.

That night they went to the Russian Ballet. *Petrouchka*, with Nijinski and Karsavina, and whether Aunty and Uncle Arthur enjoyed it or not Veronica had no idea, but they were in such a daze of happiness that they didn't care where they were. Veronica enjoyed it enormously. Rather a shock, Stravinsky, after Mozart, but when one was used to it, a very pleasant shock.

Next day Aunty and Uncle Arthur were married. Bride and bridesmaid wore couture dresses made up in frantic haste while Chanel swore terribly in French, and Bridget, the only other guest, wore a dress of yellow silk and a gold and opal bracelet, both bought in Cairo by the purser's assistant. She looked delightful.

'Do you miss him?' Veronica asked her.

'No,' said Bridget, 'but the bracelet's nice.'

Marriage on a short-term contract indeed.

Not like Aunty's. She positively glowed with happiness, and Uncle Arthur looked ready to burst. The ceremony in the *mairie* was dour, if anything, but the contract was for life, that was the point, and the two of them didn't just accept it, they were ecstatic. Then lunch at the Closerie des Lilas and more Krug, and her first taste of caviar, then back to the Crillon for the only proper bridal night Aunty would ever have, and God knew she deserved it. She, Veronica, was going to the opera, chaperoned by Bridget.

As Bridget brushed her hair Veronica said, 'He's gorgeous, isn't he?'

'The only man I've met who deserves her,' said Bridget. It was the accolade.

'I hope you'll like the opera,' said Veronica.

'All part of the job,' Bridget said.

But in fact she did like it. It was *Prince Igor*, and its savage beauty, music, costumes, décor, delighted her.

'I bet the Mahrattas were like that,' she said.

And perhaps they were, thought Veronica. The feel of a horse beneath her, and she yelling Hi! Hi! Haii! as the horse leaped in an arc like a waterfall.

The next day they took a train to Calais, then the ferry (thank you Baby Jesus for making the sea so calm), then on to London. Without the sables I think I would have died, she thought, but I *have* the sables, and Uncle Arthur said there were lots and lots of theatres and opera and ballet in London. Concerts too. But first there was the Savoy. They had something called a Riverside Suite, and there was a contraption of steam pipes to heat it so that one didn't need the sables, or even a Kashmiri shawl.

'It's true,' said her aunt. 'But I hate taking it off.'

'The sables you mean?'

'Of course the sables. Or the mink or the silver fox

come to that.' She giggled. 'Arthur likes me to take everything off.'

'Who can blame him?'

Her aunt kissed her. 'So sweet,' she said. 'What I mean is if we turn that contraption on full I'll be able to oblige him.'

'As a good wife should.'

'What a darling you are,' said her aunt, and produced cigarettes.

'I've been thinking,' said Veronica, and blew out smoke. 'When it gets a little warmer, *if* it gets a little warmer, what it would feel like to walk around in sables and nothing else – except for Russian boots of course.'

Her aunt looked at her round-eyed. 'That's a marvellous idea,' she said. 'But mind I'm coming with you. You can't go out like that unchaperoned.'

'Dressed the same?'

'Well, of course,' said her aunt. 'Except I might wear the silver fox instead. After all, you had a necklace and I had a ring.' She chuckled. 'Let's do it,' she said, then added hastily, 'When it's warmer.'

They were in Aunty's bedroom which was sumptuous and elegant, as a bedroom for honeymooners should be.

'Where's Bridget?' Veronica asked.

'In conference,' said her aunt, 'in the drawing-room. She and Arthur are working out how much money will cost tomorrow. Such a relief.'

'Relief, Aunty?'

'She and Arthur get on. You and she get on. There was a time when I was worried sick, but it all worked out well, didn't it?'

Veronica said, 'It all worked out splendidly, Mrs Nugent.'

'Oh, you,' said her aunt, and dabbed at her eyes that were misty with happiness. 'There's a tea dance downstairs,' she said. 'Want to take a look?'

'Why not?' Veronica said.

'Yes, all right,' said Aunty, 'but mind—'

'No ninepins,' said Veronica. 'I promise.'

13

She kept her promise, despite the fact that Mark turned up, but he was sober and penitent, and there was nothing to drink but tea.

He'd been in London for a week: not that he'd funked meeting Sir Charles, though he wasn't looking forward to it. It wasn't that. At the last minute his general decided it just wasn't on to give a chap leave just because an old chum had asked him to, dying or not, so he'd thought of a few errands for him to perform and so Mark kicked his heels in the India Office, the War Office, even the House of Lords for some reason, with all the time in the world to think about when he'd last danced with Veronica and what he'd done to her, and what she'd done to him come to that. Accident or design? he wondered, but he'd never know. He could hardly ask her. And anyway, who could have taught her to do such a thing? Though the answer to that was obvious. Making the punishment fit the crime, so to speak. Very Poppy Villiers . . .

His tasks were done at last, and the next day he would take the train to Newcastle, but before that he had to see Veronica. Had to. Despite what he'd done, despite Maude

Lippiatt, he still wanted her, even when he made love to Maude. It was all wrong of course, not just bad form and an insult to Maude, though he rather suspected she knew. And the girl was a half-caste, and one just didn't, unless she was like her aunt, which he was sure she wasn't.

Still he had to see her; to talk if possible: to try at least to explain. The *Daily Messenger* said they were all staying at the Savoy, which didn't surprise him. Nugent was shockingly rich after all. He would go and try his luck, though whether he would have the nerve to send a message to her room he rather doubted: but his luck was good. She and her aunt were at the tea dance, drinking Earl Grey and watching the dancers, laughing together as they so often did. 'Lovely and charming aunt with her equally lovely and charming niece', the *Messenger*'s gossip column had said. Well, that was true enough, but then it had gone on to talk about what it called 'obvious nobility of manner', and 'distinguished Iberian connections'. That would be Goa of course, but he'd never met a Goanese nobleman. Or woman, come to that. *Get on with it, Beddoes. It's what you came for, after all*. He went to them.

'Good-afternoon, ladies,' he said.

Veronica's laughter died at once, but her aunt continued to smile.

'Captain Beddoes, how nice,' she said. 'Have you come to take tea with us?'

'If I may,' he said, and she motioned him to a chair. 'It's what I came for after all, but I hadn't hoped for such delightful company.'

For a little longer Veronica stayed silent, impassive,

and then with a visible effort she relaxed.

'Are you in London for long?'

'I go North tomorrow,' he said, and she smiled. The best news you've had all day, he thought.

The band embarked, rather tentatively, on a foxtrot, and Mark stood up. 'May I?' he asked. Veronica looked at her aunt.

'Yes, off you go while I order more tea,' said her aunt, then added: 'Arthur will be along soon.'

In other words she's telling me I won't have to put up with his nonsense for long, thought Veronica. Kind, *kind* Aunty.

She looks gorgeous, thought Mark. They both do. New frocks and shoes from Paris. New jewellery too, then he embraced her with all the decorum he could muster: not a finger out of place.

'I was hoping I'd find you here,' he said.

She stiffened at once, but danced on.

'How did you find out I was here?'

'Read it in the *Daily Messenger*,' he said. 'I should think half London knows about you. Your aunt and you have made quite a splash.'

The stiffness vanished, and she was once again supple and easy to hold, and as impersonal as that nurse in the Sussex hospital. All the same, he had to say *something*.

'I've come to apologise,' he said.

'Whatever for?'

Had she really forgotten? Whether or not she had, she was going to prolong the agony.

'Last time we danced I didn't behave very well. I'm most awfully sorry.'

'Didn't you?' she said. 'Usually you dance quite well.'

'I don't mean that,' he said. 'I—' But the words simply wouldn't come.

She put down the red-hot iron and reached for the stiletto instead.

'Oh yes, now I remember,' she said. 'You were a little bit tiddly. But don't give it another thought. I know I shan't.'

A cup of tea and a cucumber sandwich are all you'll get, he thought. If you want anything else you'll have to visit Maude Lippiatt. It was a disgusting thought but he knew he'd go. The girl he held could drive him to it every time.

Veronica bought a copy of the *Daily Messenger* and read it in her room. 'Nobility of manner', 'distinguished Iberian connections', the whole lot. It was all so silly it made her want to giggle, but what was the point? Then Bridget came in and she chose a dress by Poiret, and Bridget did her hair.

'Champagne in the drawing-room,' Bridget said. 'Unless you want something else?'

'Champagne's fine,' said Veronica. But just one glass. That night she intended to read some Latin: Virgil, and Virgil was tricky. Not like Caesar . . . She went into the drawing-room. The Poiret gown was blue, and with it she wore darling Nicholas's sapphires. Aunty checked them both and smiled, but Uncle Arthur looked at the newspaper she carried.

'So you've read about yourself,' he said.

'It's so – ridiculous,' said Veronica, then her hand went to her mouth. 'Oh, dear,' she said. 'Did you do it?'

'I didn't write it, no,' said Uncle Arthur. 'But I had it written.'

She said gently, 'May I ask why?' Impossible to be rude to Uncle Arthur, and not just for Aunty's sake. For his own.

'Maybe I should answer that,' Aunty said, and Uncle Arthur nodded.

'Your uncle and I were talking,' Aunty continued, 'and I told him about that chat we had. You know – Mark Beddoes and the other sahibs. I hope you don't mind?'

'Of course not, Aunty,' said Veronica.

'Good girl. Well it occurred to us – Arthur and me – that what you needed more than anything else was a holiday from being a chee-chee, so Arthur got some people in the *Daily Messenger* to write that nonsense.'

'Like a bad novel,' said Veronica.

'A lot of people like bad novels,' Uncle Arthur said, 'and anyway it doesn't actually *say* anything, does it? Just sort of hints. The rest is up to the reader's imagination.'

'So if the reader imagines that we're some sort of fairy-tale princesses from Portugal, they're not going to think we're bloody chee-chees, are they?' Aunty asked.

'People like Mark Beddoes would know,' said Veronica.

'Who would listen to them?' said Uncle Arthur. 'The *Daily Messenger* sells two million copies a day.'

Veronica chuckled. 'Thank you, Uncle Arthur,' she said, and kissed his cheek. 'I wonder what they would say in Kalpur?'

'Who cares?' said Uncle Arthur. 'One of the nicest things about being rich is I can take care of my nearest and dearest – so mind you and Poppy speak Portuguese now and again.'

'We could start tonight,' said her aunt. 'Arthur and I were thinking of going to see *Chu Chin Chow*. Want to come?'

'Not tonight,' said Veronica. 'I have to catch up with some reading if you don't mind.'

'What reading?'

'Virgil,' said Veronica. '*The Aeneid.*'

'Good God,' said Uncle Arthur.

Facing Sir Charles was every bit as bad as he'd expected it to be. It wasn't just that Sir Charles detested him – Sir Charles detested everybody – he simply didn't know how to react to such unrelenting hatred except by shouting, and how could he do that? His uncle was obviously dying. Hence the doctor, who sat through the whole tirade.

'Took your time getting here,' said Sir Charles.

'India's a long way, uncle.'

'Both my sons served in India too,' said Sir Charles. 'Of course they didn't get a DSO or an MC or a couple of wound stripes, but at least they went to India. They can't any more, of course. Not like you. Because they're dead.'

'I nearly died a couple of times myself,' said Mark.

'Nearly doesn't count,' his uncle said.

Mark opened his mouth, the doctor looked at him, and Mark stayed silent. What was the point?

'I'm sane, you know,' his uncle said. 'Got the devil of a temper, but I'm sane.' He turned to the doctor. 'Isn't that right?'

'Indeed you are, Sir Charles,' the doctor said.

'He's even put it in writing,' his uncle said. 'It's just – I'm never pleased to see anybody any more. Wasn't pleased to see you. Or him.' He scowled at the doctor. 'I don't expect I'll be pleased to see my Maker – if I ever do.' He scowled again at the doctor. 'Cut along for a few minutes,' he said. 'There are private matters to—Cut along!'

The doctor left them.

'Nosy beggar,' said Sir Charles. 'Still, he kept me alive till you got here. Know why I sent for you?'

'No, uncle.'

'Dear God I believe you mean it,' said Sir Charles. 'It's because you're my heir, you bloody fool. It's all in the will. You get the land, the shares, the house, the coal mines. The lot. I suppose you thought I'd leave it to a cats' home?'

'It crossed my mind.'

'Oh, did it? And did it also cross your mind that when I'm gone you'll be Sir Mark Beddoes? The seventh baronet?' For whatever reason, it never had.

'The blood tie,' his uncle said. 'It's everything. The title should have gone to Francis or Tim, but it didn't. It's going to you. And so is everything else. You're a lucky beggar, Mark, wound stripes or not.'

He stirred in the bed. Suddenly he looked like men that Mark had seen in France, men to whom death was very close.

'One more thing,' his uncle said. 'I've been having you watched. You see a lot of Maude Lippiatt they tell me. Nothing wrong with that – only no wedding bells. She's far too old for child bearing. Now I want your word on that.'

'You have it, uncle,' said Mark.

All that he could think was, Now that she's a Portuguese princess, I can marry Veronica.

London was wonderful, well of course it was, and the Savoy even better because of the way it was heated. Lots of maths and literature and music of course, but theatres, concerts, ballets and opera too. It was all most satisfactory, and she and Aunty even managed their stroll clad in nothing but fur coats, fur hats and Russian boots, which for some reason gave her aunt an urgent need for Uncle Arthur's company.

Later she said to her niece, 'Didn't it make you randy too?'

'What would have been the point?' said Veronica.

'Why do it then?'

'All those sahibs,' said Veronica. 'Those jolly decent chaps. Looking at two attractive women without the slightest idea that the only other thing we wore under the coats was perfume. It made me feel marvellous.'

'Power?' her aunt asked. 'Or just laughing at them?'

'I suppose power came into it,' said Veronica, 'but I enjoyed the laughter more.'

Her aunt sighed. It was time Veronica had another man. More than time. Mark Beddoes wasn't all that bad. She had no doubt that he was ashamed of his feelings, but that was the way all sahibs were. The point was that the feelings were there. He was mad for her. If only he had some money as well . . .

At last they set off for the North, and Uncle Arthur being Uncle Arthur, they set off in style. No elephants with howdahs, but the vast Rolls-Royce that Uncle Arthur had had shipped from Calcutta that was much nicer than an elephant. More comfortable and very much faster. Heated, too, which was more than the elephant would have been. A splendid lunch, too, in an old and beautiful hotel; and Aunty and Uncle Arthur combining to make her laugh; joking and teasing in the nicest way. As if they were my parents, she thought. Parents who loved me.

The estate agent who had rented the house to Uncle Arthur called it a period gem, and it was all of that, Veronica agreed. A pretty, elegant house for her pretty, elegant Aunty, with formal gardens that were well-maintained but beginning to tire. It was September, after all. No bulbuls, no mustard flowers, no lilies about to burst. But Uncle Arthur hadn't rented the house for its elegance. He'd chosen it because it had central heating and lots of telephones.

'I know you two,' he said. 'One shiver and you'd be off back to the Savoy.'

After a couple of weeks 'getting used to the house' as Uncle Arthur called it, he asked them what they thought of it. It was almost as full of servants as a house in India, and the furniture had the same pretty elegance as the building itself, and they told him so. Veronica had a bedroom and a study of her own, and there was a Steinway in the music room. Her bedroom even contained a painting by a Frenchman called Fragonard, a girl on a swing. (She really must make a start on painting and sculpture.)

'Your college won't be like that,' Uncle Arthur said. 'All

the same you ought to see the head dragon soon. We'll have her to lunch. Send the car for her. That is if you still want to go.'

'Oh, yes,' said Veronica.

'When?' her aunt asked.

'The academic year usually starts in October,' said Veronica.

'You can go whenever you like if I'm paying,' Uncle Arthur said, but they settled on October.

Dr Rattle felt imposed upon. After all, it was she who was principal of St Winifred's College, and if there were any discussions about admissions it was up to parents and guardians to come to her, not she to them, especially if they had far more money than was good for them, gained no doubt by ruthlessness and exploitation. (Dr Rattle was of the Left in her political views.) Then again, the girl concerned was some sort of foreign royal, or so she was given to understand. Portuguese, was it? Gratifying that she should wish to attend her college, but did one need a royal at St Winifred's, or even want one? Dr Rattle, who had been at Oxford at the same time as the Prince of Wales, rather doubted it. Royals could be – almost by their nature – a Very Disruptive Influence . . .

On the other hand, this millionaire or giant of industry or whatever he called himself had sent a car for her, a Rolls-Royce no less, and there was to be lunch, which was bound to be better than the one she usually ate. (The food at St Winifred's was not good.) And later she could let fall from time to time that she had met HRH or whatever she called herself; might even be able to boast that she had sent her packing. She hadn't quite made up her mind about that.

The car turned into a driveway and she found herself looking at a house that was bigger than St Winifred's: considerably bigger, which was infuriating. On the other hand it was exquisitely beautiful, and its formal landscaped gardens commanded respect even in autumn. She would be able to allude to them, too, whenever the opportunity arose.

The chauffeur pulled up by a flight of steps, then came round to open the car door. As he did so a footman opened the door of the house, a butler stood waiting.

'Dr Rattle?' he asked, and the doctor nodded. She always had difficulty in communicating with domestic servants: disapproved of them in fact. The badge of servitude. But what could one do?

'Mr and Mrs Nugent are expecting you,' said the butler. 'This way, madam, if you please.' He set off in front of her and at once their walk became a procession. Oh, my God, Dr Rattle thought, will I be expected to curtsey?

From a distant room there came the sound of a piano, played rather well, then the butler entered another, and Dr Rattle followed, to find herself looking at the most stunningly beautiful woman she had ever seen: a woman for whom the house was a perfect setting.

'Dr Rattle, madam,' the butler said, and somehow contrived to disappear like a conjurer.

'Doctor, how nice,' said Poppy Nugent, and rose to greet her. Cashmere twin-set, Dr Rattle noticed, a skirt that had been made in Paris, like the diamond necklace she wore, and on the third finger of her left hand, above her wedding ring, the biggest diamond she'd ever seen – and her skin a glowing, rosy gold colour that must surely be unique. She must be like that all over, the doctor thought, then called herself to order. Rattle, that will do! – because a man also came to greet her, a man in well-worn, elegant tweeds: stocky and genial and as clever as they come by the look of him, and until he'd moved she hadn't even seen him.

'I'm Nugent,' he said, 'and this is my wife. So glad you could come.' And then he smiled, and the smile said it all. You've seen her, the smile said, but I've got her. But all I want to do is look, thought Dr Rattle, though I can't achieve a smile that says so.

'My pleasure,' she said. The butler came back with a bottle of champagne. 'I hardly think—' Dr Rattle began.

'Oh, please,' Nugent said. 'It isn't every day that we entertain a distinguished scholar.' He turned to his wife. 'Dr Rattle is the author of *Kant And Some Thoughts On Kierkegaard*,' said Nugent.

'How nice,' Mrs Nugent said again, and contrived to look at once bewildered and adorable.

Well, at least he's done his homework, Dr Rattle thought. Perhaps I should have done mine.

From outside the door a woman's voice called out in a language she didn't know, and Mrs Nugent answered. Another language she didn't know, but possibly Portuguese, then the unknown replied, and this time she spoke in the same tongue as Mrs Nugent, then came into the room. Dr Rattle's first thought was, This is ridiculous, for the newcomer was every bit as beautiful as Mrs Nugent, and she too wore a cashmere twin-set and Paris skirt. No ring, no diamonds, but a necklace of heavy gold with a large and flawless ruby.

'I might have known,' Arthur Nugent said. 'Pop a champagne cork and poor old Mozart goes out the window.'

'It was Haydn actually,' said Veronica, 'but you're right in principle.' Then she went to sit beside her aunt, and Dr Rattle almost moaned aloud. The same perfection of face and figure, the same rosy gold colour: together they were like a pair of erotic book ends.

'Our niece Veronica Carteret,' Nugent was saying. 'Dr Rattle.'

'How nice to meet you,' Veronica said, but to save her soul Dr Rattle couldn't say the same. To meet Veronica might be ecstasy: it might equally well be the nethermost pit of hell; but it could never be nice.

'You wrote *Kant And Some Thoughts On Kierkegaard*,' said Veronica. 'I finished it yesterday.'

'I hope you enjoyed it,' Dr Rattle said.

'Well, no,' said Veronica. 'But then I don't think you wrote it to be enjoyed. I mean it's not exactly Jane Austen, is it? On the other hand there was some jolly good stuff—'

Seven out of ten, Dr Rattle thought bitterly. Could do better.

'But some of the Kierkegaard bit was rather obscure. I wonder if you could explain—'

'Not now,' Arthur Nugent said. 'Not with Pol Roger.'

All Dr Rattle could think was, Damn the girl. She's right. Some of the Kierkegaard bit *was* obscure. Inexcusably so. She sipped her Pol Roger. It was delicious, of course, but it didn't quite ease the pain of Kierkegaard's obscurity. Or hers. Mrs Nugent offered cigarettes and Dr

Rattle refused. Veronica took one.

'At St Winifred's we rather frown on smoking.'

Veronica accepted a light from Uncle Arthur.

'Particularly among those *in statu pupillari*,' said Dr Rattle, and again Mrs Nugent achieved that look of adorable bewilderment.

'She means students,' said Veronica.

'Indeed I do,' said Dr Rattle, 'though we prefer to call them undergraduates.'

'After lunch,' said Uncle Arthur, in the voice of a man who means what he says.

Veronica considered Dr Rattle. Mannish suit, a bit on the tubby side, but not much in the way of pomelos, and one for the ladies, but not, she thought, a toucher. Not like those bitches in Kalpur all those years ago. She could handle Dr Rattle. Dr Rattle would be no trouble at all.

Dr Rattle discovered that she was sweating, which was not very nice, and puzzling, too. Outside the ground had only just begun to recover from the frost of the previous night, and yet here it was so hot. Well, of course it was, she thought. A log fire that crackled and roared, central heating turned on full blast, and yet those two exotic princesses were layered in cashmere. Mrs Nugent had even produced a shawl . . . But it wasn't just the fire or the radiators, it was the way the younger woman looked at her. First appraisal, then satisfaction, Dr Rattle thought, as if I had been a problem that was really quite simple. No foreign royalty for me: especially not that one, and quoted Shakespeare to herself: 'That way madness lies.'

'— Quite a simple lunch,' Mrs Nugent was saying, 'but

I hope you'll enjoy it. We're rather proud of our chef.'

'I'm sure I shall,' Dr Rattle said.

'Potage Solferino,' said Mrs Nugent. 'Whitebait. Roast duck and green peas. Floating Island pudding and cheese and biscuits. It doesn't do to overeat at lunch-time.'

Dr Rattle would never be quite sure whether Mrs Nugent was being ironic or not but she enjoyed every mouthful, and the claret, of which Veronica drank at least her share. Really, the child simply would not do.

When they had finished, Nugent said, 'Poppy, take Veronica to the drawing-room and test the coffee. Dr Rattle and I will settle our bit of business. We won't keep you waiting long.'

When the two lovely creatures left he turned to the doctor, his manner polite and amiable as it always was. 'Well, now,' he said, and Dr Rattle knew at once that he would show her no mercy. No mercy at all.

At first Dr Rattle couldn't believe what Nugent told her. To find a place for the girl in return for an endowed scholarship – nothing wrong with that. Not a bribe exactly – heaven forbid: a quid pro quo, but Nugent wasn't offering that.

'But what you're saying,' said Dr Rattle, 'is that your niece should be our first Nugent Scholar.'

'Exactly.' Nugent smiled at her as if pleased by her ready understanding.

'But I can't do that,' Dr Rattle said.

'Why not?'

'For a scholarship there should be an examination. A competitive examination.'

'Not competitive,' said Nugent. 'There simply isn't time

– and if you insist on it I'll have to look elsewhere.'

He means it, thought Dr Rattle. St Margaret's, Fairfax, Bishop's, they'll be queueing up.

'But I'll tell you what I'll do,' said Nugent. Damn him, thought Dr Rattle. He even sounds magnanimous.

'I'll send her to your place to take an exam, and if you don't think she's up to it – well, neither of us is the loser.'

He was still smiling, still quite merciless. On the other hand the sum he had mentioned for the scholarship had been handsome indeed.

'More than fair,' Dr Rattle said, and then: 'There is just one more thing.' Nugent smiled, and waited.

'There is a rumour in circulation that Veronica, and indeed your wife, are of royal blood. An Iberian connection I believe.'

'Ah,' said Nugent. 'You've been reading the *Daily Messenger.*'

That hurt. It really did. What Dr Rattle admitted to reading was *The Times*, but one had to keep in touch somehow.

'Rather indiscreet of them,' said Nugent. 'Not something we want to make a song and dance about as it happens.'

Illegitimate, thought Dr Rattle, delighted.

'Morganatic marriage,' said Nugent, dashing the cup from her lips. 'They're much happier living here – a couple of typical English roses.'

This was a concept so outrageous that Dr Rattle wanted to scream, but how could she? He was offering the college thousands of pounds.

14

Aunty drove with Veronica to St Winifred's in the Rolls-Royce. Uncle Arthur and Bridget were in London selling money. Or was it buying? Aunty wondered. Not that it mattered. Either way Uncle Arthur just went on getting richer. Neither the Rolls-Royce nor its chauffeur thought much of the college, built before the war of brick already black with soot, and stone adornments that were really a mistake no matter who had ordered them. Probably Dr Rattle, thought Veronica, and found the idea pleasing. The porter took one look at their car and conducted them himself to the principal's lodging.

Dr Rattle looked at them and was glad that the vacation had not yet ended. It was true that they were both as beautiful as ever, but the aunt wore sables and her niece wore mink, and a pair of diamond ear-rings that would have endowed another scholarship. She led Veronica to her study where the examination papers waited, and Veronica took a gold fountain pen by Cartier from her handbag and loosened her coat, but made no effort to take it off. What was the matter with the girl? Dr Rattle wondered. I ordered a fire specially. Veronica waited until the principal had left, then piled all the remaining coals on the fire, and studied the paper. Maths for the most part, which made sense. When forced to choose she had said that she would specialise in maths, though in fact she intended to specialise in anything that took her fancy . . . A Latin unseen. A Portuguese unseen. A bit of Victor Hugo, and a Shakespeare sonnet. She looked at the maths again. The bitch. There was a question on spherical trigonometry, and girls weren't supposed to know about spherical trigonometry, especially convent-educated girls. But then Dr Rattle didn't know about Sister Clare, not to mention darling Nicholas.

Dr Rattle had told her she could have three hours, but she went back to the principal's drawing-room in two, and did her best not to smile. Dr Rattle had obviously been trying to extract personal details from her aunt and failing miserably.

'Too much for you, my dear?' the doctor asked.

'No no,' Veronica said. 'I've finished. It was just rather chilly in there.'

Dr Rattle went to collect the papers and take them for assessment. The fire in the study roared up the chimney . . .

'Well?' her aunt said.

'They weren't doing me any favours,' Veronica said, 'but then I didn't want them to.'

'You finished so quickly,' her aunt said.

'The maths was easy,' said Veronica, and winked. 'I had a special tutor for the maths.'

'Who?'

'Captain Hepburn,' said Veronica. They were still gig-

222

gling with laughter when Dr Rattle came back, followed by a maid who brought tea.

It was a tricky one, Dr Rattle thought. The three fellows – maths, modern languages, English literature – were all agreed that the girl was outstanding. The best chance of a first the college could have, and after all she did possess a Senior Cambridge with nine distinctions. But even so, she'd built a fire that could have burned down the college, and she'd written her answers with a gold pen. Not to mention the mink coat. Dr Rattle thought of her other undergraduates. Veronica would be a Very Disruptive Influence Indeed. Firmly she closed her mind to everything but Nugent's largesse.

'I am happy to tell you,' she said, 'that Veronica has acquitted herself most creditably. The first Nugent Scholarship is hers.'

But she didn't look happy at all.

Once inside the car, Aunty said, 'God, that tea was awful.'

'Ghastly,' said Veronica.

'Not exactly the Savoy,' her aunt said, 'and I bet the rooms aren't either.' Veronica was silent. 'How will you survive?' her aunt asked.

'It'll be better than Kalpur,' Veronica said, 'and if I'm hungry – let's see what this pub of Phipps' is like.'

Phipps was their butler, who had recommended a hotel where the champagne was really quite drinkable, and the food not entirely despicable either.

They went into something called the lounge, where ninety per cent of the clientele was male. Some were dons, Veronica thought, some were clergymen, and many were both. As the two women came in all conversation died, and the head waiter came to tell them that unaccompanied ladies were not admitted, then became aware of the sables and the mink, and the glint in Poppy Nugent's eye that said You start anything and I'll phone my husband and he'll buy the hotel and fire you.

'Yes, ladies?' he said.

'Krug,' Aunty said. 'Non vintage.'

'I'm afraid not, madam,' the head waiter said, and they settled for Pommery. The head waiter departed, crushed.

'So now you're a Scholar,' Aunty said.

'Do you mind?'

'So long as you're happy.' *Darling* Aunty. 'But from what you say it's three whole years.'

'If I don't get bored,' said Veronica, and her aunt brightened. Then Mark Beddoes came in. Really he looks quite happy for once, Poppy Nugent thought. Such a change.

'Captain Beddoes,' she called. 'Do come and join us.' And of course he did. Where Veronica was, there he had to be. The head waiter brought another glass, and looked far more cheerful now that they had acquired a gentleman.

'Only Pommery I'm afraid,' said Poppy Nugent, 'but it's not all that bad really.'

The head waiter left them, crushed once more.

'It's delightful to see you, captain,' Poppy Nugent said. 'Isn't it Veronica?'

'Mm,' Veronica said.

Hardly ecstasies, thought her aunt, but the poor fool is delighted to be at the same table.

'Actually I'm not Captain Beddoes any more,' said

Mark. 'Or I won't be shortly. I sent in my papers. My uncle died, you see.'

'How sad,' said Poppy Nugent.

'Well, it was,' said Mark, 'and both his sons were killed in the war and I – wasn't. So now I'm Sir Mark Beddoes. He left me his estate, too. And the house, and I'm going to live here and write a book about India.'

It seems that you're rich, Poppy Nugent thought, and looked at her niece, but all Veronica could think was: Now Victoria will want to marry you and live happily ever after, and we can't have that.

Poppy Nugent smiled at the new baronet. 'If you've nothing better to do perhaps you'd care to dine with us,' she said.

'But he's rich now,' said Aunty.

'He's a rich sahib instead of a poor one, but he's still a sahib,' said Veronica, 'and anyway I'm rich too.'

'All I meant was he wouldn't have to come cadging off you,' said Aunty, 'but he'd still do everything you tell him.'

'I don't want him to do *anything*,' said Veronica. 'Not a thing.'

'Just go to that ghastly college?'

'It's where the knowledge is,' said Veronica.

'There aren't any men there.'

'I'll find one when I want one,' said Veronica. 'There's no rush.'

She seems so sure, her aunt thought, but why shouldn't she be? Then the car turned into the drive and she reminded herself to thank Phipps for his advice about the hotel.

* * *

Sir Mark arranged a shooting party. It was a good way to renew his contacts with the local landowners: as he invited Arthur Nugent, it was also a good way to renew his contact with Veronica. All three of them accepted: Nugent for reasons of his own, aunt and niece because their attitude to the local gentry in their native habitat was rather that of naturalists towards some exotic yet amusing species of fauna. Mrs Beddoes received them. She was acting as her son's hostess and took them to their rooms. Aunt and niece kept their coats on throughout. There was no central heating.

They had brought Bridget with them of course, this time to play the role of upper servant. How could such born aristocrats exist without an upper servant? – and anyway Bridget mingled with all the other upper servants, which made her a very useful spy. But even with Bridget's help, getting dressed took ages. There was so much to wear. First a garment called a brassière, though the French called it a *soutien-gorge*, bought in Paris and extremely useful for keeping the pomelos in place and restraining them from wobbling about at inappropriate moments, then a new kind of silk drawers called knickers, then a silk vest and woollen knickers, and a woollen shirt like a man's, woollen stockings, a tweed coat and skirt, and leather walking shoes called brogues. And still she was only just warm, even inside the house. Veronica went to join her aunt, who was dressed as she was and huddled in front of her bedroom fire.

'Where's Uncle Arthur?' Veronica asked.

'Out with the rest of the guns,' said her aunt. 'We're supposed to go and watch.'

'It'll be even colder outside,' said Veronica.

Her aunt rose. On her face was the look that said she'd made her decision, and anybody who didn't like it was at liberty to lump it.

'I'm going to wear my furs,' she said.

'I doubt if the memsahibs will,' said Veronica.

'To hell with that,' said her aunt, so, when they went to the shoot, Aunty wore her mink and Veronica her silver fox. They looked about as inconspicuous as two orchids in a jam jar full of bluebells, and at once the tongues began to wag, which was one reason why they'd done it. Besides, they were warm.

The men lined up, waiting for the beaters, and watching Arthur Nugent. He looked all right, they agreed, gaiters, boots, neat and inconspicuous shooting jacket, but his guns betrayed him. Purdeys, the most expensive guns made. Only a first-rate shot should flaunt a pair of Purdeys, not some jumped-up shopkeeper who was still in trade. Even his loader looked disgusted.

Aunty said in Portuguese, 'They don't like him.'

'Any more than they liked us,' said Veronica in the same language, but Aunty smiled unperturbed.

'They think he'll make a fool of himself,' she said, 'but Arthur never makes a fool of himself.'

Then the beaters put up the first birds, the guns began to bang, and Nugent proved that his wife was right. His shooting was as good as his guns. Once he had three pheasant falling at the same time, and his loader was beaming as if he'd had a quid on a Derby winner at 33 to 1.

'Do they do this all day?' Aunty asked.

227

'Till the light goes.'

'I think we should go indoors soon,' Aunty said. 'There's a piano somewhere. You could play me some Chopin till lunch-time. Mozart as well if you like.'

'I think we're supposed to have lunch outdoors,' said Veronica.

'To hell with that too,' said Aunty.

They went indoors and shed their furs, replacing them with Kashmiri shawls – her aunt wore two – and Veronica played waltzes and mazurkas and a Mozart sonata on the piano in the drawing-room. It was there that Mrs Beddoes found them, and Veronica ceased to play: joined her aunt beside the fire.

'You found the shooting disagreeable?' Mrs Beddoes asked.

'Cold,' Poppy Nugent said.

'Really?' said Mrs Beddoes. 'This autumn's considered to be an exceptionally mild one.'

'Good God!' said Poppy Nugent. Veronica thought it would be a good idea to buy hot-water bottles before she went to St Winifred's. *Lots* of hot-water bottles.

'But if you don't go outdoors you'll miss lunch,' said Mrs Beddoes.

'No, no,' Poppy Nugent said. 'We'll have ours in here.'

How to explain that it just wasn't done, not on the first day of a shoot? That to suggest such a thing would out-rage butler and cook alike, besides creating a vast amount of trouble? On the other hand Mark seemed absolutely besotted by these two birds of Paradise, especially the younger one, and had made it clear that their every whim must be indulged. Such a pity really, when one considered that Victoria Lippiatt adored him, and was obviously just right for him. Dear child. She really must have a word with Maude. Mrs Beddoes struggled not to sigh.

'I'll have a word with Cook,' she said, and left them.

After lunch, served by a delighted younger footman whose distaste for the outdoors equalled their own, Veronica put on an extra pair of woollen knickers, then jodhpurs and riding boots. Mark had left word at the stables that she could ride whatever she liked – even he had his uses – and she picked out a mare called Mavourneen, a strawberry roan with a white blaze on its forehead, just like Ashoka, and took her for a canter in a paddock behind the stables. She discovered that she bestrode a treasure. A little light, but high in courage, and well up to her weight. There were hurdles in the paddock and she tried the mare over them. She was as deft as a cat. I'll buy her, she thought. Keep her in stables at Durham in term time. Mark wouldn't refuse to sell – not to me. All the same it might be a good idea to let Uncle Arthur do the actual bargaining. According to Aunty no one could haggle like Uncle Arthur, except possibly Bridget, and upper servants couldn't possibly haggle with baronets.

'Of course I'll do it,' Uncle Arthur said. 'Does he know?'

'I sort of hinted,' she said. A blunt demand would have been too much, even for Mark. 'He got the idea it's a present.'

'Could be,' Uncle Arthur said. 'Christmas isn't that far off.'

'No, please,' said Veronica. 'I want to pay for her myself.'

He looked at her. 'Up to something?' he asked.

'Just being independent,' said Veronica.

She went to the stables next day, to find that Mavourneen already had visitors. Darling Victoria and her mummy and Mark. Victoria stroked the mare's soft muzzle and murmured endearments, but she was too late. Far, far too late.

Behind her Veronica said, 'You like my horse?'

Victoria spun round, scowling, and that was a mistake. If one was pretty, and Victoria was, one should make the most of it.

'*Yours?*' she said, and that said it all.

'Mm,' said Veronica, and smiled her best smile, hoping that the fact that she wore two vests and three pairs of knickers beneath her riding togs wouldn't be too obvious, then walked up to Mavourneen and offered her an apple. The mare took it at once. Both of them knew that quite soon she would earn it.

'Dear Mark sold her to my uncle last night,' she said. 'She's a prezzie for winning a scholarship to St Winifred's.' A lie of course, but a lie that would inflict a lot of pain; then a groom appeared and led Mavourneen to the mounting block.

Mrs Lippiatt looked at her daughter, who was still scowling. Mark, of course, was looking at Veronica whatever-she-calls-herself. Oh *dear*, she thought. She and Mark's mother had already had a 'little chat', as Mark's mother called it, about Victoria's suitability. Not that Mrs Beddoes knew anything about her affair with Mark, at least she didn't *think* she did, but whether she did or not the time had come to end it: look about for a suitable widower. But even with a clear field, what chance would her daughter have? Especially if she scowled all the time.

From the shelter of a beech tree Poppy Nugent watched her niece ride. She wore at least as many garments as Veronica, and the mink and fur hat and Russian boots, and she was cold, but all the same she had to see Veronica. Walk. Canter. Gallop. That was a horse that knew its business: and then Veronica put her at the hurdles and yelled aloud. Hi! Hi! Haiii! . . . But it wasn't because the mare was unwilling. She flowed over the jumps like mercury. It was more, she thought, that Veronica and the mare both enjoyed it.

There was movement near the paddock, and she watched from behind the tree. Sir Mark, and Mrs Lippiatt whom she rather liked, and that missy baba of hers with a scowl on her face that would stop a clock. Pity really. She was quite pretty. Not in Veronica's class but not bad: but if she scowled like that she'd be useless at honeymoons.

Veronica was preparing for her bath when her aunt came in. Layer after layer. What a busy time darling Nicholas would have had . . . Her aunt had already changed and looked adorable, as always. Green that night, with emeralds. Mrs Lal's best.

'I saw your horse,' Aunty said.

'Darling Aunty,' said Veronica. 'How sweet of you to go out in the cold.'

'Well I thought it was,' said Aunty. 'But it was worth it. A couple of thoroughbreds the pair of you. And what a lovely colour she is.'

'Another bloody chee-chee,' said Veronica, and her aunt chuckled, then produced cigarettes as Veronica shrugged herself into a dressing-gown like a tent. 'What's her name?' she asked.

'Mavourneen,' said Veronica. 'It's Irish. Means my darling. I looked it up.'

And there's another thing, her aunt thought. She looks like that and rides like that and spends half her life in a library. Still, she's a credit to Arthur and me.

'You know the Lippiatts are here?' she said.

'Yes.' The word came out like a bullet.

Oh, dear, her aunt thought. I'm glad I'm not a Lippiatt. 'The mother's all right,' she said, 'but the girl was scowling. Such a mistake.'

'You're looking scrumptious tonight,' said her niece. 'As usual.'

'That's because I've done nothing all day.'

You can do nothing more elegantly than any other woman alive, Veronica thought, which is more than I can.

'I'm jolly well going to look scrumptious too,' Veronica said.

But not because of some chap, thought her aunt. Because of the missy baba. Oh dear, what a waste.

'Of course you'll look scrumptious,' she said. 'You never look anything else.' Then Bridget came to tell her that her bath was ready.

A dress of yellow silk, darling Nicholas's gold and ruby necklace, the Indian gold bracelets Aunty had bought her years ago, and Bridget had applied her make-up with all her skill, so skilfully in fact that at first glance she seemed to be wearing no make-up at all. The next day was Sunday and there would be no shooting, and that night they would dance. Veronica went to the mirror and looked at herself. O Kali, she thought, you have been good to me till now. Please don't leave me quite yet.

'All that fuss over that little chee-chee bitch,' said Victoria.

'If Mark wants to sell her a horse that's his business surely?' said her mother. At least I *sound* calm, she thought.

'Of course he didn't want to sell it,' Victoria said. 'He wanted to please her.'

'That's his business too,' her mother said.

Her daughter continued unheeding: 'And all this rubbish about them being Portuguese royalty,' she said. 'Well, at least we can nail that lie.'

'No,' said her mother.

'What do you mean no?' Her daughter's voice was shrill.

'Lower your voice, child,' Mrs Lippiatt said. 'By no I mean that if you start making mischief in that quarter we'll have Arthur Nugent for an enemy, and that's the last thing I want.' Except to give up Mark as my lover, she thought, but it's more than time I did. Face it. 'And besides,' she continued, 'if we make trouble for Mrs Nugent she can make far more trouble for us.'

'What on earth do you mean?' her daughter asked.

'Your father's suicide,' said Mrs Lippiatt. 'You did know it was suicide?'

One look at her daughter's face was enough. Of course she knew.

Uncle Arthur's entrance into the ballroom was a triumphal progress. The best shot in the room and a bird of Paradise on each arm. Of course he triumphed. And then he triumphed even more. Sir Edward Kitson came up to him. Sir Edward Kitson, former Secretary of State for India, former Home Secretary.

'Arthur,' he boomed. 'You and I must have a word later.' Sir Edward had a voice like cannon fire and everyone present heard it. Aunty was in ecstasies, and went off at once to dance with Uncle Arthur. Veronica was looking at a small, rather furtive man by the buffet. It was Rollo Sandyford. Easily, taking her time, she went to the buffet for a glass of champagne. If Rollo had any ideas about Aunty and her it would be best to hear them at once. She couldn't bear hanging about. He came up to her, but it wasn't her he came to look at, she was sure. It was the ruby.

'Miss Carteret,' he said. 'How delightful to see you. Do come and meet a friend of mine.' He helped himself to champagne and a glass of fruit punch, then led Veronica to where his friend sat. And such a friend, thought Veronica. A big man he must have been once, but now he was no more than skin and bone covered in a Savile Row evening suit that no longer fitted because he was so thin.

'Miss Veronica Carteret, Miles Armstrong,' Sandyford said, and the tall, thin man looked at her, blinked, then looked again.

'You'll forgive me if I don't get up,' he said. 'I haven't been well, you see.'

'Not well,' said Rollo. 'He was wounded three times, Miss Carteret. Very nearly died.'

Of course, she thought. So many of the young men she met limped, or had eye patches, or an empty sleeve. Armstrong had none of these, but he looked as if he had no time left at all. Poor man, she thought. Handsome, and obviously rich, and about to die. And Rollo Sandyford's friend, which was the strangest thing of all.

'Here you are, old chap,' said Sandyford, and gave him the glass of fruit punch. Not even the consolation of alcohol. 'You won't mind if Miss Carteret and I take a spin on the floor?'

Veronica looked at him. He minded very much because he too would have liked to dance with her, and he had no more chance of holding her in his arms than of riding the winner of the Grand National.

'Shall we?' Sandyford asked.

'If you ask me nicely,' said Veronica. Armstrong's lips twitched in what might have been a smile.

'Please dance with me,' said Sandyford. He really must have something to tell me, she thought, and let him hold her.

It was a waltz and he did it really rather well, and no fumbling hands either, just a lot of babble about the splendour of Armstrong's country house nearby and why he'd been obliged to leave the army. He couldn't afford it, it seemed. Not in peace time.

Across his shoulder she saw Mrs Lippiatt and darling Victoria come in, and darling Victoria at once started looking around for Mark, but Mark was doing a duty dance with a rather plain girl who should not have been allowed to wear mauve.

'—had a surprise before I left,' Sandyford was saying.

'Really?'

'Had a visit from an uncle of mine. A painter. Rather a

famous one – Matthew Burton. I wonder if you ran across him?'

He suspects, but he isn't sure, Veronica thought. And oh so crude.

'I don't think so,' she said. 'I'm sure I would have remembered since you say he's famous, but I much prefer music to painting.'

The dance ended and she left him. Mark abandoned the mauve disaster and moved towards the Lippiatts. Saying good-evening no doubt, thought Veronica, but good-evening was all that darling Victoria would get, for the time being anyway, and walked towards her aunt. Mark spotted her at once, nodded to the other two women, and came to her.

'Am I still forgiven?' he said.

'Of course.'

'Because if I am I'd rather like the next dance.'

Another waltz, perhaps because so many of the dancers were no longer young: cronies of that uncle who had so obligingly died and turned Mark from a poor sahib to a rich one.

'It was so sweet of you to sell Mavourneen to my uncle,' she said, and smiled. Darling Victoria was watching of course.

'My pleasure,' said Mark.

And mine, Veronica thought. Uncle Arthur robbed you blind.

When the dance ended, she nodded to Victoria. There, the nod said, you can have him for now. I've done with him.

Aunty was flirting elegantly with Sir Edward Kitson,

while Uncle Arthur looked on. Sandyford was doing his best to be charming to the mauve disaster. She must have money, Veronica thought, and went to sit out with his friend.

He was polite but by no means effusive. There was no repetition of that first gratifying blink. The fact intrigued her: irritated her too. It was the first time she'd failed to persuade a man to show off his tricks since she'd been fourteen years old.

'Have you known Mr Sandyford long?' she asked.

'Since our schooldays.'

The sahibs, she knew, attached great importance to school.

'You were at school together?'

'No,' he said, and she thought: Is that all I'm going to get? but he added: 'Our parents were neighbours.'

'You were in the army too?' she asked.

'The Brigade, actually,' he said.

She knew perfectly well what the Brigade was, but had made up her mind to make him tell her. It was like pulling teeth.

'The Brigade of Guards,' he said. 'The Coldstream actually.'

That made him the most tremendous swell: streets ahead of Rollo, or even Mark.

'And you were wounded in France?'

'Indeed I was,' he said.

All in all it was a relief when Mark came up and offered to take her in to supper, and so refreshing to see darling Victoria looking furious again. Almost as good as pistachio burfi – not that there was any.

When Bridget came to her room to brush her hair and put away her dress they gossiped about the dance, and the nine partners she had had not counting Uncle Arthur and Sir Edward Kitson.

'You did well to dance with him,' Bridget said.

'The rest were all young,' said Veronica.

'Rich too,' Bridget said, and sighed. It was such a waste. Veronica had been meant for honeymoons every bit as much as her aunt.

'All except Rollo Sandyford,' said Veronica.

'You keep away from him,' said Bridget. 'He's trouble.'

'He said he left the army because he was broke.'

'That was part of it,' said Bridget, 'but he was broke because he couldn't cheat at cards and snooker any more.'

'Who told you that?' asked Veronica, amazed.

'Sir Mark's valet,' said Bridget. 'Used to be his batman only Sir Mark bought him out.' She winked. 'You learn all kinds of things below stairs.'

'Do tell.'

'Well, it seems Sir Mark was his company commander – whatever that is – and got wind of what Sandyford was up to, and somehow gave him the idea that he was hopeless at snooker, only he isn't. He's brilliant. So he and Sandyford played and Sandyford lost and owed Sir Mark hundreds of pounds. Still does. And Sir Mark said he wasn't to gamble any more till he paid off his debt. Only he can't. Not that Sir Mark needs the money – now he's got all this.'

'Is that why Rollo came here? To ask if he could gamble?'

'He came to try to borrow money,' said Bridget, 'but Sir Mark just laughed.'

For once, however briefly, Veronica approved of Mark Beddoes.

'His friend's nice,' she said, as her aunt came in.

'Whose friend?' she asked.

'Rollo Sandyford's.'

'Rollo Sandyford with a friend,' said Aunty. 'And a nice one, too. It seems so unlikely. Who is he?'

'That tall, thin man,' Veronica said. 'The one who didn't dance. You saw me sitting out with him.'

'He looked so ill,' said her aunt.

'I think he's dying, Aunty.'

Poppy Nugent looked at her niece, then away. 'How sad,' she said, then: 'I expect that tick Rollo's sponging off him.'

'He'll be lucky if he does,' said Bridget. 'Might manage the odd fiver and a roof over his head for a bit, but the housekeeper here used to work for his mother, and he's a shrewd one, she reckons. Very shrewd. Dying or not.'

Aunty opened her bag, and took out her cigarette case, offered it round. 'I've got some news for you,' she said, and produced her lighter. 'Arthur and I are going up in the world.'

Bridget looked bewildered. How can you go up in the world when your husband's a millionaire?

Veronica said, 'Is it something to do with Sir Edward Kitson?'

Good girl, her aunt thought. You're shrewd, too. And then: Leave that. Stick to the here and now. 'It's a secret for the time being,' she said.

'We both know how to keep a secret,' said Bridget.

'Of course,' said Aunty. 'That's why I'm telling you. In the New Year's Honours List Arthur's going to be made a baron. We'll be Lord and Lady Nugent.'

Veronica got up, turned to face her aunt, and curtsied.

'That's quite enough of that,' said her aunt, but Veronica went to her and hugged her.

'I think it's wonderful.'

'Me too,' said Bridget, and hugged her in her turn.

'It takes a bit of believing,' said her aunt. 'When you think of what I did and what I am – never mind what I will be—'

She had the bewildered look again, the one that made her even more beautiful, but this time her eyes were misty.

'Never mind what you were,' Veronica said. 'Uncle Arthur wanted you the first time he saw you, and now he's got you, and you've got him, and I think it's wonderful.'

'Hear, hear,' said Bridget, and Aunty cried a little, and did it as she did everything else. Quite beautifully.

More house parties and vests and woollen knickers on top of silk ones because Uncle Arthur seemed to be the only man in Northern England who had heard of central heating. Still, there was often dancing, and lots of houses had stables, but none of the horses were a match for her wonderful Mavourneen. Quite often there was Miles Armstrong, too: still desperately ill, gravely attentive, yet with so very little to say, but still polite. Why does he bother? Veronica wondered, but the answer came at once. Because he knows he's dying, and this is his last chance, and whether he's bored or not it's the way his life had always been, apart from the war, and therefore he sits and nods and smiles, but always with the barriers up, because what's the good of commitment when you know you're going to die? Yet oh how I long to reach out to him, Veronica thought, but it's impossible. That *bloody* war. Sucking the life out of him like a spider devouring a fly. And all he had for company was that ghastly Rollo.

There were compensations, of course. Mostly darling Victoria when she was having a success with Mark. All she had to do was look at him and he'd go to her at once. Iron filings to her magnet, leaving darling Victoria to scowl, and once – what bliss – to hurry out of the ballroom to weep. Aunty noticed it, of course, but she said nothing. It could be argued that Mark had asked for it, and the missy baba had certainly asked for it. She thought of the phrase in the Bible and the bitch of a nun who had walloped her for forgetting it. 'As you sow . . .' that was it. 'As you sow, so shall you reap.' Well, the pair of them were reaping now, because her niece would always abandon Mark as soon as the missy baba responded to the torment, though very often after that she would go to sit with Miles Armstrong, and there was simply no point.

15

October came at last and it was time to go to Durham
and St Winifred's, and Bridget fretted because she would
have no maid, not even an ayah, and even offered, heroic-
ally, to stay behind and do the job herself: but how could
she keep a maid in the sort of punishment cell the college
would call a bed-sit, Veronica wondered, and said no,
because Aunty would need Bridget, and also because she
had no intention of falling in love, and so she wouldn't
need Bridget.

They took her in the Rolls-Royce, which was very good
for her prestige, and Dr Rattle had to welcome her personally because Uncle Arthur was there. His wife was wearing sables, but even muffled up as she was, she couldn't
have exuded sex more if she'd been stark naked, Dr Rattle
thought, though all she did was smile at her vaguely.
Even so, a lot of the student body found excuses to loiter
by the Rolls-Royce, and look inside and marvel, then
marvel even more when Veronica emerged. Her fur coat
was mink, and she huddled into it even though the sun
shone. Her aunt and uncle walked her to the college gates,
embraced her, and set off for the south of France where

the sun shone much, much more. Aunty wept a little, Veronica noticed, and indeed it would be the first time they had been separated for so long since that magic day when Aunty came into her life. Her very own good fairy. Even so, Veronica wept not at all. There was so much to be done . . .

At least the little fiend had settled down to a course of study, thought Dr Rattle. Mathematics, and French and Portuguese language and literature. Spanish too. Already her Spanish was more than adequate, so that when Veronica developed the habit of strolling into other lectures, history say, or art or music, there was nothing Dr Rattle could do to prevent her. St Winifred's was a place of learning after all. The dons liked her because she was good at everything she undertook, quite often better than the girls whose main subject it was, and so a lot of the girls detested her, but did nothing about it. For some reason they were afraid of her, too. The remainder of the girls adored her, almost they wanted to *be* her, and that was even more worrying. *Most* unsatisfactory, but what could she do? Her uncle had been more than generous, and Veronica was far and away the best hope they had for a first three years hence.

In bed together for the last time, she thought. Once it's over the pink silk tea-gown will be cut up for dusters. Not that she would give up sex completely, but Mark's successor would marry her, and he wouldn't be like Mark. Make it memorable, she thought. He mustn't forget you quite yet, even if that little Eurasian's got him writhing in torment whenever she feels like it. And then there's

Victoria, too . . . but she closed her mind to that, and got down to the business in hand.

Later Mark said, 'Never?'

'Never again,' said Maude.

'But what have I done?' said Mark.

The male ego, she thought. I'm nice to you and I want you, so why close your legs? Never mind the chee-chee, who to be fair was absolutely gorgeous. Never mind my own daughter come to that. Best leave it.

'I'm being courted,' she said, 'I don't think he realises it himself yet, but I am.'

'Some chap wants to marry you?'

'Some chap *will* want to marry me, given time.'

It won't be me, he thought, and not just because I promised Uncle Charles. I want to marry Veronica – but not to have Maude in bed when he needed her would be a confounded nuisance.

'Who?' he asked.

'Really Mark, as if I'd tell you,' she said. 'All the same, it's just like the poet says.'

'What poet?'

'I forget,' said Maude, 'but I remember the words.

'Since there's no help,
Come let us kiss and part.'

'As a matter of fact you can do rather more than kiss if you're feeling up to it. It's the last time, after all.'

Somewhat to her surprise she made a friend. Jenny Lawson, the girl in the room next to hers. Quite pretty really, and capable of looking much prettier if she could coax Bridget into teaching her how to do her make-up; and fair, which was a distinct advantage. A virgin too, Veronica was quite sure. No lily-bursting for her, not yet anyway, but that was her own affair. She was studying French and Spanish, which was another advantage. They could practise together, and she was good at gossip too, and thought Veronica the most exciting girl she'd ever met. Altogether a most satisfactory friend, though she really should do something about her clothes.

Then Mark turned up: some rigmarole about writing a biography of Lord Clive, and invoked some blue-stocking or other who had left St Winifred's a remarkable collection of East India Company records, so it might well be true. Accompanied by Dr Rattle he went to her room to invite her to lunch. She was with her friend Jenny.

'I am rather busy,' she said, and Jenny stared.

'Please,' said Mark. 'I've so much to tell you.'

Veronica spoke in French to Jenny.

'Do I have a seminar this afternoon?' she asked.

Really, poor Miss Lawson might as well be her secretary, Dr Rattle thought.

It seemed she hadn't, and so she said, 'All right,' then shrugged. I *must* learn to shrug like that, Jenny Lawson thought. Just like Theda Bara. Veronica turned to Mark and said, 'So long as it's somewhere nice and doesn't take too long. We haven't even started on Calderón yet. But I'll see you at the porter's lodge in ten minutes.'

Mark and Dr Rattle left, and Veronica examined herself in the mirror. The dress was good: red silk and demure but by no means plain, the gold hoops just right, her make-up more than adequate for Mark. She opened her jewel case and took out the gold bangles and heavy gold bracelet Aunty had given her. Jenny gasped.

'What's wrong?' Veronica asked.

'Nothing,' Jenny said. 'It's just – you look wonderful.'

Really, friends were delightful things to have, Veronica thought, and then: Not the mink. Not with that shade of red. It will have to be the silver fox. She took it from its cupboard and Jenny gasped again.

'You must be frightfully rich,' said Jenny.

'So so,' Veronica said. 'My aunt's richer, and my uncle's rolling in it, bless him.'

She took out cigarettes and offered one to Jenny, who looked warily at the door.

'Don't worry,' Veronica said. 'The doctor will be far too busy sucking up to Mark to come nosing round here. He's a baronet.'

Jenny accepted a light from a Cartier lighter.

'But won't you keep him waiting if you finish that ciggie?' Jenny asked. 'You told him ten minutes.' Veronica shrugged again, and Jenny thought: I wonder if she even knows she's doing it? I wonder if she'll teach me?

'Stop worrying,' Veronica said. 'He's used to it.'

Jenny's third gasp was the loudest of them all.

When she returned Jenny was still there, the Calderón text ready and waiting. 'How was it?' Jenny asked.

'We went to the Castle Hotel,' Veronica said. Durham's best.

'Was it marvellous?'

Veronica considered. It hadn't been the Savoy, or the

Crillon, or the P&O boat come to that, and probably Jenny wasn't all that rich, though her dresses weren't cheap, just wrong.

'Very nice,' she said. 'We drank champagne.'

'You didn't!'

'Pommery,' Veronica said. Jenny was staring at her in amazement. 'They didn't have any Krug,' Veronica explained. 'Not even Pol Roger.'

'But female undergraduates aren't allowed to drink alcohol in public,' said Jenny.

'Oh, that,' said Veronica. 'It's ridiculous. I mean I didn't get sloshed or anything, and I like champagne. Anyway – do I look like a female undergraduate?'

'My God no,' said Jenny.

'There you are then.' She locked her door and produced cigarettes, and they settled down to Calderón.

The term went by quite briskly, she thought. Lots of Calderón and Camoëns, and Mozart always there when you wanted him. Jenny too, and Mavourneen to ride. And Mark . . . In a way Mark was rather a pest, but he had his uses. The food at St Winifred's was awful, and he took her to all the nicest places for lunch in Durham and Newcastle. Matinées too, at Newcastle's Theatre Royal. He tried hard for an evening performance and dinner, but she said he'd have to ask Dr Rattle and he knew at once that it was hopeless. Evening performances were no place for virgins: even technical ones like herself.

'But what do you do?' Jenny had asked her.

'Eat.'

'And Sir Mark?'

'He proposes to me. Marriage I mean.'

'And you turn him down?'

'Every time,' said Veronica. 'I mean he knows a lot about Lord Clive, but he's not what I'm looking for in a husband.'

By the look on her face Jenny wasn't so sure, so she hired a car and chauffeur and had themselves driven to Newcastle for lunch. Still no Krug, but a Veuve Clicquot that was pleasant enough. It at least gave Jenny enough courage to ask about the shrugging.

'I just do it,' she said. 'It's part of me.'

'It doesn't embarrass you?'

'Of course not,' said Veronica. 'I've got a mind and I've got a body. What's embarrassing about that? Are you after some chap? Is that it?'

'Not in particular,' Jenny said. 'Perhaps in general.'

Oh, I do like my friend, Veronica thought. Witty too, and yet somehow sad.

'I tell you what,' she said. 'Why don't you come and stay with us for a while in the vacation and I'll give you some deportment lessons – or my aunt will.'

But with your clothes on, she thought. You're nowhere near ready for a Captain Hepburn yet.

Then term was over, and Aunty and Uncle Arthur, just back from Cannes, came over to collect her. The south of France was certainly warmer than England, Aunty said, but they had this wind called the Mistral that was *most* uncomfortable. Much better to stay indoors in Northumberland with the central heating going full blast, but of course they didn't. They went to London and the Savoy instead, to shop for Christmas at Harrods while Uncle

Arthur and Bridget went to meetings. It seemed that Bridget enjoyed meetings every bit as much as Veronica and her aunt enjoyed Harrods.

Over lunch one day Veronica asked, 'When will he be a lord?'

Her aunt said softly, 'New Year's Honours. It's the most tremendous secret.'

'I've kept it,' Veronica said. 'Promise.'

'Of course you have,' said her aunt. 'What do you want for Christmas?'

I want Miles Armstrong, Veronica thought, but not the way he is now.

'Whatever you think I deserve,' she said, and then, 'I've been thinking of buying myself a present. A motor car.'

'Better leave it to Arthur,' said her aunt, and then: 'Won't that annoy Dr Rattle?'

'Bound to,' said Veronica, and her aunt giggled.

'We'll get Doughty to teach you,' she said. Doughty was their chauffeur.

'Be a change from Mavourneen,' said Veronica. 'Dr Rattle doesn't like her, either.' She began to tell her aunt about her friend Jenny, and Aunty listened in bewilderment.

'What's wrong?' Veronica asked. 'She's very nice.'

'I've no doubt she is,' said Aunty, 'but it seems so strange. You making friends with a missy baba.'

'But that's just the point,' said Veronica. 'She isn't a missy baba. Never been anywhere near India. Oh, I daresay she could tell you the principal rivers and cities and mountains – she's rather good at geography – but she's never been. I doubt if she even knows I'm a bloody chee-chee.'

'Would you mind if she did?'

'That would be up to her,' said Veronica.

'Let's go shopping,' said her aunt.

'Let's go to Fortnum's,' said Veronica. 'We've been to Harrods three days running.'

There were concerts too, the theatre, and *Don Giovanni* at the Opera, and between shops Veronica made a start on the art galleries. Aunty preferred to remain in ignorance, but Veronica discovered that there was an awful lot she didn't yet know about painting and sculpture, and she rather suspected that they would be just the sort of thing Miles would talk about – if he ever got better.

One day when she returned from the Tate she found her aunt alone, lying on her bed. Uncle Arthur and Bridget were out selling money. Veronica ran to her.

'You're not ill, are you?' she asked.

'Not that I know of,' said her aunt, 'but I may be pregnant.' Veronica hugged her. 'Thank you for that,' her aunt said, 'and I must say you do smell nice—'

'Chanel,' said Veronica.

'—but the thing is, it's early days yet and I'm not absolutely sure.'

'But do you want a baby?'

'Oh, yes,' said her aunt, and there could be no doubt she meant it.

'There could be complications,' said Veronica. 'About its colour I mean.'

Her aunt shrugged, and Veronica thought I really must get her to give Jenny lessons.

'Arthur says he doesn't give a damn,' said her aunt, 'so I don't give a damn either. Do you give a damn?'

'Certainly not,' said Veronica.

'That makes it unanimous,' said her aunt. 'But not a word to Arthur. Not yet. Not till I'm sure.' She hesitated, then said almost shyly, 'It won't affect us. You and me, I mean. We'll still be the same.'

'I know that, silly,' said Veronica. 'I'll just have a new cousin, that's all. Except that I'll be so much older I'll be more like his aunt. Or hers.' She smiled. 'My turn to be Aunty.'

'What a sweetheart you are,' said her aunt.

Veronica thought of Mark. 'Sometimes,' she said, then thought of Jenny instead. 'There's something I want to ask you,' she said, and told her aunt about Jenny's need for deportment lessons.

'She sounds sweet,' her aunt said at last.

'She is,' said Veronica. 'I told you.'

'But all this make-up and deportment stuff—'

'She just wants to look prettier,' said Veronica. 'She could, too.'

'She's not after honeymoons then?'

'No no,' said Veronica. 'She wants to look prettier with her clothes *on*.'

'Do my best,' said her aunt.

A couple of balls to go to, a concert at the Albert Hall and a visit to Bond Street, then back to the North. Christmas in Northumberland: the central heating on full and snow outside she thought belonged only in Dickens – or on Christmas cards. Mass, too, because Aunty's baby had turned out to be a false alarm, and this time even Aunty thought it best to go and ask for help.

And such a mass. It was in the private chapel of Lord Beamish, a Catholic peer and a snob who sat on one of the same boards as Uncle Arthur. Not that he knew Uncle Arthur was due for a peerage. That secret was well kept. Aunty and I are what he's being snobbish about, Veronica thought. The Portuguese royalty. He hinted and hinted to find out who their parents were – or was it their grandparents? – but they said their lips were sealed. How could they be anything else? All the same the *Daily Messenger* had done its work well.

The house was vast and rambling, with masses of sculpture and paintings, including a Holbein she recognised at once without being told. It was also very cold. Two of everything again and a vast supply of Kashmiri shawls, and Bridget doing her upper servant turn, to find out who else would be coming. Just the family on Christmas Day – Lord and Lady Beamish, handsome, stupid son, plain, sad daughter, and the priest who'd said mass, but on Boxing Day there was to be a ball.

'They'll all be there,' said Bridget. 'Sir Mark and his mother, Mrs Lippiatt and the missy baba.'

'Good gracious,' said Veronica. 'I thought they lived in London.'

'They do,' said Bridget. 'Mrs Beddoes invited them. They say Sir Mark isn't all that pleased.'

'No Rollo?'

'Keep still,' said Bridget, who was brushing her hair. 'He hasn't been invited.'

'I know.'

'And who told you, may I ask?'

'He did,' said Veronica. 'He came to see me at St Winifred's.'

'He's got a nerve,' said Bridget.

'He hasn't, actually. It was more like desperation. He owes money all over the place and some of his creditors found he was staying with Miles Armstrong so he had to do a bunk.'

'But why come to you?'

'He's got an idea there's a portrait of Aunty and me in the altogether. He's not absolutely sure, but the painter's his uncle you see, and Matthew Burton does rather specialise in naked ladies, so he asked for what he called a loan.'

'And did you give him one?'

'Of course not,' said Veronica.

'What did Poppy say?'

'Nothing,' said Veronica. 'I forgot to tell her.'

Rollo Sandyford it seemed was of no importance whatsoever.

'The butler's after me,' said Bridget.

'Are you after him?'

'Not me,' said Bridget. 'I'm a cut above butlers these days. I'm a financial consultant.'

The ball was a great success, according to the *Daily Messenger*'s gossip column, and indeed she had enjoyed a great deal of it. Delightful to see Miles again, and wonder whether he had dragged himself to Lord Beamish's house because he knew she might be there. But at least she could sit out with him, and sure enough a lot of the talk was about painting and sculpture. It seemed that he was mad about the ancient world. Greeks and Romans. More research . . . There were the missy baba and Mark to take care of too, but it was Christmas after all. She did just enough to make sure that darling Victoria's evening was ruined.

Back to their own place then, Stanton House, and the interminable debate about whether Uncle Arthur should buy it or not. Uncle Arthur rather doubted that it was grand enough, but Aunty and Veronica argued that it seemed to be the only house in the county with central heating. Then Jenny arrived and Aunty approved at once, and so, thank heaven, did Bridget. Jenny for her part blinked when she saw aunt and niece together; all that glowing gold: but Aunty reached out to her, drew her to stand between them, and Uncle Arthur grunted approval at the contrast, for already Jenny was showing improvement: hair styled more daringly, and a dress that was far more dashing than anything she wore at St Winifred's.

'It's a pleasure to see you here,' Aunty said, 'and in such a pretty dress.'

'My great aunt died,' said Jenny, 'and left me her all. Not vast sums – but so sweet of her. Daddy did the probate.'

'Your father's a lawyer?' Uncle Arthur asked.

'A solicitor,' said Jenny. 'In Tunbridge Wells.'

Uncle Arthur will be on the telephone first thing, thought Veronica. Uncle Arthur left nothing to chance . . .

'I wanted to use the money towards my education,' said Jenny, 'but daddy said we weren't quite ready for the workhouse yet, and mummy said it was high time I bought something frivolous.'

'And you did,' said Aunty. 'Good for mummy.'

Time for presents. Jenny had bought Veronica a book of mathematical puzzles, which made Aunty blink in her turn. For Jenny Veronica had bought a bottle of French perfume, and Aunty gave her some bangles of Indian gold.

'But I can't,' said Jenny. 'I brought nothing for you.'

'Hush child,' said Aunty. 'How could you? You hardly knew I existed. Now put them on and we'll leave Veronica to her puzzles and make a start on this deportment business. Come along. Shoulders back.'

And shoulders back it was, Veronica noticed, as Aunty led her from the room. Not exactly pomelos, she thought, but a lot better then peaches. Jaffa oranges, say.

It was a super holiday. Jenny knew how to ride, and even though the ground was too hard for hunting, which she longed to try, there was one brief thaw, and Jenny hired a chestnut hack from the local riding stables, and borrowed a pair of Veronica's jodhpurs. Veronica had Mavourneen brought back by train from Durham. Jenny coveted Mavourneen at once, which showed she knew about horses, but never once did she say so, which proved she was her friend. In gratitude Veronica showed her how to yell at the gallop, and together they tore across the paddock, took the hurdles side by side. Hi! Hi! Haiii! Jenny's voice a joyous scream, as loud as her own. No dulcet missy baba tones for her.

Then it was New Year and a quiet night, because of what was to follow. *All* the newspapers, *The Times*, *Morning Post*, *Telegraph*, *Messenger*, all of them, and in every one Lord Nugent. Services to fund raising during the Bengal famine, she read. Money for an orphanage in United Provinces, and that she knew to be true. It had been Aunty's idea, and some of it was her money, and half the orphans were girls. Services to education, she read. Could that be my scholarship? Is my darling uncle to be a baron because he kept it in the family? But what did it matter? Uncle Arthur was a Lord and even more wonderful, Aunty was a Lady. Baron and Baroness Nugent of Wedderburn. She hurtled down to breakfast and there they were: Uncle Arthur in tweeds as usual, and Aunty in a day dress by Worth and a new diamond necklace grand enough to live with her engagement ring. Doubtless she'll earn it at bedtime, she thought, because like Kali, Aunty always pays her debts, good *and* bad, and anyway she adores Uncle Arthur.

'Oh, you darlings,' she said. 'It's marvellous.' She kissed them both. 'And *such* a necklace.'

'Hardly the thing to wear at breakfast,' said Aunty, 'but Arthur wanted to show me off now I'm a lady.'

'You were never anything else,' said Veronica.

'Good girl,' Uncle Arthur said, and Aunty thought she might cry, but Jenny came in and they oohed and aahed all over again instead.

Baron and Baroness Nugent of Wedderburn. That was something else to think about, because Wedderburn was the place where her father had been born, but now was not the time, because the baron and baroness were giving a ball to celebrate their elevation to the peerage, and all the local gentry were invited. Almost all accepted, because although almost all of them despised Lord Nugent, they had no doubt that the ball would be magnificent.

Bridget came to dress Jenny and Veronica. They were in Veronica's room, Veronica by the fire, Jenny by a window which Veronica had allowed her to open very slightly.

'I know it's too soon,' Bridget said. 'But I've still got Poppy to dress, and myself. I'm not an upper servant tonight.'

'What are you then?' Veronica asked.

'Business consultant. Lord Nugent insisted.'

'Oh super,' said Veronica.

'Who's first?' said Bridget.

Veronica took off her dressing-gown and Jenny's eyes widened. Her underwear was on the skimpy side – no wonder she stayed by the fire – but her figure was remarkable. Not Rubens, not nearly as gross as that. Titian perhaps, or Giorgione. Bridget held her dress, Veronica got into it and waited as Bridget did up the buttons. It was a wonderful dress, Jenny thought: a creamy yellow, paler than her skin, that flowed rather than clung to her figure.

'What jewels?' said Bridget.

'Just the rubies.' Bridget nodded approval, and took ear-rings and a necklace from the jewel box. Rubies set in gold, Jenny noted, and such a gold: yellow as buttercups. Heavy, too. They must be worth a fortune: especially the necklace.

Bridget wrapped a towel round her neck and began on her make-up, as sure and deft as a painter, and gradually the character of Veronica's beauty changed: lips more red, cheeks with a hint of rouge, eyes with a hint of shadow beneath, eyebrows plucked to elegant arcs. No longer a beautiful blue-stocking, thought Jenny, or a beautiful horsewoman either. Simply a Beauty, whose destiny was the ballroom and the men within it whom she would tease and torment as she had Sir Mark.

'There,' Bridget said, and took away the towel. Veronica looked in the mirror.

'How lucky we are to have you,' she said and wrapped a shawl round her shoulders: sat by the fire.

'Now you, Miss Lawson,' Bridget said.

'Do call her Jenny,' said Veronica.

'Yes please,' said Jenny.

'Come along then, Jenny.'

That of course was the tricky bit. Her underwear wasn't as flimsy as Veronica's, but it wasn't exactly voluminous either, and she felt shy.

Bridget picked up her dress. 'I don't want to rush you,' she said, 'but if I don't go to Poppy soon she'll start to fret and we can't have that, tonight of all nights.'

Jenny took off her dressing-gown.

'Oh, how pretty you are,' Veronica said. 'Isn't she, Bridget?'

Bridget looked at her like a butcher examining meat on a slab, and then she smiled. 'Very nice,' she said. 'Now let's get your dress on.'

The same treatment as Veronica's, she found. The painter's expertise with rouge and lipstick, the same

ruthless use of eyebrow tweezers; but even that was gratifying when she looked in the mirror. Not Veronica of
course – who could compete with Veronica? – but at least
a young lady who could be at ease in the most elegant
ballroom; her natural habitat, you might say. Her gown
was of blue and white, cut to her figure, but not too
tightly. With it she wore little sapphire studs in her ears,
and a necklace of pearls. Bridget looked her over carefully: a painter whose work was finished, but who was
not completely satisfied.

'Very nice,' she said again, 'but there's something
missing.'

Veronica went to her jewel box; took out Captain Hepburn's sapphire bracelet. 'This,' she said.

'Just the thing,' said Bridget.

'But I couldn't,' said Jenny.

'But you will,' said Bridget. 'You'd be a fool not to, child
– and you were never a fool.' She slipped the bracelet on
to Jenny's wrist. 'Now I'd better go and see to Poppy
before she starts screaming.'

When she'd gone Jenny said, 'It's very good of you.'

Veronica shrugged. 'You're my friend,' she said. 'It suits
you.'

'Thank you,' said Jenny, and then: 'I say . . . About
Bridget. What is she exactly?'

Veronica pondered the question. 'One of us,' she said
at last. 'Bridget. Aunty. Me. And now Uncle Arthur, too.
She helps him with his business. She's good at it. Must
be – or Uncle Arthur wouldn't let her near.'

'But just now she was a lady's maid,' said Jenny.

Sometimes she's rather more than just a maid, Veronica thought, but I can hardly go into that. 'She's good at that, too,' she said. 'She just sort of belongs. Aunty and I couldn't cope without her.'

They went down early. Lord and Lady Nugent were waiting to receive their guests and the band was playing. Strauss, 'Morning Papers'. And not bad. Not bad at all. The best that Uncle Arthur could buy, in fact. He looked splendid in his tailcoat, noble even, and Aunty looked gorgeous, like an orchid that had found its way to Northumberland by mistake, and yet managed to be happy. A scarlet dress by Chanel, and the new diamond necklace, the incredible diamond ring. Veronica curtsied, and Jenny did the same: demure little dips that were entirely without irony, and Aunty knew it. Her eyes took in the dresses, the jewellery, in one comprehensive glance, noting without comment the sapphire bracelet.

'Two little beauties,' she said.

'Three,' said Uncle Arthur, and Aunty smiled.

Then the guests began to arrive. '*Le tout* Northumberland,' as Veronica said, making Jenny giggle, though indeed it wasn't a bad haul of the nobility and gentry: Lord Beamish and his unfortunate family, Sir Edward Kitson, Sir Mark Beddoes and his mother, and Mrs Lippiatt and her daughter, too. No way not to invite them, Aunty had said. They were Mark's guests. Not that I'm bothered, Veronica thought. I'm bored with that game, and then: Now that's enough Vera Higgins or Veronica Carteret or whoever you are. You sound like a cat who's bored with teasing a couple of mice, but at least you haven't killed them and eaten them. She smiled at them instead, which terrified the missy baba.

Dances then, with the son of a duke, the son of an earl, the heir to a shipping fortune. They all came flocking, but goodness how correct they were. She had no need of Aunty's trick, and anyway she'd promised. Jenny was a success, and quite right too, she thought. She looked positively edible. How nice it was to have a friend . . .

From the corner of her eye she saw Mrs Lippiatt approach Aunty, while Uncle Arthur did his duty by Lady Beamish. If that bitch is rude to Aunty, she thought, and then: But no. She won't be. She's nice really, only rather sad.

'Congratulations,' Mrs Lippiatt said.

'Why, thank you,' said Poppy Nugent, 'but it's all Arthur's doing after all.'

'He's a very lucky man,' said Mrs Lippiatt, and then: 'Do you mind if I ask you something?'

'We'll see,' said Poppy.

'Did you know my husband committed suicide?'

'I guessed.'

'Because of you?'

'He wanted something I wouldn't give him,' said Aunty. 'Seemed a silly reason to kill himself. It doesn't bother me.'

'Quite right,' Mrs Lippiatt said. She looked to where Mark was dancing with Jenny. 'Your niece's friend is very pretty,' she said, and sighed. Poppy looked at her. 'No doubt you'll have heard that Mark and I were very close friends,' Mrs Lippiatt said.

'There was a time when I heard all sorts of things,' Poppy said, 'but not any more. And even when I did, I kept them to myself whenever I could.'

'Now we're hardly more than acquaintances,' said Mrs Lippiatt, and looked to where her daughter was dancing with Lord Beamish's son.

Veronica made her way to Miles Armstrong. It was a ritual now, sitting out with him: a ritual that was dreadfully sad, but had nevertheless to be observed. On her way she noticed that Jenny was laughing in Mark's arms, and that Victoria, in Lord Beamish's son's arms, was not.

'How are you this evening?' she asked.

He sipped at his soda water and she sipped her champagne. It was so damned unfair.

'The same,' said Miles. 'Physically that is, but rather happier than usual.'

'I'm glad,' she said. 'But why?'

'Two reasons. Your aunt really does know how to give a party, and you're here sitting with me.'

She waited, but he said no more. Of course not, you fool, she thought. He knows how ill he is. He *can't* say any more.

'Thank you,' she said, and then: 'Tell me some more about Athens.'

He looked at her warily, but already he had begun to realise that when she asked for knowledge it was because she wanted it, as a child asks for a sweet, and so he told her about the Acropolis and the Parthenon, and Delphi not far, and how they must have looked in the time of Pericles. From there, inevitably, he spoke of Aspasia.

'His mistress,' he said, 'if you'll allow the expression.'

'Actually I knew that,' Veronica said. 'I looked her up once in the encyclopaedia.'

Before he could ask why, Sir Edward came up to claim the waltz she'd promised him.

'Good of you to sit with young Armstrong,' he said.

'Not good at all,' said Veronica. 'He knows so much.'

He looked at her, but it seemed that she meant it. Perhaps it was true then, what Arthur Nugent had told him. She might well have a first-rate mind, and in that body, too. 'He had a damn good war,' Sir Edward said.

'He's paying for it,' said Veronica.

'Rather more than most,' Sir Edward said. 'Except the dead, perhaps, but the dead don't feel pain.'

'And he does?'

'Not always,' said Sir Edward, and thought: Dear God. How did I get into this? But I can't fall back on frivolity. Not now.

'He won the Military Cross,' he said. 'Twice. What they call an MC and bar.'

'That means he was brave.'

'Almost unbelievably so,' said Sir Edward.

My first hero won a VC, she thought, and even if it was posthumous at least I slept with him first.

'Don't you think my aunt looks gorgeous tonight?' she said, and Sir Edward relaxed. He could fall back on frivolity after all.

When the dance ended she went to where Jenny stood talking to Mark and Victoria and young Beamish. Deliberately she went to stand beside Jenny: the fair and the dark, each in the first flower of beauty. It was what she and Bridget had planned after all.

'Two of you,' Mark was saying, 'who can look like that and dance like that. From St Winifred's.'

Jenny shrugged, and young Beamish's mouth fell open. Aunty really had taught her well. 'You think we should look more like Dr Rattle?' she asked.

'Good Lord no,' said Mark.

Soon Victoria would be sulking, and that would never do. That wasn't the way to play this hand at all.

'Good-evening, Victoria,' she said. 'How pretty you look tonight. Don't you think so, Mark?' Almost Victoria's mouth fell open too, but not quite. She was far more shrewd than young Beamish.

'Yes indeed,' said Mark, and looked at them all three. 'The three Graces,' he said, 'and such elegant grace.' Victoria smiled instead, and then the band played once more and Mark very nearly ruined it by asking her, Veronica, to dance, but the heir to a shipping fortune scurried over to remind her she'd promised this one to him, so Mark had to ask Victoria and the day was saved.

The heir danced quite well and kept his hands in the approved places, and once or twice he made her laugh, but even so, she thought, even when you inherit, I bet Uncle Arthur will have more money than you. Then Bridget floated by in the arms of Sir Edward. She wore a dress of a delicate pink, and her purser's gold and opal bracelet, and Sir Edward wore the look of a man who had just consulted the menu and couldn't wait for the first course. Darling Bridget's right, she thought. She's a cut above butlers these days. Or even pursers' assistants.

At last she had to dance with Mark: no help for it. He was a guest after all, and he was sober this time. Unfortunately he had a plan, and when they sat out he explained it. His research at St Winifred's on his book was over, so why shouldn't they go to India and do more research there? She pointed out that every gossip in the Raj would have a field day.

He looked appalled. 'I didn't mean that,' he said. 'I want you to go there as Lady Beddoes.'

She could have destroyed him in a single sentence. The word chee-chee alone would have done it, but once again a god intervened, and a goddess too. Baby Jesus and His Mother.

'But Mark,' she said gently, 'I've only done one term at St Winifred's, and I do so want to take my degree.'

It may even be true, she thought.

'I could wait,' he said. 'Honestly. We could just be engaged.'

'It's a big thing, being engaged,' she said. 'I think perhaps I'm a little young for it.' A honeymoon yes, but not an engagement.

'I shan't give up,' said Mark.

She smiled at him and thought, You never do.

He left her then because it was his turn to dance with the earl's plain daughter, and she began to think about this religion business, remembering the temples in India: not just Kali's, but Vishnu's also, where sex was celebrated with triumphant couplings. Not that it was lust, not in the temples: it was life; just as the Last Supper was life; life before death.

But the Supper too meant paintings and statues, and a Baby just like the temples, because that was what the temples were for, and the couplings. The Christians were more discreet, especially in their art. Music like Bach, and even the carols. Words, too. A glory of Latin prose that the English of all people had translated into their own tongue, and made even more glorious.

She'd been translated, too: from Vera Higgins to Veronica Carteret: chee-chee bint to baron's niece. Vionnet gown, satin shoes, gold and rubies. And that's enough serious reflection for a ballroom, she thought, but she needn't have worried. Victoria came over to speak with her. Veronica signalled to a waiter to bring champagne, and what could Victoria do but accept, because she was the one who wanted a word. It could not be easy, thought Veronica, not after she so viciously insulted me, and I so viciously repaid her. She deserved a little courage.

'It's about Mark,' said Victoria.

Of course, of course. Do get on.

'You don't want him, do you?'

'Not in the least,' said Veronica.

'And yet you encourage him.'

'And you want me to stop?'

'Please,' said Victoria, then gulped at her wine.

'Then I will.'

'You promise?' Victoria sounded incredulous.

'I'll dance with him if we're at the same ball, and if there's a play in Newcastle I want to see and he invites me I'll go, but I won't encourage him.'

It would have to do. 'Thank you,' said Victoria, and Veronica left her, to sit with Miles Armstrong and learn about Mitylene.

When the ball ended, Jenny and Veronica went to Veronica's room to talk about it, and at once Veronica swathed herself in a Kashmiri shawl.

'It was wonderful,' Jenny said.

'Not bad at all,' said Veronica.

'How can you say that?' said Jenny. 'Champagne and a wonderful band, and the most delicious food.'

'All the balls we go to are like that,' said Veronica. 'It's because of Uncle Arthur being rich, you see, and now he's a lord as well. So when it's his turn, he does have to make rather a splash.'

'Tidal wave,' said Jenny. 'And some very nice men, too. Talking of which, Sir Mark—'

'What about him?'

'I thought him very nice, that's all.'

'You danced with him rather a lot,' said Veronica.

'He asked me rather a lot,' said Jenny. 'I can't think why you dislike him so.'

'Not dislike,' said Veronica. 'He's just – not my type.'

That sad Mr Armstrong's your type, Jenny thought, but what's the point of that? What a waste of my beautiful friend.

16

It was time to go to London again, and they took Jenny with them to catch her train to Tunbridge Wells, then on to the Savoy. Uncle Arthur had to be made a lord officially: sworn in or inducted or whatever it was, and Aunty and Veronica were allowed in to watch. Aunty looked ready to burst, and Veronica felt a kind of joyful pride in them both. Later Uncle Arthur took them out to dinner, and Veronica made an interesting discovery. Lords, particularly lords who were also millionaires, could always get the best table in a restaurant.

'Pity Bridget couldn't be with us,' Lord Nugent said. (Collectively Poppy, Veronica and Bridget were referred to by the local back-biters as the Nugent harem.)

'A knight in Newcastle instead of a lord in London,' Veronica said, and Aunty giggled. 'She'll enjoy herself,' she said, 'and so will the knight.'

Back to Northumberland then, to prepare for the new term, and Veronica found that Miles Armstrong had invited her to lunch. Aunty was dubious.

'Just the two of you?' she said. 'I'm not too sure.'

Uncle Arthur said, 'Do you want to go?'

Keep it casual, off hand, Veronica thought. 'I do rather,' she said. 'He knows an awful lot about the Greeks and Romans.' Aunty snorted.

'Let her go,' Uncle Arthur said. 'The Greeks and Romans can't harm her. They've been dead for centuries. Young Armstrong can't harm her either. The poor feller can hardly stand up without help.'

And so she went.

Another vast mansion, but no ancient lineage, no title like the Catholic earl's. Miles's grandfather had made his fortune out of beer: Armstrong's Anchor Ales. She remembered that her father had been fond of them, until it was time for the whisky.

There was no beer at Miles's table: only champagne for her and water for him, but a very splendid table it was: rosewood, and rosewood chairs, all designed by Hepplewhite, in the little dining-room where a dozen people could dine with ease, and with a butler and footman to serve them. A master-servant ratio that was Indian in its lavishness. The food was good, too. Game soup, turbot, roast chicken, bavaroise, and Miles ate almost none of it, though he talked easily enough at first.

'What do you read at St Winifred's?' he asked her.

'Maths and modern languages,' she said.

'Not classics?'

'The nuns at school taught me Latin, but that's all. I go to music lectures though, and history, and English Literature sometimes, and next year I'll do some fine art, too.'

'Quite the polymath,' he said.

'Perhaps not yet,' said Veronica. She was by no means

270

sure what a polymath was, but he smiled, so her answer must have been a good one.

'But doesn't your principal object to you wandering in and out like that?' She shrugged. It couldn't possibly affect him, poor man.

'I believe she does,' she said, 'but I can't think why. I mean it doesn't mean I neglect my maths and languages. As a matter of fact—'

'Yes?'

'I'm sorry,' said Veronica. 'I was about to say something boastful.'

I want to know everything about you while I still can, he thought. 'Please say it.'

'I came out top in both in the end of term exams,' she said.

'Good for you,' he said. 'That isn't boasting: just a statement of fact.'

'You were at university too, I take it.'

'Oxford. I read Classical Mods – Latin and Greek. Then I dabbled a bit in Ancient History. Not Greats. That's Ancient Philosophy. It would have taken too long and I wanted to travel.'

'And did you?'

'Indeed I did.'

The meal ended and he asked if they might take coffee at the table. She agreed at once. The poor darling man simply didn't have the strength to walk back to the drawing-room.

'May I ask you something?' she said.

'Of course.'

'Your name. Why Miles? It's so unusual.'

'It's Latin for a soldier. *De Bello Gallico* and all that.'
She nodded. 'And I was a soldier – for two and a half
years. Though of course I wasn't to know that when the
parson splashed cold water on me and I yelled the place
down. Or so I'm told.'

'Then why?'

'It was my mother's father's name. He was a viscount,
and permanently broke to the point where he had nothing
left to sell but his daughters. Even to brewers. So here I
am. Miles Robert Christopher Standish Armstrong.'

'Then why didn't they call you Bob?' she asked.

'Because my mother considered it a name one gave only
to terriers,' he said.

She laughed, and he smiled at her, and she remembered
what her aunt had said about laughter, just before her
first love, but there was no sense in considering that. He
couldn't do it, and that was the end of it. Change the
subject.

'Have you known Rollo Sandyford long?'

'Since I was a boy,' he said.

'But you weren't at school together?' She couldn't
remember. Champagne had its drawbacks.

'No.'

Very emphatic, that 'No', but then Aunty had told her
that rich Englishmen were very odd about their schools.

'My father bought a house in Berkshire. Rollo's people
were our neighbours. We used to meet in the holidays.'

He looked at her again, but this time there was no
smile: only regret, or even shame, but then who wouldn't
feel shame in having to admit that Rollo had once been
a friend? He looked exhausted, too. It was time to go.

'No, wait, please. Just for a moment,' he said. 'There's something I want to tell you.'

She waited.

'I'm going to London quite soon,' he said. 'To a hospital. St George's. There's a surgeon there who thinks he can help me. New technique. He seems pretty sure it'll work.'

Six to four, he'd said. But why tell her that? My beautiful polymath . . .

'An operation?'

'Third time lucky,' he said.

'But won't it be dangerous?'

It was his turn to shrug. 'A bit,' he said, 'but not as dangerous as leaving those lumps of shell inside me. At the moment I'm hardly more than a walking scrap metal yard – not that I walk very much. It's worth a try.'

Better than being as I am, he thought. No matter what.

'Mark Beddoes had shrapnel in him too,' she said, 'but I gather yours is rather worse?'

'Just a bit,' Miles Armstrong said.

How gallant they all are, she thought, and then: But damn it, he *is* gallant. He's got two medals to prove it.

'I wish you a quick recovery,' she said, and rose. She was going to kiss him, very gently, but that *bloody* butler came in and told her her car was waiting. She had never wanted to kill a butler before.

'Promise me you'll let me know when it's over?'

'Of course,' he said.

'Honestly?'

'Honestly. Goodbye.'

She shook his hand and followed the butler to the door. On the way home she thought: I'm glad I came in the

Rolls with Doughty to drive me, because quite soon I may cry, and I couldn't cry and drive my Austin 7 at the same time. 'Goodbye'. That was what had done the damage. Not 'See you soon', or even *'Au revoir'*. Goodbye. Like a door slammed shut: locked, bolted, barred. She had fallen in love with him, and the fact had to be faced, but she hadn't the remotest idea how he felt about her.

The thing was to find out more about him. Not in Durham. All they seemed to know about in Durham was differential calculus and Lope de Vega and what time Evensong was. She went to her aunt, and told her everything.

'But he's so ill,' Aunty said.

'He's found a surgeon who might cure him,' said Veronica, and at last, as she said the words, her control gave way and she burst into tears. Aunty scooped her into her arms, and soothed.

She doesn't believe it, she thought, and who could blame her? If ever I saw a dying man . . .

'Hush now,' Aunty said. 'Dry your eyes and we'll smoke a cigarette and you can tell me what it is you want me to do.'

Veronica shuddered, then used her handkerchief. 'I must look awful,' she said.

'Bridget would slap you,' said Aunty, 'but I shan't tell her.' She offered a cigarette. 'Just tell me.'

'There's something else,' Veronica said, 'beside his wounds. I know there's something, but I don't know what it is. If I did—'

'Well?' said Aunty.

'At least I'd know what I was fighting. And even if he

274

died, I'd know what he was like.' The tears were very close once more.

Her aunt said, 'What you need is a detective.' Veronica stared at her. 'You don't like the idea?'

'It isn't that,' Veronica said. 'But suppose he told someone?'

'We'll get one who's discreet,' said Aunty.

'But I wouldn't know where to start looking for a detective.'

'Of course you wouldn't,' said Aunty, 'but I bet Arthur would.'

'But would he do it?'

'After I've talked to him,' said her aunt. 'You're his favourite niece after all.'

Veronica jumped up and embraced her.

'Cupboard love again,' said her aunt, and then, her arms still about her niece, she said, 'You're really sure you love him?' Veronica nodded. 'More than Captain Hepburn?'

'Captain Hepburn was all happiness and laughter,' Veronica said. 'This is all sadness and tears, but it goes down deep.' Deeper than the pleasure Nicholas and I shared, even deeper than the fact that he died. Her lip trembled.

'Not yet,' said her aunt. 'Don't cry for Miles Armstrong yet. He told you himself there was a good chance.'

Veronica's head came up, her shoulders squared.

'Good girl,' said her aunt, and then, 'Is it next week you go back to that college of yours?'

'Yes, Aunty.'

'Like living in a block of ice. Did I tell you Arthur and I are off to Egypt?'

'Five times,' said Veronica. 'Second honeymoon?'

'It's never not a honeymoon with Arthur,' Aunty said. 'But we've got to go to Wedderburn first. Want to come?'

Uncle Arthur had to go to Wedderburn because he had sold some money to a shipyard owner there, and if he hadn't the shipyard would have had to close, and so Wedderburn was *en fête*, and had invited its most famous son, Lord Nugent, to join in the celebrations. The invitation came from the Mayor of Wedderburn himself: his name was Joseph Higgins.

One of the many delightful things about Uncle Arthur was that you could ask him questions without having to be devious. She asked him if he could find out if Joseph Higgins had had a relative called Michael, and if so could he do it without, so to speak, alarming the natives? Uncle Arthur was delighted to oblige: he adored being devious, bless him.

Both Veronica and her aunt dressed with care. It was Aunty's first really public appearance as a baroness after all, and besides, she too wanted to take a look at Joseph Higgins, who, it seemed, was Veronica's uncle. As for Veronica, she didn't know why – it was impossible to analyse why – but she knew she had to go, and looking her best, too. A Chanel dress of that deep and subtle pink, diamonds at her ears and neck, and the sables, because Aunty had decided on the silver fox, and a taffeta suit the colour of white gold, and sapphires. Veronica went to Aunty's dressing-room to be inspected, but all Aunty said was 'Scrumptious as ever', then looked at their painting that hung above the cheval mirror.

'Either way we still win,' Aunty said.

'Too cold for that way,' said Veronica, 'and maybe the mayor doesn't deserve it.' Aunty chuckled.

When they arrived the mayor in fact gave the impression of a man who had quite recently been struck by lightning. The whole thing was altogether too much for a devout Roman Catholic socialist of sternly moral principles. First the Rolls-Royce and chauffeur, then the nobleman in frock coat and top hat, and then the two unbelievably beautiful women whose furs alone were worth the cost of a whole Wedderburn street. It was true that he also wore fur (it trimmed his mayoral robe), and a gold chain come to that, *but these two were foreign royalty*. All he could do was bow and bow, until Uncle Arthur took pity on him and murmured, 'They're supposed to be incognito, Mr Mayor. Let's get on with it.' They climbed the steps to the Town Hall, a building of elaborate, even sumptuous ugliness, while press cameras flashed, and the crowd oohed and aahed at the sight of such riches.

'Open your coat,' said Aunty. 'Let them see how scrumptious you are,' and opened hers.

'I'll freeze,' said Veronica.

'Arthur's speech won't take long,' said Aunty. 'He promised.' Veronica opened her coat.

Indeed Uncle Arthur didn't take long, but the mayor did, and the two trade unionists who proposed and seconded a vote of thanks took even longer; and all the time the mayor's wife, the mayoress, stood beside the two of them, rigid with terror, like a rabbit menaced by two incredibly beautiful ferrets. But it all ended at last with a call for three cheers for Uncle Arthur, and very loud and gratifying cheers they were, then the favoured few walked into the Town Hall, the mayor's wife between them as if on her way to the scaffold.

Aunty said in Hindi, 'Why is she so nervous? It's a party.'

In Hindi Veronica replied. 'It's us,' she said, 'and if we speak a foreign language she'll be even more frightened.'

'She'll think it's Portuguese,' said Aunty. 'And why should she be frightened of us?'

'Just look at the other women,' Veronica said, and Aunty looked, and said, 'Oh,' because Aunty was never a fool.

What Disraeli had called the two nations, Veronica thought, the rich and – not the poor exactly – but the lower-middle class and – what did they call them? – the superior artisans, that was it. All dressed in their best of course, but what a poor best it was compared with Lanvin and Chanel, and that's not being snobbish, thought Veronica. It's true. Only the shipyard owner and a handful of others had any idea of what it must be like to be rich as she and Aunty were rich, and come to think of it, even the shipyard owner owed a fair whack of the shipyard to Uncle Arthur. As Bridget said, If you buy money you have to pay for it, and money never comes cheap. Still, he went out of his way to be nice to Aunty and herself: he was still in business after all.

The two nations began the serious business of having a good time, because to most of the people there it was a serious business. Heaven knew when they'd have another party like this one. Princesses, and beer and sandwiches for the superior artisans, Veronica noticed, and lemonade for their wives (or a discreet shandy when no one was looking), sherry and daintier sandwiches for the lower-middle class, but for them champagne and *bouches à la reine* obtained from heaven knew where. From what she had seen of it Wedderburn didn't look as if it had many French pastry chefs. Gritty and grimy was Wedderburn, smoke blackened buildings and an air of unrelenting poverty – and her father had lived there. It was a pleasing thought.

She went to the mayor. (The mayoress was crouched in a corner while Aunty told her what a beautiful city Lisbon was. Aunty had never been to Lisbon.)

'I came to say thank you for a lovely party,' Veronica said.

'Pleasure,' said the mayor, and yet he doesn't look as if he's enjoying it, thought Veronica, and then suddenly knew why. It's because he's a socialist and there's class distinction even in the food and drink.

The mayor swallowed his champagne as if it were medicine. 'Good of you to come, Miss er—' he looked about him wildly. Lord Nugent had explained the incognito business, but he hadn't told him her name.

'Carteret,' she said. 'Veronica Carteret,' and offered her hand.

He took it cautiously. His is strong and rough, she thought, because mayor or not he's worked with his hands ever since he left school, and what's wrong with that?

'Have you always lived here?' she asked.

'All me life,' said the mayor.

Cautiously she worked the conversation round to family matters: his wife, his children, his siblings.

279

'Three sisters,' the mayor said.

'No brothers?'

'Just the one, but Michael died. In India.' No obvious sign of regret, but a hint of satisfaction perhaps that the mayor too had a relative who had been to exotic places.

'What was he doing there?'

'Army,' said the mayor. 'He was in South Africa too. In the Boer War. We had high hopes of him one time.'

'Really?' said Veronica.

'Rose to the rank of corporal,' said the mayor. 'Chance he'd be a sergeant – but he never did. He went properly to the bad, our Michael.'

A waiter brought more champagne and the mayor swigged because he didn't know he should sip. Far more used to beer, thought Veronica, but champagne was heaps better for loosening his tongue.

'Took his discharge in India because drink was cheaper there. He wrote and told us so. From a place called Kalpur. Then two years later he wrote to say he'd married a native woman. It was terrible.'

'That he'd married a native?'

'The way he wrote about her,' said the mayor. 'Not even respect, never mind love. And anyway, she was a good Catholic so she can't have been that much of a native.'

'Did they have children?'

'If they did he never told us,' said the mayor. 'We took turns writing to him at first, but he never answered, so in the end we just gave up. Then the War Office wrote to say he was dead. Him and his wife.'

'How sad,' said Veronica. 'And your sisters?'

The mayor brightened at once. 'All done well,' he said.

'Our Mary's a nun and Bridie's a schoolteacher and Concepta's married to Tommy Farrell and helps him run the Crooked Billet.' He smiled at her puzzlement. 'Pub,' he explained.

Then the shipyard owner came over. 'Lord Nugent tells me you're a clipping rider, Miss Carteret,' he said, and the mayor smiled and left them to join the councillors and drink beer. Horse talk was not for him. Equestrians were toffs. All the same, it seems that I have two uncles and three aunts, and both my uncles are nice, thought Veronica. She wondered what Miles would say if she described them. Probably ask if they could read Latin, and come to think of it, the nun well might, and very possibly the schoolteacher too . . .

17

Her dictionary defined a polymath as 'one who knows many arts and sciences', which was quite a compliment really, but not the one she wanted from Miles Armstrong. Still, it was a nice thought to take to the university. She went there in her Austin 7, despite Aunty's frantic forebodings. Uncle Arthur had simply asked her to take him for a drive in it and told Aunty not to worry. Doughty had taught Veronica well.

It was odd, Veronica thought. When she'd ridden in the gymkhana, it was Uncle Arthur who had worried. Aunty hadn't turned a hair. And now they were on their way to Egypt: not that she would get into any mischief. Miles Armstrong was an even more effective chaperon than either of them . . .

She arrived at Durham Station in good time to collect Jenny, and the porter crammed Jenny's trunk on top of her own. They began to gossip as soon as they set off for the college. There was so much to catch up on.

A lot of heads were turned as they drove through the city's streets. There weren't many women drivers in Durham. The female undergraduates looked for the most part envious, the men admiring. When they reached the college lodge Dr Rattle was just emerging, which was unfortunate, thought Jenny. Dr Rattle looked neither envious nor admiring: simply outraged. Veronica, who was describing the dress she had worn at Uncle Arthur's celebration dinner, seemed unaware that Dr Rattle was even there.

Not even the grace to look ashamed, thought Dr Rattle. But of course she hasn't. I doubt if she knows the meaning of the word. First a horse. Now a car. What next, I wonder? A motor boat on the river? . . . But Dr Rattle had received a letter from Lord Nugent, which informed her that he was well pleased with Veronica's progress, together with a strong hint that there could be further largesse if his niece achieved a first. Another eight terms of purgatory, thought Dr Rattle, but even so she must be strong, brave, enduring. *St Winifred's needed the money.* She set off to take tea at St Martha's. There was no point in allowing the little fiend to upset her. Indeed, there were reasons to commend her, not least her remarkable scholastic ability. Outstanding, in fact. Lord Nugent's cheque was as good as in the bank. It was just that Veronica would not obey any rules but her own, and accept no authority but her own either, and after all *I* am the principal of the college . . . It just isn't fair . . .

The porter and his minion humped their luggage to their rooms, then Jenny went to Veronica's and made tea.

'Egypt?' she said.

'Because it's warm there,' said Veronica. 'It damn well isn't here.' She lit a cigarette.

'You shouldn't,' said Jenny, and Veronica shrugged.

'I'll open a window,' she said, and looked out. 'But not now.' It had begun to snow. She would need all her hot-water bottles that night.

The snow fell day after day, and at night it froze, the cold grew more and more intense, until at last occurred what Jenny would for ever afterwards think of as the Seminar Incident. The seminar was in French, and held in a room at the other end of the college. Both Jenny and Veronica had prepared for it – nothing to worry about there – it was how to get there that was the problem. It was so cold. When Jenny called for Veronica she was ready in good time (she wasn't always), the relevant books in a briefcase. A model student, in fact. It was how she was dressed that was the problem. Russian boots, silver fox hat, silver fox coat.

'But you can't go like that,' said Jenny.

'Of course I can,' Veronica said. 'I'm *cold.*'

'You're supposed to wear a gown.'

'I forgot,' said Veronica. 'Thank you for reminding me.' She took her gown from its hook on the door, and put it on top of the silver fox. Jenny stared, round-eyed.

'Now what?' said Veronica.

'It looks a bit odd,' Jenny said, and so it did, but being Veronica it looked enchanting too.

'At least I'm not cold,' Veronica said, and they went to the seminar.

Miss Evadne Winthrop of Cambridge and the Sorbonne stared aghast at the vision that confronted her.

'Is this some kind of joke, Miss Carteret?' she asked.

'No,' said Veronica, and the rest of the seminar gazed at her avidly. This could turn out to be good.

'Then why—' Miss Winthrop began.

'Because it's cold,' Veronica said. 'I can't think properly when I'm cold.'

Evadne Winthrop looked at her. Portugal, she thought, and Goa too, if gossip was right. Of course the girl was cold, and it was vital that she think properly. Vital for the seminar.

'In that case,' Evadne Winthrop said, 'I think it would be better if you wore your gown under your coat.'

'Certainly,' Veronica said, and smiled. Miss Winthrop was of course enslaved, and the seminar began.

Veronica and Jenny dominated it, not because they wanted to, but because they couldn't help it. The day's subject was Victor Hugo's *Waterloo*, to be discussed in French. Jenny and Veronica discussed it pitilessly, remembering from time to time to pause, so that the other four members of the seminar might have a word. The other four members much preferred to leave it to Jenny and Veronica. Then the door opened and Dr Rattle came in to remind Miss Winthrop of a fellows' meeting that evening, and there was Veronica: Russian boots, silver fox hat and coat, chattering in French as if the seminar room was a café in Montparnasse. Oh, dear God, Dr Rattle thought. Almost she said it aloud.

'Why aren't you wearing a gown, Veronica?' she asked.

'I am wearing a gown,' Veronica said, and opened her coat to prove it. It was perhaps the most lascivious gesture Dr Rattle had ever seen, but she was glad that she had seen it, and she rather suspected that the little fiend knew it.

'You cannot attend a seminar improperly clad,' said Dr

Rattle, and Veronica shrugged, and put Victor Hugo, her notebook and her pen in her briefcase.

'What *are* you doing?' Dr Rattle asked.

'Leaving,' said Veronica. Miss Winthrop was appalled. The seminar had been going so well.

'I hardly think—' she began. 'Miss Carteret really does feel the cold.'

Veronica smiled at her once more. 'It's perfectly all right,' she said. 'It's about time I wrote to my aunt and uncle anyway.'

Dr Rattle felt as if a mule had kicked her. The little fiend held every decent card in the pack. Even if she were sent down she wouldn't give a damn, but Lord Nugent would.

Miss Winthrop looked at her watch. 'As it happens,' she said, 'our time is almost up. Perhaps we can leave it there for now.'

As Jenny shut the door of the seminar room, Miss Winthrop and Dr Rattle were already quarrelling.

Mark still lingered, of course, not like a bad smell, rather more like a room full of tobacco smoke that hadn't been properly aired – but even so he had his uses. When she was hungry for instance, which was rather a lot of the time. The food at St Winifred's was still atrocious, and she hated eating out on her own, and Jenny wasn't too keen about being treated, because she couldn't invite her back, and anyway she'd spent five years in a girls' school where the food was at least as bad as it was at St Winifred's. Mark was useful for the theatre, too. The Theatre Royal in Newcastle was what was called a Number One

Tour, and there she could watch Shakespeare and Shaw, and even Congreve, and memorise all the naughty jokes to tell to Aunty . . . But he came back too often: when she wanted to play Mozart, or solve a mathematical problem or read Camoëns. When he was a nuisance she sent him away.

Once she wondered why Mark was allowed to be a nuisance – by Dr Rattle that is – but the answer was obvious at once. There had been a time when Aunty had thought that Mark would be just the man for her, and had no doubt told the doctor that he might come courting, then when Veronica had said that Mark was nothing of the sort, Aunty had forgotten to say so. Not that it mattered, Veronica thought. I'm perfectly capable of saying so myself, and if Dr Rattle's bewildered she shouldn't be. She's supposed to be a philosopher after all.

There was an interesting development, however. If she turned Mark down too often, he went to Jenny. Nothing wrong with that. Mark was a normal male after all, and Jenny a very pretty girl – once Bridget and Aunty had done their work – who had gone out of her way to make sure that Veronica had no proprietorial rights. A bit hard on Victoria Lippiatt perhaps, but that was just another way of saying that sometimes things worked out for the best . . .

She began a letter to Bridget, now living in a flat in Knightsbridge, rather a grand one: keeping an eye on Uncle Arthur's affairs while the sun still shone in Egypt.

Another seminar with Miss Winthrop. Corneille this time, and goodness how he did go on, until once again there was an interruption. Dr Rattle's secretary this time.

Perhaps not quite so bad, Miss Winthrop thought, but even so it amounted to persecution, particularly as Veronica was once again the target. Not that the dear girl seemed in the least concerned . . .

'There is a telephone call for you,' Dr Rattle said. 'From London. It concerns a Mr Armstrong. And really I must say, Veronica—'

Veronica went at once to the telephone.

Am I not to be allowed even to complete a sentence? Dr Rattle wondered, but the answer was obvious.

'This is Veronica Carteret,' the little fiend said.

'Miss Carteret, this is the surgery ward sister at St George's Hospital. I have been asked to tell you that Mr Armstrong has had his operation, and that so far he is making good progress.'

'Thank you very much,' said Veronica, and replaced the ear-piece.

'While I concede that to show concern for a friend is of course admirable,' Dr Rattle began, but Veronica lifted the ear-piece again, and asked for a number, a *London* number.

'Harrods?' she said at last.

It would be, Dr Rattle thought. She even knew the number by heart, but that was not surprising.

'Roses,' the little fiend was saying. 'Caviar. Champagne.' All the things he'd said he liked in fact, but Dr Rattle was not to know that. More like an orgy than a sick bed, she thought. Once again Veronica replaced the receiver.

'Veronica,' Dr Rattle began.

'Thanks awfully for the use of the phone,' Veronica said, 'but I must get back to the seminar. It's Corneille. He's rather—' she sought for a scholarly word that would impress Dr Rattle. 'He's rather exigent,' she said.

When she left Dr Rattle suppressed the urge to scream and scream, and did something useful instead. The nursing sister had told her, after she had asked, that Miles Armstrong resided at Lammington Manor. Dr Rattle went to the section of her book shelves reserved for works of reference, and in five minutes she had him. Winchester and a first at Oxford, so he was by no means a fool. Then a spell in the Coldstream, which was why he was in hospital, no doubt. And all because of beer. To Dr Rattle such things were important. She was a gossip of virtuoso performance, and besides, everything about Veronica was important.

Poor Sir Mark, she thought. No roses and champagne and caviar for him. Only the occasional gift of her presence when she could be bothered, like a bone tossed to a hungry dog. Could the little fiend really be in love with this Armstrong? Dr Rattle doubted it. The little fiend loved Thales of Miletus and Mallarmé and Mozart, all safely dead and preserved in print, but that apart she loved Veronica – and possibly Lord and Lady Nugent, because they were rich. Even so there had to be some reason for all that munificence. Dr Rattle hoped that Lord Nugent wasn't about to lose his money.

Veronica spent Easter in Seville. Holy Week. The Semana Santa. Aunty and Uncle Arthur had ventured out of Egypt at last, and suggested that she join them. Dr Rattle hadn't sounded all that keen, but how could she object? Veronica was a Catholic when she remembered, she was studying Spanish, and staying with her aunt and uncle. All Dr Rattle could do was issue dire warnings about her conduct when she went aboard a cruise ship that stopped at Malaga, but she'd shut her up at last by saying that her uncle's assistant was sailing with her as chaperone. Not that she was. Bridget was still hard at it in London selling money, and no doubt taking a break from time to time by making Sir Edward's a life of bliss.

There had been opportunities for naughtiness on board ship, though nothing in darling Captain Hepburn's class, but she couldn't be bothered, not when she had Miles to think about. She had received a letter from him, just one, and the poor darling must have been feeling ghastly when he wrote it, to judge by the ink blots and the shaking hand, and the lines not straight. It didn't even tell her very much: just that the operation had been a success despite the handwriting, and that he was grateful for her good wishes, and her gifts. She didn't want gratitude, but it seemed that it was all that she would get.

He had disappeared. St George's Hospital had no forwarding address, and nor, more ominously, did the butler at Lammington Manor, that vast mansion in Northumberland. That was a lie, of course. It had to be: but there was nothing she could do about it. Veronica thought wistfully of Jagadir Singh, far away in Calcutta. People would tell Jagadir Singh *anything*. Usually all he had to do was appear. Veronica thought that she might cry, then decided against it. There was simply no point in crying.

She thought about Mark instead. She had met him at yet another ball after the end of term, where the earl's son and the shipping heir had pursued her vigorously,

but not sufficiently so for her to use Aunty's trick. The
trouble was that she wasn't chaperoned, which made her
'fast'. Not that she gave a damn. Her only reason for
going to the stupid ball was to ask if Mark had heard
from Miles – or even Rollo. Rollo might know.

Getting him to dance with her was no problem, and
Victoria managed not to look too furious. After all, Veronica thought, I promised. She asked him as they waltzed.

'Miles Armstrong?' said Mark. 'Isn't he in some hospital
in London?'

'Is he?' she said vaguely, and then: 'Do you ever see
Rollo Sandyford these days?'

'Never,' said Mark. So that was that.

Later she was part of a group that stood chatting and
drinking wine. Darling Victoria was there, of course,
because she could never be *quite* sure of Veronica, and
anyway the absence of Jenny was an opportunity not to
be wasted.

Suddenly Mark said, 'St George's.'

She did her best to look puzzled.

'The hospital in London where Miles Armstrong is,'
said Mark.

'Oh,' she said. That bitch Victoria was giving her the
oddest look: mocking or pitying? A bit of both, probably.
For two pins she'd – but no. She'd given her word after
all. It was a terrible ball.

Aunty and Uncle Arthur were waiting in the Customs
Shed, and Easter was late that year: warm enough for
Aunty to manage without her shawl, except in the eve-
ning, and then it was a Spanish one. They kissed, then

went out into the street, followed by a porter with her cases, to where a car waited: rather a smart car with a uniformed chauffeur.

'It's good to have you with us again,' said Aunty.

'Indeed it is,' Uncle Arthur said. 'Have they been working you hard?'

'Not too hard,' Veronica said. 'If only it wasn't so cold all the time.' She told them about the silver fox coat and the academic gown, and Uncle Arthur roared. Aunty smiled a little, but then looked grave. She's thinking, thought Veronica. About me. But she won't say anything till we're alone.

They gossiped all the way on the road to Seville, and when they arrived an elegant carriage with two horses and a liveried coachman awaited them, which Veronica considered rather eccentric until she noticed that almost every other rich person in the city also rode in a carriage, though not all were as elegant as Uncle Arthur's . . .

It stopped at a café near the cathedral, and Uncle Arthur left them. 'You two catch up with your gossip,' he said. 'There's a chap I want to see.' He went inside the café.

'Tact?' Veronica asked.

'Billiards,' said Aunty. 'It's a sort of craving with him. Just as well he's good at it. He hates to lose.'

They chattered all the way to their hotel, where Uncle Arthur had rented a suite. The best hotel, and no doubt the best suite. Uncle Arthur was even better at spoiling Aunty than he was at billiards. A maid, too. Consuelo. Aunty set her to unpack, then led Veronica to the suite's sitting-room and offered cigarettes.

'You look sad, darling,' she said.

'I am,' said Veronica.

'That Miles of yours?'

'Yes, but he isn't mine,' said Veronica. There was a catch in her voice, but then she clenched her fists. She wouldn't blub in front of Aunty.

Her aunt nodded, approving. 'Want to tell me?' she asked.

'Oh, please,' said Veronica, and out it all came: the lunch, the phone call, the letter.

'And no forwarding address?' her aunt said at last.

Her niece shook her head. 'He just vanished,' she said.

'Can you think why?' she asked.

'Maybe he doesn't like me,' said Veronica.

'Maybe pigs fly,' said her aunt. 'He's got eyes in his head. Of course he likes you.'

'Then why did he run away?'

Aunty shrugged. 'You'll find out when he comes back,' she said.

'You think he will?'

'Oh, yes,' said Aunty. 'If you don't believe me, go and look in the mirror.' Veronica realised yet again how she always felt better after a chat with Aunty.

'How's Jenny?' Aunty asked, and Veronica told her about Jenny and Mark.

'More tears for the missy baba,' Aunty said.

It was Veronica's turn to shrug. 'That's up to her,' she said, 'but I don't think Jenny's all that serious. She just wants somebody to practise on.'

'Good for her,' said Aunty, and then: 'The report came. From Arthur's detective. Would you like to see it?'

'Oh, yes,' said Veronica.

She took it to her bedroom. The maid had finished, and the only sound in the world was the ticking of the clock by her bed. Veronica opened the envelope that had been stuck down and sealed. Darling Aunty and Uncle Arthur. They hadn't even taken a peep.

She began to read. Nothing in his earliest years except the usual: nanny, prep school, ponies, and then public school. And then Rollo, but not in term time. Rollo it seemed was far too thick for Winchester. But in the vacations, a schoolboy affair. How dreary it sounded. Giggling and fumbling. That it had had its effect on Miles was obvious, but not on Rollo. From what she read it seemed that at one point Rollo had considered Aunty's line of business, and why not? The little bugger was pretty, and when he was younger no doubt even prettier. Not that he was that way inclined, she was sure. Look at the way he'd kept pestering Aunty: though that, Veronica thought, was because of status rather than lust: membership of the most exclusive club. For Rollo sex would always be a commodity to be traded in.

Then he came into money and became a dashing soldier instead, till the war came and went with no assistance from Rollo, who had contrived instead to lose almost all his money and sent in his papers because he was far too poor even for an infantry regiment. He had an uncle called Matthew Burton, the detective wrote. A distinguished painter. Well, hardly distinguished, Veronica thought, but he knew how to paint one in the altogether.

Miles. After Winchester he'd gone to New College and read Classics (which they called Classical Moderations), and Classical History. In the summer he played cricket; in the winter he hunted. No close friends, the detective had written. Very tactful . . . He'd done well at Oxford, it seemed, but he became restless and spent a lot of time travelling: Italy, Greece, the Levant, looking at old buildings. And then the Coldstream.

India too is full of old buildings, she thought. He should have gone there. We could have had a honeymoon. But that was foolish: Miles wasn't for honeymoons. Then what was he for? Could it be for life? Perhaps that too was foolish. It could just as well be for death. She would go with Aunty to pray, she thought (Aunty still wasn't pregnant, and prayer her last resource), but it would have to be the cathedral. There was no temple of Vishnu in Seville.

She took the letter in to Aunty, who was changing for dinner, helped by Consuelo. Aunty took one look at Veronica and told the maid to come back later.

'Do you want me to read the letter?' she asked.

'Oh, please.'

Aunty read it straight through and then looked at her. 'Well?'

'I don't know,' said Veronica. 'I don't even know where to begin.'

'Then I'll tell you,' Aunty said. 'You may know more about maths and Mozart than me – of course you do – but when it comes to men I'm the expert, wouldn't you say?'

'Of course,' said Veronica.

'And I wouldn't lie to you any more than I would lie to Arthur. Do you believe that?'

Veronica nodded.

'You think he's queer, don't you?' Aunty said.

'It says so in the letter.'

'It says he used to be queer. When he was a schoolboy. Half my clients used to be queer when they were schoolboys. It didn't stop them coming to me. And it also says "no close friends". Queers always have close friends. The closer the better. Can you imagine Matthew Burton without close friends?'

'But he ran away,' said Veronica.

'And I think I know why,' said Aunty. 'Because he's ashamed.'

'Ashamed?'

'Because he used to be like that and now he isn't.'

'But that doesn't make sense,' said Veronica.

'Men often don't,' Aunty said. 'Even Arthur. Besides, look what the poor chap's been through. All those medals and wounds and being at death's door for years, then an operation that could have killed him, then you on top of everything else. Do you suppose he could think straight after all that? But I bet you he hasn't run far, and, what's more, I bet you'll find him. Or he'll find you. Only don't rush him, child. Not yet. I don't think he's ready to be rushed. What do you say?'

'Oh, Aunty,' said Veronica, and embraced her, and wept just a little, but not because of sorrow.

Aunty hugged her and said, 'Now you go and choose a dress, and I'll send Consuelo in to help you to tittivate after she's finished with me. I want you looking your best. Arthur says we're going somewhere special.'

But as Veronica chose a dress she found herself

thinking: Suppose Aunty's wrong? She never had been, not when the subject was men, but it was possible after all, and Miles had disappeared as soon as he was able to move. Nothing for it but to decide which dress was her prettiest . . . She chose one by Callot in a deep, deep blue, Captain Hepburn's diamond necklace, and diamond drops for her ears. Darling Nicholas had escaped her too, but at least he hadn't wanted to. And that's quite enough of that, she thought, as Consuelo came in to dress her and was at once delighted because she was not only young and beautiful, she spoke fluent Spanish as well. The other beautiful lady spoke only Portuguese.

When she joined Aunty, Uncle Arthur was there too, and she knew at once that he had won his billiards match. A cat gorged on cream. He and Aunty were drinking sherry and he poured her a glass, taking the bottle from an ice-bucket. Cautiously she sipped. It was very dry indeed.

'I know,' Uncle Arthur said, 'you'd sooner have champagne. Maybe we'll find you a glass later. Spanish stuff. Not bad though.'

But Veronica was looking at a shawl that lay on the sofa. Black silk embroidered with a pattern of roses, and a long, long fringe.

'Oh, that's divine,' she said.

'Like it?' Uncle Arthur asked.

'It's beautiful,' said Veronica.

'Just as well,' said her aunt. 'It's yours.'

Veronica hugged her again.

'You'd better hug Arthur too,' Aunty said. 'He paid for it.' And Veronica did so. 'Tomorrow we'll buy mantillas,' said her aunt. 'We'll look good in them, and anyway we'll need them since we're going to church.'

That night they went to a reception at the British Consulate: lots of eligible young men, both Spanish and English, some of whom could dance quite well. Mostly the Spaniards talked about their king, whom nobody seemed to like, though they liked her well enough, and said so. They liked Aunty too, but Aunty could cope with that. When it came to chaps, Aunty could always cope. She pretended to be terrified of Uncle Arthur, approaching him with a kind of nervous flutter that made Veronica want to giggle, despite her sadness, and Uncle Arthur was splendid too, muttering darkly and scowling at any man rash enough to ask Aunty for more than two dances: and for *her* protection there was Aunty. Young ladies of her quality were never left unchaperoned in Seville. Spain was the land of the *duenna* after all.

Later, much later, they went by carriage to a restaurant, the guests of a rich Spaniard and his wife and son, a Spaniard who thought he might be even richer if he could persuade Uncle Arthur to sell him some money. The son was quite pretty, rather like a darker Rollo, but with a much better appetite, and with me for dessert, Veronica thought, but there was no need to worry. Not only would Aunty kill him, his father would too. Don Ramon was after half a million pesetas. The food was good, hot and spicy: there was even a dish called paella which was made with rice – a sort of pilau – and there was a gypsy dance troupe who danced with a fierce elegance that was marvellous to watch, and who tried to sell them carnations between dances. If only Miles had been there.

As Consuelo brushed her hair, Aunty came in yawning, already in her dressing-gown, but ready for a gossip. Aunty was always ready for a gossip.

'What a night,' she said, and produced cigarettes.

'You too,' said Veronica. 'What a performance. Terrified little wife indeed. I was dying to laugh all the time. Has Uncle Arthur gone to bed?'

'Making notes,' Aunty said. 'He hasn't decided about Don Ramon yet. What did you make of his son?'

'Bit of a weed.'

'We'll find you another one tomorrow,' Aunty said. It might have been a new hat.

'Will it all be like that?' Veronica asked. 'Carriage rides and restaurants and dancing?'

'Shopping too,' Aunty said. 'But not the bull fights. Not for me anyway.'

'Nor me,' said Veronica. All that blood and killing would make her think of Miles.

Next day they bought mantillas: elegant black lace and tortoiseshell combs to support them. Consuelo was enchanted, and insisted they try them on then and there, and why not? Half the women in Seville were wearing mantillas, as they sat in carriages or behind their caballeros on horseback. That was what the Semana Santa was: riding or being driven, or watching other people riding or being driven: going to church or a flamenco café, or listening to some street orator denounce the king. Goodness, how they detested him.

Good Friday was solemn of course, and Holy Saturday too, but on Saturday at midnight they sat on the balcony of their suite that overlooked the square, and watched as a huge rocket thrust upwards into the sky, then burst in a great cascade of lights. At once more fireworks erupted, bands played, guitars throbbed, wine was passed from hand to hand. Once again the serious business of pleasure had begun.

On and on it went. On and on and on. Men and girls in Spanish costumes like paintings by Goya, and Andalusian horses that looked well enough, but none that she would have swapped for Mavourneen. At least Aunty and she had their mantillas, and wore them to go to the cathedral that was packed out, but Don Ramon knew the cardinal archbishop, who had reserved seats for them, like a box at the opera she thought, but even so she prayed that Uncle Arthur would give Aunty a baby, then as a kind of postscript she prayed for Miles: prayed that even if she never saw him again he might be well.

That was about it, really. Feasting and drinking, cathedral and carriage drives. (No horse-riding; no sitting meekly behind some man. When she got on a horse, she was the one in control.) In between she read and re-read the detective's letter as if concealed in it somewhere there might be a clue to where Miles was, which was nonsense. On the other hand she responded to the account of Miles's time in the Coldstream. How brave he had been. Both the men in her life had been heroes, but darling Nicholas was dead: little more than a memory. Now there was only Miles, or there was nothing.

18

They left Spain at last, by ship once more, and the sea
was kind and calm (both she and Aunty were terrible
sailors), and there was lots and lots of dancing. Soon it
would be time to go back to Durham, and examinations.
Time to see dear Jenny again, and poor old Mark. Jenny
seemed to have gone off him too, and Veronica at once
asked why.

'Philip,' Jenny said.

'Philip?'

'Philip Martin,' said Jenny. 'He's a barrister. Gray's Inn.
What they call a junior.'

'Rich?'

'Not yet,' Jenny said, 'but daddy reckons that in a
couple of years he'll be doing very nicely, and in five he'll
be rolling in it.'

In a couple of years Jenny would be Miss J. Lawson,
BA (Dunelm), the gyves of St Winifred's struck from her
wrists.

'I take it he's smitten,' Veronica said.

'Mm,' said Jenny. 'Me too.' Veronica kissed her. 'So you
see,' said Jenny, 'I really can't have Mark cluttering up

the place any more than you can.'

Veronica made a most difficult decision: a magnanimous one too. 'Better let Victoria have him,' she said.

After that it was just lots and lots of work, with Mozart and Mavourneen as occasional treats. (Dr Rattle was inclined to fuss about Mavourneen. She didn't want her most promising – and lucrative – scholar's health threatened by what she described as a dangerous animal, but Veronica telephoned her aunt, who wrote at once to inform Dr Rattle that for Veronica horse-riding was essential, though for what none of them was sure.)

One day on the way to the library she met Mark. His Lord Clive researches were finished, it seemed.

'What will you do now?' she asked him, and he looked disconcerted, even shifty.

'Go to India,' he said at last.

And why not? she wondered. Why all this furtiveness?

'Soon?' she asked.

'Couple of months,' he said, and then, with the air of a rider taking a tricky fence: 'I'm going to be married, so India will have to wait until after the honeymoon.' Even the word made her want to giggle.

'Anyone I know?' she asked him.

'Victoria Lippiatt.' He said it like a man expecting a blow.

So he'd finally found a girl to sail away with. First he'd tried her, and after that she was pretty sure he'd tried Jenny, but with darling Victoria he wouldn't even have to try. Even so: 'I wish you both every happiness,' she said, and it was worth it if only to see how astonished he looked.

All the same it took a bit of thinking about. If Aunty's gossip sources were correct, and they almost always were, Mark had been rather involved with Victoria's mother not all that long ago, and she'd rather liked Mrs Lippiatt. Too bad if she was hurt, but Aunty had the answer to that too when she told her. Mrs Lippiatt had just become engaged to a recently retired Indian Army colonel. Arthur had read it in *The Times*. 'All's Well That Ends Well' for some, she thought, and went back to the detective's letter.

When he'd first told her Miles had looked at ruins she had been impatient: seen him as a sort of pale, ineffectual poet mooning about among broken columns, but it hadn't been like that. He'd measured, taken photographs, made excavations, written monographs, even a book, before the war came. The Great War. The War To End Wars. They had better ask Kali about that, she thought. He must have been an extremely strong, fit man, the detective wrote. After what hit him he should have been dead. For once Aunty's wrong about a chap, she thought. It's been too long. Months and months. It seems that he is dead to me; or I to him.

She took a walk, past a cricket field and a match that was all sharply pressed white flannels and decorous applause, to the river where large men in funny shorts submitted to the chivvying of midgets they could have crushed with one hand, and opened her text book. Corneille. He was difficult and he was dreary, but that was just the point. Quite a lot of examinees would avoid him if they could. There could be rather a lot of extra marks in Corneille. She slogged on as if a midget were chivvying her.

Before the examinations her aunt came to take her to lunch, but beforehand they sat and gossiped in Veronica's room, and Aunty marvelled that anyone could exist in such squalor.

'It's sort of a tradition,' said Veronica. 'Goes back to the Middle Ages. Nuns do it all the time.'

'You know how I feel about nuns,' said Aunty, so Veronica changed the subject to Jenny and her new chap.

'I like Jenny,' Aunty said. 'Better bring her too.' So Veronica went to invite Jenny to lunch, and while she was gone Dr Rattle, who was aware of everything that moved in St Winifred's, sent the parlourmaid to invite Lady Nugent to take sherry. Lady Nugent had discovered in Seville that she detested sherry, but went even so, swallowed a glass as if it were quinine, then took her niece and her friend to lunch in Durham's best hotel, the Castle, the one where the lawyers ate during the Assizes. Private room, too, which meant they could drink champagne. Jenny adored it. She adored Aunty too, but that was no novelty. Anybody with any sense adored Aunty.

They ate and drank a lot, and laughed even more, until over the sweet Aunty said, 'Did Veronica tell you we're off to Cap d'Antibes?' Jenny nodded. 'Why don't you come too?' said Aunty. 'Bring your chap. The villa's big enough.'

'I'd love to,' said Jenny, 'but I don't know about Philip.'

'You'd be all right, I promise you,' said Aunty, who had had rather more of the champagne than her guests. 'Bridget will be there too.'

Jenny, blissfully ignorant, said, 'He's so frightfully busy you see. He wants to get on.'

'Quite right, too,' said Lady Nugent, 'but come if you can.'

They drove back in the Rolls to St Winifred's, and Jenny sat up very straight, because so many people were watching, and envying, then kissed Lady Nugent *au revoir* and left her to say goodbye to her niece.

'Really Aunty,' said Veronica.

'But what did I say?' Aunty said.

'Bridget will be there indeed. She isn't like that.'

'She will be one day,' said Aunty. 'She'll have to be.'

'Not yet,' said Veronica. 'She's a virgin. She may not want to be – I don't know – but she is.'

'You make her sound like a missy baba.'

'Never that,' said Veronica. 'She's my friend.'

'Tell her to keep up her horse-riding,' said Aunty.

The examinations came and she sat them all like a good little student. The maths was fine, because for her maths was always fine, but the language papers went well too, until the Portuguese Unseen. She'd been on time for all the other papers because Jenny, besides being her friend, and sweet and pretty and clever, was also very good at remembering appointments. Veronica was hopeless at remembering appointments, so Jenny would always collect her and take her to the examination. The trouble was that Jenny wasn't studying Portuguese, and Veronica forgot to look at her timetable, and exercised Mavourneen instead.

When she got back the uproar was tremendous. Like something out of Wagner, she thought. (She detested Wagner.) Miss Winthrop, Professor Acuña, Dr Rattle, all roaring away. Dr Rattle in the role of Brünnhilde, *of course*, and roaring even louder than the others.

When they paused for breath Veronica said, 'If I'm being sent down, I'd better go and pack – and perhaps you'd be kind enough to telephone my aunt and ask her to send the chauffeur to collect me.'

There was a long, long pause, and at last Dr Rattle said, 'Perhaps you and I should have a talk on our own, Veronica.'

Veronica shrugged. Even in riding kit the effect was noteworthy. Certainly Professor Acuña found it so.

Dr Rattle said, 'This is really rather serious, you know,' and this time the little fiend didn't shrug. Mannish shirt and jacket, jodhpurs and riding boots, and she still contrived to look as beautiful as she was clever.

'Tell me why you failed to turn up,' said Dr Rattle. 'Were you afraid you might not do well?'

'Of course not,' Veronica said. 'I forgot. And anyway—'

'Yes?' said Dr Rattle.

'My horse needed the exercise.'

For the ten-thousandth time, chanting it in silence as though it were a mantra, Dr Rattle told herself: St Winifred's needs the money.

'You've been overworking,' she said. 'Studying until almost dawn.'

'That would be stu—'

'Let me finish, Veronica,' said Dr Rattle. 'Studying until the everyday realities became confused. You thought tomorrow was the day of the Portuguese Unseen, not today, so when the opportunity came for fresh air and exercise you took it, in the firm belief that it would help you on the morrow. Am I right?'

'I suppose so,' said Veronica, and shrugged once more. Dr Rattle waited grimly, but then it occurred to Veronica that, for whatever reason, Dr Rattle was throwing her a lifeline. 'I had one of my headaches too,' she said. 'Rather a bad one. Fresh air's the only thing that works.'

'Excellent,' said Dr Rattle. 'That it worked I mean. I shall speak to the examining body and I have no doubt that they will allow you to sit the paper tomorrow. A different paper, of course. There must be no suggestion of collusion with your fellow students. You really are causing a great deal of trouble, Veronica.'

'I quite often do,' said Veronica. 'Just like my aunt.'

Dr Rattle's fists clenched. 'Tomorrow I shall conduct you to your examination room personally,' she said, and did so. All that was missing was a ball and chain, thought Veronica.

The doctor had even talked of gating her for the rest of the term, but that was ridiculous. How could she possibly be cooped up in college when there was a ball to which she and Jenny had been invited: rather a grand one, in the Castle?

'But how did you make her change her mind?' Jenny asked.

'I told her I *had* to go to this ball,' said Veronica.

'Had to?'

'I explained that my uncle was keen on it because the sons of two of his colleagues would be there. Sort of a business thing.' She lit a cigarette, and Jenny opened the window wider. After all they were in her room.

'Is it true?' she said.

'It could be,' said Veronica. The shipping heir and the viscount would be there, and both their fathers were specially nice to Uncle Arthur and Aunty, which meant that they wanted some of Uncle Arthur's money, even though they'd have to pay for it.

'Honestly you're the giddy limit,' said Jenny admiringly.

'I don't see why,' said Veronica. 'I do almost everything she tells me, and there aren't any rules about horses or motor cars. I know. I looked it up. And what's more I only wore that fur coat because I was cold. I usually am in this place.'

'And you do work hard,' said Jenny.

'Yes, but I enjoy it,' said Veronica. 'What will you wear at the Castle Ball?'

It *was* a good ball, and she wore a dress of a blue so intense she thought of the Indian skies that she longed to show to Miles, and the captain's sapphires and a corsage instead of a necklace. Darling Jenny looked divine in pink and white, and pearls that no doubt her mother had decreed to emphasise her virginal status. Both the shipping heir and the viscount danced quite well, and did their best to monopolise herself and Jenny. She was dancing with the viscount when Dr Rattle arrived in a dress of a quite stupefying puce and a garnet set in urgent need of cleaning.

When the dance ended Jenny said, 'Dr Rattle's here.'

'Of course,' said Veronica.

'Checking up, you mean?'

'What else?' said Veronica, and turned to their partners. 'Come along chaps,' she said. 'Time for you two St Georges to meet the dragon.'

But it was a dragon with no fight left in her. The very names of their partners was enough. Altogether a most delightful ball.

19

It would be nice to go somewhere warm, she thought. Dr Rattle had asked her where she was going and Veronica had told her: first Paris (the Crillon), and then Cap d'Antibes. The information horrified her, which was puzzling, until Veronica remembered that Dr Rattle considered all Frenchmen libidinous in the extreme, and France was full of them after all. She seemed to think that Veronica would travel the whole way on her own, which was nonsense. Aunty wouldn't ever have permitted it.

She and Jenny travelled together to London and drank champagne in the dining-car, and Jenny became rather squiffy and tearful because she wouldn't see her friend for absolute ages, until Veronica reminded her that she would be seeing Philip Martin instead, and Jenny cheered up at once . . . From King's Cross Veronica took a taxi to Bridget's flat in Knightsbridge, and it really was frightfully grand, if rather full of what one might call memorabilia of Sir Edward Kitson: but if Bridget didn't mind why should she? and anyway Bridget was frightfully grand too, and prettier than ever. Soon she'd be far too grand for baronets, never mind butlers.

313

The two women embraced, and settled down to a long and enjoyable gossip in Hindi because Bridget was afraid she might forget it and it was more than possible Uncle Arthur might send her to India on business. As it was, she had to complete some negotiations in London before she would be free to go to Cap d'Antibes. Rather a bore in a way, though dear old Kitters didn't think so. It came as no surprise to Veronica to learn that dear old Kitters was considering a visit there himself. In her turn Veronica described her continuing skirmish with Dr Rattle.

'There was a time when you would have been straight round to Kali's temple, if Durham had such a place,' said Bridget.

'I don't need Kali for Dr Rattle,' said Veronica, 'not when I've got Aunty and Uncle Arthur.'

Next day she took the boat train to Dover and the ferry to Calais, then on to Paris and the Crillon where Aunty was waiting. More hugs and kisses.

'How pretty you look, child,' Aunty said.

'Look who's talking,' said Veronica automatically, and then, because you could say anything to Aunty provided you were honest, 'but something's bothering you, isn't it?'

'I'm still not pregnant,' Aunty said. 'Poor old Arthur's exhausted.' Veronica giggled. 'Yes I daresay,' said Aunty, 'but I'll have to start Bridget making love-potions soon. As it is I have to see a doctor tomorrow. Poor old Arthur. Some mornings he can hardly get out of bed.'

'What a way to go,' said Veronica. This time it was her aunt's turn to giggle.

Next day there was a telegram from Dr Rattle. Veronica

314

had done splendidly in every subject, especially maths and the Portuguese Unseen. Jolly good, Dr Rattle had said. It was her only comment.

'Hardly opening the Krug, is it?' said Aunty. 'Never mind. I'll do that. Then we'll go to Cartier and buy you something nice before I see my doctor.'

'Just being with you's enough,' Veronica said. 'You don't have to.'

'Arthur would kill me if I didn't,' Aunty said.

'He wouldn't be strong enough,' Veronica said.

'Now that's enough,' said Aunty. 'Let's go and drink that Krug.'

Something nice turned out to be a pair of sapphire ear-rings to complement Nicholas's bracelet, and afterwards Aunty sent her back to the Crillon, determined to face the gynaecologist on her own. Adamant in fact.

'Just the way I am,' said Aunty. 'Afterwards I'll tell you, but I don't want you with me. I love you, but I don't want you with me.'

Veronica knew that voice, and went to take tea at the Crillon, and yawn over a fashion magazine; then Rollo came up to her.

The extraordinary thing was that it didn't surprise her. Apart from the absence of Miles, life had been good: exam results, Seville, Paris, sapphire ear-rings. There had to be some grit in the oyster to produce a pearl like that, she thought, and there it was. A rather shabby piece of grit, too. A suit elegant enough but too well worn, a shirt that should have been at the laundry. He didn't belong at the Crillon.

'May I join you, Veronica?' he said.

'Miss Carteret,' said Veronica.

'I'm sorry, Miss Carteret,' he said, and she waited. It didn't take long. 'I heard that you were here.'

'How?'

'A friend of mine drove you here. He's a taxi driver, you see. Rather well born for a taxi driver, but down on his luck like so many of us.'

Russian, she thought. A count maybe, or a general. A colonel at least. Again she waited.

'When he described you I knew it must be Ve— Miss Carteret. You're unique.' As he spoke he was looking at her ear-rings as if he knew just the pawn shop to take them to.

'The thing is,' Rollo said, 'that I'm rather down on my luck too, and I was wondering—' His voice, or was it his nerve? failed him.

'You were wondering,' Veronica said helpfully.

He gulped, then ploughed on. It should have been manfully, but that could never be true, she thought. Not of Rollo.

'I saw my uncle again,' he said. 'Matthew Burton.' She took a cigarette from the case in her handbag, and a waiter appeared like a genie from a bottle to light it for her.

'I have absolutely no interest in your relatives,' she said.

'You did in this one – and your aunt, too. He swears he painted you both with no clothes on.'

'Mr Sandyford,' Veronica said in her kindest voice, 'are you sure you're quite well?'

'He did, I tell you,' said Rollo. 'He showed me a pencil

316

sketch. Your aunt was lying down. You were kneeling. A bird was perched on your finger.'

The bastard did it from memory afterwards, Veronica thought. Jagadir Singh knows all there is to know about searching people.

'Hardly the way for a peer's wife and niece to behave, Miss Carteret. What would happen if the press got hold of a story like that?'

'You would be sued,' Veronica said.

'But as I've told you, I'm broke.'

'Your uncle isn't. You told me once before how famous he is. If the *Daily Messenger* went after him he'd deny every word if he has any sense. He's got a lot to lose after all.'

'I haven't,' said Rollo.

'Oh, but you have,' said Veronica, and blew out smoke, not quite in his face. Rollo found that he too wanted a cigarette, but was much too frightened to ask for one. 'When you were in Calcutta, did you ever meet Jagadir Singh?' Veronica asked. 'He was my aunt's *chokra* – her watchman – among other things.'

Rollo hadn't, but his uncle had, and had made a sketch of him, also from memory. Rollo had thought it unbelievable, but his uncle had assured him that if anything it was understated.

'Big,' said Veronica dreamily. 'Enormous even, but by no means fat. Muscular would be the way to describe him. Incredibly muscular. Once he used to be a wrestler, but of course he had to give that up.'

'Why?' said Rollo. His voice was a croak.

'He hurt his opponents too much,' Veronica said. 'He's

a homosexual, you see, with what are called rather specialised tastes. You'd appeal to him, I'm sure.'

'What on earth do you mean?' This time the voice was a squeak.

'If you tell lies about my aunt and me we'll send for him,' Veronica said. 'We'll pay him of course, but he'd probably do it for nothing. You're quite pretty you know, especially when you're frightened.'

'Do what?' said Rollo.

'Whatever he felt like,' said Veronica.

'I won't say anything,' said Rollo.

'Very wise,' Veronica said, and Rollo got up from his chair. 'Wait,' said Veronica, and Rollo waited. He was terrified.

Veronica took a hundred franc note from her wallet. The appalling little tick in front of her had once at least tried to be nice to Miles, not that he was with Miles now. She was sure of that. Even so, a hundred francs would last him a day or two. He might even have his shirt washed. She crumpled the note into a ball and threw it to him.

'Thank you,' Rollo said.

'Thank you, Miss Carteret,' said Veronica.

'Thank you, Miss Carteret.'

She didn't tell Aunty: there seemed no point, not when they were so happy. All the time they gossiped; in Paris and on the Blue Train, about Bridget and her baronet, Durham and Dr Rattle, Jenny and her barrister, and about the clothes they'd bought, because they had lingered rather in Paris, and there was one rule Aunty held to above all others: money earned was there to be enjoyed, and they had both earned theirs by dispensing pleasure every bit as much as Uncle Arthur had earned his by dispensing money.

At last they arrived at the villa and Veronica loved it. Of course I do, she thought. It's like going back to India. Cool and shady, with long verandas: there was even a tank, though here one called it a swimming pool. And a garden like India too. Orange trees, lemon trees, hibiscus, roses, oleander; everything in fact except bursting lilies . . . Bridget had already arrived and was full of stories about dear old Kitters; and Uncle Arthur, who kissed her cheek and grinned at her and said, '*Mi princesa portuguesa.*'

'But that's Spanish,' she said.

'I did a deal with Don Ramon,' Uncle Arthur said. 'Only fair to learn a bit of the lingo.'

'About the party,' said Aunty, and looked at Uncle Arthur. He nodded.

'Party?' said Veronica.

'Just a few people in for drinks to celebrate your exam results,' said Aunty. 'We'll give a proper one in a week or so.'

'But Jenny won't be here by then,' Veronica said.

'We'll give another one when she comes,' said Aunty. 'But this party will be just a few old friends and enemies.'

'Enemies?'

'Sir Mark and Lady Beddoes.'

'*Lady* Beddoes?' said Veronica. 'Oh – you mean Victoria.'

'I do indeed. That's if you don't mind?'

'Of course not,' Veronica said. 'If she gets nasty we can always organise a gymkhana.'

Aunty chuckled and said, 'Her mamma is here too. She's engaged to a retired Indian Army colonel these days as you know, but he's away in Delhi. Court of Enquiry or something. Not that she'll be a problem. I rather like Mrs Lippiatt.'

'Me too,' Veronica said. Her aunt looked at her fondly.

'Common sense as well as brains,' she said. 'The rest will be the usual Riviera riff raff. But rather fun.'

'There is one other,' said Uncle Arthur.

'Indeed there is,' said Aunty, and went to her niece and put her arms about her and smiled as if Veronica was eleven years old and it was her birthday and it was time for pistachio burfi. 'Miles Armstrong,' she said.

Veronica squeaked as if she really were eleven years old, then said, 'He's here?'

'He's in Nice for the moment,' said her aunt, 'having a check up.'

'You mean he's ill?'

Her aunt touched her cheek. 'No,' she said. 'He's fine. Honestly. But after what he's been through you can hardly blame him for having a check up.'

Veronica wanted to cry, but forced herself to concentrate on what to wear. For Miles she must look her absolute best. Thank God Bridget was there to help her.

In the end she (and Bridget) decided on a dress of pale blue silk with much darker blue beading and the sapphires: bracelet and necklace, and her new ear-rings, nothing spared.

'Rather a lot for a drinks party,' said Bridget.

Veronica looked at her. 'I think you know why,' she said, and Bridget smiled.

'Of course I do,' she said, 'but I'm not going to waste my breath telling you not to worry. Of course you'll worry. Only don't let it show. Remember the missy baba will be watching.'

Veronica's head came up at once as Aunty came in. She was also rather too well dressed for a drinks party – cream silk by Vionnet and diamonds – but she too knew that the missy baba was coming. *And* her mother.

'I'd better go and put on something special,' said Bridget.

'Just pretend that dear old Kitters is coming too,' said Aunty.

'Oh you,' Bridget said, and left, not quite running. Aunty chuckled, but stopped at once when Veronica asked, 'How did you find him?' This was serious after all.

'I spoke with Arthur,' she said. 'He put that detective on to him – the one who looked into his background. I hope you don't mind?'

'Of course not,' said Veronica.

'No, not you,' said Aunty. 'He was on a tour of the South of France. Got as far as Cannes. Arthur and I drove over and bumped into him by accident. I told him it wasn't very nice of him to disappear like that after you'd gone to all that trouble to keep in touch.'

'And what did he do?'

'Agreed. He's taken a hotel room here for a week. But don't rush him. You can make him stay longer.'

'Yes, of course,' Veronica said, but it wouldn't be as easy as that.

He arrived early, and almost she didn't recognise him, he looked so well. His dinner suit looked as if it had been made for him, rather than a man twice his weight, and he looked brown, too, like a sahib. His doctors must have decided that the sun would be good for him. He came to speak to Aunty and Uncle Arthur. Veronica was with them, but her aunt and uncle moved away almost at once to greet more newcomers. Darling Aunty. Darling Uncle Arthur, too.

'I owe you an apology,' he said at once.

'Never mind that,' she said. 'I know how ill you were. It's wonderful to see you so well.'

A waiter brought them drinks and she sipped.

'It's wonderful to be so well,' he said. 'Especially now.'

Slow and easy, she told herself. Don't rush him. She smiled instead, her best smile, then the quartet Uncle Arthur had hired played a one-step.

'Dance with me,' she said.

'I'm afraid I'm not awfully good,' he said. 'It's been a long time.'

'I'll help you remember,' she said, and took his glass and her own, put them down, and went to his arms.

None of Aunty's tricks, not on him. Of course not: but the language of her body was as eloquent as Camoëns' Portuguese, and she knew it, and somehow contrived to make him relaxed yet happy. He even remembered how to dance.

When it was over she said, 'There ... It wasn't that bad, was it?'

'It was wonderful,' he said. 'Only—'

'Only what?'

'Oh, nothing,' he said.

I mustn't think I've won, Veronica thought, because I haven't. Not yet.

Then Sir Mark and Lady Beddoes arrived with Mrs Lippiatt in tow, to be met by Lord and Lady Nugent. Darling Victoria had obviously decided to be gracious and condescending and put everyone at their ease, Veronica thought, then realised too late that it was tricky for a baronet's wife to be gracious and condescending to a baroness. She strolled across to join them, leaving Miles on his own. It was dreadful, but she mustn't rush him. Only he could set the pace. She waited for the missy baba to put her at her ease.

'How well you look,' Victoria said.

'And you.'

'Married life,' said Victoria. 'It suits me.'

'Really?' Veronica looked from the missy baba to Sir Mark as if she found it hard to believe.

'Anyway,' Victoria said, 'I'm sure you'll find that out for yourself one of these fine days.'

Mrs Lippiatt glared at her daughter, who continued oblivious.

'Oh yes,' she said, as Veronica twisted the bracelet on her wrist that was much much better than anything she was wearing, 'you should marry quite well once you've finished at that school of yours.'

'Come and dance,' said her husband.

Uncle Arthur went for a duty dance, and a young Frenchman approached Veronica. Just as well, Veronica thought. The missy baba mustn't think I want only Miles. Not yet.

Mrs Lippiatt turned to her hostess.

'My dear, I'm sorry,' she said.

Aunty shrugged. The cream silk could have been designed precisely for Lady Nugent's shrugs, and Mrs Lippiatt blinked.

'Not your fault,' said Lady Nugent. 'I know that.'

'Can we talk?' Mrs Lippiatt asked.

'For a little while. I still have other guests to speak to.'

'It's – she's insecure, you see,' Mrs Lippiatt said. 'She wanted him and now she's got him, but she's still insecure.'

'Because of Veronica?' Mrs Lippiatt nodded. 'But my niece doesn't want Mark. Never did.'

'He wanted her.'

Now there was honesty, Lady Nugent thought, because he got you instead, and you know I know it.

'A lot of men do,' she said, 'but Veronica isn't in a hurry.'

She's in a hurtling rush, she thought, but why should I tell you?

'She won't – do anything?' Mrs Lippiatt asked.

'Of course not,' Lady Nugent said, 'any more than I will.'

But Mrs Lippiatt's obstinate honesty persisted. 'You could if either of us hurt you really badly,' she said.

Lady Nugent spoke very softly. 'Because of your husband you mean? And his suicide?'

'And the fact that I intend to marry again,' said Mrs Lippiatt.

'I wish you happy,' said Lady Nugent. 'Don't worry. I keep my secrets,' and moved to meet two new arrivals.

Mrs Lippiatt sighed her relief. If that idiot daughter of

hers could contrive to stay silent until the end of the evening there would be no trouble. Lady Nugent would keep her secret, she was sure of it, but then Mrs Lippiatt had just discovered that she liked Lady Nugent . . .

This time he came up to her and asked her to dance. He moved smoothly, easily, but he was wound up tight. We're still not there, she thought. Wherever it is we're going.

'We have to talk,' he said.

'Yes, but not here,' she said.

'God no,' he said. 'What I have to tell you – it's personal. Is there somewhere we can be alone? – That is if your aunt won't mind?'

'Aunty trusts me,' Veronica said, and thought: Whatever I do.

'Come to tea tomorrow,' she said. 'Aunty and Uncle Arthur are going to Nice. Bridget will be about, but she won't bother us.'

In fact Bridget was laughing and twirling in the arms of a man with the same air of money and power as Sir Edward. Was her friend collecting them?

'I'll look forward to it,' he said, and yet still sounded reluctant. Even so she smiled at him.

Mark asked her for the next dance, and she smiled at him too, because darling Victoria was watching and in this world one pays for one's pleasures.

After the party she went to Aunty's dressing-room for a chat. Uncle Arthur was still downstairs talking about the price of money, but there was no sign of Bridget. Aunty was undressing by herself.

'No Bridget?' Veronica said.

'Out courting,' said Aunty. 'With her new chap.'

'Who is he?'

'Cartwright? Owns a lot of coal mines. High Sheriff of somewhere, too. Derbyshire would it be?'

'She's a busy one,' said Veronica.

'Isn't she though? I don't mean doing it, though she probably quite likes that, too. It's being next to all that wealth she really enjoys – and knowing it has to be nice to her. But she'll have her work cut out when dear old Kitters is here too.'

'Does she want to get married?'

'Of course not,' Aunty said.

'Because she's a bloody chee-chee you mean?'

'Partly that,' said Aunty. 'She's a sensible one after all. But it's more because she enjoys working for Arthur. Between that and her chaps our Bridget's having the time of her life.'

She took off her knickers and looked round for her dressing-gown. It was still all there, Veronica noticed. All still very firmly in place. Just as she was in the picture of the two of them that now hung on the wall behind her in front of the safe. Aunty sat on the stool before the dressing-table, and Veronica began to brush her hair.

'Poor Arthur,' Aunty said.

'Why poor?' Veronica said.

'He still tries, you see,' said Aunty. 'Tries very hard.' Veronica giggled. 'Yes, I daresay,' Aunty said. 'All the same I bet you'll be off to see your Miles first chance you get.'

'There may not be a chance,' Veronica said.

'Not this chee-chee nonsense?' Veronica shook her head.

'Of course not. You're Portuguese royalty after all. So what is it then?'

'I'm not sure,' Veronica said, 'but I will be tomorrow. He's coming here for tea and a chat.'

'Just take it slow and easy,' Aunty said. 'It'll all be fine. You'll see.'

There isn't a thing Aunty doesn't know about chaps, thought Veronica. All the same, I wish I had her confidence.

'He looks nice now he's well,' said Aunty.

'He is nice. Clever too,' Veronica said.

'Then that makes two of you. All the same, if things turn out the way I think they will, mind you go to see Bridget first.'

In other words no babies before wedlock, thought Veronica. But as Jenny had once said, chance would be a fine thing. She looked at the picture of the two of them.

'Bit of all right, weren't we?'

'We still are,' said Aunty, and winked. 'That's why our chaps try so hard.'

Veronica giggled again, but even so her sleep was uneasy.

20

Miles arrived looking elegant: lightweight suit, Wyke-hamist tie. But Miles could always manage to look elegant, even when, as now, he also looked as if he were about to lead his troop or whatever it was in a charge against German machine-guns. They took tea in the garden, and Bridget, who really was her friend, was nowhere to be seen.

'I think you know how I feel about you,' he said, 'but there's something else I'll have to talk about first. Something not very nice. Downright nasty, in fact.'

A Hindu would say that it was all in his karma, his destiny, she thought, and that none of us can help our karma; but Miles didn't believe that any more than she did. Suddenly she remembered Jagadir Singh, and could not think why, though she knew beyond doubt that it was bad to remember him just then. He too was her friend, but now was not the time.

He was talking about Rollo, and the adolescent – love? passion? sex? that they had shared. As if it mattered. It must have been ten years ago at least, but even so she tried to look as if she'd known nothing about it. And anyway, she thought, what a lot of fuss about nothing. 'Much Ado', in fact, but it wasn't nothing to him, and now it was up to her to kiss it better. When he had done there was a silence, until she said: 'That's all?'

'All?' He sounded amazed, perhaps even irate that his great confession should be made to sound so trivial.

'What I mean,' she said, 'is that it's over and done with. You don't do it with him now, do you?'

'Of course not,' he said. 'It was over before I went to Oxford.'

'Then – forgive me, please – but why did you tell me?'

'Because I couldn't bear you to find out any other way,' he said, and indeed he had a point. Rollo would most certainly have told her if he knew that Miles was now hers. He would be furiously, frantically jealous, not because she had Miles's love, but because she might have his money.

'If it's over then it's best forgotten,' she said.

'You mean that, don't you?' She nodded. 'Then let me tell you that I—'

'No,' she said. 'Later – if you want to. It's my turn now. Cigarette please.'

He produced his case and lit one for her, and she dragged the smoke deep down.

'Did Rollo talk about me when he met you?' He nodded. 'And my aunt?' Another nod. 'I adore my aunt,' she said.

'Me too,' said Miles, 'but not quite in the way I adore you.' She could have kissed him then, but slow and easy Aunty had said, and slow and easy it would be.

'I had an affair in Calcutta,' she said. 'Just one.'

330

'Rollo seemed to think that there were rather more,' said Miles.

'He lied.'

'Yes,' said Miles. 'He's good at lying.'

'My – friend is dead,' said Veronica. 'He was a hero like you.'

'You mean killed in the war?' She nodded. 'Medals and things?' Another nod. 'But why did you say like me?'

'Medals and things,' she said. 'Wounds. Being close to death, only he got too close. But my friend and I – what we had was a sort of friendship with our bodies. What the French call an *amitié amoureuse*. If you and I are going to continue being together I shall want rather more.'

'Of course,' said Miles. Yet still he sat there.

'Well then?'

'I don't know if I can,' said Miles. 'After Rollo I sort of went off the whole idea.'

'There's only one way to find out,' said Veronica, and held out her hand.

'You mean now?' His voice was a squeak.

'You're a hero,' she said. 'You can't be afraid of a little thing like me.'

'I'm terrified,' he said. 'You see I never—'

'Sh,' said Veronica. 'If you talk any more we'll never do it.'

She took his hand and drew him to his feet, and Bridget watched them go and smiled. It would be all right. Veronica had been to see her first. What a lucky young man Miles Armstrong was, she thought, but then from what

Veronica had told her he deserved a bit of luck. She looked
at her watch. When Poppy and her lord got back she was
going out to dine with what Poppy called her coalman
but then maybe she deserved a bit of luck too.

He stood inside the bedroom door and looked at the
bed as if it were an instrument of torture rather than o.
pleasure. Ah well, there was a reason for that and it was
her business to help him after all.

'Don't you want to touch me?' she said.

'I ache to touch you,' he said. 'It's just—'

'Sh,' she said again and went into his arms and kissed
him on the mouth. Slowly, reverently almost, he
embraced her, then his arms tightened about her, and
she knew it would be all right.

'What now?' he said at last.

'First you take your clothes off, then you take mine off
and then we'll see. Only try to go slowly, my darling
Make it last. That's what you want, isn't it? To make i
last?'

'My God yes,' said Miles.

And he did. He was – what was the expression? –
tabula rasa: a blank page, on which she had to write th
delight of love, and slowly and carefully she did so: equ
ally slowly, equally carefully he responded. Perhaps, sh
thought later, it was because he was a scholar: knowledge
all knowledge, was to be first acquired, then used: but i
wasn't scholarship that explained the tender cunning c
his hands, that knew from the beginning how to cares
and squeeze, or the quickness of his response when i
was her turn to touch. It might be something he was bor
with, she thought, like perfect pitch ... But oh, how h

332

loved to touch her, and that was as it should be. She was there to be touched.

As they rested he said, 'I've never been so happy.'

'I'm glad,' she said.

'I'd no idea a woman could be so beautiful. I'd seen the statues, of course, in Greece, Italy, all over the place: but they were the ideal. You're reality.'

His hands reached out to cup her breasts like a hungry man at a banquet.

'You do love the pomelos, don't you?' she said.

'Pomelos?'

'These,' she said, and her hands came over his, gently squeezing. 'It's another word for grapefruit.'

He looked at them. 'It's right if you're talking about their shape,' he said, 'but when it comes to texture and colour it doesn't do them anything like justice.'

'You like their colour?'

'Of course,' he said. 'It's the same as the rest of you.'

His hands reached out to them again – like a greedy schoolboy, she thought, and oh, how I love his appetite.

'On the other hand,' he said, 'there's another way that they're like grapefruit. The ones in a restaurant anyway. They each have a cherry on top.' His fingers teased and pleased and he said, 'You don't mind my saying that?'

'I adore your saying that,' she said. 'You can have a nibble if you like.'

Carefully, tenderly, lovingly he did so. Darling Miles.

When it was time to go they bathed together the Indian way, kneeling in the bath, pouring water over each other, turning a jug into an improvised shower, and he enjoyed it so much it almost started him off again, but when he was dressed he became nervous, furtive even.

'I'll have to go downstairs,' he said.

'Well of course.'

'But I can't,' he said. 'Somebody might see me.'

Impossible to explain that not only would Bridget stay out of sight, she'd keep the servants out of sight, too: but being a scholar and a hero he found a solution to his problem. Of course he did. Near her balcony was a lemon tree, and he swung from one to the other then down to the ground and blew her a kiss. Like Douglas Fairbanks, she thought. All that was missing were the cloak and sword.

Softly he called up to her, 'Darling – when can I come back to you?'

'Whenever you like,' she said.

'Tonight?'

'If you can climb the lemon tree,' Veronica said.

Her aunt came to her room as soon as Bridget set off to dine with the coalman. 'Slow and easy I don't think,' she said.

'But it was,' said Veronica, 'once we started – and before that there were problems.' She told Aunty how Miles had confessed about Rollo and the adolescent cavortings, because you could tell Aunty anything and know the secret would be kept.

'Nasty little bugger,' she said, then brooded. 'You thought it was now or never, so to speak,' she said at last.

'Yes, I did,' said Veronica, 'and it turned out to be now.'

'Will I be hearing wedding bells?'

'If it were just up to him, yes,' said Veronica, 'but for the moment I prefer things as they are.'

'Why?'

'I love him and I need him – for his body I mean – just as he needs mine, but I have to be quite sure he's got over Rollo.'

'Or even some other chap,' said Aunty. 'Quite right.'

'It's really a rather splendid body,' said Veronica. 'But oh, Aunty, the scars. All over.'

'Did it put you off?'

'Of course not,' Veronica said. 'They're *his* scars.'

Her aunt smiled. 'Good girl,' she said. 'When will you see him again?'

'Tonight,' said Veronica.

'*What*?' For once in her life, Aunty was shocked.

'Don't worry,' said Veronica. 'He'll use the back stairs.' She took her aunt to the veranda, and showed her the lemon tree.

'Damn it,' said her aunt. 'Between you and Bridget it's just like being back in Calcutta.'

Veronica giggled, and after dinner she played Uncle Arthur's favourite Chopin pieces, and then a little Mozart too. Uncle Arthur was developing a taste for Mozart, which just went to show what a super uncle by marriage he was, she thought, then closed the piano lid and went to prepare for bed, and Miles.

This time he wore an open-necked shirt and flannels and was naked in no time at all, and then it was her turn, but when they embraced he still let her lead in their love dance, but goodness how quickly he learned. When they rested once again he talked of Aunty.

'She knows, doesn't she?'

'Well, of course,' said Veronica.

'And she doesn't mind?'

'Why should she? You're what I want and I've got you. She's not a memsahib you know, any more than she's a Portuguese princess. We're Anglo-Asians. Chee-chees.' He winced. 'English-Irish-Mahratta-Goanese. And the Goanese means I'm part-Portuguese, which means I'm part-Arab, too, because all Portuguese are.'

'All those pigments to make one perfect colour,' he said, and kissed her shoulder that was scented and sleek.

'That's nice,' she said, 'but let me finish telling you. Being as she is, when I developed this – affection—'

'*Amitié amoureuse*,' he said.

'Whatever it was – she didn't just leave me to get on with it. She taught me first – she and Bridget. Do you believe that?'

'I knew somebody must have,' he said, 'because of the way you are.'

'It wasn't my chap,' she said, 'if that's what's worrying you.'

'Why should it?' said Miles. 'I didn't even know you then.'

She stroked his face. 'We had a lot of pleasure together but it was Aunty and Bridget who taught me how to have it. Does that shock you?'

'It delights me,' he said. 'It's part of you.' And then because he couldn't help it, he had to know: 'Your chap – it was that navy hero, wasn't it? Captain Hepburn? He won a VC.'

'Posthumously,' she said. 'And you've got two MCs and thank God they're not posthumous. But how did—'

'Rollo told me,' said Miles.

336

'Oh, sod Rollo,' she said, then her hand went to her mouth, but he was laughing.

'It never quite came to that,' he said, and kissed her.

'I think I'm going to teach you some more about touching,' she said at last. 'Ladies first.' She took his hand and showed him how easy and pleasant it was to make his beloved cry out loud in delight.

In the bath she said, 'I want to ask you something.'

She was holding him in a way he specially liked and he said, 'Not while you're doing that.' She let him go. 'And anyway,' he said, 'I'd sooner play waterfalls.' He took the jug, poured water over her breasts and watched it cascade downwards.

'Do listen,' she said.

'Sorry, miss.'

Just like darling Nicholas, she thought. How lucky I've been. Twice. Even Aunty was lucky only once.

'It's your name,' she said.

'Miles?' he said. 'It's Latin for a soldier. I thought we established that the day you had lunch with me: when I thought I might die, but even then you made me happy.'

'Miles Robert Christopher Standish Armstrong,' she said.

'You remembered that?'

'Of course,' she said. 'It's you. When it's you I remember everything. What I want to know is – why Miles – when you've got all those other names to choose from? Unless you like it of course.'

'Not specially,' he said. 'It was my mother's father's name.'

'And Robert?'

'That was my dad's.'

'Then why—?'

'My mother wasn't all that fond of my dad,' said Miles: which might be the reason for Rollo, she thought, or part of it.

'I like Robert,' she said. 'Do you?'

He nodded. 'I liked my dad,' he said.

'I know it's too late to change your name in public, but when we're alone I should like to call you Bob.'

'My mother once said it was a name appropriate only to terriers,' he said. 'I told you.'

'But would you like it?'

'Woof, woof,' said Miles.

One morning Aunty told her that she was pregnant, and Veronica rushed to her and embraced her.

'How's Uncle Arthur?' she asked.

'Having a lie-in,' said her aunt. 'On his own for a change. Tired but happy you might say.' She took a spoonful of her boiled egg and said, 'We ought to give another party.'

'To celebrate the fact that you're pregnant?'

'We don't have to tell the guests, but yes,' Aunty said. 'Also to celebrate the fact that you're not.'

'I do what Bridget tells me,' said Veronica.

'Well of course,' said Aunty. 'You're a sensible girl – but even Bridget isn't infallible.'

She made a face. Infallible made her think of the Pope and church, and the fact that God had heard her prayers and she'd have to say thank you. It was only polite. Still, she and Veronica could wear their mantillas to

338

church like the rest of Portuguese royalty. She bit into her toast. 'Has that chap of yours proposed yet?' she asked.

'He never stops,' Veronica said, and for once looked smug.

'Well then?'

'If I fall pregnant I'll marry him, of course,' said Veronica. 'I'll marry him anyway in time.'

'You'll have to explain that,' Aunty said.

'It's Durham,' said Veronica. 'Not the languages. I've learned them and they're here – ' she tapped her forehead ' – and that's that. It's the mathematics. I adore that.'

'More than Miles?'

'I adore him, too, and he adores me, but he adores Hellenic art too. We're two of a kind.'

'That's as maybe,' said Aunty, 'but suppose he gets restless?'

'Suppose I do?' said Veronica, and her aunt chuckled.

'Two of a kind is right,' she said.

'Miles wants to have a talk with Uncle Arthur,' Veronica said. 'To explain things.'

'Better him than me,' said Aunty. 'Maths and Hellenic art and two in a bed. Still, if anyone can understand it Arthur can. He understands most things. But let him rest a while. He'll need all his strength for this one – especially the Hellenic art. He's pretty good at maths.'

'And two in a bed,' said Veronica. 'He's just proved it.'

It was her aunt's turn to giggle.

Miles called next day to take Lord Nugent to lunch in Nice. A very formal, very correct Miles in a lightweight suit and a Guards' tie, who drove up in a hired car with a chauffeur. Uncle Arthur was equally formal, equally correct, but with just the slightest hint of weary exultation. Aunty, Veronica and Bridget spied on them lovingly and watched them go, then Aunty turned to Bridget.

'Now,' she said, 'tell us all about your coalman.'

'He really is rather nice,' said Bridget. 'Rich, too.'

'So I should suppose,' said Aunty. Bridget was wearing a diamond brooch a duchess might have envied.

'A bit possessive,' said Bridget.

'The way he spoils you he's entitled to be,' said Aunty. 'Married?'

'Not just at the moment,' said Bridget. 'He wants me to marry him.'

'And will you?'

'No,' said Bridget. 'I'm having too much fun selling money.'

Aunty looked smug. Right again.

The young feller knows about restaurants, Uncle Arthur thought: he's chosen the best. Knows about getting down to business, too. As soon as the aperitifs were served Miles asked, 'When do you want to ask your questions? Now or after the meal?'

'Best get it over with,' Lord Nugent said.

'Fire away then.' The words were said calmly enough, but he looked as if he were about to go over the top at the head of his guardsmen.

'Do you want to marry my niece?' Nugent asked.

'Hasn't Veronica told you?'

'I want you to tell me.'

340

'The answer is yes,' said Miles. 'More than anything in the world.'

Nugent nodded. Point taken. 'She's not in a hurry to marry you,' he said.

'Mathematics,' said Miles.

'You understand that?'

'Yes,' said Miles. 'I do. She's a natural-born academic. It's a disease there's no cure for. I know. I'm that way myself.'

'Then you don't mind?'

'I'd sooner she married me,' said Miles. 'But that would be awkward. A married undergraduate, and a female one at that . . .' He sipped his vermouth. 'So long as she doesn't leave me.'

'She won't do that,' said Nugent. 'Can you support her?'

'Easily,' said Miles, and handed over a sheet of paper. Assets and liabilities. The former far in excess of the latter, Nugent noted. There was money in beer: enormous money. Even so the young feller had sense. He'd not only anticipated the question: he'd written down the answer. Slowly, cautiously, Lord Nugent began to like Miles Armstrong.

'She's got money of her own,' he said.

'So she told me. We'll save it for our children.'

Schools, thought Nugent. Nannies, governesses, ponies.

'There may be a problem about their colour,' he said.

'Portuguese princesses' children don't have problems,' said Miles.

'I must remember that,' said Nugent.

Miles thought for a moment then offered his hand. 'Congratulations, sir,' he said.

Nugent took it. 'Thank you, my boy,' he said, 'but we're keeping it in the family just for the moment.'

'Thank *you*, sir,' said Miles. The use of the word family in that context was just what he needed. The lunch, too, was splendid, even if Nugent had to try hard not to yawn as it neared its end.

'Just about perfect,' he said to Poppy. 'Straightforward, direct. Clever, of course – but with common sense too. And he adores her. Can't wait to be married. I could have drawn up the blueprint for him myself.'

'Did you mention the lemon tree business?' his wife asked.

'How could I?' he said. 'The way you and I carried on.' He yawned.

'You can take a nap in a minute,' Poppy said. 'God knows you've earned it. Just tell me one thing.' He waited. 'Do you think they'll be happy?'

'Just like us,' he said.

'I do love you,' said Poppy. 'Go on. Off you toddle. I might just join you later.' He looked wary.

'No rape,' Poppy said. 'Promise. Not unless you're in the mood. The doctor said I should rest in the afternoons, that's all.'

'I'll help you,' said Nugent, and headed for the stairs.

When he'd gone Lady Nugent whistled like a mynah bird, and Veronica came in from the veranda.

'You managed to hear all right?' said her aunt.

'Yes, I did,' Veronica said. 'Oh Aunty.'

Her aunt held out her arms and she ran to them. 'I'm so lucky,' Veronica said.

Her aunt stroked her hair. 'Poor little orphan, that's what you are,' she said.

'I'm not poor,' said Veronica, 'and I'm not all that little – and how can I be an orphan when I've got you and Uncle Arthur?'

'We're lucky too,' said Aunty.

Yet there was something lurking, Veronica thought. An obstacle, perhaps even a threat. One black cloud in a sky of flawless blue. She asked Bridget about it, because Bridget could pick up signals like that even faster than she could, but all Bridget could say was that it was there: not what, or why, or who. The only thing she could do was be ready, but it wasn't easy. The cloud might be small, and yet it was all around her.

But she still had Miles, that was the point. That night as always he came to her, climbing the lemon tree as easily as if it were a flight of stairs, and as ardent as ever, perhaps even more so after surviving the ordeal of his interview with Lord Nugent.

As they lay together Veronica asked, 'Was he nice to you?'

'Yes, he was,' said Miles-now-Bob, 'but I bet he could be formidable if I crossed him.'

'But you didn't.'

'Of course not. I said all the things he wanted to hear. I love you, I want to marry you, and I'm rich.'

'Are you?' Veronica said. 'I'm glad. I like being rich.'

'Weren't you always?'

'When I was a little girl I was poor and it was ghastly. I didn't know what having money was till Aunty took me on.'

He began to stroke her, enjoying her rounded smoothness as he always did. It would be kisses soon. Would it be polite to say thank you to Baby Jesus and His Mother? she wondered. Vishnu, she was sure, would be delighted for her. Then it was her turn to touch and kiss, and he was ready for her. She mounted him.

'This is new,' he said.

'I think you'll like it,' she said, and then, 'Oh, you do. You like it enormously.' He wanted to laugh, but what she was doing was too delicious even for laughter . . .

In the bath he said, 'I've been thinking.'

'Yes, Bob.'

'About Durham. Did you know I nearly took a job there?'

It was all in the detective's letter, but darling Bob must never know about the detective's letter.

'No, I didn't,' she said.

'There was a lectureship going. Hellenic studies. Rather my sort of thing.'

'But you didn't take it.'

'I joined the Coldstream instead.'

Her hand reached out to touch the scars that were still so visible.

'You really don't mind them?' he asked her.

'You're my hero,' she said. 'All heroes have scars.'

'Or else they're killed.'

He was thinking of poor Nicholas, she knew, but even so the black cloud hovered once more, until he said 'Would your aunt mind if I took you to Nice tomorrow?'

'I shouldn't think so,' said Veronica. 'But why Nice?'

'I want to buy you things,' said her darling Bob.

'I'll enjoy that,' she said, and then, 'What things?'

'An engagement ring for a start.'

'I'll ask her at breakfast,' Veronica said, knowing that Aunty would be all for it.

It was a wonderful day out: the chauffeur and the limousine, a splendid lunch, and then the shops. First a jeweller's to buy an engagement ring because that would make them respectable when they visited the other shops, but it would have to be one that fitted, said Bob, and almost she giggled, because how could they be respectable? And such a ring: a great cluster of diamonds and rubies set in white gold that palely gleamed against her honey gold skin. Then on to another jeweller's for a wedding ring. For this she wore her engagement ring to show she was respectable, and Bob bought her a diamond and ruby necklace too, because she had behaved so respectably. Then with engagement ring and wedding ring on her finger they went to the boutiques: Erté and Poiret, Vionnet and Callot and Chanel: then on to the underwear shops for knickers and things: all silk, and all delightfully indecent.

'But it's such a waste of time,' said Veronica. 'When we're alone they won't be on five minutes.'

'I'll enjoy taking them off,' said Bob. She kissed him, then took him back to the villa for tea, and Aunty and Bridget and Uncle Arthur oohed and aahed at the engagement ring and the necklace.

'Of course I'll only wear it when we're together like this,' Veronica said. 'I could hardly wear it at St Winifred's, could I? All the same we *are* engaged.'

345

Uncle Arthur looked with approval at his nephew-to-be by marriage. Smart young feller is right, he thought. That engagement ring's as effective as a pair of handcuffs.

'We ought to give that party we talked about,' said Aunty. 'Celebrate your engagement, too.'

'But—' Veronica began.

'Not tell anybody. Just celebrate,' said Aunty. 'Just like we'll celebrate that I'm expecting. It's about time we had another party.'

'The missy baba and her mother and Sir Mark?' Veronica asked.

'They'll help to fill the room,' said her aunt, 'and anyway I like Mrs Lippiatt. I told you.' She turned to Bridget and grinned: 'We'd better have the coalman too.'

Miles-now-Bob left them to rest before his evening's labours then changed into his tree-climbing outfit, and Veronica took Aunty and Bridget upstairs to show off the new dresses. Both women had a good eye, and approved of every dress. After that she showed them the underwear.

'Well, well,' Aunty said. 'It looks like your honeymoon's going to be a long one.'

'Maybe two years,' Veronica said.

'Two years!' said Aunty. 'The poor man will be in a worse state than Arthur when he totters down the aisle.'

'It's all rather up to you,' Veronica told Bridget.

'Do my best,' said Bridget, 'but there aren't any guarantees.'

'If only I wasn't so mad about maths,' Veronica said and Bridget looked bewildered.

'Who would have thought it?' said her aunt. 'All those years ago when I came and collected you in Kalpur, poor little scrap – that you'd end up like this?' She gestured at the riot of silk and lace on the bed.

'It was all you – and Bridget,' said Veronica.

'It was you,' said her aunt, 'and what's more you deserve it.'

'They tell me he's rich,' said Bridget.

'Rolling in it,' Veronica said. 'It's gorgeous.'

'Arthur reckons he could buy and sell Mark Beddoes half-a-dozen times,' said Aunty. 'How upset the missy baba will be when you finally make an honest man of him.'

21

The removal of the new underwear was a great success; a pleasure shared in fact, because he was happy and so she was too, but then the touching began, and she was happy anyway. Later he said, 'About Durham.'

'It's weeks away,' she said.

'If you're going back there, I want to be there too.'

'But how can you? You can't just rent a house there – not when you've got that vast mansion twenty miles away.'

'One of the men's colleges – St Luke's,' he said. 'Do you know it?'

'They gave a Bach recital last year,' Veronica said. 'It was rather good.'

'They want a tutor in Classical Studies,' he said. 'I thought I'd apply.'

'What happened to the one they had?'

'He went to Harvard,' said Bob.

'Why?'

'Money. Not all classical historians own breweries. It was all in the ad in *The Times* I bought when I took your uncle to lunch. "Because Dr Playfair has progressed to a professorship at Harvard . . ." Showing off, you see.'

'Dr Playfair?'

'The college, too. Anyway I thought I'd try and see what
happened.'

'We'd have to be awfully careful,' she said. 'There
wouldn't be much chance for any of this.' She stroked him
the way he specially liked and he did everything but purr.
'I daren't risk being sent down.'

'Of course not,' he said. 'I just want to be near you,
that's all.'

'Mind you,' said Veronica, 'that doesn't mean we
couldn't do it sometimes – if you're clever and careful,
that is. And you are clever and careful.' She eased herself
to him. 'I'm just clever.'

That was the way it was. Silk knickers and perfume
and love that was just about perfect, because by now she
had taught him all the tricks she had learned in the
Kama Sutra: all the ones that were anatomically possible,
so to speak: lilies bursting all over the place – and he
loved it. Not only that but he was so strong. He could
pick her up and carry her as if she were no more than a
parcel from Harrods marked 'Fragile' and she loved it.
All that strength and none of it menacing: no reason for
fear, only love. Him holding her, and she with an arm
round his neck. He loved it too.

'Like a god and goddess in an Indian temple,' she
said.

'We must go there,' he said, and she kissed him.

'So strong,' she said. 'You should have rowed in one of
those boats. Like the ones they have in Durham.'

'We had eights,' he said. 'In Durham they only have

fours. And anyway I did row – for my college.'

'I bet you looked sweet in those pretty little shorts,' she said.

Carefully, cautious not to hurt, he smacked her bottom and she yelled discreetly, and that was the way it was: just about perfect.

The night of the party came and she had to choose her dress herself because Bridget had a migraine, and when Bridget had a migraine it was agony. At last she settled on a Vionnet dress of a rich green silk that glowed like jewels; cut on the cross, and with the pleated skirt that Vionnet did so well. No emeralds. Hers were too dark for the dress's summery lightness: diamonds, that was the thing: Bob's necklace and engagement ring – but worn on her right hand; and poor Nicholas's ear-rings because Bob had told her he didn't mind, and he wouldn't lie: not about something as important as that. Aunty's Indian bracelets, and a handbag of white silk with a green-leaf design by Lallement, and she was ready. Time to call on Aunty.

'How gorgeous you look, child,' Aunty said.

'Look who's talking,' Veronica said again. Aunty wore Poiret dress of a red like roses, and a necklace and bracelet of diamonds and rubies. She looked at Veronica's right hand.

'So it's still a secret,' she said.

'On account of the missy baba,' Veronica said, 'but I'll wear it on my left hand when it's just the family.'

'He's a sweetheart,' said Aunty. 'The best compliment I can pay you is you deserve him.' She looked at the little

French clock on the dressing-table. 'Better get down
there, I suppose. Poor Bridget.'

'She's not worse?' said Veronica.

'No no. It's just the coalman's driven over from Nice to
be with her.'

'She's still not up to it?'

'She's in agony,' Aunty said.

Veronica and Aunty and Uncle Arthur received their
guests, and tried not to be too gracious, because everyone
knew that Aunty's parties were the best in Cap d'Antibes.
Darling Bob was late, which was worrying, and when he
did arrive it was more worrying still. With him were Rollo
and a tall, foreign-looking man who was thin and yet
menacing, somehow. Like a knife blade. Rollo went at
once to Aunty.

'Lady Nugent, do excuse us,' he said. 'Vladimir and I
happened to drop in on Miles and he was just about to
come to your party. He insisted you wouldn't mind if we
came too.' By the look on his face her darling Bob had
insisted on nothing of the sort.

'Yes of course,' Aunty said. Veronica thought: If Jagadir
Singh had been here she'd have had you thrown out.

'May I present Vladimir – Count Solokov – Lord and
Lady Nugent and their niece, Miss Veronica Carteret.'

Veronica and her aunt inclined their heads, and Uncle
Arthur grunted, by no means convinced of the count's
nobility.

He's queer, Veronica thought. He has to be. No normal
male could look at Aunty as if she were part of the furniture. Nor me, come to that. Rollo's gone on the game.

'Help yourselves to a drink,' Uncle Arthur said, as if the only alternative was to take themselves off. They went.

Bob turned to her uncle. 'I'm sorry, sir,' he said. 'I didn't mean to invite him at all. He just seemed to think I did.'

'He clings,' said Aunty.

'Like tar to your shoes,' said Uncle Arthur.

Bob took her off to dance. 'You believe me, don't you?' he said. 'I truly didn't want him to come here – or that weird friend of his.'

'Of course I believe you.' How to explain that for her there would have been no problem in telling Rollo to go away and take his friend with him? She looked to where the two of them were eating canapés: rather a lot of them.

'They look hungry,' she said. 'Are they both poor?' The thought was cheering. Certainly their dinner jackets had seen better days.

Bob said, 'He hasn't asked for a loan. Not yet.'

'He will,' said Veronica. 'How did he find you?'

'They're staying in Nice,' said Bob. 'There was a piece in the local paper about your aunt's party. Some of the guests, too. Mark and Victoria. Me amongst others. So they came down here to look for me.'

'Definitely a loan,' said Veronica.

But it wasn't. The two of them ate an enormous amount and drank quite a bit, but they were among the first to leave. In fact Veronica thought they had left even earlier, but they came back in from the garden for more canapés, more *bouches à la reine*. Young love, thought Veronica. A kiss and a cuddle in the moonlight.

Mrs Lippiatt had seen them, too. 'A most unsatisfactory young man,' she said.

'All of that,' said Lady Nugent.

'He didn't—' Mrs Lippiatt hesitated. 'He didn't *gate-crash*, did he?'

Lady Nugent looked at her approvingly.

'I suppose he did,' she said, 'but there are enough strong men here to throw him out if it should be necessary.'

Mrs Lippiatt looked at Miles Armstrong, who was dancing with her daughter, no doubt because Veronica had told him to. He really did look formidable.

'Indeed there are,' she said.

At last the guests were all gone and the four of them could sit on the terrace for one last drink and cigarette, and hold a post-mortem on the party. Despite Rollo's presence and the possible count's it had been a good one, not least, said Bob, because Veronica and her aunt had been the most beautiful and best-dressed women there by far.

'The only reason I came,' said Nugent. Both men scored maximum points.

'How's Bridget's migraine?' Veronica asked.

'I went up ten minutes ago,' said Aunty. 'It's worse if anything.'

'Poor darling,' said Bob. He and Bridget liked each other.

'The coalman didn't look too happy,' Veronica said.

'He will be in a day or so,' said Aunty. 'Bridget's head aches never last.' She rose to her feet. 'Time I was off,' she said. 'We mothers-to-be need our rest.'

'So do fathers-to-be.' Uncle Arthur too rose from his chair as Veronica and Aunty kissed.

'I'd better be off soon,' said Bob, as the other two left.

'No tree climbing tonight?' said Veronica.

'This is hardly my Tarzan outfit,' he said.

'You can make up for it tomorrow,' Veronica said.

'You can bet on it.'

They finished their cigarettes, then rose and kissed: a delightful end to a delightful evening, until the scream. Never in her life had Veronica heard Aunty scream, but she knew that it was her, knew too that there was anguish in the scream, and terror.

'Oh, my God,' she said, but Bob was already running hard for the villa. Behind her there came a sound like footsteps on gravel, but by then she too was running, cursing the skirts of her dress, her only thought of Aunty.

On the stair landing by Aunty's bedroom the first horror was waiting: that bastard Solokov, unconscious and somehow weird looking, and Bob beside him, the handle of a knife showing from his side. She wanted to stop, *of course* she wanted to stop, but from Aunty's bedroom there came a sort of hammering sound, and Aunty had screamed. She ran on into the bedroom, and Aunty lay there, battered and bruised, and breathing in a snoring way that was somehow frightening. The hammering came from Uncle Arthur's dressing-room. There was a chair tucked under its handle, forcing it shut. She pulled the chair away and pulled the door wide. Uncle Arthur stood in its frame: he'd been using another chair, trying to break the door down.

'Tell me,' he said.

'Aunty,' said Veronica, 'and Miles. Aunty's unconscious.

Miles has been stabbed. Solokov's with him. Unconscious.'

Uncle Arthur went to look at his wife and, unconscious or not, kissed her oh so sweetly. 'Show me your chap,' he said.

She did so and he went to him, felt his wrist. 'Not dead,' he said, 'but he needs a doctor. Quick.' He went to Solokov next.

'Not unconscious,' Uncle Arthur said. 'He's dead.' She knew then why Solokov looked so weird. His neck was broken.

Dimly she became aware that two more men were looking at her from the stairs: their chef and butler. The butler held a poker, the chef his largest knife.

She said in French, 'There has been a robbery. One of the robbers is dead, and a guest is – hurt. Go and warn the other servants that the police will be here soon.'

Uncle Arthur said, 'You'd better phone them, and when you do, tell them that the mayor was here tonight, and the prefect of police. And tell them to bring a doctor who knows about knife wounds.'

'And Aunty?'

'Phone her doctor after you've talked to the police. His number's on the telephone table.'

She went down to the phone, and the police said they'd be there at once and indeed they would, she thought. Monsieur le maire *and* monsieur le préfet. Doctor Jannot also said he'd come at once, but then Uncle Arthur was a millionaire.

She went back upstairs, to where Uncle Arthur knelt by her darling. 'They're coming,' she said, and then, 'Oughtn't we to pull the knife out?'

'The quickest way to kill him,' said Uncle Arthur, and he would know, she thought. According to Aunty his early days had had more than their share of violence. She went into the bedroom, where Bridget was sponging Aunty's forehead.

Before she could speak Bridget said, 'My headache's gone.'

'You knew there was something?' Veronica asked.

'Not what it would be,' said Bridget, 'but I had this feeling that there would be something bad – though I never dreamed it would be this. The poor darlings.' She looked at Veronica. 'You haven't cried?'

'I mustn't,' said Veronica. 'Not yet.'

The police arrived then, the discreet and intelligent sort of police appropriate to the needs of a millionaire who knows the prefect and the mayor. With them came a surgeon who knelt by her darling, touched his wrist and said, 'Hospital. At once.'

She had expected it. Already he had acquired that former look: the look of a man who would die if the operation failed.

The senior detective asked to see the bedroom, which was reasonable enough. She had said it was where the safe was, after all. The trouble was that it had been covered by the picture of Aunty and herself in happier times and far fewer clothes: but when they went in the picture wasn't there: just the slate grey of the safe door against the peach-coloured wall.

'A little obvious, mademoiselle,' said the detective. Veronica translated to Uncle Arthur.

'Usually it's covered by a picture,' Uncle Arthur said,

'but I'm having it valued. It's one that I treasure.'

Hidden it, she thought. What a gorgeous man he was, but what did it matter? What did anything matter, if anything happened to her darlings?

The detective looked at the safe door. 'I think your friend was too quick for the thief,' he said. 'I doubt if it's been opened.' She told Uncle Arthur.

'Wouldn't matter if it had,' said Uncle Arthur. 'It's empty. A Boy Scout could have opened it with that gadget they use for taking stones out of horses' hooves. I keep my valuables elsewhere.'

'And you've checked?'

'I've checked,' said Uncle Arthur. 'Nothing's missing.'

The detective looked at him with approval, and perhaps a little bafflement, too. Englishmen weren't supposed to have that kind of logical practicality.

The obstetrician arrived, and then the ambulance. Both doctors insisted that there would be no point in Veronica or Bridget or milord going with them. That night milady and monsieur would be – what was the word? – inaccessible, but they could come tomorrow, and if there was any change, no matter what the time, they would be told. That would have to do, and all three of them knew it, and Veronica kissed Aunty and her darling, and Uncle Arthur walked downstairs behind the stretchers. Only then did Veronica's control break. She gave a great wail of anguish and the tears came, and Bridget took her in her arms and hugged her and hugged her.

When Uncle Arthur came back he brought cognac and three glasses, and waited until Veronica's grief had faded to quiet tears, but even then she clung to Bridget.

Uncle Arthur said, 'It's three in the morning. We must rest.'

'I couldn't,' said Veronica.

'For their sakes,' Uncle Arthur said and she nodded, freed herself from Bridget at last, and lit a cigarette from the box by Aunty's bedside. Uncle Arthur poured out cognac.

'I don't like that stuff,' said Veronica.

'Just as well at your age,' Uncle Arthur said. 'It's a sleeping draught,' and Veronica drank.

'I suggest we don't talk now,' said Uncle Arthur. 'We're too damn tired. In a state of shock, too. We'll talk in the morning.' He looked at Veronica's glass that was still half full. 'Get it down you, girl,' he said.

For the first time he's talking to me as Aunty talks, Veronica thought. Mummy and daddy. She finished the glass and her head swam, but she was sleepy too.

'Bedtime,' said Bridget. 'Come along.' As if she were nine years old.

Even so it was easy to give in and be led down the corridor to her room and be helped out of her clothes and have her nightdress slipped over her head, the sheet tucked in. She was asleep almost at once. There were nightmares, of course, but what could you expect after what that bastard had done to Bob and Aunty? Then there was that other bastard who'd escaped. Between the nightmares, when she was no more than half asleep, the ideas began to come, but it would be better to save them for tomorrow. She closed her eyes, and waited for the next horror to invade her dreams.

They rose early and met at breakfast, tried to persuade

each other to eat; but soon it was just cigarettes and coffee. At least there had been no phone calls, which presumably meant no change. The best we can hope for, thought Veronica.

'Sandyford was in it too,' Uncle Arthur said.

'Well of course,' said Veronica. 'After Aunty screamed I heard someone running away down the path. Who else would it be?'

'Lookout,' Uncle Arthur said. 'Not even up to punching and kicking a lady, never mind knifing a strong, fit man. He behaved very bravely, that chap of yours.'

He very often does, thought Veronica, then forbade herself to cry, and lit another cigarette instead. 'We must find him,' she said.

'How can we do that?' said Bridget.

'A detective.' Uncle Arthur nodded. After all he and Veronica had used a detective before, but he wouldn't say so, not in front of Bridget.

'You mean a private detective?' Bridget asked. 'But half the police in the South of France will be looking for him.'

'When they're not doing other things,' said Veronica. 'Our detective would have only one thing to do – and a big reward if he's successful.'

'But where will you find a detective in France?' said Bridget.

'I'd better have a word with the mayor,' Uncle Arthur said.

'The mayor?' said Veronica.

'He owns a perfumery in Grasse,' said Uncle Arthur 'It's quite successful really, but he's a bit short of ready money at the moment.'

'So he is,' said Bridget. For the first time since the robbery she smiled.

'And what do you want us to do when we find him?' Uncle Arthur asked.

She had thought about that too, between the nightmares.

'It depends on what happens,' Veronica said. 'If Miles were to die, or Aunty loses her baby, then he must be punished. If both things happen he must be punished twice as much.'

'And if neither happens?' Uncle Arthur asked.

Veronica shrugged. 'Hurt a little, then let go.'

'You've been thinking of Kali again,' said Bridget.

'Praying,' said Veronica. If Kali listened and the prayer was answered she would have to arrange for garlands in the goddess's temple in Calcutta: perhaps the one in Kalpur too.

Nugent had lived long enough in India to know who Kali was. The goddess of revenge, destruction: and his niece, scholar of her college, leading mathematician of her year, good Catholic too when she remembered, had said and meant that she had prayed to a Hindu goddess whose only attributes were death and suffering. Not only that, but Bridget, another good Catholic, was neither surprised nor appalled. It would take some thinking about, but not yet.

'I'd better get on to the mayor,' he said. No problem there. The mayor spoke English.

'Did you pray to Our Lord too?' Bridget asked.

'Oh, yes,' said Veronica. 'And His Mother. There's a chapel in the hospital. We can pray there too if you like.'

'Don't forget to wear a hat,' said Bridget.

At the hospital there was no change, except that Aunty drifted in and out of consciousness. She had been savagely beaten and kicked, the obstetrician said: broken ribs, extensive bruising, including the stomach . . . Darling Bob was still unconscious. They had extracted the knife, cleaned the wound, stitched him up, and he had scarcely moved.

'So many stitches,' the surgeon said. 'He has had an operation recently?'

'He was hit by shrapnel in 1918,' Veronica said. 'Rather a lot of it. They tried to get it out but it wasn't a success, not completely. Then earlier this year they had to try again. Otherwise he would have died,' she said.

'And this time it was a success? He was well?'

'Perfectly well,' said Veronica. 'Until last night.'

But he doesn't look well now, she thought. He looks as if he's dying all over again.

22

Veronica and Bridget went to the chapel, and there Nugent
joined them and said the Lord's Prayer because it was the
only one he could remember, and then, over and over,
'Please God let her be all right.' At last he sat back and
looked to where Bridget and Veronica still knelt, saying
the rosary. I mustn't think of Kali, he thought. Not here: it
would be blasphemy, but even so he knew that he would
not deny Veronica what she wanted. He had no doubt it
would be what Poppy wanted, too. The only problem,
he'd thought earlier, would be who would administer the
punishment. He could hardly ask the mayor to help him
with that, but Veronica had the answer at once.

'We must send for Jagadir Singh,' she said.

The detective came to them after lunch. (An omelette
and salad which none of them wanted, but which they
had to eat, as Bridget had said. Without food they would
be weak when they must be strong.) Veronica approved
of him at once. He was neat and contained and clever,
and his suit and watch told her that he was successful,
too. Bridget and Uncle Arthur also approved: he spoke
excellent English.

363

'Which of you will tell me?' he said. 'Forgive me but it will be best if there is only one of you who speaks.'

Uncle Arthur motioned to Veronica, who told him, and Jean Luc Guestier listened with an intensity she could bring only to mathematics.

When she had done he said to the others, 'Do you both agree?' and they nodded. 'So,' he said, 'we have a rich young man who became a poor young man.'

'Not rich,' said Uncle Arthur.

'Not by your standards,' Guestier said, 'but at least – what do you say? Comfortable. A regular officer in a good regiment of the British Army before the war – he would need money to be that.' He looked again at Uncle Arthur. 'I know this you see because I was a captain in Intelligence. We often worked with the British Army.' He turned to Veronica. 'Now your fiancé, mademoiselle,' he said, and Veronica gave him full marks. Guestier had seen at once that the ring was now on the third finger of her left hand. 'He also was in a good regiment?'

'The Coldstream Guards,' said Veronica.

'*Crème de la crème*,' said Guestier. 'And rich, too.'

'He still is,' said Veronica.

'And for some time he helped this – Sandyford. Financially, that is to say. But eventually Captain Armstrong decided that he no longer wished to support him.'

'Nothing wrong with that,' Uncle Arthur said.

'Certainly not,' said Guestier. 'Young men should support themselves, but from what you tell me Sandyford would not be all that good at it. He is handsome, you say?'

The truth had to be faced. She wanted Rollo found, and Guestier might do it.

'Pretty,' Veronica said.

'And this *soi-disant* Russian count was a *pédéraste*?'
Veronica nodded. 'How do you know?'

'He danced with me,' Veronica said, and Guestier
thought: *Bien sûr*, mademoiselle. That is all it would take.
'But Sandyford was not?'

'Sex didn't bother him,' Veronica said. 'What he wanted
was money.'

'Not to make it,' said Bridget. 'Not a business or a
company. Just to have it and be kept, like a pekinese on
a silk cushion.'

Another expert, thought Guestier. Their opinions are
always of value. Then milord, too, grunted agreement,
and that made three.

'And they had come from Nice?'

'Bo – my fiancé told me so, and Solokov had a Nice
newspaper,' she said. 'There was a piece in it about my
aunt and uncle's party.'

'There are quite a few White Russians in Nice,' said
Guestier. 'Most of them are respectable. Some have
money, some work as taxi drivers, or waiters, or maids.
A small group are not. They live off the earnings of prostitutes.'

'But how could Solokov do that?' said Uncle Arthur. 'He
was queer.'

'Quite easily,' said Guestier, 'if some of the prostitutes
are boys.'

'Ah,' Uncle Arthur said, and nodded approval. Monsieur
Guestier is now on the list of his consultants, Veronica
thought, and quite right too.

'It is not much to go on but it is a start,' Guestier said,

'and one must begin somewhere. If you will excuse me, I will begin now. I have three men to assist me and we'll go—'

'Only three?' Veronica said.

'Three good men,' said Guestier. 'Very good men in fact. Far better than a dozen mediocrities.'

'Quite right,' said Uncle Arthur.

Each day they went to the hospital, as Aunty got better and her darling got worse: not that anyone told her about Bob, but she had eyes: she could see. On the other hand Aunty really did look better: sitting up, the bruises fading, but nobody had yet said anything about the baby and whether it was alive.

When at last she was allowed to say more than 'Much better darling' and 'Thank you for the flowers', she reached out her hand to Veronica.

'I think your chap saved my life,' she said.

'But how could he?' Veronica said. 'He never ever reached your room.'

'As he came up the stairs he was yelling,' Aunty said. 'Roaring like a tiger. Solokov stopped kicking me and used his legs to run away instead. And much good it did him, Arthur tells me. Without Miles I'd be dead.'

And Bob would be safe and well, Veronica thought. But how can I choose between the two people I love most? It's all up to Baby Jesus and His Mother now.

When they returned to the villa it was to be told that the prefect had phoned. Every effort was being made, his message said. No stone was left unturned.

'He hasn't found a bloody thing,' Uncle Arthur said.

But then Guestier phoned. 'I am in a café in Nice,' he said. 'It's rather public, but I think I have found something that may interest you. Would you care to join me?'

'We would indeed,' Uncle Arthur said, and Guestier gave them directions.

It wasn't a very nice café, but then it wasn't in a very nice neighbourhood. It was where Rollo lived, however, which meant he must be really poor, and that at least was pleasing.

'He lives in a house close by,' said Guestier. 'A rather nasty house which he and Solokov shared with two prostitutes. No doubt Solokov was their pimp.'

'Pretty ones?' Veronica asked.

'Certainly not.' Guestier seemed shocked. 'In this quarter nothing is pretty. But see for yourself. One of them is sitting by the mirror drinking coffee.'

Veronica looked once, then away. Not pretty at all.

'She is the better looking of the two,' said Guestier.

'Good God!' said Uncle Arthur, and then: 'Sandyford's pretty.'

'You imply that Solokov may have pimped for him, too. It is very possible.'

How Rollo must hate me, Veronica thought. Once Bob loved him – or at least thought he did – and he has nothing, and now Bob loves me and I have everything – or I will if darling Bob survives.

'Shall we go?' Guestier asked, and they rose at once.

These three are formidable, Guestier thought: even the women. Perhaps especially the women.

It really was a nasty house, thought Veronica. But then Rollo is nasty too. Close by, two men sat drinking beer at a pavement table of a café even more deplorable than the one they'd just left.

'Your men?' Uncle Arthur asked.

Guestier nodded. 'The third is watching the back of the house. Even if he runs he won't get away.'

'He won't run,' Uncle Arthur said, and turned to Veronica. 'Let me do the talking this time,' he said.

'Yes, Uncle Arthur,' she said. Whatever the group he would always be in charge, and yet she loved him now for much more than just Aunty's sake. Guestier banged on the door with his fist – no knocker, no bell – and Rollo appeared almost at once. Waiting for one of his whores to bring him some money, thought Veronica.

Uncle Arthur said, 'I think you'd better invite us in. We can hardly talk on your doorstep.'

Whatever else he might be, Rollo was a realist. He couldn't withstand Lord Nugent, let alone the dangerous-looking Frenchman with him: let alone Veronica and Bridget come to that. He turned and led them into the house, to what seemed to be drawing-room and dining-room combined. Off it was another room that seemed to be furnished largely with an unmade bed. He shut its door.

'Please sit down,' he said.

Uncle Arthur looked at the furniture. 'We'll stand,' he said. 'This won't take long.'

Rollo waited, terrified.

'We've come to do you a favour,' Uncle Arthur said. ' know it seems unlikely after what you've done to us—'

'I don't think I follow you,' said Rollo, and Uncle Arthur sighed. Not only a coward, said the sigh, but a fool as well

'Four days ago you were an accessary to an assault on

my wife, and on my niece's fiancé. Miles Armstrong may die. My wife was pregnant and may lose her child.'

'I didn't know that,' said Rollo. 'Honestly I didn't.'

'Just listen,' Uncle Arthur said. His voice was patient, like that of a maths teacher trying to explain the theorem of Pythagoras to a none too bright fifth former.

'There was no reason why you should know it,' he continued. 'Nor did you take part in either assault. You kept watch. But when you heard my wife scream you ran away.'

'I don't know what you're talking about. Honestly,' said Rollo.

'I saw you,' Veronica lied. Just three words, but it was like a sentence of death.

'Do you have a cigarette to spare?' he asked, and Uncle Arthur gave him one. He smokes as if he's about to face a firing squad, thought Veronica, and in a sense perhaps he is. All the same, lies are very useful things when one is dealing with stupid people.

'I didn't agree to any violence,' Rollo said at last. 'Please believe that. I have great respect for Lady Nugent, and once Miles was my very best friend.'

'Just get on with it,' said Uncle Arthur.

'Yes, well – during the party Vladimir managed to slip away upstairs and saw the safe. We were broke, you see. I don't mean hard up. I mean broke. I doubt if we had ten francs between us after we'd paid our train fares. So we went to your place to ask Miles for a loan.'

'Why bring Solokov?' Uncle Arthur asked.

'He really was a count,' said Rollo.

'Snobbery,' said Uncle Arthur. 'Always goes down well

at parties.' But his voice was indulgent and Rollo risked a smile.

'But you didn't ask for a loan,' Veronica said.

'I saw you and Miles together,' said Rollo. His eyes were on her ring, on the third finger of her left hand.

'So you tried to steal instead,' said Bridget, and Rollo blinked. Another bloody chee-chee talking to me as if I were dirt, he thought, but then look at how she's dressed compared with me. To her, maybe I am dirt.

'You could have lived off your whores,' said Veronica.

'They're useless,' said Rollo despairingly, and Uncle Arthur threw back his head and laughed: even Bridget smiled.

'They'll never find the pair to you,' said Uncle Arthur. 'All the same I'm going to do you a favour.'

How much? Rollo wondered, and what will I have to do for it?

'Jagadir Singh is with us,' Uncle Arthur said, and Veronica looked at him, puzzled. This was far too early.

'*Jagadir Singh*?' Rollo sounded horrified.

'You've heard of him then?'

'My God, yes.' He remembered the night when his Uncle Matthew, drunk for once, had described what it was like to be body-searched by him. 'But I thought you'd left him in Calcutta?'

'Lady Nugent decided that we needed a watchman, and indeed we did, but he arrived just a little too late. He doesn't like you, old chap. Doesn't like you at all.'

'You mean he knows that Vladimir—'

'And you,' said Uncle Arthur. 'He knows it all.'

'But how could he possibly?'

'I told him,' Uncle Arthur said.

'*You told him*? And you call that a favour?'

'Not that, no,' Uncle Arthur said. 'The favour is this: he doesn't know where you are, and I haven't told him. Not yet. If I did he would tear you apart.'

'Would that have bothered you?' Rollo asked.

'Your death wouldn't bother me in the slightest,' Uncle Arthur said, and Rollo winced, as the other man continued, his voice still pleasant, unhurried, 'but I'd hate to see him go to the guillotine for killing scum like you, so I'm going to ask this gentleman,' he nodded at Guestier, 'and his assistants, to be your bodyguard, just in case someone lets slip where you are. If that's all right with you, monsieur?'

'Perfectly,' said Guestier.

'Of course we could hardly expect you to move in here,' Uncle Arthur said in that same pleasant voice, 'with two ugly whores and a pretty one. If you could rent a flat somewhere—'

'I know just the place,' Guestier said.

'Splendid,' said Uncle Arthur. 'If you wouldn't mind turning your back for a moment.'

'Of course,' said Guestier. Of the five people in the room, only Rollo had no idea what was going to happen next. Unhurried, picking his targets, Uncle Arthur punched Rollo twice in the stomach, left and right, and Rollo screamed, then fell down on his knees in agony.

'After all,' Uncle Arthur said, 'you could hardly expect us to let you off scot free, now could you? But at least you now have some idea of what my wife went through.'

* * *

They went to a café in a much nicer part of Nice, one recommended by Guestier, where some sort of snack meal was always available, and Veronica could phone the hospital. No change for Bob, but wonderful news for Aunty. She hadn't lost her baby. Uncle Arthur told her to phone Aunty's favourite florist's shop and transfer its entire stock to Aunty's room.

'She'll love it,' said Veronica. 'All the same I'm glad you made Rollo scream.'

'Me too,' said Bridget, 'and if I may say so, what a clever way to keep Rollo in captivity.'

'He doesn't even think it's captivity,' said Veronica. 'The idiot thinks it's safety. What a clever uncle I've got.'

'At least we'll know where to get our hands on him if anything happens to Miles,' Uncle Arthur said, 'but if our prayers are answered I don't think we need bother Jagadir Singh, do you?'

'You were a more than adequate substitute,' Veronica said.

Next morning they went to visit Aunty, who lay in what was more like the opening salvo in a battle of flowers than a room in a hospital.

'Arthur, you idiot,' she said fondly. 'They've had to put them in every ward. They even ran out of vases. I had to pay for new ones. Give me a kiss.' Uncle Arthur kissed her. 'You are a sweetheart,' Aunty said, and turned to Veronica. 'There are some in Miles's room. The chapel too. I saw them.'

'You saw Miles?' said Veronica. 'He looks dreadful doesn't he?'

'He's still with us,' Aunty said. 'Hang on to that.' Then

quickly, because Veronica might cry again, she said, 'I saw the chapel, too. They took me there in a wheelchair.'

Bridget looked startled.

'Yes I know,' said Aunty, 'but I had to say thank you for my baby to Our Lord and His Mother. Just because some of His servants turned out to be bloody sadists there's no need to be rude.'

Then the surgeon came in and spoke to Veronica. 'I think you should see Monsieur Armstrong,' he said. 'Five minutes only. I shall come after—' But already Veronica was up and running, because five minutes was all she had.

He lay on the bed, white as the sheets that covered him, and his eyes were open, but was that a good sign or a bad one? He looked so *ill*. She moved towards him and knelt by the bed.

'Bob,' she said. 'Bob, my darling.' She was in agony, until she saw that he was smiling.

'Woof woof,' he said, and she knew that it would be all right. His face no longer had that waiting for death look, and his hand was warm, would soon be strong. Oh thank you Baby Jesus, Blessed Virgin, for what you have done. My darling will live and Aunty still has her baby.

'There's a secret,' said Bob. 'Maybe I shouldn't tell you but I want us to have secrets.'

'I know how to keep them,' Veronica said.

'Your uncle told me when I gave him lunch. He's giving more money to St Winifred's.'

'Another scholarship?'

'A fellowship this time. Mathematics. It'll be yours if you get a first – and you will.'

'The Lord Nugent fellow?'

'Lady Nugent,' said Bob.

Darling Uncle Arthur. He knew exactly how to show his love, and to make life hell for Dr Rattle. She leaned over to Bob and kissed him carefully, gently on the mouth before some bloody butler or doctor or whatever it was could come in and tell her not to.

Heroes, she thought. My life's been filled with heroes. Even my father. He'd been a brute, but in South Africa he'd been a hero, too. And darling Nicholas, and Uncle Arthur, and darling, darling Bob. Even Mark had medals . . .

'Hurry up and get well,' she said. 'I've remembered another one.'

'Another what?'

'From the Kama Sutra.'

'Oh marvellous,' said Bob. 'I can't wait.'

'You'll have to,' she said. 'You'll need all your strength for this one.'

First he would pick her up and carry her when they were naked, like Shiva and Vishnu, but did they have scented oil in France? Not that it mattered. Bridget would know how to make her some, and until Bob got his strength back there was always differential calculus.

'I do love you,' she said.

He looked at the ring he had given her. It was on the third finger of her left hand and he smiled, delighted that it should be so.

'And I love you,' he said.

And then the bloody doctor came in.

Leading Lady

James Mitchell

Jane Whitcomb has been fighting Felston's battles for years, organising hunger marches, building clinics and using her privilege in aid of others. But her restless energies and genuine desire to help are little use against the onslaught of the Great Depression. Loving Jane, banker Charles Lovell too does his bit for the coal miners and ship builders of Felston, but fails to make much of an impression. Until, that is, Jane's film star best friend invites them out to Hollywood. From there they travel on to Mexico and Charles secures a contract to build a destroyer for the Mexican government – a contract that might just save Felston from ruin.

The 1930s bring marriage and a luxuriant lifestyle to the Lovells, but there are rumblings of discontent in Spain and at home and suddenly they find themselves embroiled in the rise of Fascism, the scandal of Edward and Mrs Simpson, and the Spanish Civil War. Jane is tumbled back into a war zone at the behest of the *Daily World*, back to the kind of war that first brought her face to face with the heroic men of Felston.

Praise for James Mitchell's writing: 'Terrific story, a guaranteed page-turner' *Daily Mail*; 'A novel of stature and insight, and immensely enjoyable' *Sunday Telegraph*; 'Genuinely enjoyable' *Daily Telegraph*; 'A clever chronicle, sharply, confidently, elegantly done, with panache and skill' Elizabeth Buchan, *Sunday Times*; 'Sharp, gripping and intelligent, this novel . . . will thrill you to bits' *Cosmopolitan*

FICTION / SAGA 0 7472 4354 9

An Impossible Woman

James Mitchell

Creator of *When The Boat Comes In*

1929. A New Year and the champagne is still flowing, the music still playing for Jane Whitcomb. Wealthy, attractive and adored, she has no right to feel dissatisfied, but ever since her heroism in World War I, she has been uncomfortably aware that there are more important things to do than dance the night away.

Helping Felston, for instance, the North East town that was the home of her dead fiancé and is now in the grip of the worst depression in history – the Kingdom of Rags to Jane's Kingdom of Riches.

When the Wall Street crash plunges Felston into yet deeper poverty, Jane pulls out all the stops to raise more money, even agreeing to a Hollywood film of her adventures in wartime France. But money alone is not the answer. She organises a Hunger March from Felston to London – three hundred weary miles by ex-soldiers, herself among them, to show the world how a town is dying of neglect. It is a magnificent gesture, focussing all eyes on the tragedy. But it is barely over when Jane goes to Spain and there sees the gathering clouds of an even greater disaster – the Spanish Civil War.

Many men love Jane, rich and powerful ones among them, but she remains elusive – too intelligent to settle for less than the best. Courageous, determined, unconventional, by the standards of her time she is simply . . . *an impossible woman*.

'A clever chronicle, sharply, confidently, elegantly done, with panache and skill' *Sunday Times*

'Terrific story, a guaranteed page-turner . . . should be his biggest bestseller' *Daily Mail*

'A novel of stature and honesty and immensely enjoyable' *Sunday Telegraph*

FICTION / SAGA 0 7472 3919 3

A selection of bestsellers from Headline

LAND OF YOUR POSSESSION	Wendy Robertson	£5.99	☐
TRADERS	Andrew MacAllen	£5.99	☐
SEASONS OF HER LIFE	Fern Michaels	£5.99	☐
CHILD OF SHADOWS	Elizabeth Walker	£5.99	☐
A RAGE TO LIVE	Roberta Latow	£5.99	☐
GOING TOO FAR	Catherine Alliott	£5.99	☐
HANNAH OF HOPE STREET	Dee Williams	£4.99	☐
THE WILLOW GIRLS	Pamela Evans	£5.99	☐
MORE THAN RICHES	Josephine Cox	£5.99	☐
FOR MY DAUGHTERS	Barbara Delinsky	£4.99	☐
BLISS	Claudia Crawford	£5.99	☐
PLEASANT VICES	Laura Daniels	£5.99	☐
QUEENIE	Harry Cole	£5.99	☐

All Headline books are available at your local bookshop or newsagent, or can be ordered direct from the publisher. Just tick the titles you want and fill in the form below. Prices and availability subject to change without notice.

Headline Book Publishing, Cash Sales Department, Bookpoint, 39 Milton Park, Abingdon, OXON, OX14 4TD, UK. If you have a credit card you may order by telephone – 01235 400400.

Please enclose a cheque or postal order made payable to Bookpoint Ltd to the value of the cover price and allow the following for postage and packing:

UK & BFPO: £1.00 for the first book, 50p for the second book and 30p for each additional book ordered up to a maximum charge of £3.00.

OVERSEAS & EIRE: £2.00 for the first book, £1.00 for the second book and 50p for each additional book.

Name ....

Address ....

....

....

If you would prefer to pay by credit card, please complete:
Please debit my Visa/Access/Diner's Card/American Express (delete as applicable) card no:

Signature .... Expiry Date ....